DEMONS & THIEVES

Brae Wyckoff

Demons & Thieves
KWA Publishing
©2018

Printed in USA

ISBN: 0-9997890-8-2
ISBN-13: 978-0-9997890-8-7
Library of Congress Control Number: 2018901147

Editor: Zannie Carlson
zanniecarlson@gmail.com
www.zanniecarlson.com

Map created by Michelle Keyser
mkeyser777@gmail.com

Cover art by Sharon Marta of Marta Studios
http://www.martastudios.com

Other books written by Brae Wyckoff

The Horn King Series
The Orb of Truth: Book #1
The Dragon God: Book #2
The Vampire King: Book #3
Sword of the Elements: Book #4 (Coming Soon)

Children's Book Series
The Unfriendly Dragon
The Mountain of Gold (Coming Soon)

www.BraeWyckoff.com

CONTENTS

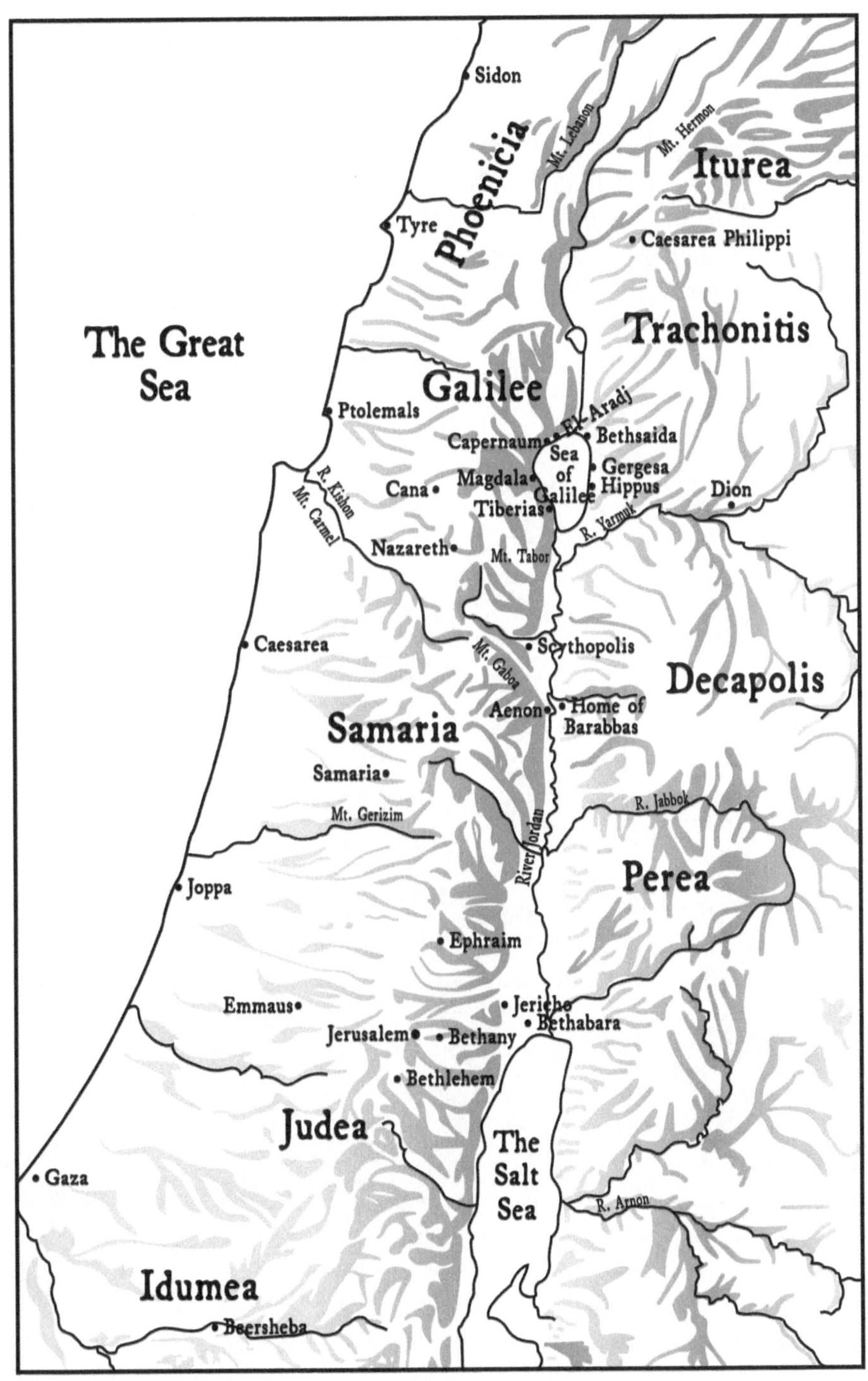

Sidon
Phoenicia
Mt. Lebanon
Mt. Hermon
Iturea
Tyre
Caesarea Philippi
Trachonitis
The Great
Sea
Galilee
Ptolemais
El Aradj
Capernaum
Bethsaida
Sea
of
Galilee
Magdala
Gergesa
Hippus
Cana
Dion
Tiberias
R. Kishon
Mt. Carmel
Nazareth
Mt. Tabor
R. Yarmuk
Caesarea
Mt. Gilboa
Scythopolis
Decapolis
Aenon
Home of
Barabbas
Samaria
Samaria
Mt. Gerizim
R. Jabbok
River Jordan
Perea
Joppa
Ephraim
Emmaus
Jericho
Jerusalem
Bethany
Bethabara
Bethlehem
Judea
The
Salt
Sea
Gaza
R. Arnon
Idumea
Beersheba

Eden's locked gates the Thief has opened wide,
By putting in the key, "Remember me."

—Eastern Orthodox Church

PART I
The Beginning

CHAPTER 1
SAVE OUR CHILD
TWENTY YEARS BEFORE THE CROSS

"Is she...going to die?" the man asked, his voice strained, barely audible. Evident in his cracked tone was the deep pain of a man on the edge of losing everything. His face was distraught, his brow wrinkled as he looked into the eyes of the physician. Tendrils of brown hair, saturated with sweat, clung to his forehead.

He looked over the doctor's shoulder to see his wife in the next room, grimacing in pain, laboring intensely to deliver his child.

"I'm sorry, Nestor, the baby has not turned. She has lost a lot of blood."

The husband turned back to him and said firmly, "By the gods, do something, *anything*!"

But the doctor could only quietly retreat to his patient. Two of the town's women, one was the doctor's wife, stood on either side as the contractions continued to force her to push, causing more damage inside her body. One gripped her hand, speaking soothing tones to her, while the other wiped a cool, wet cloth over her forehead, making sure there was always a supply of fresh water available.

The husband fell to his knees in anguish and called upon the gods he had served his entire life. "If there was ever a time I needed you, Zeus, Aphrodite, it is now. Hear me. Take my life instead of hers. Do not let my child be raised without a mother!"

As he continued to plead, some of the words caught in his throat and were unintelligible, as spit and snot caught in the web of his beard. Not caring, he pressed on with his prayers. The lamps cast eerie shadows throughout the home, a dwelling sparse of belongings and space. His wife screamed again. He looked through the doorway to see her lurch in pain like never before. "No! Do not take her!" he begged.

Just then, the wooden door behind him burst open, letting in the cold, howling wind from outside. The fresh air melded with the smell of the birthing blood and burnt fish sitting in the pan beside the fire, forgotten since the labor pains began. A man, face wrapped with muslin, entered quickly and closed the door. He rushed to the husband's side, flinging the cloth scarf away from his face. His olive skin was damp and his lips pursed behind his groomed black beard. His dark brown eyes were filled with sympathy as he looked at his childhood friend with great concern.

"Nestor, my friend, I'm here. What news of Vena?"

The husband clutched him, pulling him lower. Tears flowed and he swallowed hard. More screams came from the bedroom and the man glanced quickly to ascertain the situation.

"Philos, the god of death calls to her," said the husband.

"No, my friend. We must call upon the other gods to contest this. They will answer."

"To whom do they answer, Philos? They are gods. They don't need us. I am a poor man with no inheritance to offer. I came from nothing and will leave with nothing, for if my wife and child pass, then I will follow them this night or the next."

"You speak not of yourself, Nestor. The child could still live. What of your child then? Who will raise it?"

The husband snorted sarcastically and said, mockingly, "The gods will raise it. They take us and use us however they see fit with no regard for our requests and pleas."

"Anger has blinded you."

Nestor abruptly grabbed Philos, pulling his face close. Anger seethed from him as he growled through gritted teeth, "You know nothing of what I feel! My wife and child are at the mercy of the gods who hold silent in their glorious castles in the heavens!"

There was a long moment as the two men matched each other's stare. Philos looked hard into Nestor's eyes. One had splashes of gray and blue while the other was brown. Nestor's friend said, "I am indebted to you ever since you saved my life at the river those many years past. Tonight, let me return the debt to save her in another way."

"What other way, Philos?"

He whispered, "There is a god that resides outside the Greek elite that has been known to answer the prayers of a father."

"What god do you speak of?"

"The name escapes my mind but there is a soothsayer nearby that professes to know this deity. It is a woman who lives outside of town and keeps to herself. Let me go to her and beseech her to come with her god."

Another guttural scream startled them and they looked at the scene unfolding in the next room.

Without wasting another moment, Nestor said, "Go and bring this woman. I have nothing to lose."

The friend stood, wrapped his face in the scarf, unlatched the door, and stepped back out into the dark night.

Nestor rose and rushed to his wife's side, kneeling gently to take her hand. "My wife, I am here for you."

His voice seemed to calm her a bit. She pushed away the damp cloth, one of the women had placed on her forehead, and swallowing with difficulty, said, "The doctor won't tell me, but you have always spoken truth to me. Will our baby live?"

He tried to hide the pain of the question. As she slumped back, Nestor leaned toward her and whispered, "I will not let you or the baby die. I swear it."

"You are not the gods, my love." She coughed and grimaced in pain as another contraction hit her. Again, she wailed and then settled back to labored breathing.

Nestor said, "I am no god but I will go to further lengths than the gods themselves to save you, Vena." He leaned in once more and said firmly, "Upon my very life, you will live."

She screamed again, even louder than before, clutching the bed and arching her back. Nestor caught the eye of the physician inspecting his wife's progress. The doctor's lips pursed and he shook his head slightly. Intently focused on his patient, he waved his hand to his wife, "Bring me more water and another cloth."

Nestor turned his attention back to Vena. There was a defiant edge to his voice, "Upon my life, you will live."

Broken, pained, and tired, she uttered, "I trust you husband, but save our child if choice be made. Save our child."

CHAPTER 2
THE DECISION

The night waned and Nestor's adrenaline slowed; the dark-bearded Greek rested his forehead on his wife's shoulder. The doctor's exhausted wife, battle-worn blood-soaked apron across her lap, was on the other side of the bed. Dipping a torn cloth into the water bowl, she wrung it out and wearily dabbed the forehead of the semi-conscious patient. The room smelled of burning herbs, a clump of which smoldered on a small table in the corner. The smoke slowly rose, lingered, and eventually dispersed. A haunting silence had fallen upon the bedroom, none willing to speak or make a sound for fear of awakening the resting woman. She had bled and screamed for hours and now a fever had gripped her body.

The doctor sat in a wooden chair, shoulders slumped, arms resting on his thighs while maintaining a sorrowful stare upon the couple before him. He knew underneath the blanket was a large amount of blood, even now soaking through the straw bedding and dripping to the floor below. His own appearance was that of a man who had done great battle. If another bout of contractions were to come, he feared he would not be ready for the task. There was nothing left inside him. Hope had gone hours ago and he was uncertain if the baby was even alive at this point. He silently thanked the gods for taking the baby, if that be the case. He silently prayed, *"Goddess Tyche, bringer of favor, take the child home to be well with you and spare the wife."*

Not a second later, the front door flew open. The door scraped over the uneven floorboard, causing a screech to resound loudly through the silent house. The doctor's wife scrambled around the bed waving her hands to be quiet as two people entered.

Nestor, alerted by the sudden commotion, lifted his head and turned toward the door. The weary doctor waited, not moving anything but his eyes, thinking it to be more town women with supplies.

Nestor's best friend, Philos, had returned. Stepping in behind him was an enchanting female—high cheekbones, long eyelashes, plump lips, piercing green eyes. She wore strange jewelry upon her neck and silver earrings that curled around her outer ear and draped to her shoulders. Her hair was covered by a blue shroud of silk. Nestor was enraptured by her beauty and he could not stop staring at her. She stared back, not gazing away in shyness. Her persona radiated confidence as she slowly, seductively, unwrapped her shawl, releasing long, raven-black hair, straight and luxurious.

"Nestor," his friend called. "She is here to help."

Nestor stood and walked toward him, leaving his wife's side.

Intrigued, the doctor shakily bent forward to get a better look into the other room. A sudden jolt of realization came upon him. He quickly stood and charged into the front room. "She is a witch doctor! Get out!" The doctor's wife clutched his arm and tried to get him to quiet down but he pushed her hand away.

Philos stepped in between them and held the physician at bay with his palm planted against his chest.

The doctor continued, "She knows nothing of the gods. She brings trouble."

She spoke with a calm timbre, "And yet your gods did not prevent me from coming. The only trouble I see is your patient at death's door."

"Nestor, what do you say?" Philos asked. "I will do as you wish."

Silence befell the room as Nestor gazed at her in contemplation. He slowly raked his eyes across the room, as if to peer into each person's soul, trying to discern the answer to the choice before him. Nestor pleaded with the doctor, "Is there another way? I beg you to tell me!"

The doctor started to answer but held his tongue. With lips pursed, he placed his hands on Nestor's shoulders, "I am doing all that I can. I beseech the gods on your behalf and pray they answer, but I plead with you not to release the dark magic she will impart upon your family."

After a long moment, the mysterious woman stepped between them to enter the room where Vena lay dying.

"I am familiar with your gods and they have called upon me before," she said.

"She speaks the truth, Nestor," Philos said. "I heard a story from a traveling Samarian who claimed he witnessed her workings to save a man from death. This is how I knew of her whereabouts."

"What is your name?" Nestor asked, following her to the bedside.

Standing at the foot of the bed, she put out her palm and waved it slowly over the dying wife. "Her life is faint, but the child is strong."

"Your name, woman." Nestor's voice was low and demanding.

She turned with a smirk, "Maman Brijett. Most call me Mother."

The physician stepped forward, "This is not the way, Nestor. Do not overstep what the gods have ordained."

Nestor turned sharply, spittle coming from his mouth, "Do not overstep? My wife clings to life while the gods mock us! They do not care!"

"You speak out of anger," the doctor tried to appease.

"This is not anger, this is rage!"

Nestor's wife groaned suddenly and began to move, bringing all eyes upon her. Pain once again wracked her body and her face contorted, but this time there was something different. Vena's eyes were wide and fixed on something above her. Nestor followed her gaze and saw nothing but the shadowy ceiling.

The physician took charge once again, "Move aside, witch." He snapped his fingers, getting his assistants' attention, "Help me."

Nestor grabbed his arm, "No. You have done all you can, Doctor. It is time you leave, for my fate with the gods does not involve you any longer. Now go."

The frazzled doctor's wife, wisps of graying hair escaping her scarf, stood frozen in place, unsure what to do.

"Nestor, please," the doctor begged.

"No, you must go. Go now!" Nestor took a step back, making room for him to leave.

Philos, following Nestor's decision, gently grabbed the doctor's arm, helping him to the door.

Maman Brijett said to the other women, "You are not needed either."

Two younger women backed away, averting their eyes from the

enchantress. One knocked over the bowl of fresh water, causing it to splash everywhere. The wooden vessel bounced until finally settling.

Philos closed the door behind them. The sorceress gracefully moved closer to Nestor's wife, pulled herbs from a pouch at her side and sprinkled them over Vena. This settled the woman. Maman Brijett inhaled deeply, closing her eyes as she leaned over the bed. She weaved her hands back and forth in synchronized movements.

Maman began to chant in an entrancing language that neither Nestor nor Philos understood. *"Eldrvarya wyndys aiedail letta foyur coynrs. Arucane Astori darkyneid heyartis eldrvarya haldthin."*

A crack of lightning startled the mesmerized men. Drops of rain pelted the rooftop, quickly growing into a torrent that filled the street. Maman pulled away the covering to reveal the naked wife. Philos quickly looked away but found himself slowly peering back over Nestor's shoulder. Mesmerized, the men watched Vena's stomach stretch as the baby pushed, reshaping the skin. The wife broke into a heavy sweat with drops forming on every surface of her body. She was stuck fast, motionless, almost wooden. Maman reached into another pouch along her belt. She brought out a mustard colored dust, which she spread over the mother's exposed belly, and then upon her forehead.

The witch doctor turned to Nestor, "Put out your hand."

"Why?"

"Just do it! Do it now!"

He fearfully held out his hand which she quickly grabbed with one of her own. With the other, she pulled forth a small blade. She ran the knife over his palm, cutting him. He flinched, but she held him in place, directing his bleeding hand over his wife. Blood dripped onto her belly and mingled with the yellow dust. She pushed his hand away. Nestor retracted in pain, still staring at the witch doctor, surprised at her strength.

A new chant came forth in the same mysterious language, *"Wyrdfell synto Vae, nosu dauthleikr blaka stryn. Arucane Astori powyr ai ryvialed dauthleikr Astori vaymynt rykeived."*

A second bolt of lightning cracked and Maman gasped. Her face grimaced and she slowly turned to face the men who waited with held breath.

"Come, Philos."

He stuttered with surprise, "M-m-me?"

She lurched, grabbed hold of him, and yanked him with an unnatural strength to stand next to her. "Put out your hand."

He looked at Nestor who could only stare back with bewilderment.

"Do it now before it is too late!" she commanded.

Philos shakily brought out his hand. She grabbed it and sliced it across the palm. Blood trickled out and fell upon the woman's belly. As soon as it hit her skin it fizzled like water on a searing pan. The witch doctor pushed his hand away, smiled and nodded her approval. A strange ethereal smoke began to form, moving up, then side to side, and twirled around the two men. It entered their lungs and their eyes rolled back into their heads.

Philos and Nestor's feet slowly lifted two inches from the ground. Their arms were limp as their backs arched. The dark smoke writhed around them, seductively moving its tendrils over their bodies.

Nestor's wife suddenly lurched upright and shrieked, jarring both men from their trance. They dropped to the floor with a crash. Nestor scurried to her side. The witch doctor yelled at her, "PUSH!"

Vena's scream became a growl as she did as instructed.

"Push!" Maman commanded again and again. Each command invoked the woman to growl in pain and push. Drops of sweat slid down Vena's forehead and veins of stress bulged along her temple and neck. The smell of mustard and blood permeated the room. Vena lurched forward, gripping the edge of the bed in strained controlled grunts.

"I can see it! The baby is coming! Keep pushing!" Maman Brijett gripped the crowning head to help pull the baby out. "One more!"

Vena fell back in exhaustion just as the baby finally came out. Maman held up the child for them to see. The umbilical cord was wrapped around its legs like shackles on a prisoner. She cradled the child for stability, cutting the umbilical cord. The rubbery cable slid loose and fell to the ground.

"Will she live?" Nestor whispered.

"Take hold of your son."

Nestor, fighting tears of relief mixed with joy, took hold of his child. He looked at this tiny being in his hands. The baby calmly looked back at him. Nestor was struck by the life he saw in those eyes, as well as the fact that one of them was mismatched like his own. "My son...you are my..." He choked back his crying and repeated, "You are my son."

Maman Brijett gathered her belongings and headed for the door. Philos stopped her. "Will she live?"

She looked back at the woman lying in the blood-soaked bed. Just then the new mother coughed and her eyes opened. "She lives," the enchantress smiled as she stepped around him to leave.

"Wait, what about payment?"

She stopped, turned to face him, "You have paid plenty, Greeks of Hippus." She turned away and departed into the night. Philos wasn't sure, but he thought the door closed behind her by itself. He shrugged it away when he heard the baby cry.

Nestor brought his son to his wife, who pulled the sheet back over herself and was now sitting up. She gave her husband a tremulous smile as she reached out to take hold of her baby. Vena's lips began to quiver as she gazed at her son.

"Nestor, he has your eyes." She looked at Nestor, affectionately smiling, and then back to her son. The baby began to root around, so Vena guided him to her breast to nurse. Nestor leaned down and kissed Vena on the forehead.

"His name is Dismas." Nestor was barely able to speak. He embraced his beloved wife and child gently, and let the tears come.

"Dismas," she whispered. "Our son."

CHAPTER 3
THE TURNING

Thud! Thud! Thud!

Unceasing pounding against the wooden door jarred Nestor and Philos out of their daze. They looked at one another nervously. The knocking continued and each rap made the men cringe. They cupped their ears and tightly closed their eyes as if each thud caused severe pain.

"We know you are in there, Nestor!" a voice yelled. "It's been three days since the baby was born! Just open the door, so we can make sure everything is all right!"

"That was the doctor, but who is with him?" Nestor wondered. He pointed toward the door and Philos immediately went to it, not to open it, but to push himself against it, should they try to break it down. Nestor went into the bedroom. Flies buzzed about the fetid bed, feasting on the decaying matter. Small larvae wiggled through the tangled mess of blood-soaked bedding. A rancid smell like that of a dead animal permeated the confines. A cloth was covering the single window in an attempt to block out any light. Through the filtered shadows, Nestor scrambled to his wife's side, who now sat in a chair in the back corner.

"My love," Nestor said, his voice strangely raspy. The baby was suckling at the mother's breast. The right arm lay limp at her side and her head rested back against the stone wall awkwardly. Her face hidden in the shadows.

"My love," he said again, "They come for us. What do you wish us to do?"

He grabbed hold of one of her limp hands, bringing it close to his chest. He leaned in to hear her answer. There was no movement nor response from Vena, yet Nestor listened intently as if someone was speaking to him.

Nestor pulled away, nodding in response to an unspoken answer, "Yes, protect the child. He is special. Yes, yes."

The baby slid away from the breast and began to cry. Nestor's lip curled and he growled. He positioned the child back again to quiet him, but Dismas continued crying, and soon it became a wail. The smell of soured milk wafted and then faded quickly as it was overtaken by the aroma of death.

More pounding baraged the door. "Nestor, it has been days now without a word of your situation. We are concerned for your wife and child!"

Nestor suddenly roared. It was animalistic. It was unnatural. Philos joined him in the roar and together the sound caused the foundation of the building to shake. A different voice outside commanded, "Get back, get back! Step away!"

The shaking caused the baby to fall to the ground. Nestor immediately stopped and looked down at the helpless screaming three-day-old. Nestor's head cocked slowly to the left studying the wailing child. His eyes narrowed and his upper lip began to quiver, rising up on one side to expose dried blood-encrusted teeth.

He whispered through tight lips to his son, "You are weak. I will show you true power."

Suddenly, louder, more intense pounding came. Thud! Thud! Thud!

Just then someone outside yelled, "By order of Rome, open the door!" The voice was deep and militaristic.

Philos peaked into the room where Nestor stared at the squirming baby, who had stopped crying. "Master, what do we do?"

Nestor jerked out of his trance and looked about to get his bearings. The chaotic orchestra of buzzing flies intensified, soothing him and he calmed. "Let them come." His voice was shallow and the tone suggested pain—deep emotional pain. "Let them come." He grabbed hold of his head with both hands, suddenly thrashing his body around. "Get out of my mind!"

The door splintered open, letting in piercing sunlight. Roman soldiers clamored inside, one after the other. Each abruptly stopped to cover their mouth and nose as the intense smell of death and fecal matter assaulted them.

"Halt!" a guard commanded, pointing at Philos. They could not see Nestor or the baby, who were around the corner inside the bedroom. Philos turned toward them. His eyes flinched at the light. He fell to his knees and began to cry uncontrollably, "Help...me."

"By the gods, what has happened here?" one incredulous soldier said under his breath.

The doctor ran in behind the guards, "Where is she?" He pushed past the soldiers and stood over Philos who was now curled in a ball, crying.

"We are here," a raspy voice said from the back recesses of the bedroom.

"Nestor? Vena?" The doctor peered inside while covering his mouth and nose. The buzzing of the flies increased as he entered the horrific scene. Trickles of light fluttered in as the wind caused the heavy draping to move, casting ghoulish shadows over the dead mother. Vena, the ashen gray color of death upon her, sat in a chair at the back wall next to the covered window. His eyes were diverted when the baby cooed.

"By the gods," he stammered in shock.

A guard, the apparent leader, peaked over the doctor's shoulder and said, "What is this evil?"

He looked back at his other four men who stood uneasy, but ready, and pointed at Philos. They quickly grabbed him, lifting him up by his arms and holding him in place. "You are under arrest until we can discern what has happened here." Philos did not resist. Instead, his head slumped down as if passed out. The guards continued to hold him in place.

The doctor quickly tore the makeshift drape away from the window to let the full light enter the room. He then used it to cover the naked woman from head to toe. Her eyes were still open. Lifeless. Dark. A soulless stare. The doctor shivered as he covered her face, knowing this scene would haunt him all the days of his life.

Nestor sat in the corner shadows. He buried his face in his knees, hiding from prying eyes. The once strong and vibrant Greek was not who he used to be. Dirty and malnourished with dark circles around his eyes; Nestor was now a shell of a man.

The doctor bent down to pick up the squirming baby but before he could grab hold of him, Nestor charged with a speed that shocked everyone. "Stay away from him!" Nestor pushed the doctor away with such violent force that the man flew into the adjacent wall and crashed to the ground. He moaned in pain.

Two guards entered the room and went to subdue Nestor, but he threw them back like ragdolls. The lead guard slashed with his sword and sliced the side of Nestor's ribcage, exposing flesh through his clothing. Blood gushed out of the wound. It was a blow the soldier knew to be fatal. The other soldiers held their positions next to their prisoner while the felled guards scrambled back to their feet and picked up their swords.

Nestor fell back and slumped to the ground.

"I've never seen such strength before," one soldier said shakily.

"You will quiet yourself," the captain ordered. "Help the physician."

They assisted the doctor back to his feet, "Are you all right?"

"I will be fine." Once settled on his feet he picked up the baby and cradled him. Dismas began to cry.

"Doctor, get that child out of here!"

"What of Nestor?"

The Roman officer looked at him grimly. It was a look the doctor was accustomed to seeing. The knowing that Nestor would not live.

The physician looked upon the baby as he hurried out the building, "May the gods take any memory of this from you, child."

"Take the body and Philos back to the barracks," commanded the captain.

"Yes, sir."

Before the men were able to take a step toward Nestor, the flies massed around his body. It was as if they came out of thin air. They formed a blackened spinning sphere, buzzing so loudly it forced the guards to step away and hold their hands up to shield their ears. The sphere of insects suddenly lurched toward the men in the form of a demonic face and then it retreated back to the faceless sphere once again. The soldiers scurried backwards toward the front of the home. Their leader also tentatively backed away, but held his ground.

"Neleus, what is this madness?" one guard said to the captain.

He did not respond, nor did he look away from the body now covered by the insects. Instead, his eyes narrowed in disgust, transfixed at the sight. The other men moved Philos outside into the street. One sentry coughed as he took in fresh air and then almost vomited while holding himself steady against the adjacent building across the narrow street. Another kept his sword ready in attack position while the remaining two held Philos captive.

A few other soldiers, who had been waiting outside in case they were needed, said, "What happened in there?"

The one holding the sword quietly began to speak, "It's not natural," he mumbled. "It's just not natural...not natural...the flies... all the flies."

"Efrem, calm yourself," one of the men said.

A nervous sweat beaded and then ran profusely down his forehead and his tanned skin turned ashen. "It's not natural. The...the flies. It's not natural."

The captain remained steadfast, still standing in the entryway of the bedroom. He watched as some of the flies landed on the body while others buzzed about in a frenzy. The stalwart warrior who had seen the gruesome battlefield many times over was startled nearly out of his skin when Nestor suddenly flinched and sat straight up. Flies covered Nestor's face, entering in and out of every orifice. The captain could not believe his eyes when Nestor stood. The abomination had not used his hands to push himself up but instead had stood supernaturally, like a wooden board being lifted up at one end.

Neleus raised his sword. He was confident in his skills and training, having been in many battles, but unsure as to what he was fighting, as this was no mere man.

"What is it?" the nervous guard spouted toward his captain. Neleus looked over at his soldier for the briefest moment and then looked back at the monster before him to see Nestor holding his side where he was wounded. The flies had mysteriously vanished. Neleus' eyes darted around the room and he saw not a single insect where there once were thousands. It was eerily quiet.

"Help me," Nestor coughed and then slumped forward. Neleus instinctively dropped his sword and caught Nestor before he hit the ground.

"Guards!" Neleus ordered, "Get in here and take them to the courtyard. I want them both shackled in restraints."

They paused, but he boomed, "NOW!" and they responded. Each one grabbed an underarm and dragged him out of the home and into the street where Philos was being held. The captain exited and then led the way back to base.

The two sentries holding Nestor did not notice the single fly exiting his left nostril and then quickly entering his right. His eyes fluttered back into his sockets revealing only the whites and his head rolled to and fro as he was dragged away.

Nestor tried to speak but the only phrase the guards could hear was, "Who am I?"

The soldiers looked at one another, clearly concerned. They marched hastily to get this crazed man locked in chains as fast as they could and be done with him. Tonight, they would drink these evil memories from their mind and pray to their gods for protection from the curse that had befallen Philos and Nestor.

Nestor, in a daze, repeatedly whispered, "Who am I?"

CHAPTER 4
THE TOMBS

"ARE THEY SECURE?" the voice said nervously.

Sweat and grime covered the face of the Roman soldier who had just entered the quarters. His arm securely cradled his helmet against the thick leather armor around this chest. He was attempting to calm himself as if he had just come from the battlefield.

"Yes, Commander Fortus. It took ten of us to subdue but one of them after they broke the first restraints. They are now bound in chains on the wall outside for the time being. I have posted guards with clear instructions to keep everyone away."

The commander massaged his temple to alleviate the bad headache that had resulted from this entire ordeal. "We don't have the resources for this. I need everyone watching the north and east roads. Damn bandits have been reported in the area."

"Yes, Prefect. I will assign the guards as instructed."

"Wait, the chains," he paused. "They will hold?"

The soldier had not made eye contact until now. He exhaled slowly, "Yes, sir, the chains will hold."

"Then take those men and secure the north and east road."

"As you say, sir," the soldier replied obediently as he turned to leave.

"Wait!" The commander interrupted. "Have Lucius' team position troops on the south road as well."

"But we don't have enough men."

"Do as I say! These bandits love to use trickery and rarely follow any rules of engagement. They are barbaric and will die as such."

"As you say, sir." He bowed and retreated from the small room.

The commander went to his water bowl to wash his hands and face. He rested his arms on the edge, and massaged his neck, letting the water dribble down his back. His nose almost touched the water in the basin.

The pressure of maintaining the region with no support weighed heavily on him. And the report of the unusual evil disturbance in town with these two Greek men now in chains did not sit well in his stomach. The stress was getting the best of him. Cool water dripped into the basin and he focused on the relaxing sound it made. A strange screeching noise interrupted his momentary relief, beckoning him to look outside. *"What is that noise?"* he thought.

Fortus stood upright and slowly walked outside to hear more clearly. *"Those aren't jackals. I know their incessant cries well, for over a year now, since coming from Rome. No, this sound is more animalistic, with a tinge of...what?"* he thought.

The commander grabbed his red cloak and slung it around his neck. He was no fighter, though he had seen his fair share of bloodshed with the backstabbing of men to rise to the top. Fortus' battles were within the political arena. His rise through the ranks had come because of his father's influence. With the combination of that, as well as the *untimely* deaths of a few key individuals, he had been able to ride upon his father's stature to the position he now held. Eight months ago, he was assigned to oversee the region now known as Decapolis. Ten ungodly towns on the fringe of Arabia.

Again, the screech came from beyond the courtyard. No other personnel were in the vicinity and the large, reinforced double-door that led out was half open. He heard a few of his men talking loudly but he could not make out their words. He stepped closer to the open door. A guard hurried by in a blur, which caused him to halt in surprise, but he continued on, drawn to the haunting cries.

Then he heard the words that chilled him to the bone, "They have broken loose!" It was his nightmare come to life. He knew deep inside his soul that this would happen. A premonition he had wished away. *"What in all the gods had come upon this Decapolis town?"* The echo of his father's words flashed through his mind, *"Always be prepared."* He remembered asking as a boy, *"Prepared for what?"* Then he received the backhand lash that changed his perspective forever. He looked up at his dominant and commanding father and heard his stern voice say, *"The unexpected. Always be prepared and never be caught flat-footed."*

A piercing, unearthly scream startled him back from his thoughts. A soldier hurried by him just before Fortus took the final step through the open doorway. Suddenly, a warrior crashed into the wall, stirring a flurry of dust. This soldier wasn't running. He had been thrown. His heart raced and the sweat dripped freely from his brow. Fortus had no contingency, no plan. He needed to witness what monster lurked around the corner. These demon-men his soldiers paraded into headquarters earlier must have transformed into creatures of immense size. Beasts sent by the gods to test him. *"What is it? I must see it."*

He stepped beyond the door and turned to the right to see the two Greek men, once bound in chains, freely tossing his soldiers aside with ease. A strange buzzing sound, like that of bees, emanated from their direction but he could not see any source to support the sound he heard.

The taller Greek spoke, his abnormal voice reverberated, "We are many!" He waved one hand in an arc as he spoke. The broken foot-long piece of chain clanked against the manacle attached to his wrist.

More soldiers flooded into the courtyard bearing spears and shields. The Greek men, who were not mere men any longer, focused their gaze upon Fortus, who had just entered the courtyard. They pointed simultaneously and spoke in unison, "You, Commander of the Weak! You will receive us or die."

Shakily, Fortus responded, "Who are you?"

Both demon-men shouted, "Silence!" The earth trembled underfoot.

It was their eyes. Even in the waning sunlight, he could see that they shimmered an unearthly orange.

"We will destroy you, lest you sacrifice to us. For we were sent to shroud this region with the darkest of glory."

"You were...sent?" he questioned.

A spear suddenly launched from behind the shield-bearers. It sailed in, perfectly aimed, at the former Nestor. He did not move until at the last moment his hand miraculously caught it in flight. The demon-man snapped it like a twig and screamed hideously in rage causing warriors to cup their ears.

"Regroup!" an officer yelled. "Prepare spears!"

A score of men readied to hurl at the signal to release.

"Halt!" Fortus yelled. "All of you halt!"

An uneasy quietness fell upon the courtyard. The soldiers obeyed and waited for their orders. Fortus walked toward the Greeks uneasily. It was as if he was resisting an unseen force that was pushing him forward.

"Back away, let them be!" he resigned. There was a noticeable grimace on his face as he gave the orders.

The men glanced at one another, uncertain whether this was a trick. But how could it be? Their commander gave them an order and the Roman way was to obey. One-by-one they backed away and opened up a path for the two demon-possessed men to exit. Soldiers held their breath as they walked past them. The demon-men turned to and fro in an agitated state of mind, sometimes lurching toward a warrior, causing the Roman to flinch and flare his shield. Roman soldiers wanted to fight and showed no fear or backing down. The chapped, dry-skinned faces of the warriors creased in disgust as they watched the Greek men leave the courtyard of the great Roman citadel of Hippus. Rome doesn't know defeat. This was instilled into every one of them.

Nestor and Philos departed and so did the presence of evil that enveloped the area. The commander did not give any orders, but instead walked back to his quarters solemnly. His men followed a step or two then stopped and watched their leader close and latch the door to his office. Orders shot out from the next in command, "Back to your posts! I want men on the north and south roads!"

Another order came on the heels of the last, "Officer Neleus!"

"Yes, sir."

"I want your patrol to follow them. Do not engage, but do not lose sight of them. Have a messenger report back."

Neleus nodded, "Yes, Lucius." He hesitated.

"What is it, Neleus? Speak freely."

"What are we doing, Lucius? Those things need to be put down."

"I know. I will speak with Commander Fortus." He placed his hand on Neleus' armored shoulder. "Don't engage them. Just monitor. Do you understand?"

"I understand."

The sound of sandaled soldiers bearing shields, spears, and swords was heard moving out. A calmness returned and order was restored.

Commander Fortus, hands covering his face, wept. "I am weak. I am not worthy, Father," he said through muffled tears. He could hear his father's words in his mind, *"You are a failure. A disgrace to our family."* He was right and there was nothing he could do about it. He whispered, "You sent me here, didn't you Father? This godforsaken station out in the middle of nowhere. You sent me here to die."

A single fly buzzed around his left ear and he swatted it away. Fortus froze in place after swatting the insect to see the tall demon-man standing before him. The Greek's dark beard was matted with blood and saliva. His eyes glowed a reflective orange. Fortus stared in horror.

"Do not speak, only listen," the demon whispered, his words echoing around Fortus. "We will make you strong, Commander of the Weak. We are many and this region was given to us. Your weaklings will be ordered to stay back from the tombs. You will bring us an animal sacrifice every day. Do you understand, Commander of the Weak?"

Fortus nodded.

The chamber door rattled, causing Fortus to jolt. A soldier pounded on it three times in quick succession.

"Sir, I need to speak with you right away!"

The demon brushed Fortus' cheek with his hand and then brought one finger up to his lips and said, "Shhhhhhhh. We will make you strong. We will make you known and feared across this land. We will protect you, as you protect us." Nestor backed away into the shadows of the darkened corner of the room.

"Prefect, are you in there?"

No answer.

Lucius yelled out to his soldiers, "Something is wrong! Open this door!"

Several minutes elapsed. Whispers ensued outside the reinforced wooden door. Suddenly, it flung open as two warriors slammed a heavy steel-tipped wooden beam into it, breaking the locking mechanism. They let go of the leather handles and it clanked loudly to the ground. Light filled the room where the shadows once lurked. The commander sat motionless on his chair, eyes fixated on the empty corner of the room. The demon was gone.

"Get the physician!" Lucius barked.

He rushed to Fortus' side and said, "Sir, the two men are being tracked. We must plan an assault."

The commander snapped out of his trance and, trembling, said, "No! No, there must not be an assault. Take...take those soldiers and..."

"And what?"

Fortus hesitated. He could hear his father's voice in his mind, *"Hesitation is for the weak. Confidence, regardless of right or wrong, stands the test. Now stand up and speak with authority!"*

"Prefect? What are your orders?"

Fortus made eye contact with Lucius and stood, never disconnecting from his stare. Fortus' voice slow and deliberate, "Back away. Leave the two Greek men alone. They are not to be touched. Set up a post at the top of the hill to the tombs but do not go any closer."

"Yes, sir," Lucius responded hesitantly, "We will have the men make sure they don't come out of those tombs."

"No, the post is to keep the town people away. No one is to harm those Greek men."

"But, sir..."

"Do you understand me? No one!"

Lucius fought to acknowledge the orders.

Fortus leaned in close, "Are my orders not clear enough? Do you need to be relieved of duty?"

Lucius swallowed hard, "As you command."

Fortus broke away and stepped past Lucius. "Our focus is still on those bandits. We will clean the region of their filth once and for all. I want twenty crosses made and I want them filled by the end of the week. Do you understand me?"

Lucius nodded.

"The thieving bastards will fear us by month end. This I vow," the commander said as he exited his chamber. The sunlight waned as he walked out. He stopped and turned around to face Lucius and the other soldiers. "The times have changed and we must change with them. Today wasn't a loss. In fact, it was a great victory." Fortus smirked as he watched the bewilderment of his men.

Fortus turned and walked away briskly. "Yes, a great victory!" he yelled for all to hear.

The men stood dumbfounded. Fortus knew he would use this supernatural force that just took residence within his region. Over time, wielding this new power, his father and Rome itself would hear of his great exploits and finally take notice.

PART II
DISMAS

CHAPTER 5
TEN YEARS LATER

I KNOW THAT THEY *are there. Hidden. Waiting for me. This isn't the first time I've seen them. Dark, wispy shadows that hide outside my room. Their red eyes give them away. Yes, they are there, waiting for me, but I know that if I stay inside they will not enter. I know to remain. Or they have taught me to stay. I know not.*

I don't dare step out. There is pain out there. It is unknown what lies beyond this cell I chose to stay inside. I can imagine nothing but the worst of nightmares. They never come inside, only wait outside.

I've learned that my physical body is sleeping in the world created by the Greek gods, while my spirit never sleeps in this other dark realm. Do the gods know of this place? They must know. Why do they allow this torment to befall me? I'm only a child and know not the thoughts of the immortals. Their ways are not ours, even though we long to be with them.

I hear something. What is it? Sounds like scratching. I am afraid. They have never come inside before. The latch to the door, it's moving. I don't want to believe it. My last defense is to close my eyes and curl myself in the corner. I can hear the creak of the metal latch lifting. I cover my ears and don't believe.

By the gods, where are you? The horror of this place. I can hear the door opening, ever so slowly. I cannot help myself, I peek and there it is, the red eyes. They want to kill me. No, not kill, consume me. I can feel my lifeforce being pulled on. My soul has no filters and flashes of death enter my mind. Bloody appendages litter the ground. I see my head, eyes wide open, lifelessly staring back at me. The mouth, my mouth, of my dismembered body speaks, 'Your pain, your fear, your soul, is mine.'

The ten-year-old boy suddenly awoke from the nightmare, gasping and lurching up from his bed. Beads of sweat trickled down his forehead and his dark brown hair was matted to his skin. If he could grab his heart to calm the erratic pounding, he would. His hand rubbed his bony chest.

Another boy woke up next to him, "What is it, Diz? Another nightmare?" He sat up to comfort him. He was older but not by more than two years. A bright, full moon was visible through the open window, lighting up the small room.

"Gestas," he whispered, "do you believe the gods exist?"

"What are you talking about? Did you catch the fever that father has?"

"No, I just…"

"It was only a nightmare, Dismas."

"It was different."

"What do you mean?"

"I don't know. I'm scared, Gestas." He felt tears well up, but quickly wiped them away before his brother could see them.

Gestas grabbed him and pulled him close. "It is going to be okay. Father will not let anything happen to you or me. I promise."

"But father is sick," he whimpered.

"Shhh, I will protect you." Gestas stared into the distance while holding his little brother in an embrace. He bit his lower lip, unsure of the future, hoping he would be able to keep his promise.

It weighed heavily upon him having to help with his father's business while father recovered. If only the gods had not crippled his leg at birth then he could have done the work of ten men.

"Go ahead and lie back down."

Fear gripped Dismas and he shook his head. Gestas grabbed his brother by the shoulders and said, "You do not have to sleep, just lie back down." His little brother couldn't relax, but he laid down as instructed.

Suddenly, there was an urgent knock at the front door. It was loud enough that they could hear it from their bedroom in the back. Both startled, Dismas sat straight up and Gestas froze in place. They listened and could hear muffled conversation. It was their mother and a male voice talking.

Gestas moved to look but Diz grabbed him, "No, Gez, don't leave me. It's the monsters from my dream."

"Monsters are not real. I am just going to look." He pulled away and crept to the door. Diz held his breath, intently watching his older brother. With one or two steps you would never know that Gestas had a limp, but it was very noticeable when he walked any distance.

"What do you see?" Diz whispered.

"Shhh, nothing yet. Wait, it's, it's…"

"It is what?"

"Roman soldiers."

"Why?"

"I do not know. I have only seen them at the swine farm. Never here." Suddenly, Gestas stiffened.

"What happened?" Dismas asked.

"Mother closed the curtain to the kitchen where they are. I saw at least three. I am going to get closer."

"Closer? Do not go, Gestas."

"Diz, it is our home. We will be fine."

"I have heard of Romans pulling people from their homes."

"Father always says, 'The best way to get over fear is to dive right into it.'"

"I am scared."

"And I will protect you. They cannot see us and we will be quiet."

Dismas waited two long seconds and then slowly slid from the bed. He grabbed hold of his brother's hand. They both slipped through the door and silently made their way to the curtained doorway leading to the kitchen. They could hear them more clearly with only a piece of fabric separating them.

A soldier with a grizzly voice said, "I don't care what you say, woman. Commander Fortus will have his time and we will have ours."

Their mother replied, with fear in her voice, "My husband is not well. Could Fortus see to it another time, I beg?"

Chuckles from several men answered her question. A new voice entered the conversation, silencing the room. It was smooth and eloquent, not one of the soldiers. "I most certainly will not be put off another night, my dear."

The guards stood at attention, "Commander."

A portly man just below six-foot stature entered the domain. He was not in regal attire as this late night visit wasn't notated by any scribe.

"At ease, men," the red-cloaked Commander Fortus instructed. "Now, where is he? I take it he is in his room."

"I beg of you to send for the physician," the mother pleaded.

"The physician has already been here. I need to assess the situation to see how sick your husband truly is."

"He has not been able to work for weeks now."

"This I know to be true. Another reason I have come. Now, men please stand guard while I parley with the man of the house."

"Yes, sir."

Fortus entered the husband's bedroom, closing the door behind him. Gestas whispered into his brother's ear, "Watch Mother and the soldiers. I am going to listen in on what's happening in Father's room."

Diz shook his head in fear, but Gestas moved by him. Stopping a few paces away, he cupped his ear against the wall. Dismas watched a few seconds and then heard the guards speaking to his mother, which pulled his attention away from Gestas.

"Get us something to drink, woman. We are thirsty."

He heard her rummaging for cups and ladling water. The grizzly voice said, "We are not asking for *water*, woman."

Meanwhile, Gestas could hear the conversation between Commander Fortus and his father.

"Your business, or should I say our business, suffers daily with your absence."

His father spoke, but his voice was so weak that Gestas was unable to hear through the wall.

"My dear man, you look and sound horrible," Fortus responded. "Let me be plain. Should you die, your business falls to me. Now, our relationship is not public due to the law forbidding a Roman soldier to own a business, as you are quite aware. I'm here to understand your contingency." There was a pause and then Fortus said, "Karpos, this is the time where you say something to my liking."

Father began to speak, but Gez was unable to hear him once again. *"How was this possible that his father had been working with Fortus, the Roman constable of the region?"* The ramification of this insight was beyond his twelve-year-old mind.

Fortus, the one who governed all of Decapolis, spoke, "I see. Your sons are not of age to own and manage such an undertaking. Your pig farm supplies this entire region, Karpos. Do you understand the magnitude of the situation that I am facing? I'm not sure that you do so I have another plan that is to my liking." Fortus paused and said, "You will initiate a partnership with Clavius."

Father raised his voice, "No, never!" Gestas heard father coughing and the creaking of the bed as father fell back against it, his remaining strength sapped.

Clavius Sedontin was the epitome of betrayal within the family. Clavius was Father's brother and 'stole', as Father put it, the family business when Gestas was two and Dismas was a baby. A plague, as the story was told, hit the swine in the region and destroyed everything. Father started from scratch, resurrecting himself over time, forever distancing himself from the brother who betrayed him. Clavius' name was never spoken within the family. Last they heard of him was years past when they were told he had become a drunkard in the southern towns of Decapolis.

"I understand your position," Fortus said, "but it *will* happen. If you resist for any reason then I cannot ensure the safety of your family."

The threat hung in the silence like a noose slung over a tree. But what Fortus said next shook him to the core.

"Your wife would not be safe alone. Your crippled son, how long do you anticipate he will last? What if others found out about your bastard child, Dismas, and who his true father is?"

He heard his father respond, "You cannot do this. Please, I will do whatever you want, but promise me you will take care of my family. Let them live in peace." Then father went into another fitful cough.

"Peace is in high demand in a region such as this. Times are changing, my friend."

Gestas thought deeply about what he was hearing. The clear threat to the family weighed heavy enough, but he locked onto the latter statement. Gestas looked at his brother, who was listening to the soldiers and their mother in the other room. He stared at him, shocked. *"Dismas isn't my true brother? Who was his father, then?"* Thoughts and questions rattled around his brain. Diz noticed him staring. The boys locked eyes. Gestas focused on Diz' mismatched colored eyes. One eye was brown while the other splashed greens and blues. No one else in the family had those eyes.

A slap caused them to snap out of the moment. Then the yelling began.

"You will do as commanded, Greek wench!" the soldier said. "Or I will beat you to death!"

Mother was crying. Gestas hurried to Dismas' side and peered through the curtain. A chair was knocked over and a drink spilled, the liquid dripped from the table onto the floor. Three other soldiers scooted their chairs back and stood. Mother held the left side of her face and looked down at the ground in subservience.

Diz noticed the lead guard nod to another. This single nod initiated action. Mother was grabbed by her arm and tossed toward the other men. She was quickly grappled and then shoved face first onto the kitchen table. Cups and plates spilled and fell to the floor as she tried to resist.

"Now we will show you Roman hospitality," the grizzly voice said while lifting mother's robe. One soldier cupped a hand over mother's mouth to muffle her scream. The lead soldier positioned himself behind her.

"Nooooo!" Gestas shouted and charged into the room, taking the soldiers by surprise. He slammed into the man and thrashed his arms back and forth in rage. They let go of mother as they repositioned themselves against the new threat. Once they understood that it was a mere boy, they began to laugh heartily. The soldier took the blows from the child as Gestas continued to pound his fists against his leather armored chest.

Mother began to get up from the table but the soldier that was being hit by her son quickly backhanded her and said, "I didn't tell you to get up, woman." She toppled into a ball at another soldier's feet.

Gestas was grabbed and lifted to eye level by the unshaven Roman soldier. Gez looked into the steel-grey eyes and noticed the small scar above his right eye. His teeth were yellowed and his gums looked inflamed. Gez swung at the hideous monster, hitting his jaw, causing a a trickle of blood to gather at the split of his mouth. The man licked at it and smiled. Blood covered his yellow teeth, making the soldier look even more grotesque.

"Not bad, boy."

Gestas tried to swing again, but the soldier was ready. He blocked it while simultaneously letting him drop to the ground. Gestas' weak leg gave out and he fell back in pain. The soldier's leather sandaled foot was raised high to stomp on him.

Dismas, like a blur, ran through the black curtain, slid under the soldier's foot and punched his testicles. The man doubled over and fell to the ground.

"Get him," he commanded through gritted teeth while cupping himself with his hands.

The other soldiers responded and tried to grab the ten-year-old, but Dismas was quick and agile. The boy eluded them by going under the kitchen table. One soldier grabbed the edge and flipped it over, sending dishes flying everywhere. Pottery shattered and shards slid in all directions. Diz was gone from underneath.

Gestas yelled, "Get out of here, Diz!"

He was already at the front door when Fortus came out of Father's room and bellowed, "Enough!"

His voice stopped everyone except Dismas, who ran into the starlit night.

"Captain, get your men and prepare my horse."

The soldier stood up slowly, still in pain, nodded to his men, and they left.

Fortus came to their mother's aid, helping her to her feet. "My dear, I do apologize."

She looked at him fearfully.

"Do not be afraid. All is well. Once your husband gets healthy, then everything will be all right once again."

"Will the physician come?" she asked, tentatively.

"No, he is not needed. On the morrow, another person of importance will be here. His name is Clavius."

She was clearly stunned, "Clavius? Why? Why him?"

"I have discussed the matter with your husband and he is in full agreement. Clavius and he have some business to attend to and you, my dear, will be a good wife and make sure he is welcomed. Offer him something to eat and drink, and you will ensure they are not disrupted by your unruly children."

There was a long pause, "Do you understand?"

"Yes," she said shakily.

"Good. I would hate to bring those ruffian soldiers back with me for another visit." He grinned and said, "Well, I must be off. This was a productive meeting and I thank you for your hospitality."

Fortus exited and the room was silent.

"Are you all right, son?" She came to Gez' side and hugged him.

Gestas didn't respond and she quickly said, "What's wrong? Are you hurt?"

His eyes slowly connected with hers and he said, "Who is Dismas' real father?"

CHAPTER 6
THE PROMISE

TEN YEARS BEFORE THE CROSS
-DISMAS-

SEVERAL DAYS HAD passed since the incident with the Roman official and his savage guards. Gestas, this morning, was inside father's room alone for quite some time, while I lingered in the kitchen, wandered outside, and then came back. All the while mother tried not to look at me, remaining busy preparing food, washing clothes, and tidying up the home. I had a strange sense that something was not right. The smell of roasted pig and baked bread, my favorite meal, filled the air. Everything was as it should be but there seemed to be a hidden mystery. It had to be the private meeting with Gestas.

"Mother," I said nervously.

"Yes, Dismas."

"What's going on?"

"What do you mean?" she paused.

"I don't know. Ever since those men came, things have been different."

"Different how, son?" She wasn't making eye contact and remained busy cleaning a pot, scraping out the burnt leftovers caked at the bottom.

"I don't know. It's just…"

"Why don't you go outside and play for a bit."

"When will Gestas come out of father's room?"

She peered over at the closed door, and said, "When the door opens."

"But when will—"

"No more questions. Now go or I will have you help me clean these dishes." She grabbed a nearby broom, giggling, and stabbed at my rear end to push me away with the stiff bristles.

I reluctantly walked toward the front, knowing that mother's playfulness masked a deep pain inside her. Suddenly, the door to father's room opened and Gestas walked out, closing the door behind him, but not all the way. Father coughed in the background. I held my breath, frozen in place, the secret meeting gnawing at my curiosity. Father had private meetings with us both periodically, but never like this, and not for so long.

I broke the silence, "Is father okay?"

Gestas looked at me with uncertainty. It was a look I'd never seen from him before.

"What is it?" I pressured.

My older brother hobbled over to the kitchen table, his left foot turned in from a deformed bone at birth. He grabbed his walking stick, and then made his way out the front door. I looked at Mother, who gave me a feeble smile. I could tell she wanted to comfort me, but whatever burden she carried prevented her from being able to do it.

"What is going on? You all know something and you're not telling me what it is!"

Silence.

"Is Father going to die?"

Silence. Mother's eyes became glassy with tears.

I began to cry, "Mother, what's going to happen?"

From the back room, father's voice resounded, "Diz, come." This prompted a hacking cough.

Mother brought her hand to her mouth. She fought to hold back tears.

I was frozen in place and looked at Mother for an answer, wiping the tears from her face.

With a cracked voice, she said, ever so softly, "Go to him."

I turned and faced Father's room. *"What awaited me behind this closed door?"* My mind brought back the nightmares. The shadow creatures awaited my family, and perhaps they were in there now and wanted to show me their power by taking Father away into the valley of darkness. I felt my knees wobble with each step. I saw my trembling hand reach for the door as if I were out of my body, watching myself.

In the dimly lit room, Father laid in bed. The smell of burnt sage couldn't mask the lingering scent of sweat and I could almost taste blood in the air. Candlelight danced slowly against the stone walls and I flinched at the shadow creatures that lurked in the dark corners of the room.

"Come closer, son."

I approached the left side and Father's hand reached for me to grab hold. His hand was rough, cool, and clammy.

"Let me look upon you," Father said. He liked to stare at us and especially liked my unusual mismatched eye color. "I always felt blessed by the gods for giving you double-sight."

"What do you mean, Papa?"

"Your eyes are the eyes of two different people. You are able to see things differently than others. The gods have granted you great insight. I have seen how you watch people and speak once you have discerned their heart."

"It is a curse, Papa."

"No, not a curse, a blessing." Father gripped my hand tighter and pulled me closer. "Don't forget that, son. It is a blessing." He suddenly let go and turned away to cough violently. He pulled out a cloth from under the covers to put over his mouth.

"You are bleeding," I whispered, clearly noticing the splotches on the cloth.

Father settled and looked at me. He smirked as he said, "As long as I'm bleeding, I'm still alive."

"What's happening, Papa? I don't want you to—"

"Only the gods know, son."

"Then why aren't they answering?"

"Have you been beckoning them?"

"Yes, Papa, daily."

"The gods are not to be beckoned, son. They do as they please. It is best to serve them and beg for mercy."

"I don't need them. I need you."

"You will need them. Someday, you will need them."

"Today is someday."

"That's my boy. Always in the present."

"You taught us that it is the here and now that matters."

"Yes," he sighed. "But never stop believing in the future. There are things in life that won't make sense. People won't make sense. You will make many choices and it's those moments, those choices, that will define you."

I couldn't understand what my father spoke of but answered according to what I knew he wanted to hear, "Yes, Papa."

He took another labored breath. "Now, I have something for you." He reached behind him, dislodged a loose stone in the wall, and slid it away. Father grabbed something inside the dark alcove and held it hidden in his hand before slowly revealing it to me.

"I had it made special for you."

I looked at it in amazement. The candlelight reflected off of the glazed wood, casting shadows over the carved edges.

"Take it," he said.

I took it in awe and strained in the light to pick out the details of the sculpted wood figurine. It rested majestically in my palm while my other hand caressed its features.

"The desert lion represents your strength and determination, my son. I believe it will also be your guide in the future, a future I am not sure I will see much longer."

"But Father, the gods, they will save you. I know it to be true."

"I believe you are right. They can save me if they so choose. Now go and show your mother your gift and ask her to come and tend to me. I am very tired."

I looked away from the gift and embraced my father as if it would be the last hug I would ever receive. I tried to force those thoughts from my mind. Slowly, I turned toward the door, but stopped and said, "Father, what did you speak about with Gestas?"

"He had questions for my ears only."

I wanted to press further but decided not to and turned to walk out. Before I could call for Mother, Father said, "Dismas?"

I turned back, "Yes, Papa."

"I love you, son. I always have, since the moment I laid my eyes upon you, and I always will."

I couldn't resist. I ran to him, lunging into his great embrace. Moments later, he whispered, "Now go and be the man I know you will become. And remember to listen to your brother."

"I will, Papa." Tears streamed down my face as I turned away, knowing this might be the last time I spoke with my father. I called to mother and she quickly darted past me, closing the door behind her. The wood figure in my hand was smooth and I marveled at the craftsmanship. In a strange way it brought me peace just looking at it. The desert lion posed proudly and I imagined it looking out into a valley somewhere, surveying the land he reigned over within the animal kingdom.

I whispered, "What god do you worship?"

It did not answer me. I clutched it tightly as I headed outside to look for my older brother, determined to find out what was spoken to him by father.

Gestas wasn't hiding, but was instead quietly looking off into the distance. We would often come out to the naturally formed sand pillars, a stone's throw from our home, and pray to the gods. We imagined that the gods once walked there and the pillars signified the remains of an ancient temple. Gestas' left arm wrapped around one such column and his left cheek rested against it as he looked off into the open valley. Hundreds of pigs were being shepherded by our father's workers in the distance. I was used to the rank smell of swine fecal matter that kicked up with the breeze and whistled through the four-pillared make-believe temple.

I said softly, "Gez?"

No answer.

"Father gave me this." I presented the wood figure in both hands.

Gestas did not turn around and said, "I don't care."

"What did father give you?" I was fishing for information.

"He gave me plenty."

"Of what?"

Gez turned and faced me. Dried tear tracks were evident. "You wouldn't understand." Gestas stared at me with an intensity I had never seen before.

"What is it?"

Gez shook his head, "Nothing."

"But what did father say to you? You were in there for so long."

"Stuff. Nothing. I don't know." Frustrated, Gestas turned back around to face the pig farm and clutched onto the column once again.

"Are you praying to the gods?"

"I want to be alone, Diz."

"He can't die, Gez, the gods won't allow it."

Gestas turned sharply to face me, "The gods? They don't care about me or you or father or anyone else! What are we to them? We are just pawns to be played in their game. Do you want to know what Father asked of me? He wanted me to promise him something."

"What promise?"

"Don't you understand, Diz? The promise to take care of you, like a brother, no matter what."

"But we are brothers, Gez. Aren't Mother and Father going to take care of us?"

"You saw Father. The sickness comes to take him away. Soon it will only be us."

"Don't say that! The gods will save him."

"Just leave me alone." Gestas turned and walked away.

A distant scream froze us both instantly, stealing my breath away.

"Gez, it's Mother!"

His eyes narrowed and he said sharply, "Like I said, the gods don't care, Diz."

"Gez, she needs our help! Come on!"

He shook his head and walked away. Where was he going? Why wasn't he running toward home? Something was wrong and yet he walked away when mother needed us most.

I ran home. Mother was wailing against the closed door to her room. I could see spots of blood on her apron.

"Mother?" I said tentatively.

Her arms opened to usher me in. I ran into them and she clutched me so tightly I almost couldn't breathe. My voice was muffled, "What's wrong?"

She continued to cry and all I could do was hold on to her. Deep down inside I knew that Father was gone, but I didn't want to believe it. Nestled against my mother's shoulder, I lifted the wood figure up so I could see it as my mother cried. Again, the peace returned to me.

"The gods must care," I thought. *"Did they not take father to a better place; a place without pain?"*

I prayed to the gods in my mind, *"If any god out there would hear my plea, then please save my father. Bring him back to me and I promise to follow you all the days of my life."*

CHAPTER 7
CHOICES

-DISMAS-

THE 'OLD TOMBS', as they were known, along the shoreline of the Sea of Galilee, were never to be visited. Father would tell us the stories. He said, *"Two demons were sent by the gods many years earlier. To this day no one knows why they came."* I loved Papa's storytelling. Gestas and I would curl up next to one another by the fire. I remembered that night he told us about the demons. I think that was the night my nightmares began.

"Only rumors existed among the communities, but I saw the beasts face-to-face," I remember him saying. *"Where poets recited prose drawn from curious imagination to tell their tale, I had firsthand knowledge."*

Gestas would interrupt, *"What happened, Papa?"*

That night, Father leaned in close to us as the shadows of the room danced about, mimicking the flickering flames. His breath was heavy, lips closed, eyes narrowed and he paused such a long time that I was uncertain of time itself. *"One of the demons stared at me,"* he continued. *"Its eyes red and full of hate, but I would not look away."*

"Why not, Papa?" Gestas asked.

"Fear is what they feed upon. Fear is what brings them from the dead. I would not show any fear so I narrowed my eyes like this." Father gave us a menacing look and his face tightened in anger. I remember leaning away from him with my brother. *"This was my battle to win or lose. I*

chose to win, not for myself, but for my family." I will always remember what he said next, *"I stared down fear to protect my family. To protect you."* His eyes pierced us with spears of intensity.

Mother sat nearby watching and said, *"Karpos, maybe it's too much for them."*

Father leaned back and responded, *"They are ready, Dora."*

"Yes, Mama, we want to hear this," Gestas said.

Father continued, *"There we were, face to face, locked in a battle within our minds. I could feel its dark tentacles trying to break in,"* Father pointed to his head. *"But my anger, propelled by the Greek god Zeus himself, strengthened my defenses. I yelled, 'By the power of Zeus, I banish you to the tombs of the underworld of Hades where you will never be released and forever condemned!'"*

Father paused and Gestas blurted, *"What happened?"*

"To this day, these demons walk the Old Tombs and feed off the fear of those who wander too close."

"Are they real?" I asked.

"As the flesh on your body. Yes, they are very real. You two are never to go to the Old Tombs."

"Were you scared, Papa?" Gestas asked.

"Of course I was but I wouldn't show them. Remember, don't show fear to anyone in this world or any other. You either control the demons around you or the demons will control you."

Cool air whipped through the crags, howling a haunting wail, pulling me from my memories. The priest mumbled words before the small gathering, which I paid no attention to. Friends from town, business associates of father's pig farm, Mother, along with me and my brother stood just outside where Father was wrapped in linen. Others were laced throughout the small trails on the sloped rocky hill behind us. The clergyman performed the coins ceremony, placing them upon father's eyes to pay the boatman for passage across the River Styx. The tomb entrance was then covered with rocks. Those gathered slowly dissipated. Some clustered in small groups to talk amongst themselves. Others approached the tomb to place small statues of the deities they worshipped at the sealed entryway, asking for a blessing for our departed father.

Mother grabbed the back of our necks and nudged us to walk. With heads down, we walked sullenly in silence toward our home. Not too far into our journey, a most unpleasant voice caused us to halt. It was father's brother, Clavius Sedontin, my uncle.

Clavius' voice was sultry and it sickened me to hear it, "Good tidings, Dora. Children," he nodded with a smirk.

"Not here," she pleaded.

Two Roman guards revealed themselves from around a large boulder to bring more tension to the threatening situation. Mother scoffed and drew us closer. We were out of sight of anyone from the funeral, but I knew a scream would echo far off, bringing the villagers running.

Clavius said, "Let's not make this any more difficult than it has to be."

"Meaning, what my husband built is to be handed over to you?"

"Well, that part is already done, as I now hold the deed with his signature signing it over to me. I'm here to make sure you and your sons are taken care of, as per our arrangement." Clavius pulled forth a small leather pouch with the drawstrings pulled tightly. The clang of coin resounded as he jiggled it in his hand.

"Your first payment."

She glared at him with suspicion, "Why here? Why now, Clavius?"

"I was on my way to pay my brother respect when we happened upon you. It seems it was fated by the gods." He put his hands up in the air and looked around as if to spot the deities hovering above them.

"You expect me to believe that?"

"I expect you will believe whatever you want to believe." Clavius walked by and dropped the bag of coin at her feet. He leaned in close and whispered, "I will see you soon, Dora."

The red armor and regal helmets worn by the Roman guards escorted Clavius as he walked out of sight toward the burial location.

I picked up the bag and opened it to see several pieces of silver.

"Leave it, Dismas," Mother said firmly. "It is money from Hades itself."

I tossed it away like it carried the plague. It fell between some rocks, spilling out the silver. The sparkle of the metal intrigued me and ignited my desire to obtain it. I stared at it as my mother pulled me away toward home. I brought my lion figurine from my pocket and rubbed it with my forefinger and thumb. Bringing it closer to my mouth, I whispered, "Protect me from Hades."

———✦———

A FULL WEEK after the funeral passed. It was the Greek day of the week called Hemera Dios; the day of Zeus. Mother led us through the marketplace, stopping to barter for fruit, bread, and some meat.

"Mother, don't we have food at home? Father always had meat at home." I asked.

She continued to try to barter the merchant down in price, but he wasn't budging. A shift had happened since father's death. The people in the marketplace used to wave and greet us openly but now it seemed as if it pained them to show any emotion or even a simple gesture of good tiding. I could see the frustration building on mother's face. It was the same face she had when Gestas and I were fighting at the kitchen table. Gez tried to pull mother away, but she paid him no attention as her shrill voice became louder, as did the merchants.

Then her countenance softened. She took a deep breath and closed her eyes. Looking at the man, she said calmly, "Please Kotus, the boys." She gestured toward Gez and me.

"Bah, Dora. Don't do that. You know that is not good business."

"Oh, is good business causing innocent children to suffer?"

They continued to spar back and forth like two warriors swinging swords, but not to kill. Gestas and I were diverted by two younger street children who wore dirty robes and had no sandals. Smudges on their faces and knotted hair told us they came from the poor section of town. The two rag-tag boys, probably the same age as Gez, rolled dice on the ground. One pointed and laughed while the other sighed and turned to face the crowd of buyers and merchants. He waited for a moment and then sprinted out of the alley and slammed into an older man carrying a satchel of bread. Fresh-baked spear-like loaves spilled out onto the ground. While the man was distracted and entangled with the younger boy, the second crept in between the people who gawked at the spectacle and began to steal from the nearby vendors and the patrons.

Gestas and I were astonished at what we had just witnessed. The boy filled the hidden pockets of his robe and then slipped away, back into the recesses of the buildings. The other boy, however, was getting a severe beating by the man with a thin stick called a 'thatch'. He covered his face and took the swipes across his back. Then the man stopped and began to pick up his dirty bread. He wiped off the dust and placed them back into his pack, all the while mumbling profanities and curses under his breath. The crowd began to disperse.

Gestas turned to me and our eyes connected. We exchanged a

hidden language between us, one brief moment, that would end up affecting us for life.

I looked at Mother, who continued to bargain for the meat with the last coin she had, while my brother telepathed his desire that we embark on a life of crime like the two raggedy boys.

Gestas leaned in and whispered, "Diz, we can do this. The gods favor your speed. It's a gift and the gods have gifted me with my injured leg."

"What do you mean? This isn't right."

"In whose eyes? Look around, they have plenty to spare."

"No Gez, we can't do this. Let's go back to the hills and search again for the coins."

"They're gone, Diz. You know that. Do it for Mother. She is lost without Father."

I watched her arguing with the merchant with whom she'd done business for years. I could only begin to understand the depth of pain on her face, but knew that the loss of Father was indeed great.

Gestas tapped my shoulder, "Follow my lead, brother."

"Wait!" But it was too late. Gestas hobbled out to the middle of the street, maneuvering between people, then suddenly fell to the ground in dramatic fashion. His walking stick clattered away from him and he held his leg, grimacing in pain. People stopped and knelt down to assist him. More people gathered. Vendors looked on and tried to raise their heads higher to peer over the crowd.

I glanced around to see what was near. The meat dangled above me on the line but just a step further there was a fruit cart. Merchants' eyes were transfixed on the spectacle and I slowly lifted my shaking hand toward the mound of figs before me. I heard voices in my head telling me not to, but the overwhelming desire for food and to help mother weighed heavily on my ten-year-old heart. Not to mention the immense pressure my brother had just placed upon me to do my part.

I clutched the lion figure in one hand, while I snatched two figs, then a third, fourth, fifth. I didn't stop until my pocket was filled. I never looked around to see if anyone was watching. I focused solely on the food, fully expecting someone to grab me and beat me to death with a thatch, but no one did.

Mother yelled, "Gestas!" She rushed over, pushing people aside to get to her son. "What happened?"

"I fell and hurt my leg."

I was behind mother now and peered around to catch my brother's eye. Gestas locked eyes on me for a second and then went back into his act, fake clenches of pain contorting his face. Slowly, he subsided.

"I feel better. It must have been a cramp. I'm fine."

She helped him to his feet while I retrieved his walking stick. The crowd slowly dispersed and we went home, mother empty-handed while my pockets were full.

One never knows how a single moment can affect a lifetime. The week following the death of our father, the lack of money, the fear of what was to come, and our unknown destiny led to a single reactionary decision. This path seemed less like a choice and more like the only option.

Darker times were coming. Darker times had already come.

CHAPTER 8
DARK TIMES

-DISMAS-

Two months had passed since my father's death. Hard months. Long months. I clutched the lion figurine close to my chest as I thought of Papa sharing stories with Gez and me. I chuckled when thoughts of the past began to weave inside my mind. Father had a way of capturing our attention, only to find out it was just a bad joke that really only entertained him. He said he loved to see our faces scrunch up in contemplation. Father had such a deep laugh. I miss him greatly.

I looked down at the lion figure and said to it, "I wish you were still here, Father." This was his final gift to me and somehow I felt connected to him through it. Perhaps the gods had allowed father to live inside this carving; at least that was my prayer. My throat tightened as I tried to swallow, fighting the emotions. I whispered, "Father, are you in there? I need you."

"You still talking to that thing?"

Startled, I turned to see my brother limping around the large boulder I sat against. "What do you want, Gez?"

"I just came to let you know our favorite Uncle arrived." Gestas turned and walked away.

I stopped breathing. Clavius brought a heaviness upon me that no one else had ever done. This one man nearly destroyed Father when I was a babe and now haunts our family, but why? What does he want? *"It's the pigs,"* I thought to myself. *"He was taking the family business all over again."*

I leapt to my feet and scrambled to catch up with my brother.

Gestas and I entered to find Roman soldiers standing on either side of the entry. Clavius sat at our kitchen table with filthy booted feet propped upon it, throwing olives one at a time into his mouth. He had a sinister smirk and his countenance was evil. My home, our home, felt dirtied by his presence.

"Ah, the children are home, Dora," he said, mid-chew.

Mother turned from her cooking and with a forced smile quickly tried to usher us back out.

"No, let them stay. They need to hear this just as much."

We looked at one another, uncertain as to what news he brought, but knew instinctively that it would be of no good.

"Please, Clavius. This is not the arrangement."

With no regard for the muddy mess his boots left on the table, he lowered them and stood. "The arrangement is whatever I see fit."

She pulled us close to her, maintaining a submissive posture. She whispered, "It will be okay. I promise."

"Yes, it will all be okay," Clavius mocked, waving his hands in the air. Clasping his hands behind his back, Clavius crossed the kitchen, kneeling down to speak to us face to face. With condescension, as if speaking to a two-year-old, "It was your father's wish that I take over the family business. Did you boys know that?"

Gestas farted loudly. I usually would laugh, as he had the ability to do this almost on command, but now was not the time. Gestas was making his disrespect known.

Mother pulled him in tighter. "Gestas, stop it."

Clavius didn't flinch and continued, "Not only am I the owner, but he also wanted me to take care of his family."

"We don't need you," I brazenly responded. I felt my chest puff up a bit as I stood my ground.

He stood upright, all pretense of kindness gone, "Is that so? Well, the papers that these fine soldiers hold in their hands say otherwise and since I'm a Roman, law-abiding citizen. I must comply."

I glanced at the soldiers. Their faces were ruddy and scarred with experience. Their military bearing spoke of years of training and fine particles of dust appeared to be embedded into their skin as if it were another layer of armor itself.

Gestas said sharply to Clavius, "You're a traitor to the Greeks."

One of the soldiers eyed him and got ready to backhand my brother, but restrained himself once Clavius took a step closer.

"I forgot to mention one other thing written on this parchment that he holds. It's of minor consequence but perhaps it might be of interest to you."

We were frozen waiting for what was to come next. No one moved. No one breathed. Seconds ticked by.

"Your father agreed to the ancient Greek tradition of epikleros."

I looked at Mother but her face revealed nothing. I spoke softly, "What is—?"

He cut me off, "Epikleros? Well, it is an interesting tradition. When a husband passes away, then *all* of his belongings are to be inherited by the brother. *All* possessions."

Mother said, "You already have the business. Just go and leave us be."

I watched as his eyes slowly graze Mother's body up and down. "Yes, the business is one thing of many. What about the house?" He swung his arm gesturing to the walls around them.

With gritted teeth, she said, "Just take it."

"What about the slaves?" He paused and then said softly while leaning closer to Mother, "And what about his wife?"

She gasped and clutched us closer, "Never!"

The Roman soldiers suddenly grabbed Mother and ripped her away from us. I watched in horror as one guard blocked us and the other dragged her into Father's bedroom. She thrashed, kicked, and screamed. I stared at Clavius in shock. My mind could not process what was happening. It was a nightmare I waited to awaken from, but never did. I locked eyes with that soulless man as time stood still. In slow motion, Clavius turned and walked into the bedroom. The Roman closed the door and stood guard while the other held me and my brother in place. I couldn't hear, my surroundings blurred, and I felt dizzy.

Suddenly the grip of the warrior released and I saw my brother yelling at me. I could read his lips, "RUN!" But I couldn't. I was stuck. My brain had forgotten how to send messages to the rest of my body. My brother pushed me and I fell backward toward the door. The guard was scrambling to get back up and the other was approaching.

Suddenly, I could hear Gez and I no longer felt like I was

underwater. Energy coursed through my body like it had been hit by a lightning bolt.

"RUN, Diz!"

I did just that. I don't remember opening the door but found myself running toward the dark, shadowy mountains. The sun blared behind them. They looked like they were on fire and all I wanted to do was run into that fire.

I don't know how far I ran. My mind wanted me to continue, but my legs gave out causing me to crumble to the ground. I cried and cried until I was crying without any tears, moaning and groaning the pain that wracked me. It wasn't just pain, but also anger so strong that it hurt my body to not release the rage. I clawed the hard packed sand until my fingers bled. This was going to be my grave, dug by my own hands. Sand crumbled the deeper I went until I could scoop chunks away. It was cold and soft and I envisioned it becoming my blanket, wrapping around me and chilling my body as I traveled the road to the River Styx. The gods had cursed my family and me. I longed to fall asleep and never wake again.

❖

"GET UP!"

Someone kicked me and my eyes burst open to see the silhouette of a man looming above. The sun was rising and I could hear the shore of the sea in the distance. My teeth chattered as the chilly morning air enveloped me.

"I said, get up!" He leaned down and grabbed my tunic and yanked me to my feet.

It was the Roman soldier I had left behind. He had found me but I did not care.

"He's over here. Bring the other one," he called out over his shoulder.

My brother Gestas was dragged and tossed by my side.

"Diz, are you okay?" he asked me.

I stared at him. I knew that nothing mattered and that we would soon be joining Father in the realm beyond.

"Let's hurry it up. This place is not right. It is cursed," the soldier said.

"Shut it, Kye. I will hold this one so he doesn't run again. You kill him and I will kill the crippled one."

Kye stepped forward, unsheathing his dagger. "My pleasure. The quicker the better."

His blade was about to slice my throat open. I could feel the cold steel nick my skin. My brother tried to free himself from the heavy, sandaled foot that pinned him down, but was only able to watch—his breath stuck in his throat.

It's hard to explain what happened next, but a sound, not of this world, echoed around us, causing the soldier to pull the knife away. He frantically looked around trying to locate the unearthly source.

"It's him. I knew we shouldn't have crossed over the marker."

The sun had just emerged an hour ago and the brisk morning sunlight splashed over the terrain. This was the Old Tombs, a cursed land, now overrun with demons. Some believe the last man who was buried here, while still inside the tomb, before he began his journey to the underworld, uttered a curse that befell the area. Still, others speak of dark magic gone wrong by priests of an ancient order that disappeared a decade ago.

Another howl echoed between the hills. I spotted several sealed burial sites in the distance. A patchy fog surrounded the area.

"Let's get out of here!" the Roman said.

"Not before we kill them."

"Leave them for the beasts."

"We shall call it a sacrifice to whatever that thing is." Kye drew forth his blade and positioned it against my neck.

It was then that a creature jumped down from a rock mound to our left and raked its claws across the soldier's back, tearing through his leather armor like silk. He let go of me as he lurched back in pain. I fell to the ground and quickly looked to locate the beast, but it was gone.

Another demon sprang from the right and tackled the second warrior, knocking him to the ground. I expected something hideous but what I saw was a man—unshaven, unclothed, shackles dangling from his wrists. He had dirt embedded into his skin as if it had been years since he'd bathed. He had long, sharp fingernails, gnarled hair, and scars that covered most of his body. He stared intently and then scrambled like a cat toward me. I was frozen once again. I could feel its hot breath on my face but I could not move as it looked inside my soul. The shadow creatures from my dreams emerged in my mind.

It was the eyes that startled me the most. They were not the same. One was oddly colored just like mine. Its head tilted slightly sideways as it inspected me. Suddenly, the other demon-man grabbed the soldier's foot, whose back was bleeding, and dragged him away. The warrior clutched the ground but nothing could slow him, not even a tree base small enough to grab with his hand. In a second, he was gone. We heard a scream and then it was silent. An unearthly silence.

The demon-man before me never took his gaze away. It was as if he knew me.

"Diz," my brother said.

I didn't say anything. I don't think I could have said anything. I was entranced.

The other soldier, dazed, got to his feet and began to stumble away. Gestas whisked by me with a rock lifted in both hands above his head and slammed it into the Roman's back. He grunted as he fell. Just as the man looked back to see what had struck him, Gestas brought the same rock down upon his head. Facial bones shattered and blood spattered onto Gestas' tunic.

I wanted to say something, but couldn't. The demon-man held me transfixed. I was about to be his next victim and my only wish was that my brother could escape.

It snarled at me. The yellow rotting teeth revealed under the cracked dry lips caused me to flinch. I instinctively shielded my face. The demon noticed my precious figurine and snatched it away. He inspected it, dragging his thick, razor-sharp fingernails across the midsection, leaving a mark.

Meanwhile, Gestas raged on, lifting the rock again and again, slamming it into the back of the soldier's head. The skull caved in, releasing its contents to soak the ground around him. The sound seemed to snap the demon out of his trance with me. He dropped my figurine and leapt away into the craggy hillside. I picked up my father's gift and scrambled over to Gestas. He was lying on his back next to the gore, crying. No, he was laughing. Why was he laughing?

"Gestas, are you okay?"

He couldn't stop. I wish I could say that it was joyful, happy laughter, but it was maniacal. In that moment, it was as if the demons had stolen my brother and replaced him with one of their own.

"Come on, we need to get out of here."

I tried to help him up but he rolled in hysterics.

Firmly, I said, "What about mother? We need to help her."

This caused him to stop and regain his senses.

"Mother?" he questioned.

"Yes, Gez, mother. She is alone and she needs us."

His eyes were fixated. I saw evil inside my brother that day. Something I had never seen before. Only in looking back can I tell you that it was the look of revenge.

CHAPTER 9
A MOTHER'S LOVE
-DISMAS-

"I DON'T SEE HER."

"She is either inside or…"

"Don't say it, Gez."

"I'm not, but we need to find her."

I sat back against the rock we were hiding behind while watching our home. I pulled out the figurine. "Lead us to our mother," I said.

Gestas slid down beside me and gave me a puzzled look. "What are you doing?"

"I'm praying to Father to lead us."

"Father? He is not in there, Diz."

"You don't know that."

"Diz, he has crossed the River Styx with the other souls."

I paused for a second and then said, "I don't care. Maybe he is speaking through this to help us from wherever he is."

Gestas was about to respond, but relented. He let out a big sigh and said, "All right then. What is Father saying?"

"I haven't heard any voice yet. It's just a feeling."

"Maybe it's just you wanting to feel something."

"I don't know. Maybe."

We both stared at the figure in my open hands for a long while.

Gestas periodically peered over the boulder to look at the house in hopes of seeing mother but it was quiet with no movement.

"Gestas?"

"Yes."

"When those...demon-men attacked, did you notice anything about the one with me?"

"No, why?

"I don't know, it just..."

"Just what?"

"It just had a strange eye or something."

"Or something? Those were the legendary Demons of Ghasa. We came face to face, you quite literally, and lived to tell about it. No one will believe us."

"I looked into its eyes, Gez."

"What did you see?"

"I saw this." I pointed at my eyes.

"I don't understand. You saw yourself?"

"Kind of, in a way. It had a mismatched eye just like mine. What do you think it means?"

Gestas didn't respond and instead went back to looking at our home in the distance.

"I don't think anyone is in there."

"Gez, what do you think it means?"

"What, the eyes? I don't know." He said, evasively.

"What is it?"

"Diz, how did you feel when you looked into its eyes? I mean, did you sense anything?

"I don't know. It was like I knew him, the man or beast or whatever it is."

"Knew him? What do you mean?"

I let out a deep breath and said, "Like a connection somehow. I can't explain it."

"Come on, let's look for Mother. We can talk more about this later."

We slowly made our way toward the house, slinking and sliding behind thick shrubs and over rocks. There was still no movement. The stone structure of our home seemed more like a tomb and I prayed that Mother was not a victim lying inside.

Gestas was about to scurry to the next wall of vegetation when I suddenly pulled him back.

"What is it? Gestas asked.

"I heard water."

He froze and listened intently. "I don't hear anything."

"I don't either now, but I did. I'm certain."

"Did it sound like Mother pouring water into a jar?"

"No, it was more like running water, like…"

We both looked at one another and said together, "The washing."

—⊗—

WE SPOTTED HER, back to us, kneeling at the water that ran a little ways from our homestead, and flowed down into the Sea of Galilee less than a mile away. To our left, far off in the distance, were herds of hundreds of pigs grazing on the hillside and the sea, with a slight haze, framed the background. This was where Mother would wash our clothes, but more importantly, it was her sacred place. She came here to escape the rigors of life when she needed a break. The tall spires of the thin grass were greener here and the constant bubbling of the water churning over and through the rocks and vegetation brought a magical feel to one's soul. Whenever Mother came here, we knew not to bother her. But today was different.

"Mother?" I called from a distance.

We could see her figure hunched over. Normally she would be washing clothes but today none were seen. She did not turn when I called.

"She can't hear us," Gestas said.

"Mother!" we called together.

She froze, then slowly turned in our direction to lay her tear-filled eyes upon us. She gasped and charged toward us, lifting her robe high so as not to trip over it.

"Boys!" she called.

"Mother!"

We collided. She hugged us fiercely, resting her chin on our heads as she squeezed.

"By the gods, thank you."

"Mother, we—"

"Don't speak, I have something to tell you. It will be hard to hear, but you must."

We all dropped to our knees in the grass, ready to listen.

"Just let me look upon you. Are you all right?"

We nodded.

"The gods have spared you. The call on your life is bigger than me or your Father now."

"I don't understand," I said.

"Just listen, my dear ones. Your home will no longer be here."

I tried to say something but she hushed me and continued, "You will both travel to a new land across the sea. I have foreseen it in my dreams. The gods have revealed to me your destiny."

"The Jews live on that side," Gestas said a bit fearfully.

"Yes, son, but there are others. You will find your way and the gods will show you."

"But how will we know what to do?" Gestas said.

I chimed in and said, "Gez, Father will lead us just like he led us to Mother. Remember, I heard water?"

Gestas stared at me not saying anything. I could tell he wanted to argue but didn't. Perhaps he was starting to believe me. Gez turned to mother and said, "We can't leave you."

"Nor I, you. We won't have time to get our things, but whatever happens, you must leave and never come back."

"We don't care about anything else. We just want to be with you," I said.

She smiled and pulled me in close to her face where our foreheads touched.

"I won't leave you. Am I not always inside your heart?"

Gestas said, "I don't understand what is happening. Why is Clavius taking everything? Can't we do something? Anything?"

She looked at him and responded, "It is the way of man. Evil lies in wait inside us all. It is with the love of Aphrodite, as our guide, that we are able to walk through the evil. Those who don't follow her ways fall to the dark army encamped outside their heart."

"I sometimes have bad thoughts, Mother."

She hugged me and said, "Yes, but you did not act on them which means Aphrodite is protecting your heart. I'm proud of you. I'm proud of you both and so is Father."

I felt a brief pocket of peace in the shifting wind. I closed my eyes, nestling myself into my mother, never wanting the moment to end. But the wind came back, along with the fear of the unknown. I could smell sage and feel warm air on the back of my neck.

"Mother?" There was something in Gestas' voice that was an alert.

She looked where he stared as did I. We saw two Roman soldiers looking at us from across the creek. They were not moving. I looked behind us and spotted two more. Another pair to our right and then two more to our left. We were surrounded. But they did not advance.

Coming over the slight rise from our homestead was the man we had hoped never to see; Clavius. A pair of soldiers flanked and kept in stride with him. Clavius walked steadily with a cocky swag. He wore the smirk of a conquering king.

Mother grabbed and looked at us intently, "You must leave now. Follow the creek down to the water. Swim across the sea if you have to."

"Mother—" we tried to say but she stopped us, "I love you and always will. Now go!"

Clavius was now in earshot and said, "Boys, murder is one of the worst crimes, but the murder of a Roman soldier is even more severe than that. I have come to protect you though."

"Go!" she yelled and pushed us away. "Whatever happens, don't come back. Promise me."

We began to back away.

She said again, "Promise me?"

"We promise," Gestas said.

"Dismas?"

Reluctantly, "I promise."

She smiled through her tears and watched us as we scrambled with uncertainty away from her.

"Where are you boys going? We are about to have a family discussion." Clavius nodded to a couple of soldiers in the distance. They began quickly marching toward us.

We ran, but I quickly realized that Gez couldn't keep up due to his crippled leg.

Gestas yelled, "Diz, keep going! Go to The Well!"

"The Well?" I thought to myself. *"Is he crazy?"* I stopped and ran back to my brother, slunk under his right shoulder and began to run with him, speeding up his pace.

"You're an idiot," he whispered while hustling.

"No, the Romans will be slowed by the mud field."

The men were on a course to intercept us, but part of the creek slowed, trickling into a large grassy patch making it a slog of mud. We would get through it faster because we weighed less.

"Stay close to the water," Gestas said.

"I know."

"We need to get to The Well."

"That is not a good idea."

"It's the only way. The mud will slow them but they will catch us if we don't go into The Well."

"But we don't know what's down there."

"I know there are no Romans down there. The water has to be going to the sea. We have no choice."

I knew he was right. He was always right. What we called The Well was the slow trickling water of the creek flowing into a crop of rocks just before the edge of the cliff that led down to the Sea of Galilee. We would sit by it and throw rocks down the black hole into the unknown. We thought it was an entrance to the realm of darkness itself and would make up ghost stories together. It is where I believe the creatures that haunt my dreams come from and now I would be plunging into their realm.

The warriors hit the sludge and trudged through it with immense strength. Their strides were long and we could hear their heavy breathing as their endurance was tested. It was going to be close. We could hear the squeals of the pigs faintly as a herd drank from the water ahead and wallowed in another muddy area nearby.

"Come on. We are almost there," Gestas said.

"What about Mother?"

"No time. She will be all right."

I trusted my older brother. He wasn't strong but he was smart. My legs and arms contained more muscle than his, but his brain excelled in every area beyond mine. Together we always imagined taking on the world. That world loomed before us now, but didn't seem that appealing considering our circumstances. Our land was all we knew. We had only dreamt of exploring the outer region—the region of the Jews.

I clutched my figurine and said, "Father, protect us."

CHAPTER 10
THE WELL

-DISMAS-

THE SMELL OF pig dung and wet vegetation did not deter us from hustling along the edge of the slow trickling water down the hillside. We could see the dark group of rocks, which we called "The Well", where the water plummeted down into darkness. The rocks were darker due to the moisture and sometimes, depending on the heat of the day, they would steam.

The Roman soldiers were almost on top of us but they continued to be slowed by the mud that oozed around their sandaled feet, sucking them into its slippery grasp. Their jaws were clenched tight and their leg muscles strained as they pulled each leg out of the mud, raising their knee as high as their chest. It was the intensity in their eyes that scared me most. They were focused on their task to apprehend us. It was as if they were possessed.

Gestas said, between labored breaths while holding on to me, "We won't have time to think. We will just have to jump."

I didn't answer him. He was right. If we delayed for even a second, the men would grab us. The Well was twenty paces away and time began to slow in my mind. I could hear the clanking of the soldiers' weaponry against their leather armor and I could hear the seabirds squawking just ahead as we looked down into the sea below. They flew at our eye level. I tried to keep myself calm and not look directly at the dark opening between the rocks where the water fell. We were ten paces away.

This was a place I never imagined ever going into and now it would either be my destiny or my death. The gods surely designed it this way for they must hate us greatly.

My brother's voice was garbled in my mind as I tried to process the insanity before us. Gestas said, "You go first. I will protect you."

All I heard was, "you go first" but not the last part. One step away. Gestas released his arm from around me, looked back, and pushed me to go through. The soldiers were growling in contempt, clearly not happy about the slog through the deep mud, and reached out to grab us from just a few feet away. I froze, not able to go first into this dark hole where the shadow creatures dwelled. I felt the push from behind launch me and I knew Gestas was right there as he clutched onto my robe. We squeezed down The Well together. It was narrow but the slimy algae made the rocks slippery. I just remember holding my breath and falling for what seemed like eternity into the void. My mind imagined no end and that the feeling of falling would continue forever, but of course it didn't. We hit the rocks below. Hard. I winced in pain several times as my legs and arms became cut and bruised.

I don't know how much time went by. Sounds were muffled as my senses fought to bring me back to reality. My brother's moans and the echo of the water flowing down The Well, along with the lapping waves of the Sea of Galilee, came into focus. Sunlight hit my face, blinding me as I raised my arm to block the rays. I slowly moved next to Gestas.

"Are you okay?" my voice echoed.

"My head hurts."

It was then that I saw the darker splotch on the back of his head as he sat up.

"I feel dizzy."

"It's okay. Just stay still," I said.

Echoes of the soldiers' voices rang down the chamber.

"Do you see them?"

"I can't see anything."

"Do you hear them, then?"

"Not with you talking." They quieted for a few seconds and then one said, "They're dead."

"Are you sure?"

"No, I'm not sure. Do you want to go down and find out?"

Then it was silent except for the water cascading down. I looked at Gestas and knew he should stay put for the time being. We were inside a ten-foot-wide cave. When I sat up, the ceiling was almost touching my head. I tore the bottom part of my robe and applied it to the wound on his head. He reached up to hold it in place.

I told him, "I'm going to look out the opening. You stay here for a moment."

He didn't argue and laid back to rest, closing his eyes, while he continued to hold the rag to his head.

It took a few minutes to get to the opening where I could stand fully upright. I surveyed the area and could see the pebbled shoreline off to the left. To the right was the cliff face and open water. Either way would require us to swim but I recognized the shoreline and knew it to be the home of the demon-men of Ghasa.

There was deep water to the right and no telling how long we would have to swim before reaching a place to rest. Gestas was hurt and I was bruised and bleeding in several spots as well. The night was approaching and we would need a fire to dry our clothes and fight off the chill of the evening air. I went back to get my brother.

"Come on, Gez. It's time to get out of here."

He groggily sat up with my help. We slowly scooted down to the edge of the cave, some fifty feet away. Assisting him, we both waded into the cold water. Small waves splashed against the rocks. I pulled my brother as I swam one-handed. Father hadn't taught me how to do this but somehow I knew by instinct. Perhaps the gods gifted me with my brother's brain for this moment in time. I felt larger rocks underneath my feet periodically, which I used to push from to propel us along. And occasionally, to rest upon. Relief hit me when I felt the smaller rocks as I reached the shore. I slung my brother's arm around my shoulder. Water sloshed from our bodies as we exited the water and finally fell onto the pebbled beach. I looked around the area. Those beasts were out there but what was the chance of seeing them again on the same day? Still, I glanced around hastily seeing ancient tombs dotting the hillside. The gods cursed this land and some say the dead lay in wait for the living to wander into their domain. The problem was, I didn't wander in, but instead, chose to enter. I brought out my lion figure and held it up in front of my face.

"Protect me and my brother. Let nothing harm us."

Gestas groaned and his eyes fluttered open. Then he fell limp. I scrambled to his side saying, "Wake up, Gez. Come on, wake up."

I couldn't carry him. I dragged him up further to hide behind a large, jagged rock that had dislodged from the cliff. I leaned back against it and propped my knees up. My wet robes clung to me and it was already getting cold. Just to the right, I spotted a pile of driftwood that lay cluttered from the high tide.

I could hear my father's voice in my head, *"Diz, this is how you do it."* He had shown me how to start a fire and I recalled all the steps and began to get to work.

With the lion statue propped onto one of the stones that created the fire ring, I gathered the driftwood and piled it close. I felt strongly that Father was guiding my every step as his instructions flowed effortlessly into my mind. My brother was still unconscious.

A screech echoed down the hillside, an unholy sound, and I stopped to survey the area. Nothing. Then it was quiet again. The sun waned and was preparing to set behind the hill when I thought I spotted something move at the top of the ridge. I was unable to see anything clearly with the glare of the sunset obscuring my vision.

My father's voice spoke in my mind, *"Diz, get the fire started."*

"Yes, Father," I said out loud and then began.

The smell of the smoke wafted into my nostrils and I blew lightly on the whitewashed wood to bring the fire to life. Again, my father's voice directed me, *"Light, but steady, breath. Stay focused and will the flame to life."*

Then it happened. The fire ignited and took its first breath of the air. I watched how it ate the wood and grew. *"It is like a child,"* Father said. *"Take care of it. Teach it and it will protect you."*

I added larger pieces of wood and then felt hunger pains, but ignored them as I scooped up the figurine and leaned back against the rock. The warmth brought me peace, as did my thoughts of Father, as I rubbed the wooden idol. My eyes focused in on the flames that sprang up. Their orange and red colors intertwining, mesmerized me. At this point, nothing mattered. Father called this the 'fire gaze' and it was here where one could speak with the gods, if the gods so wished. Father called it 'communing'.

"Father, protect us," I whispered, locked in the fire gaze.

CHAPTER 11
TO THE UNKNOWN

-DISMAS-

I WOKE, STARTLED BY the unholy screech. It was a sound that brought me great fear. Morning had come and the fire smoldered, releasing gentle gasps of smoke. I quickly moved to my brother's side, "Gez, wake up."

He moaned, but remained unconscious. I pulled the rag from his scalp and saw matted bloody hair covering a gash the size of my little finger. "Gez, wake up," I said, again.

Peering around the large rock that shielded us from the tombed hillside, I couldn't see anything but I knew they were out there. The sunlight revealed what had been hidden in the night. Old tombs, some of which had crumbled open, littered the mountain. It was barren here, more so than anywhere else I had seen before. Plant life was non-existent and rocks were brittle and sharp. Hard to believe that my home was but a stone's throw from here.

Wait. I saw something. It moved about midway on the hillside. Then I saw the second demon. It stood by a cave on the edge of the slope like a sentry watching the area. They were the creatures that attacked us and killed the Roman. What were they waiting for? They must have known we were here the entire night with our fire going but they didn't do anything. I grabbed my gift and brought it out,

"Father, it was you. You protected us." I kissed it and placed it back in my pocket.

The sound of the lapping waves hitting the pebbled beach caught my attention. I noticed more driftwood, some of larger size, being rocked back and forth. An idea came suddenly to my mind. Father gifted me once again, by the gods, the intelligence of my brother.

"Come on, Gez. We're getting out of here."

With that, I started to drag my brother closer to the shore and began to pull the larger pieces of wood by his side. I tore strips of my robe and tied the wood together to create a makeshift bed. His legs dangled over the edge of my work but it would be enough, I hoped.

Throughout my building project, I glanced back to the cave and saw nothing but a black hole. I knew they were watching from just behind the veil of the shadow world they lived in.

"Father, we are getting out of here. Gez and I are—"

I stopped because a rock skittered just behind me, down the embankment. I could see loose pieces shifting and settling. I held my breath but there was no movement.

"Come on, Gez. Time to go," I said while pulling the platform of wood into the water.

Then I froze. It was them. They had come for us and now stood ten feet away. How did they make no noise getting there? I would surely have heard them walking on the pebbled shore. The taller one, skinny and naked, tilted it's head slightly as it stared at me. I locked eyes with it again. Its left eye was different than his right one, just like mine. Its hair was knotted and nasty and chunks of its beard were missing. Scabs and bleeding wounds dotted its chest, arms, and legs.

The other one stood further back on higher ground. It was also unclothed and filthy from head to toe. It spoke but with words I didn't understand. It must've been the demon tongue, as the one staring at me held up its hand and snarled in response.

I took a step deeper into the water while pulling my brother but the tall one closest to me also took a step toward me.

With a shaky voice, I said, "What are you?"

It didn't say anything. I heard a sound like a swarm of bees or flies, but saw nothing. There were no insects anywhere. Again, the other spoke and the sounds were like a carpenter sanding wood beside a crackling fire. Through the scratchy tones I thought I heard the word 'kill'.

I was knee-deep in the water and Gez' feet were dragging along the bottom. With each lap of water that came I began to inch my way out, slowly, so my steps would go unnoticed. It appeared to be working as the beastmen were not advancing. The one in front never took his eyes off me. What was it looking at? It seemed to be contemplating something, as if it was searching for a lost memory.

"I just want to leave. Please let us go. I promise to never come back."

The smaller beastman never stopped talking and saliva began to drool down its chin into its beard. The one closest to us began to roll its eyes into its head and I saw the whites fluttering in and out. Now the water was up to my thighs and I inched even more freely as Gestas' feet were free of the bottom. The buzzing was getting louder but where was it coming from?

"By the gods," I whispered. The demon furthest away began to shake rapidly in place. The outer edges of his body became ghostlike until finally shattering into tens of thousands of flies. The swarm raced towards me, a black swirl, but the closest demon man turned, brought up both hands, and snarled, causing it to stop its advance. The flies froze in place, but the angry sound of buzzing increased.

I turned in a panic and swam deeper, pulling Gez with me. I didn't stop. My legs kicked and pushed until I couldn't touch the ground anymore. We were moving further and further from the shore. When I finally looked back, the swarm was gone but the tall beastman stood at the edge of the water watching me.

It looked down at its feet and bent to pick something up. It held it in his fingers and inspected what I thought to be a rock until I reached into my robe to discover that my gift was gone. My figurine must have floated from my robe pocket when I swam away. I desperately wanted to go back for it but knew that was not possible.

"I'm sorry, Father." Tears flowed from my face. "Why is this happening to us? Gez, wake up. I don't know what to do." I sobbed.

The shore was far away now and the water grew colder the deeper I went. I could see so much of the land now and yet I couldn't see anyone. Not a soul along the coast or the cliffs. Our home was set back a ways from the top of those cliffs. I noticed the grass was greener from far away. All the land seemed greener except the Old Tombs which were gray and vacant of life. They were like scabs on the land; wounds that never healed. It was barren, dry, and ominous.

My legs were tired and I stopped to rest, slinging my arm over my brother and laying my head on his chest. The sounds of his heartbeat and the sloshing water calmed me.

Father was gone now. Every trace of him lost, except for my memories, which even now seemed distant. I don't know what happened to Mother but we promised her never to come back, no matter what. Clavius stole my father's business and land. My brother was not waking up and we were lost in the Sea of Galilee heading into the unknown.

⸎

"Come alongside them, son."

"Father, who are they?"

"It doesn't matter right now. What matters is getting them into our boat."

"Are they Samaritans?"

"No, Greeks."

I felt someone grab my robe and start pulling me up. I didn't know where I was or what was happening. The voices were distant and my eyelids wouldn't lift to see. Many hands lowered me and the smell of fish assaulted my senses, causing me to gag.

"James, help me with the other."

"Yes, Father."

More grunts and strains as they worked to lift my brother out of the sea and into the boat beside me. My eyes opened intermittently and I saw silhouettes of people with the sun glaring high above.

"Ner□," I coughed.

"Father, he spoke in Greek. You were right."

"Ner□," I said again.

"Sons, get them water while I get us back to shore."

I felt the cool liquid on my face and I drank the water. It trickled down the sides of my face as my mouth couldn't take hold of all of it. I sputtered and turned my head. Taking a breath, I asked for more. The sensation of it traveling down my throat and into my stomach was like jumping into the cold sea on a hot day. Life had come into me once again. The gods had spared Gestas and me but who are these people who speak Aramaic? I could only surmise they were Jews. My brother and I survived the Demons of Ghasa but now found ourselves at the mercy of the Jews. It is said that no mercy is to be found with them. They keep to their own. I was convinced that the water they gave to us was only to keep us alive long enough to sell us into slavery. The rumors of what these people were capable of went beyond imagination, and here we were, at their mercy.

"Patéras, voithíste mas," I said under my breath. I looked beside me to see a blurry image of Gestas just before exhaustion overwhelmed me and I fell asleep.

CHAPTER 12
INTO THE HANDS OF THE JEWS
-DISMAS-

I WOKE TO THE sound of seabirds squawking by the hundreds and men calling to one another giving instructions to tie down the boats. The air smelled different, like a mixture of fish guts and bird dung. I didn't know where I was, or the time of day, but looked around to see my brother lying beside me in a small room. There were fishing nets hanging on the walls and a workbench along two walls littered with tools. A single rickety door, weathered by the proximity to the water, hung cock-eyed on the doorframe and the warped slats created large openings for the sun to blaze inside, shooting spikes of light into the room.

"Gez, wake up."

He groaned but his eyes fluttered open. He had a new bandage wrapped around his head and I could faintly see blood seeping through.

Elated, I said, "You're okay. Thank the gods." I lunged and hugged him tightly.

Pushing me away, he moaned, "Get off of me." He looked around, "Where are we?"

"We are now in the hands of the Jews. I'm sorry. I was too weak to fight them."

"Fight them? What happened?"

"Father said to never trust a Jew. They steal and will stop at nothing to get what they want."

"What are you talking about? Father was talking business. He wouldn't do business with the Jews."

"That's not what he told me."

"You heard it the way you wanted to hear it. Now tell me what happened." He tried to sit up but fell back into the blankets, grabbing his head.

"You hit your head pretty hard, Gez. You need to rest."

"You need to tell me," he said, wincing in pain. "Start talking."

I spent the next hour revealing all that happened up to that point.

"One other thing, Gez."

"What?"

"It's gone. I lost it."

"Lost what? What's gone?"

"Father. I lost the figurine that Father gave me and, with it, any chance for us to have his favor."

"You're insane, Diz. It was just a statue."

"No! No, it wasn't! You didn't see what happened! Father protected us from the demons and sacrificed himself for us! Why don't you ever believe me, Gez!"

"Shhh, calm down. I'm sorry."

I looked away and there was silence between us for several minutes except for the sounds of the fishermen outside in the distance and the incessant birds.

"Gez?"

"Yes."

"Do you think we will see Mother again?"

"Of course we will."

Hearing his confidence brought me comfort but then I asked, "Do you think we will see Father again?"

This time he didn't answer right away but finally said, "I don't know, but I hope so."

Just then the door to the workroom opened and a small child peered inside. His dark brown eyes were wide open, along with his mouth, when our eyes connected. He slammed the door and ran away yelling, "Papa! Papa!" in Aramaic. The door bounced back and forth against the frame, lessening upon each impact.

"Diz, help me." My brother tried to get up and so I helped him to his feet. Together we hobbled over to the door and opened it. We were blasted by the sunlight, forcing us to hold our hands up to shield our eyes. Our faces scrunched as we looked around to gain our bearings. The Sea of Galilee loomed before us, but we had never seen it from this point of view so it looked completely different. Several boats were tied to the dock with about a dozen fishermen offloading nets full of fish and filling baskets.

The little boy was now at the side of a man, presumably his father, pointing in our direction and explaining what he saw. The man looked at us, waved, and began to come our way. A woman filling a basket also broke away and walked just behind him with the little boy by her side. They walked along an old wooden dock. On each side stood tall marsh grass and there were several patches of trees clustered throughout the area as well.

My brother and I exchanged concerned looks, but there was little we could do until we understood exactly where we were and the intent of these untrustworthy people.

I whispered, "Father said not to trust them."

Gez didn't respond.

The man was loud and boisterous and had a huge smile as he spoke, "Good morning, good morning!" His arms swept open wide as if he was going to hug a giant.

The woman prodded, "Ask them."

He waved back at her, still smiling, "I know, I know." His eyes never left us but I could tell he seemed uncomfortable.

Slowly, he said, "My name is Zebedee. What are your names?"

Gez and I looked at each other. This Jew spoke to us like we didn't understand him.

Zebedee looked at the woman with raised eyebrows.

She said, "I told you they don't understand our language."

He said, "Well, I don't speak theirs."

"You should have learned when I told you."

"Oh, don't start with this now, Salome."

"I do, Papa," the youngest boy said. He then stepped forward and said in butchered Greek, "My name John. What is name?"

This was a perfect time to utilize the secret language we created where we combined the two dialects that Father and Mother taught us. Greek and Aramaic. For a yes or no answer to a question, we would answer with one pig grunt for yes or two grunts for no. You start with a Greek word and then alternate the two languages utilizing the words of most importance.

I looked at Gez and said, "Father said not to trust them. They treat us like insane people."

I watched as my brother understood and responded, "We need to know where we are. Don't do anything stupid."

We saw the surprised expressions, which quickly turned to confusion, upon the Jews' faces. It was priceless.

"Papa, I don't understand them."

He quieted the child, pulling him into a protective embrace. "We," he used his arms and hands wildly to indicate them. "We are fishermen."

I repeated the word fishermen in Greek as if I understood, which caused his face to light up.

He did a broad stroke with his arm to encapsulate the entire area and said, "Village called el-Aradj. Fishing village."

"El-Aradj?" Gez questioned.

"Yes, yes, el-Aradj. Village," he said excitedly.

It was at this point that I looked at Gez, understanding now where we were. We learned of the landscape around Galilee in our studies. There were many villages and towns and this one was located just outside the city of Capernaum. Internally, I sighed with relief as this was not far from home. We weren't directly across the sea but instead, only a day or two away.

"Gez, home isn't far."

He grunted once like a pig.

"Zeb, they are possessed," the woman said in fear as she took a step back.

"No, no, my bride. These are children," he comforted.

"Greek children," she reminded.

"Oh, my Salome. No, they are children." He turned toward us and said, "And I suspect most likely from the region of Decapolis."

I thought to myself, *"This is a smart Jew."* I better be cautious.

My brother asked me, "What do you want to do, Diz?"

"I don't know. We need more time."

"Time for what?"

"Time to plan."

"Plan what?"

"Gez, we need to figure out how to rescue Mother."

I turned and made my way to a flower growing amongst the tall grass, picked it, and then brought it to the woman. She needed to trust us.

"Oh my," she said. A surprised smile replaced her fearful expression. I asked in Aramaic, "We stay?"

This caught her by surprise and she froze. She looked at her husband who waited impatiently for her to answer. She said, "Yes, yes. You stay."

The father clapped his hands together and burst out loud, "This is wonderful. James and John, prepare your room for these boys and help Mother set the table for dinner. We will celebrate tonight with our best catch of the day."

"Are you sure?" the wife asked. "We need that money."

"Nonsense, the Lord God Almighty will provide an even grander catch tomorrow. You will see. Come, come."

He ushered us along the dock to the home settled on the small rise.

Gez whispered to me, "We promised Mother that we would never return home."

"Yes, but inside my head I added something else."

"What are you talking about?"

"I promised that I would not come back until I'm ready."

Gez gave me a look that said, *'You'd better explain.'*

"We need to be trained how to fight. Jews know these things, right?"

"I don't know. They don't look like fighters to me. Our people know how to fight but Father didn't allow us to be trained."

"Trust me, Gez. We need to bide our time and find the right person to teach us."

"Diz, you live in a fantasy world."

"What is your plan then?"

He didn't say anything.

"Then my plan is what we are doing."

Gestas stared at me for a second and then relented, shrugging, "Fine, little brother. We will go with your plan."

I looked up at Gestas and said, "We are on a great adventure."

"Yes, it is big. I pray the Goddess of Luck is on our side."

With contempt, I said, "Gods? You pray to the gods? They are up there gambling as we speak that we will not make it. We will prove them wrong."

I felt a tug on my robe and turned to see the little boy called John. He said, "My name is John."

I pulled him in close as if giving him a hug, made sure the

father and mother gave an approval, and then whispered in perfect Aramaic, "I know who you are." The boy was surprised as I spoke but I continued, holding him in place as he wanted to step away, "You will not tell anyone that we know your language. If you do then I will sink your Father's boats and blame you for it. Do you understand?"

"Diz, what are you doing?" Gez whispered harshly.

I continued to scare the younger boy and said, "I have spat in the faces of Roman soldiers and have looked into the eyes of demons. Do you understand?"

He nodded his head fearfully.

"That's good. Very good. I think we will be good friends, John. Remember what I said. We don't want to hurt anyone."

"Diz!" Gestas said. Leaning in close to me, "What are you doing?"

"Father always said, 'Don't let the situation control you but you control the situation.'" I shrugged, "I'm controlling the situation."

"Welcome to my home," the father announced with arms open wide. "Come in, come in."

Together we stepped into this new adventure. This new opportunity.

CHAPTER 13
THE WAY

-DISMAS-

GEZ FOUND ME early, sitting on the pier looking out at the sea. I was lost in my thoughts and captured by the water's relentless movement and sound. It appeared to be a greener blue than I had seen in the past. The reflections caused by the rising sun seemed strange to me. Everything was different and not in a good way.

I reached out to Gestas' head, "How is it?"

He flinched away, "Don't touch it. It still hurts."

A few moments passed before I said, "It's been a week now. What do you think of our new life?"

Gez didn't say anything but instead sat next to me and put his arm around my shoulder. He always knew what I needed and when I needed it. I couldn't contain the emotions that I held onto and all of them flooded out. I cried bitterly in my brother's arms as I buried my face against his chest.

I don't know how much time had passed, but it took quite awhile before I started to relax. Periodically, I took in deep breaths, my lips quivering.

"It's okay, little brother," Gez interjected every now and then.

"How could it be okay?" I thought to myself.

I finally pulled away. We looked off into the sea and watched the many fishing boats and the men throwing their nets over while others hoisted theirs aboard, tangled with fish. I could hear the nets hitting the water which sounded like short bursts of rain. All the sights and sounds calmed me, along with having my older brother by my side.

I finally said, "Maybe we should stay here for a while, Gez."

He sat up and looked at me incredulously.

"Gez, hear me out." My palms out to calm him.

"Talk," he said firmly.

"I was just thinking, maybe we should get an understanding of what is going on and prepare ourselves to get Mother."

"For how long?"

"The other day I told you that we needed training. Look, I am just as anxious as you are to—"

"Are you, Diz?"

"Yes, I am. We need to be smart just like Father taught us to be. Patience is not a weakness."

He couldn't argue with me. Father's words echoed in my mind. We both knew that Father was always right. Oh, how I wished he was here now. Why did I have to lose the carving he gave me? That was the door to him directly, I was sure of it. He would have given us the answers we needed. Still, I remembered more of what Father had told us over the years, *"Move on. Don't waste thoughts on what cannot be changed."*

Gez sighed and said, "Are you saying we stay here with these Jews?"

"Why not? They feed us, we have a bed, and I overheard the man saying something about teaching us to fish."

"Fish? We know how to fish. Father taught us."

"Yes, but not with boats and nets."

There was silence for a long moment until my brother stirred uncomfortably.

"What is it, Gez?"

"Something else I heard."

"What?"

"I think they want us to learn..." he hesitated.

"Learn what?"

"Learn something called 'The Way'."

"The Way? What are you talking about?"

"Their ways, Diz."

"Like how to talk in their language?"

"Something like that but I think it is more."

"More than Hebrew?"

"Yes, it was the wording he used; 'The Way'. I don't know for sure, but it seemed to be more than a language."

"Gez, that is strange. Maybe you didn't hear it right."

"None of this seems right, Diz. But I'm sure all of this will help us in someway. Remember what Father said…"

I repeated with him as he was saying it because Father had ingrained it into us. "Eat the meat, spit out the bones." I remember when he first said this to us and we had looked at one another, confused. He explained that some things in life will occur that we won't like or understand or agree with but there was always something to be learned from it. I recalled what Father said, *Absorb what is good for your soul even if it was only one thing and then reject all the rest.*"

We laughed as we finished the saying. Then, all of a sudden, I was launched into the water. The cold and the shock of the sudden plunge startled a scream out of me. I came up for air frightened, kicking and clawing to get back up onto the pier. My brother laughed and pointed at me. He had pushed me in like he had done so many other times growing up. How had I not seen it coming? In that instant I hated him.

All I could do was retaliate with words. I yelled, "You stupid cripple!"

Gez hated it when I said that to him. He mumbled some profanities and walked away. The Jewish mother raced by him and helped me up. The water sloshed onto the wood and then back down between the slats to the muddy marsh grass below like heavy rain drops.

She said, "What happened? Are you okay?"

I nodded to her to let her know I was fine.

"Oh good, you scared me. Come, come, I will make you some food. You boys are so skinny."

As she ushered me back to the warm home with her arm nestled around me, I was reminded of Mother. I missed her so much. For that brief moment I was thankful to have this Jewish woman by my side. Confusion crept into my mind. Father said not to trust the Jews but yet they fed us, clothed us, and gave us a bed to sleep in. These foreigners took us in as their own and I would dare to say, 'loved us'.

Salome said, "Zebedee and the boys will be home in a little while, but in the meantime we shall have some food. Let's get you by the fire and into some warm clothes. You Greek boys are very interesting but you are still boys, nonetheless. My sons, James and John, do the same as you, or worse, more often than not."

"Or worse?" I thought. *"What could those Jewish boys have done worse than what Gez and I have done? We killed a Roman soldier. Best to keep that to ourselves. Otherwise, I am sure she would throw us off the pier herself."*

I did prod a little and asked in a deliberate slow voice in Aramaic, "The Way?"

"What is this way you speak of?" she quickly asked.

"Know not," I continued to play the slow speech.

"I don't know the way you speak of, Dismas."

I think she was holding back. She did know, but wasn't saying. We entered the house and Gez was sitting at the kitchen table with his usual annoying smirk. I looked menacingly at him as the mother led me to the fire and told me to strip off the robe. She handed me a blanket and told me to sit at the table. I sat opposite Gez and stared at him, planning my revenge. He knew it and without words told me to give it my best attempt.

The mother was talking in the other room about the foods she was preparing for dinner and how we couldn't have any of it yet. She went on explaining in a long drawn out story that I didn't care to hear. I was busy staring down Gez.

I was suddenly jarred back to reality when the mother said, "Tomorrow I will have you boys begin to learn the ways of Yahweh with James and John.

Gez nodded at me as my face flushed with shock. He whispered mockingly, "The Way."

CHAPTER 14
THE MESSAGE

SIX YEARS FROM THE CROSS
-DISMAS-

GEZ AND I had worked for Zebedee these last four years learning the fishing industry. Learning isn't the right word but instead experiencing the ways of fishing from boats to nets and everything in between. Our knowledge of the Sea of Galilee and how it worked swelled inside of us like a giant wave. We knew what to look for, when to look for it, where it was, and why it came, from fish to sudden storms.

Never once did we get close to the Gergesa tombs. We kept our distance physically, but they were always at the forefront of our hearts and minds. These four years had been hard. Zebedee and his family experienced great resistance from the other Jews for taking us in. We stayed with him for nine months before he was able to plan for us to depart his home. He secretly funded us to have a place in Capernaum and even loaned us an old fishing boat that we repaired. We earned money with the fish we brought in each day, not much money, but we learned the art of negotiating and became shrewd businessmen.

These years taught us to watch out when it came to dealing with people and money. It didn't matter whether they were Jew or Samaritan. We found that people of all walks have dark hearts. It felt like we were running a race without a finish line. That was the essence of conducting business amongst all of these Galileans.

My brother and I took our licks as we learned and at times had to eat scraps or humbly ask Mother Salome to help us. Yes, Mother Salome, a title she earned wholeheartedly. I have seen similar qualities in her as I remember from our own and see *mother* as simply the title for a person who cares for her family at all costs. She and Zebedee had risked much for us. Our very presence hurt their fishing business. The Jewish community definitely sticks to its own and refrains from mixing, at least in most of the communities surrounding Galilee. Having Greek children in their care stirred up the local religious leaders.

Religion. What a waste of time, being devoted to something they have never seen. I was once like that, but no longer. The gods, if there truly are any, are far away from our minds. These Jews, however, have some type of calling to a glorious future, unknown to anyone else but themselves. They call it the "Coming of the Messiah"; a figurehead of God who will rescue them, and only them, apparently. Another deity who only thinks about one group of people. What about the rest of us? Those first couple of months living with the Jews, all we heard about was this Messiah coming someday. I wanted to punch James, the older brother to John, and almost did a couple of times. Their Holy Scriptures were ingrained into them as they practiced daily to repeat them to the other religious zealot leaders in the community.

Gez and I hadn't forgotten about our own mother and during these years we had not squandered our time but instead trained toward our mission. Our strength had increased, along with our knowledge. We gained insight from travelers who came from Decapolis and even dealt with those trying to import pig meat into Capernaum. It was a hard sale, considering the Jews control the marketplace for the most part, and they abhorred pork, claiming it unclean to eat because of their religion. It was indeed a battle for anyone outside of their kind. The city was a melting pot of groups of people who came from Damascus down through Palestine all the way to Egypt. All the highways came in and out of Capernaum and the fishing industry was just as strong as it was in Tiberias, to the South.

Capernaum, what can I tell you about this place? It harbored a large population of over two-thousand souls and flexed double that during times of festivals. Fishing was the main source of income. In order to survive in that business, you needed to be cutthroat in your dealings, be quick to make the deals, and undercut your competition whenever possible without being caught. If you were caught, then the rest of the fishing family made outcasts of you. Everyone knew that there were unscrupulous dealings but as long as you were not caught in the act then it was okay. The better your ability to deal, the better your prestige in the eyes of everyone. There were two owners that rivaled us all, one being Zebedee, of all people, and the other, a barbel bottom feeding fish of society, called Tokhes, which meant 'ass'. A fitting name.

A few days ago a stranger came through the marketplace, a Greek from Decapolis, and we made sure to connect with him. Our usual tactic was to offer a free fish to lure people into giving us information.

"Stranger," I said in Greek as he passed by our booth amongst the dozens who were yelling to vie for his attention.

He stopped, looked long and hard at us, and then approached. "What say you?" he asked.

"I say nothing but well met, my friend."

"Don't be so quick to be calling one a friend you have not yet met, boy."

Gez stepped in and said, "Who are you calling boy, old man?"

The man wasn't old exactly but Gez was making his point. The Greek stood tall, with black hair, dark brown eyes, and had the familiar wrapped beige tunic. A dagger was sheathed at his side.

"Well, aren't you a pair," he paused and then finished, "of testicles."

"You son of a bitch!" Gez yelled as he lurched forward to grab hold of the stranger. The man didn't resist and when my brother drug him closer to his face the message was delivered.

"Your mother sends word."

We were stunned; socked in the stomach, and we couldn't breathe. What did he just say?

"Meet me tonight at the south gate."

Gez released him and without a word from us he departed, melting into the crowd of people coming and going, bartering and buying.

"Gez, did he just say what I thought he said?"

"Yes," he responded with a glazed look on his face.

I wanted to cry just at the thought of her being alive. We never talked about it openly, but it was always a possibility. My brother looked at me. We started to grin, joy welling up in our hearts for the first time in a very long while.

"She's alive!" I said.

Gez nodded excitedly, "She's alive, Diz!"

We closed up shop early that day. We broke down our booth, still filled with fish, so fast that the others around us thought we were on to something big and didn't know what to do. We could see the looks on their faces and saw that they were ready to break their booths down also, as soon as they figured out what was going on. I took the opportunity to have some fun.

"Gez, lucky that man told us about the barge coming to port. We will certainly sell all we have and then some."

Before I was even finished with my statement, I heard Abel in the next stall throwing his gear into the rolling cart and packing his things. He even told the others who were trying to buy his fish that he was closed. Gez stopped and watched for a second, then looked over at me. We burst into laughter as we continued to pack up.

Then the others began to pack. Today would be a history maker in the marketplace of Capernaum. There was no deal to be had, and all these owners would be sorely awakened to this fact the moment they looked out to see the docks with no barge in site. Oh, what joy it brought to us to turn the tables on them. If we hadn't been so excited about the upcoming meeting, we might have come right back to open shop and sell out with no competition. But that wasn't in our hearts to do. We would be incapable of doing anything more than waiting for the night to come, and to meet this stranger from Decapolis.

Our mother was alive and she had a message for us.

CHAPTER 15
PATIENCE

-DISMAS-

THE SINGLE ROOM we rented from a Syrian family was in a dungeon-like setting. Located in the back, it was originally created as a cool room to store food as it was below ground. It caught fire long ago and was abandoned. The black soot was now part of the walls. Narrow steps led out the door, exiting into the alleyway. We liked it. It was ours. It was hidden, secluded. Just like us.

"Let's go," Gez said. Dusk was upon us. The sun could not have set any slower than it did on that day. We were about to meet the stranger from Decapolis; the deliverer of news from our mother. Plans inside my head had already begun. I had visions of our embrace, of her asking us, *"Are you all right, my precious boys?"* I could smell the sweet dessert berries in her hair. She was all we had left. There was no other reason for us to go on living. To lose her would be to lose ourselves. We already lost half of ourselves when Father passed. We could not, I would not, lose her.

The air at dusk was brisk but the spring months were just ahead, along with the warmer weather they would bring with them. We could smell the leavened bread throughout the streets mixed with the lingering scent of stale fish. I'm not sure that smell would ever leave this town, nor the villages surrounding it. It took us a good year to get used to it, but now I might actually miss it.

I felt sure this was the night that Gez and I would leave to rescue mother. We were ready. Although rescuing might not be required if she was able to send a messenger.

"Gez?"

"Yeah."

"Why do you think mother sent a messenger? I mean if she is still under the thumb of Clavius, then why risk finding us?"

"I don't know. What are you saying?"

"Nothing, just thinking out loud is all."

"Come on, Diz. We will finally get some answers. We need good news for a change."

"I'm ready, my brother, believe me."

"Good. It's been four years. My hope is that Clavius choked on pig meat and died."

I laughed at that, slapping Gez on the shoulder. Our pace quickened and then there he was, the messenger. He was still in the same garb. Little had changed. His dagger was still sheathed on his side and his arms were crossed over his barreled chest as he waited patiently. His expression was stiff. There was no joy in those eyes.

Gez waved and said, "Well met."

There was no response or movement as we came face to face with him.

"So, what say you?" I asked impatiently.

He looked at me, uncrossed his arms, left one dangling to his side while his right went for the dagger. We both took a step back as he was about to draw it out but then suddenly he laughed aloud, grinning with his bright white teeth. His hands flared out empty to show us that it was a ruse.

He said, "Got you good, didn't I?"

We exhaled our collective breath and looked at one another, still unsure. Who was this man?

"Come on," he continued, while still laughing. "The look on your faces."

I thought he was going to fall to the ground in laughter but he didn't.

"What is this?" Gez asked.

"Your message," he quipped.

"We don't understand."

"Okay, boys, your mother is fine and she sent me to fetch you."

We desperately needed to hear this. His words almost didn't register.

"But who are you? Why didn't mother come herself?"

"If she came herself, then I would be out of a job. My name is Max and she hired me to find you. I have spent weeks scouring the villages, never thinking you to be in Capernaum."

"Why not Capernaum?"

"Why not indeed? I shall remind myself next time to start in the larger populated areas. I'm lucky because you could have been in Tiberias for all I knew and there are a lot of villages between here and there. More than I would like to visit."

"What happened? I mean since we left," I inquired further.

"Too much to tell, dear boy. These are dark times. The Romans flex their muscle almost daily across the lands. Bedouin bandits have increased their raids on the Eastern roads but none of that matters. Are you ready?"

"Ready? For what?" Gez said.

"To leave, of course."

"It's night. Best to leave at first light," I said.

"Nonsense. I have a camp not too far. We will settle there and then complete the last little part in the morning."

"Camp?"

"Yes, my camp. You didn't think I came alone did you? Well, I did come alone to scout out Capernaum didn't I?" He chuckled and then continued, "Just didn't want to attract unwanted eyes to a few of my comrades who quite frankly look like ruffians even to me."

I looked at Gez and he caught my glance. *"Ruffians,"* I thought. This is all too strange. But Mother was okay and that was all that mattered.

"We're ready," I said and Gez nodded.

"Good, then let us be off. Only a mile or so away."

The further we went, the more unsettled I became. I whispered to Gez, "It just doesn't seem right."

Gez surprised me by saying, "I feel it, too."

It surprised me because we rarely agreed on anything. For both of us to feel it, something was definitely off. I whispered again and said, "Time to go fishing."

"Max," I got his attention. "How is Mother's health? She always complained of headaches and such."

"Yeah, we are not far now. Just over this little rise. Oh, forgive me. I thought you asked how far the camp was."

Gez said abruptly, "I need to rest. My leg is bothering me."

Max stopped and turned about, "Come on. Just but fifty steps away now. Not far, just push a little further."

"Nah, my leg," Gez feigned.

I had seen him do this trick numerous times. We were well-acquainted with the shady side of people. And we knew when someone deflected a clear question, such as the one I had asked. Something was fishy. This Max, or whoever he was, knew of our mother but he wasn't sent by her. Just over that rise could be Roman soldiers waiting to arrest us for our crimes, or hired mercenaries from Clavius ready to haul us back.

I said to Gez in Hebrew, "Ab Arake."

He understood I had said 'father' and 'patience'. We didn't have the full language grasped but we picked up keywords which helped us get where we needed to go.

Max looked perplexed and said, quizzically, "What language is that you speak?"

"Hebrew."

"The Jewish tongue? Aren't we full of surprises."

"We've been with them for a few years now. You pick things up."

"Teach me something," Max suggested.

"Okay, say 'be-tachat-shelcha'."

Max attempted to repeat the phrase which simply meant 'up your ass' and while he butchered the words, I whispered to Gez in Hebrew, "Nagach."

Gez stood, saying in our language, "Don't make him say that!" Then he pushed me hard for that was the instruction I had given him. I plummeted into Max and he easily grabbed hold of me.

"Whoa, now boys, let's settle down a bit."

"Yeah, Gez, settle down," I said, as I took a step away from Max.

Max said, "Now what was it that you had me say there?"

"You don't want to know."

"Oh, come on now. There is no harm. We are just having a bit of fun."

"Well, 'be-tachat-shelca' translates as 'up your ass', Max."

The man reached up with his right hand and scratched at his beard in contemplation and then said, "That doesn't seem very nice, now does it?"

"Do you think lying to us is nice?"

"What's this all about?"

"Mother didn't send you."

"Now why would you say that?"

There was an awkward silence as we all stared at one another. Then Max said, "Come on, boys. Just a few more steps and—"

"And what? Your gang will grab us?"

"Gang? You boys listen to too many stories. I'm just a hired hand to bring you back."

Gez said, "To whom?"

He didn't answer. I pressed further, "How is Mother's health, Max?"

"Oh, come on now. I'm no doctor, nor would I ask her for fear of insult."

"No need to ask. You can see it upon her countenance."

"Well," he hesitated as he tried to figure a way out of the question. I was cornering him but he still had a fifty-fifty shot.

Gez increased our odds and said to me, "Diz, of course he knows of her headaches. That wrinkled brow of her always gives it away."

Max quickly followed, "Yes, that brow. That's right. I always think she's mad at me but it must be the headaches. It makes sense now. Okay, are we settled then?"

"Yeah, we're settled."

"Come on, let's go."

Max turned around and began to walk away. I scurried behind him and sliced his calf muscle wide open with his own dagger which I had stolen from him moments before. The moonlight showed the dark splotch of blood streaming down to his ankles. Max fell to the ground and screamed in pain while grabbing the wound. This would surely alert the others, but by that time we would meld into the darkness and be gone.

We knew the area quite well. Fishing wasn't the only thing we had learned these past four years. We also scouted the surrounding land to understand every facet of it.

After we had some distance between us and Max, we made our way to one of the streams and traveled with it, away from Capernaum. Whoever these people were, they would track us to the stream and then assume we went back to the town. We wouldn't, we couldn't go back there. But where would we go now was the question looming over us.

"What now, Gez?"

"Not sure. Let's get to Point View and rest on it."

Point View was what we called a group of tall spired rocks with a grove of trees both on top and at the base. We would be safe there and able to defend ourselves if need be.

I collapsed, out of breath, at my normal spot after the climb. Over the years visiting this place we had carved out a small alcove. I wrapped my robe around me tighter and closed my eyes. The wind howled through the cracks in the rock and the tree leaves rustled continuously.

Gez grabbed a loose dried branch and threw it out into the darkness in anger. I was angry, as well, but I buried my emotion.

"What happened, Diz? Who are those people? Mother didn't send them!"

"I know. We just…"

"Just what? We can't go back to Capernaum now." He took another breath before saying, "We were stupid, Diz! We shouldn't have been so close to home! We should have gone…"

"Where?"

"I don't know, anywhere, further away!"

Gestas finally slunk down to the ground against a rock, propped his knees, and sulked. Several minutes passed. I closed my eyes during the quiet.

"I think it's time," I said with my eyes still closed.

"Not sure what you mean."

I opened my eyes, "Time to go back."

He looked at me hard, "What about patience?" Gez said.

"Patience has run its course, my brother. Now it's time to get Mother."

Gez leaned his head back and closed his eyes without saying anything. It was settled then. I knew he agreed, otherwise he would have said something. We really had no choice. We needed to know. Max, or whoever he was, was a clear sign that something was amiss. There was no more patience to pull from. We had trained and learned more about ourselves amongst these foreigners over the years. The winds spoke to me that the time was about to change. We were moving from a season of patience to a season of action.

"We are coming home, Mother. We are coming home."

CHAPTER 16
WELCOME HOME

-DISMAS-

GERGESA WAS DIFFERENT, but the same. Or was it me who had changed? It was where I grew up, but being away for four years made it strange to be back. There was the sense of knowing my hometown intimately, while at the same time feeling disconnected and unsure of my place here. Gergesa was a small village the locals simply called Ghasa that held a valuable resource for the region; swine. The pig farms of my father supplied the entire Decapolis region; all ten towns on the east side of the Sea of Galilee. All the smells caused the memories to return; old man sweat, pig dung, and desert blooms.

The desert flowers had come early this year and there was nothing like seeing the brown fields turn to a glorious spray of color. As a child, when I looked upon these blooming fields, I envisioned there might be something more out there. But each season the flowers would die and like them, so would my faith. My heart bloomed one moment and then died the next.

Early morning stirred the town's people awake. Women were out first, preparing the day's meals or performing the many cleaning duties. I couldn't help but think that Mother had always done this. She was caught in the cogs of life, yet what brought her meaning? I smiled to myself as I knew she would happily say "her family."

Hundreds of townsfolk resided in Ghasa. Mainly to shepherd the pigs and work on father's slaughter farms. This town was built because of our father.

Directly south, just a couple of miles away was one of the largest of the ten towns, Hippus. It overlooked the Sea of Galilee and was a rival to the western shore city; Tiberias. Fishing boats from either city would not dare cross their side of the sea or there would be blood spilled in the water.

All in all, the ten towns known as Decapolis controlled the trade route that went from Arabia to Damascus, but did so under the protection of Rome. Although we remained a league of free city-states, we were still under the umbrella of Roman authority. It was there, under that Roman protection, that corruption had taken root. Even my own father was a participant, as big business attracted the wrong people. Father always told Gez and me that we do what we must in order to keep our family safe. He was a good man and kept the Romans away by paying them handsomely each month.

Our uncle Clavius was jealous and stripped our father's livelihood away, not once but twice; the second time literally taking his life. Clavius might not have murdered Father but his presence surely suffocated him.

Gez' voice snapped me out of my thoughts of our family history, "Hey, let's go."

We brought our hoods over our heads and with no protective walls around Ghasa, we easily entered town. Roman guards were stationed along the road and at certain posts but rarely did they walk the streets.

"I think we should start at home," I said.

"No, Clavius and his men would be watching there for sure. We should start in town and talk to some people we know. We need information."

"But who?"

"Hassi."

"What? Crazy Hassi?"

"Yes, he knows everything, Diz."

"He knows nothing and speaks in riddles."

"Father liked him. He always invited Hassi to dinner each year."

"I don't know why. He just swayed back and forth at the table while his eyes looked in different directions. He can watch two people at once. It's creepy."

"Well, while you were scared, I watched Father talk to him and get answers to questions he had about people in town. It was like Hassi was his spy."

"Really? I never saw that."

"I know. You were too scared to see what was really happening. How do you think Father knew about the workers in town forming a revolt against their lack of wages that one year? That was from conversing with Hassi."

I had no response to that. I couldn't remember any of the talks at the table when Hassi was there. I just remember wanting to leave as quickly as possible.

"Trust me," Gez said. "I'm right about this."

Gez was always right. I had no choice, really. I also had Max's dagger and would gut that fool Hassi the minute he did anything crazy, which in my estimation, would be inevitable. I nodded and then followed my brother down the narrow passages between buildings. We knew this place very well. Fine desert sand rimmed the edges of the stone buildings which brought back memories of me playing on these very streets. The way I played as a child, I was now playing for real. I clutched the dagger a little tighter.

Hassi's home was near the marketplace. It actually overlooked the small plaza from an upper room. Gestas knocked.

We could hear the muffled excitement of the fool behind the door, who said, "Visitor. Visitor."

The door opened and Hassi's broad smile faded. His deformed eyes, that never looked at anyone, shifted rapidly. His brown hair was cut in odd shapes, matted down on one side from lying on it in bed. His beard was also strangely trimmed, like he had done it himself. He wore a simple brown robe that had dried porridge dribbled down the front. His skin was smooth, having never known the rigors of physical labor.

"It's Gez, Hassi. Do you remember us?"

"I 'member," he said softly.

"This is my brother, Diz."

"I 'member."

"Good, can we come in?"

"I 'member," he said again.

Gez and I exchanged glances. "We need to talk with you about our father."

"I 'member." His eyes were twitching faster and sporadic facial ticks told us that he was extremely nervous.

"We don't have time for this, Gez," I said finally.

"Going back home right now with no information is stupid, Diz."

"Father nice," Hassi said.

Waiting respectfully at the entryway, Gez refocused and said, "Yes, that's right. Our father was nice. We need to find our mother."

"Mother nice."

I barged into the room pushing my brother and Hassi out of the way.

Gez quickly followed and closed the door. Hassi backed to the nearest wall and brought his hands up to his chest. His fingers danced and interlocked with each other, always the same pattern.

"We are sorry to do this, Hassi. We need to find our mother."

"Mother nice."

"Yes, we know but where is she? Do you know where she is?" Gez asked.

"Mother nice."

I rolled my eyes, "This is stupid, Gez. We are wasting our time."

"I watched Father do this, trust me. I just need to lead him correctly."

"Why don't you lead him to the roof and tell him to jump," I said under my breath as I took a seat at the table.

Hassi stepped forward, pointing at me. "No, mine! Mine!"

I stood up and stepped away with my hands up. "Fine, take your precious chair."

"Mine," he said more softly.

Gestas tried again, "Okay, father nice and mother nice."

Hassi repeated the word 'nice' as he continued to fidget. He sat at his table, which only had one chair. I looked around; the room had no kitchen, only a table with the chair and a bed nicely made in the corner. Nothing else. No other belongings. *How did this crazy fool survive?* I wondered.

"Who takes care of you, Hassi?" I asked. A hint of irritation in my voice.

"Mother nice."

"Yeah, we know mother is nice but who takes care of you here in this place?"

"Mother nice."

"Oh by the gods, Gez, what are we doing here?"

Through the window overlooking the plaza, my brother watched the vendors setting up their booths for the day's business. He appeared to be contemplating what to do next.

He looked at me, "We wait."

"Wait? Here?"

"Yes, this is a great spot to watch the market where Mother comes almost daily. If she is alive and well, then she would show up here."

He was right. This would be the perfect spot to watch from. No one comes to Crazy Hassi's and Hassi wouldn't tell anyone. Even if he tried, no one would understand him.

And so we watched the plaza. Mother would come between eight and nine in the morning. It was Woden's Day. If there were any day of the week, it would be this day that she would be here.

Eight-o-clock came with no sign of her. There was still time, but I was anxious. The crowd was thick, as if every person in town was here. I looked back and saw that Hassi had retired to his bed, curled up like a ball facing away from us. He mumbled words under his breath periodically, but otherwise stayed put.

Gez tapped me. I looked back out into the market. My breath was stolen away at the site. Clavius, in regal Greek attire, waltzed into the square. Four Roman guards pushed people out of his way to keep his path unobstructed. I wanted to throw myself on him from my perch, like a cat pouncing on his prey. He acted pompously, like he was a Greek god. We watched as he perused the vendor carts, stopping to pick up a few dates, eating them as he continued on without paying.

We were startled by a knock at the door. It was a peculiar knock. Three taps, a pause, then two taps, a pause, then one final knock. Hassi was no longer in bed, but was waiting at the door already.

We lunged at him to keep him from pulling it open. In mid-lunge, everything slowed as Gestas and I fell, missing our mark. Cool air and a shaft of sunlight hit us when Hassi opened the door. As I was getting up, I saw the sandaled feet under the hem of the light blue robe. I tried to see who it was, but the glare of the sunlight obscured my view. Gestas clamored over me, attempting to grapple the legs of the untimely visitor. I followed to help but then I heard my name. "Dismas?" It was the voice of a woman. I raised my hand to shield the sunlight.

"Gestas?" she said, blocking the sun as she took a step closer.

Our mother! We froze. *"I must be hallucinating,"* I thought. *"This can't be real."*

Her shock transformed to joyful surprise. For four years we had not embraced. For four years we had to envision what she looked like. For four years we were lost without her. Time stood still.

She rushed to embrace us, "Oh, by the gods! My precious boys!"

Oh, those words I had longed to hear. Her voice was like water to my parched heart, healing all my wounds.

"Mother nice," Hassi said.

Gez and I laughed. Hassi had been telling us who took care of him. Our very own mother.

She wouldn't let go of us and said, "Why did you come back?"

We didn't answer. We just held on tightly. If I were to have died right then, I would have died a happy young man.

His voice muffled, Gez said, "We came for you."

She pulled back and looked at each of us, tears streaming down her face, which was more worn than before. She had a few gray hairs laced through the black. It was obvious she was deeply sad but even amongst the horrors she must have endured, she was still beautiful. Her soft skin indicated that she was touched by the favor of Aphrodite herself.

"You promised to never come back," she whispered.

"Men came for us, Mother," I said.

Her eyes squinted as if it pained her to hear this, "What men?"

"A man named Max. We didn't see the others."

"Max?" she said in surprise.

"Max not nice," Hassi said.

"You know of him?" Gez asked Mother.

"He works for Clavius. A tracker hired from Hippus."

"Mother, what is going on?" I asked.

"Listen, Clavius promised me that as long as I...stayed with him then he would not look for you. He sent soldiers to look for your bodies and knew you were alive when no bodies were found."

"You are with him?" Gez said with disgust.

"I did it for you, both of you, to ensure your safety."

She reached out to touch our faces with each of her hands. Her expression softened and tears began to run again, "You have grown. My boys, my sweet boys, have grown. Not a day went by that I didn't pray to the gods for your protection. Gestas, look at how tall you are. You look more and more like your father." She turned toward me, "My Dismas, my sweet Dismas, you are starting to get a beard, but you look so thin, both of you." She pulled away and went into her bag, "Let me get you some food."

A voice called from the stairway outside the door, "Dora, are you there?"

It was him. The man who had stolen everything from us, who had ripped our family apart.

"Go now. Out the window with you," Mother whispered, pushing us toward it.

Clavius ordered his guards, "You wait here.". We heard his sandals scratching and sliding across the wooden steps. His steps slow but steady. "Dora, my dear," he called again.

Dora opened the door and said, "I'm here. Let us go."

"No wait, let me see this hovel I pay for at your command." He entered and saw Hassi.

My brother and I clutched at the edges of the ledge on either side of the window.

"You must be Hassi."

"Come dear, let us go."

"Dear? You have called me many things over the years, but never *dear*. I like it, but let me have the tour." His eyes raked across the room and he raised his brows. "Not really a lively place, is it? I think a home reflects those who dwell in it, don't you think?"

"It's simple," mother said quietly.

"Ah, simple, right. Simple for the simple-minded. Is that right, Hassi?"

Hassi began to fidget again. His eyes fluttered and twitched.

"I don't see why we need to pay for this poor soul to live here, Dora."

She started to protest, but he quickly raised his hand and said, "But if it pleases you, so be it. I am a man of compassion after all."

Clavius stepped toward the window. He didn't lean out, for if he did, he would have surely spotted us. Instead, he watched the crowd below.

"Look at all those people, Dora. Do you realize that they live because of us? We give them work, we give them homes, we give them food, all because of the favor of the gods placed upon me."

Mother nodded.

Clavius continued, "I thought it prudent to expand operations. I sent Max out to Capernaum."

I looked at Gez with concern. We knew Max must have spoken with Clavius by now.

Mother said, "I know not why you speak of your business with me."

"Well, I also tasked him to find me some good hands to work on the farms, as this is needed in order to expand."

"Why not fetch more from Decapolis?"

"Good question, very good question. I was looking for *experienced* hands."

"You have your ways of doing things, Clavius," Mother said.

"And you have yours, my dear wife." There was a bite in his voice now.

"Well, how did Max fair on his quest?"

"He did just fine. Actually, he was able to bring back two young men." Clavius turned and sat on the inside ledge of the window.

I could see his backside less than a foot away and could feel the evil that emanated from him. I looked at Gez to get some direction. What were we supposed to do? Below was the market and someone was going to spot us eventually. Up was the roof and, as if hearing my thoughts, Gez began to climb.

I was going to follow, but heard Clavius say, "I know they are here, Dora."

I froze. What was he going to do to Mother? Whatever it was, I had to protect her. I began to pull the dagger out, envisioning myself gutting Clavius like one of the pigs in the slaughterhouse.

Mother said, "What are you talking about?"

Just then a Roman soldier shouted from the plaza below, "Hey, you!"

Everyone looked up and saw me hanging on the ledge. Gez was already on the roof and was reaching down to help me up. Clavius peered back out the window and was surprised to see me there. I reactively thrust the dagger at him, but it only grazed his side. The weapon clattered to the ground as I lost my balance from the thrust of the blade.

Clavius scrambled back into the room, out of site. I caught my brother's outstretched hand and climbed up to the roof with his help.

"Run!" Mother screamed.

Gez and I jumped to a neighboring rooftop, scaled down, and ran the best we could with Gez' bad leg, through the small alleyways. We knew Ghasa, well, and even with Gez' limp, we were certain no one would catch us.

"I cut him, Gez! Cut him good!"

He didn't respond, but kept leading the way. I looked behind me several times to make sure we weren't being chased. Within minutes we were moving through the flower fields outside of town. Now in the open desert, we hid behind a small ridge to catch our breath. Unfortunately, we were not the only ones there. Max popped out from behind the mound of sand and rock, along with four other ruffians who wore bandanas covering their faces like bandit nomads.

Gez couldn't outrun them with his leg, and I was now weaponless. We were caught.

With open arms and his big bright white teeth shining, Max said, "Welcome home!"

CHAPTER 17
NOMADIC SUSPICION

-DISMAS-

Max limped out from behind the mound and every escape route I could see closed in that moment. We were caught. But did it truly matter? We had finally embraced our mother and I knew then that if we died it would be okay. That was not what I truly wanted, though. I wanted mother to be free.

Max flared his big white teeth in a smile and said, "I'm the best tracker in the land. I knew all your ways before I even laid sight on you in Capernaum. I know all your hideouts, all your friends, all your beliefs. I even know what you ate last night."

"How's your leg?" I asked.

Max scoffed. The other four goons drew out curved daggers, Jambiyas, a desert nomad favorite. We had trained for the last several years in many areas from boating, fishing, to languages, customs, and endurance, but the one thing that had eluded us was the art of fighting. There was no one on the corner saying, *I will teach you the ways of combat. Come with me.*

Gez said, "Clavius will betray you, just like he did his own family."

Max chuckled, "I'm sure he will, but until then, he is paying us quite well."

The others were like statues, just staring at us under their head coverings. All we could see were their eyes. The intensity of those eyes spoke of experience and readiness. There was no escape for us.

"We can pay you," I blurted out.

"With what?" Max countered.

"Clavius gave us a coin pouch."

"And where is this coin pouch?"

"We will take you to it."

Max laughed heartily, "Of course. You need to take us." His laughter faded, "You take me for a fool?"

"Yes, but that is beside the point," Gez said.

"I can snap you like a twig, cripple."

"Are you interested or not?" I brought his attention back to me.

"Why not? A little extra coin never hurt my pockets. Lead the way, boy."

I slowly turned, catching my brother's concerned eyes, but I couldn't tell him anything. I just hoped he would follow my lead. We walked around the town, keeping to the open land. Not ten minutes in, Max said, "It's a good thing we filled The Well with rock so no one accidentally falls into it."

I wasn't going to The Well, but he was making his point. Max had covered his ground, but I was taking him to the place I never ever wanted to go back to.

As we walked, Max said, "What do you want in exchange for this coin? You never gave terms."

"I will tell you when we get there."

"Of course. When we get there."

I didn't have to look back to know that Max was smiling. Another ten minutes passed.

"Are you, by chance, taking us to the *forbidden* area?" Max said mockingly.

I turned and said, "Yes, that is where the coin is."

"No amount of coin can replace my life, boy. Perhaps this coin is somewhere else and you are just trying to have your demon friends rescue you."

I had no retort. I had no more ideas. I looked at Gez and he blurted out, "At father's grave. That is where the coin is."

"Well, lead on then. See, the older they are, the wiser they are."

"That was where the coin was dropped, but we never found it. What would be the point in taking them there? It will just be a dead end. We

are dragging out the inevitable. I hope you have a plan, Gestas. I had to believe he knew what he was doing. He was right, always right."

Another ten minutes elapsed. In the distance, I could see the rock crags leading to the tombs. Father was buried there. I silently prayed to the only one who truly cared about me in the life beyond this one, *"Father, if you are there and can hear me, we need your help once again."*

I then spotted the small Roman outpost where guards were stationed to protect the tombs from being plundered. In the blink of an eye my brother started hustling toward the outpost waving his hands frantically and screaming, "HELP US!"

"This was his plan?" I followed suit.

"What are you doing?" I asked, once I was close enough to speak into his ears only.

"Diz, I will not believe that all the Roman guards are under Clavius. We need some type of protection. Perhaps we can escape into theirs."

He was right. He was always right. My brother was brilliant. Even Clavius had to have his limits. We had no choice but to find out.

Max called, "Now what are you boys up to?"

I looked back and saw Max hobbling along after us. He pointed and his ruffians began to sprint. At the same time, we saw the Roman sentries stir from the hideout, looking in our direction. Two took up their spears and approached cautiously.

"Nomads!" we yelled.

Two more guards came out and all four began to converse. It was going to be close. Either we would be dead, with the soldiers still looking on confused, or these men stationed out in the middle of nowhere would be eager to prove themselves amongst the elite Romans. Bandits in the area were a constant concern and Max's four friends looked the part with their covered faces.

I peered back to see their faces now uncovered, "Damn it!" I said.

Gez didn't hear me as he continued to yell and scream for help. All we needed was for these soldiers to detain us for questioning and then we could figure out our next steps.

Suddenly, my brother tripped and fell to the ground. No, he didn't trip on his own but instead one of Max's men caught his back leg.

Gez said, "Run, Diz! Go!"

The soldiers were still a hundred yards away. My momentum, as well as the pursuit of the other three men, forced me to continue on. No longer under the restraint of my hobbling brother, my legs took me faster than I thought possible. I'm pretty sure I run faster when frightened and I was definitely frightened.

The trackers kept up with me, but never gained. I was going to make it, but what about Gez? Max wouldn't kill him, but would use him to get to me. I had to believe that, otherwise I would turn around this instant and try to rescue Gestas.

One of the Roman soldier's said, "Everyone halt and state your business!" This particular soldier was younger and stood more pompous than the others. He must be the one in charge. I spotted a fifth Roman at the outpost, who stood ready to alert the next outpost if anything went awry.

"Thank the gods," I said breathing heavily. "These bandits are trying to take us as slaves."

He eyed me suspiciously but then looked at the men who had been in pursuit and questioned them, "What say you?"

One, with a well-trimmed beard and scar over his left eye, from what I could only imagine was caused by a blade, stepped forward and said, in a thick accent, "Our master, Max, son of Reko, has documents authorizing us to apprehend these boys and escort them home."

"He is lying!"

"Shut your mouth, boy, or I will shut it for you," commanded the Roman soldier. He looked back at the man and said, "Reko is not a name I recognize. Your paperwork has Roman approval, I take."

"It does."

"I also assume that Max is this one coming our way?"

"It is."

"The papers are fake," I pleaded.

"We shall see about that. Now, be quiet."

I looked at Gez as they approached, both hobbling, and gave him the nod that this was not going our way.

The sergeant stepped forward, "Ah, you must be Max, son of Reko."

Max suddenly lifted his hands and flashed his big, annoying smile once again, "Indeed I am. I traveled from—"

"I don't care," the soldier interrupted. Max' cheerful face slumped. The sergeant said, "Papers?"

"Yes, I've got them here." He handed the scroll over and said, "Signed by Commander Fortus himself."

"Shit," the Roman said under his breath as he unrolled the document.

This was clearly not a good sign. *"Why the Hades does Fortus care about us?"* I thought.

"It's a fake," I said.

The Roman grabbed my chin with one hand and squeezed my cheeks together painfully. "And what does a Greek boy know of fake documents? I said, 'shut up.'"

Max chuckled, calling the pompous young sergeant's attention toward him, "More than I hate youth, I hate trackers, Max, son of Reko." He let go of me and I rubbed my face.

Max sobered quickly and said, "My apologies."

"You know, Max, I was just saying to myself that I needed an excuse to get back to Hippus. I believe you have just provided that for me."

"We have our papers in order, Centurion," Max pleaded.

There was a long pause as the officer read the document. He looked up and said, "No, I think not. I will be taking these boys back to Hippus for further examination of the situation. It appears the signature is smudged."

"Let me see," Max demanded, clearly not liking the Centurion's tone.

I breathed a little easier as Gez and I made eye contact. We were going to Hippus under Roman guard; not the best option, but not the worst either.

"This is ridiculous," Max said.

"Ridiculous would be when your tracking license is revoked and you have to reapply through the magistrate."

"You know not of the importance of this nor of the status of my employer."

"Is that so? Well, you, who are clearly not Roman, don't understand the ways of the Empire. We are under high alert and all things are subject to Hippus headquarters jurisdiction when any suspicious nomads are about."

"Suspicious nomads? We are not nomads."

"Your blades speak otherwise," he nodded toward Max's four men, who held their Janbiyas at their sides.

"You cannot be serious?"

"See how serious I am. Men, take these Greek boys into custody and have them prepared for transport back to Hippus."

"Yes, sir!"

Two guards walked us back to the outpost. I could hear Max

throwing a tantrum in the background. I peered back to see the Centurion clasping his hands behind him and walking toward us with a cocky smirk.

"Thank you," I said.

He kicked me from behind, sending me sprawling. "I said 'shut up.' Any more talk, and I will have you flogged."

Gez helped me up and we walked in silence. Stretching to try to ease the pain surging through my back, I began to wonder if this was the better idea.

CHAPTER 18
THE SERVANTS
-DISMAS-

"A T LEAST OUR *hands were not bound,*" I thought to myself. We were flanked by two soldiers on horses as we walked. The Roman centurion who led the brigade sat proudly on his Arabian steed. He left the other three at the outpost to wait for the new guard exchange while he took us back to Hippus to "sort things out", as he told them. It wasn't like the others were going to argue with him. He was in charge, after all.

The centurion was young, probably twenty years of age. Not young by Roman military standards but young to be a centurion. I surmised he must know someone of high rank, perhaps his father, to move up so quickly. I respected that. Nothing wrong with gleaning from your father and gaining ground you never earned yourself. I didn't respect his sandal in my back, however. Thoughts of revenge played out in my mind to pass the time.

Gez and I exchanged glances periodically. I feared that if I said anything, the centurion would command his steed to kick me in the face. Right now, all we had to do was sidestep horse dung.

Max and his goon squad were gone, but he made it clear to us that we had not seen the last of him when he said, *"See you boys in Hippus."*

What a day. We were in Capernaum earlier this very morning, saw our mother after four years of separation, and now we were in Roman custody. How did we get here? It was still before noon and there was a lot of sun left. What else could happen?

The horse to my left stirred uneasily and whinnied while slightly lifting its two front hooves. Something had startled him.

"Whoa," the Roman said. "What is it, girl?"

He found out, as did we all, when he plummeted from his horse to the ground by my side, a dagger protruding through his cheek. I could see the tip sticking out of his ear while the blade shimmered inside his mouth. Blood sloshed out freely, puddling around him. His lifeless eyes stared blankly up at me. The horse galloped away and the other soldiers turned about trying to figure out what was going on. Gez and I huddled together. I saw a large rock next to a single desert tree and pulled Gestas toward it.

We looked around the rock and saw the two soldiers engaged with Bedouin bandits. The Romans were outnumbered. A second Roman quickly fell as one of the bandits slashed the horse, causing it to topple over. Two raiders jumped the soldier and stabbed him repeatedly with no remorse.

A dozen men in garb that covered their faces surrounded the remaining centurion. His horse spun around frantically as he tried to control the beast. A Bedouin reached to grab the reins but his hand was cut off by the centurion. He screamed in pain, holding the stump as he stumbled away. Another bandit stabbed the Roman leader from the other side, and then it was over. The young centurion fell off his horse. A few bandits kicked him to see if he was still alive. One in black straddled the centurion and buried his dagger into his chest, while letting out a victorious, high-pitched yell.

"Gez, let's get out of here," I said.

My brother was looking at something else and I followed his gaze, quickly ascertaining that we were not going anywhere. An ominous figure towered over us. Dressed in a dark blue robe, his pitch-black beard, oiled to a shine, glistened in the morning sun. A belt carrying numerous leather pouches adorned his waist, along with a curved dagger, the hilt made of a rhinoceros horn, sheathed at his side. Two other men, one skinny, the other bear-sized in girth, stood on either side of this menacing figure.

"My name is Abd al-Aziz," he said to us. His voice had a pleasant tone of confidence, mixed with a hint of sarcasm. "The question is, who are you?"

I repeated the name softly to myself, "Abd al-Aziz."

"No, that is my name. This is when you unveil yours."

I repeated his name because I had heard it before from traveling merchants coming into Capernaum. This wasn't just an ordinary bandit group attacking a Roman patrol. This was none other than 'The Servants'.

Gestas spoke, "My name is Gestas and this is my brother, Dismas."

"Gestas and Dismas. Yes, you are the ones."

"The ones?" Gez said.

"No matter. We will explain once we are safely away. Rest assured, you are in safe hands." He waved his arm in the air and the others began to call out in bird calls to one another. They had stripped the Romans of their valuables and taken the horses except for the one they had injured. That one they put out of its misery.

The Servants were not safe hands to be in. Gez and I knew this and had heard the stories over the years that came into Capernaum. They were one of the largest nomadic groups, consisting mainly of Arabs, but adopted all walks into their ranks. They were merciless to the Romans, and to anyone who stood in the way of their mission; the complete destruction of the Roman invaders.

We traveled the entire day. Gez and I didn't say a word. All I could think about was that they knew of us, referring to us as 'the ones'. Why? To what purpose? I couldn't fathom how we could be of any importance to The Servants.

We came to a hidden cave that opened up from the ground, unlike most of the caves in the area, which were inside crags of rock. To any prying eyes, it would appear to be open desert with prairie weeds and wildflowers sprouting from patches of rock. It was the perfect place to hide. We descended thirty feet on an easy zig-zag trail down. The air was much cooler and I heard the echo of water trickling further back in the cave. This couldn't be the main camp, as there were only forty men traveling with us from my count during the day, and I knew this group to be in the hundreds.

The faces we passed spoke of hardship, of loss, and of great power. Each man could take three Romans on his own. We followed Abd al-Aziz to the back of the cave where plush pillows and blankets of various bright colors brought some life to the dark environment. Torches, wedged in between rocks, were placed throughout the area, shedding light and creating long shadows. Men rested along the wall, wherever they could find a suitable spot to lie down.

"Sit," the leader said. "Let us speak with one another."

Gez and I sat down as led by the massive bodyguard who had escorted us since our capture. I looked up at the behemoth. His brown beard was braided and he wore the typical Arab head wrapping. His chest was exposed and a black sash dangled over his baggy pants. He had a large, curved sword that I had never seen before. The blade fanned out at the end of the curve and looked frightening in and of itself, but the man wielding it was more menacing in all respects.

Abd al-Aziz said, "This is Usama, my loyal friend. Over here is Mas'ud. They ensure my safety, and I ensure theirs. We are brothers, not in blood, but in the ways of belief."

With trepidation I asked, "Why did you take us?"

"Is it common to ask your mother or father why they feed you?"

I didn't say anything. I understood that this was a subtle reprimand. Father had also used this tactic.

The skinny man, called Mas'ud, to our right, pulled out a small knife and picked at his fingernails. His beard was patchy, a blend of dark and light brown, from what I had seen in the light during the day as we traveled. He did not wear a head covering and his hair hung straight to his shoulders. I could see him watching us closely, never taking his eyes off of us, while still fidgeting with his blade.

Aziz must have seen my discomfort from Mas'ud's unwavering gaze and said, "Don't worry about Mas'ud or Usama. It is the others in camp you should be watching, for they don't take kindly to strangers. We need to understand one another so as to relieve the strangeness between us. You are Gestas and you are Dismas, sons of Karpos."

This wasn't a question. It was a statement.

Aziz then said, "I am sorry for your loss."

"What is this all about?" Gez asked in frustration. He was clearly tired of the slow release of information.

"This is about you, Gestas and Dismas. We take what we need in order to survive. Taking you today was a step toward our survival."

"We are just children," Gez protested.

"Not just children. Sons of Karpos."

He knew our father.

"Father paid you, didn't he?" I asked.

"Are you hungry?" Aziz clapped his hands and instantly one of the men brought over a silver tray with dates, nuts, bread, and wine, setting it down on the floor before us. Aziz said, "Excellent. Please eat." He waved his hand over it giving us permission. The food definitely caught my attention. We shoveled it into our mouths. Aziz smiled and grabbed a handful of the nuts and slowly ate them while watching us. He poured us each a glass of wine which we slurped down.

"How do you know our father?" I garbled around two plump dates I just put into my mouth.

"Your father was an interesting man. A complicated man. Torn between two worlds."

"Our father wasn't torn. He just wanted the best for his family," Gez quickly responded.

"Yes, and that is where things get complicated. You see, in order for a man to protect his family, he needs to be physically and mentally strong. Karpos was indeed both, but the more he consumed of this world, the world outside his family, the more complications it brought upon him and his ability to protect his family."

"He farmed pigs and helped other families," Gez said.

"Yes, he did. The pigs attracted flies."

"Romans," I surmised.

"An enemy to the pig. Flies are to be killed and controlled. Your father knew this."

"But how do you know him? He never spoke of you."

"We were silent partners, just as your father silently helped the Romans."

"He paid his taxes like the others," I said.

"This goes beyond taxes. Rome, as they have done before, took control of your father's business and *let* him run things."

Gez and I locked eyes.

Aziz continued, "You see, your father was protecting his family, but found himself in a situation where he was forced to be bedded by the Roman dogs. He was also forced to deal with The Servants in order to protect his family from slaughter."

"What did he do?" Gez asked.

"He gave us information about the Romans in order to keep his family alive. He would deliver messages to us through the pigs. Since his death, we have lost this way of gaining information, and are now forced to adjust accordingly. This is where you come in."

"What can we do?"

"You know things. Your father taught you in the ways of his business and Saif al-Malik, the leader of The Servants, sees this as a benefit to us. We looked for you but did not find you, so we waited."

"Waited? For how long?"

"It doesn't matter. Tell us about Clavius."

"He deserves to be gutted like a pig," I said.

Aziz rolled back in laughter and looked at his bodyguards. "You see? You see?" he repeated.

Usama and Mas'ud chuckled with him and nodded.

"Then it is settled," Aziz said.

"What is?" I said, half smiling and still chewing bits of broken dates wedged in my teeth.

"You, Dismas and Gestas, sons of Karpos, have information and this is valuable to us. Even after death your father still protects his family."

"What if we don't know anything?" Gez asked hesitantly.

Abd al-Aziz looked at each of us and said, "How did you say? You would be gutted like a pig."

CHAPTER 19
THE GREAT LOSS

-DISMAS-

I WAS AWAKENED BY Usama, which we'd found out means Lion, but looking at this beast of a man, I think they should have named him Bear. His paw shook Gez awake and he said in a deep voice, "You follow."

As we walked the dark cave by the light of a single torch that Usama held, we could see that not one of The Servants remained. It was empty. Echoes of our steps resounded as we followed Usama who guided us up and out. As we reached the top, there was a ring of Servants holding torches that fought the slow bursts of morning winds. It was dawn and the sun was about to blaze over the horizon.

"Come," Aziz said, "It is time."

"Time for what?"

"Time for the truth."

All of the nomad soldiers turned and began to walk. Those holding torches snuffed them out in the dirt. Usama and Mas'ud trailed behind us as Aziz came up by our side.

"A large Roman contingent is on the move."

I said, "And you plan on fighting them?"

"No, we plan to watch them, study them."

Gez asked, "How many is a contingent?"

"One hundred."

"A hundred?" I said, surprised. "I have never seen that many before."

"They don't normally bring out such numbers unless they plan on striking."

"Do you know who they will be hitting?" Gez said.

"Yes and so we will watch and learn." Aziz walked away briskly, bringing the conversation to an end.

Several hours passed before we arrived at the backside of the mountain known as Gadarene. We knew this mountain because our home, along with the pig farms, was on the other side. The Bedouin hiked up single file through the crags and trails that littered the sides. They knew what they were doing and where they were going. How many times had these same people spied on our town, on our home, on me?

The shadow of the mountain was still on Gergesa, when it came into view in the distance. It was a hot day, stifling. The air was still and strange gray clouds appeared to be stationary. All of the desert warriors crouched behind rocks and peeked out to view the area. Usama forced us to keep low so as not to be seen. We were positioned next to Aziz.

"You will watch and not speak," he told us.

Not understanding why he was instructing us, we just nodded. The tone of his voice implied that we should follow his instructions closely.

A warrior near Aziz pointed to a location. Several seconds passed before he looked at the warrior and nodded. Then Aziz quietly said to us, "Remember, we watch."

I started to say something but he held up his hand and looked back at Usama. The bear-man grabbed me and Gez, and Mas'ud quickly brought gags around our mouths, tying them behind our heads. Voices muffled, our eyes widened in shock and confusion. Usama tied our hands in front of us. I looked at Aziz. He nodded and said, "Watch." We lifted our chins above the rock to look.

I saw the people gathered. The entire town of Gergesa was in the assembly area. As I continued to survey the scene, I saw Roman soldiers. Some on horses, but most on foot and in perfect rows surrounding the town. Other warriors patrolled the area on horseback looking for any desert nomads lying in wait.

The center was cleared of all people, except for two Romans standing at the whipping post. This was a place where people were tied and lashed according to their crime. Hassi was tied to the post!

A Roman commander, clearly marked by his red adorned helmet and gleaming armor laced with gold and silver, paced away from the post holding a whip. Dust kicked up as he dragged the leather tail behind him. He was talking to the people gathered and then suddenly turned and lashed Hassi across his back. We could hear the whip crack and echo against the mountainside.

Gez and I gasped and I looked away at Aziz. He was staring at me. Not wavering. Aziz' eyes, brown with a hint of green, narrowed as he said, "Watch."

I tentatively peered back. Gez was beside me, as more cracks of the whip resounded. Hassi was being whipped repeatedly and it looked like he had passed out hanging on the pole. Blood streamed from his wounds. Finally, the commander stopped and the soldiers cut the rope. Hassi fell to the ground. They dragged him off to the side.

I recognized the lead Roman when he pulled his helmet off. It was Fortus, Commander of the Roman Legion stationed in Decapolis and headquartered in Hippus. He had dealings with our father. He waved toward the crowd in front of him. We could see Clavius and a woman, who was desperately trying to break from his grasp. Wait! It was Mother! Her hands were tied behind her back. Two guards grabbed her. She kicked and screamed as they lifted her up and tied her to the post.

Usama and Mas'ud quickly grabbed us to keep us in place. I tried to plead with Aziz through my gag. I could feel tears welling up as I peered into Aziz's intense stare, surprised to see his eyes watering slightly, as if he was actually feeling compassion for my pain. Aziz whispered, "You need to watch. Let all that your eyes witness today be the spark that ignites the fire inside you."

"Please help her," was all I could manage, but he nodded to his warriors, instructing them to hold our heads in place to look.

I could hear Gez crying next to me, but instead of my tears flowing freely, they began to dry. I knew that I was going to lose the other half of myself today. Today, my mother, who I held in my arms for the last time just yesterday, would die.

Fortus continued to shout to the onlookers of Gergesa.

Clavius stood close by. Fortus turned toward my mother, my sweet mother, and brought his whip down upon her with brutal force. Each hit struck my heart. Each lash that ripped open her clothes and flesh, tore pieces from my heart and soul. I watched as lash after lash came down on this woman who loved us, who took care of us, who sacrificed everything for us. Oh, how I wish I could take her place and receive all of the pain in her stead.

Then it stopped. Fortus handed the whip to Clavius. No, it didn't stop. It had just begun, for now the lashes came from this evil man. A Greek striking a Greek. Far worse, a family member whipping a family member.

I was numb. There was no feeling inside of me. But then it came, creeping further and further. There *was* a feeling welling up inside of me; it was hatred. It was the darkness that I feared the most, along with the creatures that had lain in wait in my dreams. But now, I felt like I had become the darkness. I wanted to destroy anything and everything around me. The face of Clavius zoomed out of the darkness and mocked me, then the face of Fortus, replacing his image.

Aziz understood what was happening inside me. He whispered, "Let the fire ignite. It will be a fire that no man can put out. A man's flames come from the tragedies they have experienced in this life. Yours is called *'easim khasara'*; the Great Loss."

Mother hung from the pole. Clavius stopped his torture as Fortus gave a new command. I expected the two Roman scum to cut her bound hands, but instead, they pulled her limp body up tight against the post. Her head dangled. Blood saturated her shredded clothes and her soft, delicate skin was now torn.

Fortus continued with his speech to the people assembled as he strode up to Mother. He grasped her hair. Lifting her head up, he pulled out his sheathed blade and sliced her throat open.

He let go of her as the guards cut the ropes. Her lifeless body fell face first into the dirt.

Fortus mounted his horse. He said a few more words and then his contingent of monsters rallied behind him and marched away.

I slipped backward and was caught by the arms of Usama. Someone removed my gag, along with the rope. I couldn't look at Gez. I was lost in a shadowy world inside myself. There was no light left to guide my soul. I now walked in darkness.

Aziz whispered to me but I couldn't hear him. It didn't matter. I was dead. All of Dismas was gone. Something else had taken his place.

I don't know how long we were there but my senses slowly returned, and I found myself resting in Aziz's arms against his chest. I sat up and looked at him. All he did was nod and stare back at me. He knew the transformation had taken place.

My brother was leaning over a rock puking a few steps away from me.

Usama was next to him. Mas'ud stood off to the side, ever watchful of the surroundings. All the others were gone. It was just us on this mountain.

Aziz asked, "What did you see as you dream walked with your eyes wide open?"

Everything around me was slowed as if underwater. His words were deep and muffled.

"What did you see?"

His words formulated more clearly as he repeated himself.

"I...I saw...darkness."

"And how did you feel walking through this darkness?"

I said, "I felt like a shadow within the darkness."

Aziz nodded in contemplation. "A shadow. This is your essence now. You will now be known as 'Zill'.

"What is Zill?" I mechanically asked, not sure why. What did it even matter?

"'Zill' translates to 'shadow.' You are no longer Dismas, for he has died. Now standing before us, is Zill. We welcome you, Zill."

Mas'ud and Usama both said, "Zill," bowing to me.

"Welcome me into what? What is there for a shadow in this world?"

"That is your assignment. To find out why you were called to this world."

The old me had died. Now standing was someone new, for I had been reborn with no mother or father. I looked around at Gez, then Usama, Mas'ud, and finally Abd al-Aziz.

"Come," Aziz stood. "It is time to start your journey."

Gez was resting against the rock holding his stomach, but looked up at Aziz. Both of us were silently asking what our journey was to be. We waited for the leader of The Servants to tell us.

He said, "It is time to meet the Sword of the King; Saif al-Malik."

"What will he want from us?" Gez asked.

"To become warriors, of course."

Our final training did not come before our mother's death, but after. The final ingredient wasn't finding someone to train us, but instead finding the pain to drive us into having no choice. It would be the Great Loss that stoked the fires of hate burning inside us. I looked at each of them and the scales fell from my eyes. I could now see the great loss they had suffered as well.

A sudden realization struck me; *these* were now my family. These were my brothers, they would die for us, and now I realized, I would die for them.

CHAPTER 20
HIDDEN FEAR

FOUR YEARS BEFORE THE CROSS
-DISMAS-

WE WERE ALWAYS on the move. Breaking down camp, setting up camp, fire-building, animal-tending, patrolling the area, and fetching water and food. All of these duties brought Gez and me no discomfort these past two years. We took our place gladly and understood our roles. There was only one thing on our minds; the slow death of Clavius. It went beyond revenge now. It was our objective; our duty. We knew that the demise of Clavius was not the endgame of our life, but killing him was a stepping stone to the next level. For Gez and me to get to that next level, it would require the death of the 'Butcher of Ghasa', as we now called Clavius.

"Tell us everything," Aziz instructed. I remembered our conversations with Aziz over the last two years as they replayed in my mind. "Tell us what he eats, how he talks, who he sees. Tell us everything."

"Why don't you just kill the pigs and close the farms down?" I asked in those early days.

Aziz answered, "Because those farms and pigs bring an income to many families in the region. Those farms are a focus for the Romans. It blinds them. A distraction we use against. We don't bite the hand that feeds us. Instead, we control the hand."

The Servants were not only mighty warriors, they were also very calculating. Spies would make informational drops in locations prescribed by Aziz or he would send someone to meet an individual in one of the towns for information. They first sought knowledge of their enemies and then used that knowledge against them.

We saw this quickly, as Aziz and his group hit The Butcher of Ghasa where it hurt, which affected Clavius' relationship with the Romans, especially the commander, Fortus. Strategic supply lines were intercepted, while other times he captured messengers, causing the loss of vital information.

There would be weeks of Aziz being away on missions and many times we wondered if he would ever return. He was called *Abd al-Aziz*, Servant of the Powerful, but he was known amongst us as something else; *Khadim Almawt*—Servant of Death. As the story was told to us on many nights by the fire, before The Servants' birth, a group of nomads found a teenage boy covered in blood from head-to-toe. The boy, who held a bloodied dagger, was surrounded by the dismembered bodies of four Roman soldiers. These same Romans had killed Aziz' father and mother before his very eyes. The nomads took him in as their own, naming him Khadim Almawt.

I was caught in the 'fire gaze' as I recalled these memories. I felt a connection with Aziz because of our similar great losses.

"Thinking about that girl from last night?" Gez said as he approached me sitting by the fire.

It snapped me out of my ruminations of Aziz' moment of great loss. "Yes, and what a lovely night it was."

"Lovely? An interesting word choice. Did you bring her flowers?"

"Shut up," I said as I playfully pushed him away. "Yes, lovely. You're just jealous."

"Jealous? I think not. I had her the night before you," he said.

I laughed and threw another piece of wood onto the fire. We watched the sparks fly into the air, then quickly disappear in the chilly night air. The stars were bright and howls of desert wolves could be heard in the distance. How many nights had we done this together, sitting by the fire? *"Too many to count,"* I thought. We were living a different life. Our former life had passed away and was a distant memory as if it were a story told to us by someone else.

We both stared into the fire for a long while until I said, "You didn't seriously sleep with her the night before, did you?"

He didn't laugh and I quickly looked up at him. He gazed into the fire without flinching, then slowly looked at me.

I punched him in the arm, "You did! You bastard!"

He rubbed his arm as he laughed at me. "It's okay, brother. The question now is, 'who will she come back to?' now that she has tried us both."

"Tried us? Are you saying that she used us?"

"Why else? Do you think it was my crippled leg or your crazy eyes that drew her in?"

"That's ridiculous," I countered.

"Is it?"

"Yes, it is. I have seen the Bedouin whores who have been through camp. She is different."

Gez chuckled, "Yeah, different is the word."

"What are you saying?"

"Nothing, my brother." It was quiet between us for a minute before Gez said, "Tomorrow, Aziz picks."

I didn't look at him and said, "Yes, but only one."

"Diz, you must realize that it is only going to be one. If he picks you, then go. You have my blessing."

I scoffed, "I don't need your blessing, but I won't leave you either."

"You long to see action, Diz. What if he picks you?"

"Then I will decline."

"You would be the first to do that."

"Would you not deny the position if he picked you, big brother?"

"No, I would go."

I looked at him in unbelief, "You would do that to me? You would go?"

"Yes. Why not?"

"Well, maybe because you wouldn't want to be separated from me?"

"What do you take me for, your wife?"

"How is it possible that we are even brothers?"

Gez didn't answer, and he raised an eyebrow as he took a drink of his wine.

I said, "I realize that Aziz will not pick either of us, but the fact that you would abandon me just doesn't make sense."

"You are afraid, then?"

"No, not afraid. I'm sad, brother."

"Why? You of all people look to hide in the shadows. You have always run away, even when we were children. Even now, you fear our separation."

I punched him in the arm again, even harder than before. His drink sloshed and spilled onto him as he fell over clutching his arm in pain. I walked into the darkness of night. *"Damn it,"* I thought. *"He was right. He is always right. Why do I run? Why is it that I need my brother by my side? What am I afraid of?"*

A voice startled me, "You fear losing him." It was Aziz.

"How much did you hear?"

"I heard more than what was actually said."

"Who are you going to pick tomorrow?"

"I've watched you over these years, Zill. I've watched both of you."

He didn't say anything after that so I prompted, "And?"

He stared at me. I felt his penetrating eyes upon me even through the darkness of the night. "Tomorrow is a big day for The Servants. Hear me, Zill. A shift in the balance is coming. I have foreseen it."

"What have you seen?"

"There will come a time, Zill, that I will not be around."

"Why do you say such a thing?"

"You must hear this. I look to the future of the generations to come. Your generation will be the one to conquer our enemies, new and old. Your training these last years was not to hone your skills, but to develop your character."

"I don't understand."

"Your skills were always there. I just pointed them out and made you practice them over and over, but your character is something entirely different. It is what drives a man to the core of who he is when he comes face to face with himself."

I turned from him, "I lost myself when…they took her from me."

"You were empty but over time that emptiness has been filled. Man can never leave himself. You are still there, deep inside," he turned me to face him and touched my chest with his finger.

I looked at him for a long moment and then said, "I never see you pray for anything. Do you believe in the gods?"

Aziz' eyes narrowed a bit, his pause indicating a reluctance to say. "I believe in oneself."

"What do you do when you fail yourself?"

"You see failure but I see promise. One only fails if they never try."

"What is my future, Aziz? I feel lost."

He grabbed my shoulder and said, "It is what you make of it. I have seen many men lost to the *'shadow-walk'*, but you embraced the darkness and became the shadow. You made it become part of you instead of it overpowering you. Never forget that you play a part in this world."

"But what of the world that follows? What is next?

"Paradise for those who want it. Others," he paused, "darkness."

"Two worlds?" I asked.

"Many worlds. It will depend on what you do in this one and what you believe to be true before your final breath."

Aziz' hardened warriors were the elite. He took into his inner circle forty men, no more, no less. Tomorrow was *'The Pick'* to replace a recent loss from a skirmish on the road to the South.

"You have many good choices for tomorrow's pick. How do you decide?

I couldn't clearly see the expression on his face in the shadow of the moonlight, but I thought I caught a slight movement of his cheek. A smirk perhaps?

"One must always be ready," is all he said. With that, he left and I was alone once again.

CHAPTER 21
THE PICK

-DISMAS-

THE SERVANTS HAD gathered deep in the east, near the border of Arabia, away from prying Roman eyes. Several of the smaller tribes in the region gathered as well. It was the largest union of the most feared men in all the surrounding lands. Abd al-Aziz was going to pick someone out of the hundreds assembled to be a part of the forty top warriors. It was an elite group of fighters skilled in all aspects of warfare. With no pattern for the Romans to discern, The Servants' tactics, which ranged from small to larger raids throughout the region, brought fear to the Roman army in Decapolis.

This was not only the *'Khiar'*, the Pick, but also a time of celebration. Men, women, and children, gathered to hear the tales of victory and loss. There were also games of skill, games of chance, games of strength, and there was plenty of wine and women.

Saif al-Malik, Sword of the King, was announced with a ram's horn that spiraled high above the man who blew it. This was what everyone waited for. The tent draping was pulled aside as the great Saif exited. He wore kingly attire brought from Arabia. The flowing outer cloak of white and gray wool covered his normal *thobe*. The white *gutrah* had a double golden rope laced around it to keep it in place on his head. Gold armbands and multiple earrings added elegance and symbolized power. Silk patterned slippers adorned his feet, and with each step, one could hear the tinkle of the small bell at the curved upward tip.

Saif was escorted to the shaded area arrayed with pillows and blankets in various bright colors. A tray of food awaited and servers stood nervously by in anticipation of honoring their king. Aziz followed Saif, also dressed in regal attire befitting this occasion. It was widely believed among the warriors that Aziz would be the next king of The Servants.

The dust had settled from the day's activities and the great Saif said in Arabic, "Walsamah laha 'an tabda!"

A cheer erupted.

"Let it begin, indeed," I thought, having learned the language these last two years.

I nudged my brother, excited for what was coming. He nudged back, smiling and nodding. There were so many great candidates for Aziz to choose from. I looked at the muscled men around me, comparing them to my skinny physique. They bore bronze colored chests thrice my size. Directly across from me in the perimeter of the circle, the confident Al-Mutaraqa, the Hammer, stood stoically with his arms crossed. He would definitely be my choice if I had to replace someone.

Jokingly, Gez pointed at me to be the one picked and I pointed back at him. We laughed heartily. In the back of my mind, however, I couldn't help but remember what Aziz had told me the night before, *"Be ready."*

"Be ready for what? I'm ready to see The Forty warriors moving throughout the region as the Sword of Death continues to strike our enemy, the Roman dogs."

An eruption of cheers came from the left of us. We strained our necks to see what caused the ruckus. Two men dragged out a Roman soldier they had captured for the event. It was custom that whoever was picked would kill the Roman as an offering. This would seal his blood-thirsty, single-minded focus on the Romans as his nemesis. As I looked upon this beaten Roman, sudden images of the Romans inside our home many years ago flashed through my mind. I forced the thought away.

Aziz stood and walked out into the middle of the circle of men. The two warriors tied the Roman to a post. Aziz said loudly, "I'm against my brother!"

Aziz began his speech in the Bedouin tradition, an ancient saying now embedded into everyone's memory. We all echoed his words, "I'm against my brother!"

Aziz continued, "My brother and I are against our cousin!" Again we repeated it.

Then he said the final part, "Our cousin and I are against the stranger!"

After the words fell from everyone's lips, we erupted in a warrior yell. Hatred plastered our faces as we locked in on the Roman bound to the post. All of us wanted to storm this single man and pull him apart, letting his blood soak the ground at our feet. Blades were drawn and lifted high into the air as we screamed. Some frothed at the mouth, spittle sliding out and melding into their beards. I loved every second of it. I felt a part of something powerful. I felt invincible.

The crowd hushed and Aziz continued, "Today we not only choose someone worthy, we mark our minds with those who have fallen. Wahid Bisawt Eal, the Loud One, will be remembered."

Men looked at one another and acknowledged the most recent member of The Forty who had fallen. He was indeed a loud one, always yelling even when it was quiet. Gez and I were told that The Forty always had to instruct him to put a gag on before battle as to not alert the enemy of their position. He had fought valiantly, but was struck down by an arrow during combat with a Roman patrol along the road.

Aziz continued, "Wahid Bisawt Eal is still tormenting our enemy. When we yell, we yell with Wahid in our heart!"

Another roar resounded. When Aziz said this, I felt a shift inside me, like the spirit of Wahid had entered me. As I yelled, I pictured him yelling through me. I was suddenly uncomfortable, and looked at Gez to see if he also seemed uneasy, but my brother looked upon the ceremony wide-eyed in excitement and fascination. I refocused on the event.

Aziz quieted the people, "I am not one to belabor you with words. I will now mark the chosen." The Arab warrior walked over to the gagged and bound Roman prisoner who looked around in terror. Aziz withdrew his dagger and grabbed the Roman's arm. He sliced it open, making sure not to hit a vital artery. Aziz sheathed his blade and then wiped blood onto the palm of his hand. He would place his hand on the shoulder of the person he chose to mark. He walked around looking through the hundreds that awaited his decision.

Aziz turned toward Saif al-Malik and waited for the King to grant his approval. Saif nodded. It was time for the Pick, the Khiar.

Aziz spun around and boldly walked in our direction. This was it. Someone nearby us was about to be chosen. I lightly nudged my brother, who was also intoxicated by the moment. Wow, Aziz was looking straight at us, twenty paces away! I looked behind me to see who was in our area. What warrior did we stand next to that would receive this honor? There was one notable that I could tell. It was Sayr, the Seer. Oh, that would be a very strategic pick. Sayr had great visions that would always come true in some capacity. Yes, Sayr will be the one. Aziz was now ten paces away. My heart was pounding. This was all happening so fast. A layer of fighters who stood in front of us began to part as Aziz walked clearly in our direction toward the Seer.

Aziz lifted up his blood covered palm and I watched everything go into slow motion as his hand came down onto Gestas. My brother? The wind was knocked out of me. He chose Gez, he chose Al-Qadhif, the Thrower. Then as suddenly as he placed his hand and marked Gez, his hand lifted and he placed it on my shoulder. I looked at the blood clearly marking me and then back to Aziz in unbelief.

How is this possible? He couldn't pick two. I saw the confusion upon the faces of those around us. The warriors, big, brawny, stalwart, looked on in utter confusion, and what I thought to be disgust. Murmurs erupted all around us at this unprecedented pick. Not one, but two, were chosen.

The horns blew and the people quieted. Saif stood from the comfort of his pillows and spoke, "Aziz, what is the meaning of this?"

Even the king was confused. Aziz approached and explained, "Great Saif, I have chosen only one warrior today, though your eyes show two. Al-Qadhif is Zill and Zill is Al-Qadhif. They are one and not to be separated. I have seen in a vision that when one dies, the other will as well. They live under the same heart and as long as it beats they will fight as one."

Saif al-Malik walked out to Aziz. He narrowed his eyes. The silence was deafening as we waited for the king's response to this unorthodox replacement of the fallen warrior of The Forty. Saif nodded and said, "I accept this. Let it be as Aziz has said."

Cheers erupted and Gez and I were instantly surrounded with people praising our tribal names. "Al-Qadhif, Al-Qadhif, Al-Qadhif ! Zill, Zill, Zill!"

Gez yelled, "See, my brother, you can never get rid of me!"

I laughed and thought, *"You are right, Gez. You are always right."*

We were pushed out toward the frightened Roman and then given space. A sudden surge of cheers from behind caused us both to turn. Ushered through the crowd was a second Roman. They tied him to the other side of the same post. More cheers came and then the crowd silenced.

I looked at Gez, who was staring at me. We were elated, but also in shock. We soaked in this humbling honor and let our eyes look upon the men who surrounded us, these great men. As I scanned Al-Mutaraqa, Al-Kashfia, Sayr, Al-Kisara, Al-Shafara, and others who were not chosen, we briefly locked eyes and each of them gave their approval. Pride welled up inside of me. I lifted my blade into the air and everyone yelled. I was now in command of this audience. They waited upon me and they wanted to feast on Roman blood.

Gez and I looked at one another. We were ready for this next level in our life. We were one and nothing could separate us, not even death.

Our blades simultaneously penetrated the prisoners. We gutted them like the pigs on our farm. The pigs we killed many years ago were all a prelude to the Romans who had invaded our land, the *'strangers'* that we would kill, united with my brothers and cousins of the Bedouin way. I felt the warmth of the blood flow over my hand as I looked into the dog's eyes and pushed my blade in deeper and deeper. The Roman's eyes opened wider and wider. The smell of the blood wafted into my nostrils, and like a calming medicine, I breathed it in and closed my eyes.

The thirty-nine warriors of Aziz lifted us up into the air and passed us around. We were then brought to Saif's tent and ate the most impressive food in the land as we dined with the King. So much of it was a blur to me. I don't even remember eating, which is surprising because I love to eat. Reality came back to me when I overheard Gez and Aziz talking outside alone by the fire. It was late night and men littered the ground all around us, passed out from too much wine.

"Ah, there is the fortieth. The great Zill," Gez said.

"What happened?" I groaned, stumbling closer to them, then sitting down.

Gez chuckled. "I will tell you all about it later."

Aziz stood, "Time to get some rest, young warriors. Tomorrow we ride to familiar ground."

"Familiar ground?" I questioned.

"Diz, we are going home," Gez said.

"Home? What do you mean?"

Aziz clarified, "We have information that Fortus will be in Ghasa to meet with Clavius. You both are favored to have been picked for such a time as this. It is time we strike the head of the serpent."

"Why now? Why after all of this time?"

Aziz laid his hand upon my shoulder, "Because we have finally caught up to fate."

CHAPTER 22
THE HEAD OF THE SERPENT
-DISMAS-

THE NEXT DAY, feeling the effects of too much wine and fire talk, we groggily prepared for our mission; our first as members of Aziz's elite. Gez and I were now part of The Forty. I found it strange that all my duties and training had led me to this. Thoughts of what I would normally be doing at this time of day ran through my mind. My old chores shifted overnight and I had to turn my thoughts to my new duties as part of this elite group of warriors.

We all expressed our farewells to the other tribes and to our comrades. It was a long day of travel back to the perimeter of Decapolis. Ghasa was another day beyond that. Setting up camp without fire alerted Gez and I that we were now in hostile territory, with Roman sentries ever watchful of any light in the distance. I had longed for this. I had dreamt of this. It was difficult to sleep as the sense of danger sparked every nerve in my body.

Aziz sat next to us and said, "Tomorrow will define you."

We knew not to speak as we waited for him to say more. Aziz wanted us to digest his words first before speaking again.

"Zill, I want you to enter Ghasa and then come back to inform us of what you see. Your information will give us direction for our strike."

He looked at Gez, "You will stay with Mas'ud during the initial attack." Gez started to argue but Aziz held up his hand, "Mas'ud and you have a special assignment that will be revealed tomorrow."

Aziz observed our brotherly exchange of excitement and said, "Commander Fortus will come unattended to meet Clavius at his new home on the west side of Ghasa. We have someone on the inside who is a loyal Servant and he will give us access. We will strike fast and we will strike sure. Do you understand?"

We nodded.

"Good, now rest."

How could we rest? Tomorrow, we would finally get our revenge and the lifeblood of Clavius and Fortus would be spilled. Eliminating a commander of the Roman army would bring repercussions; The Servants would make a full withdrawal into the heart of the desert. The hornet's nest would be stirred and anyone in the vicinity would certainly be stung. We wouldn't be retreating, however. We would be celebrating.

The time had come. The sun was setting, casting a beautiful orange glow upon the land; a calm before the storm. In the morning we would bring an incursion that would rival all storms, and it would be ours to release.

The next morning dawned early and brought with it the excitement of unfolding our plans.

Aziz walked back with Mas'ud after surveying my hometown of Ghasa from our vantage point. He looked at me and said, "Now it's your turn. Do not be seen by friend or foe. We will await your return."

I looked back at Gez, who nodded, then I glanced around at the others. Their eyes spoke volumes to me. They were prepared.

I was about to head out when one of The Forty held me back, "Wait," he said. He pointed to an area. Aziz turned and looked. We tried to discern what he had spotted. Before any of us got our bearings, Aziz said, "Fortus just arrived with two soldiers cloaked in disguise. They are approaching the homestead." Aziz' head subtly bobbed in approval. "We strike now."

"What about Mas'ud and me?" Gez said. "What is our mission?"

Aziz looked around, his eyes falling upon Gez, "Our plan has changed. Today, as one, we will take the head of the serpent."

I grabbed my brother's shoulder, excited for him to join us in this historic conquest. Aziz understood Gez' bad leg, and, for him to allow my brother to come, meant he was very confident of the outcome. We all were confident. Why shouldn't we be? We had a scout in the hills to watch and signal us. We had perimeter defense for an immediate escape and we had the rest of us, twenty hardened fighters, entering the town at different points, with the others stationed inside the perimeter pretending to be merchants.

We knew this town, yet it seemed like a faded memory, distant to me. As I entered and began walking the street it felt somewhat foreign, like a stranger I had seen before but did not know. Deep down I knew what was missing; it was my heart. My heart died in this very place when I watched the men we now hunted, butcher and brutally murder my mother. It was this memory that fueled my revenge. Each step brought me closer to that fulfillment.

My hand instinctively reached for the hilt of my janbiya blade, gifted to me by Aziz. His words echoed inside my mind, *"Become one with the blade."*

Gestas, on the other hand, focused his training on knives. His accuracy in delivering these deadly weapons rivaled any in the region, which is why his name is Al-Qadhif, the Thrower. He couldn't run and fight like most, but where he lacked, he made up for in his skill in throwing knives. He was deadly accurate and his reach was far.

In the center of this small village stood a renovated temple dedicated to Aphrodite. White pillars bordered the sandstone-colored marble steps leading to the entrance. Our contact gave signal that Clavius and Fortus were inside. I saw the others surround the building and begin to enter through side entrances and cellar doors. All exits were covered.

Aziz nodded for us to go. I whisked up the stairs in long strides. My breath was controlled, and I could feel blood flowing through my body as my heart pumped rapidly. Torches were lit on sconces outside the open double door. I could see more light emanating from inside. Gez hobbled up to the opposite side, hiding behind one of the pillars which held the balcony above.

I tuned out the others and focused on the shadows that called to me. It was there that I entered. I left no trail. I made no sound. I gave no trace that I ever existed. My eyes quickly adjusted to the darkness, which heightened my senses. All my training came to the forefront of my mind.

Voices alerted me, but the words were not discernable as they echoed off the walls. A huge mosaic of the goddess Aphrodite was in the center of the floor. Small white pillars, with Greek flowery patterns sculpted into their sides, laced the perimeter of the fifty-by-thirty-foot room. I peered around the stone and saw Clavius and Fortus at the far end next to the baptismal pedestal. Candlelight danced along the edge of a stone shelf just behind it.

Aziz entered the front door brazenly. His confidence inspired me. The shawl-like black cloak fluttered behind him with each stride. His right hand rested on the hilt of his masterfully crafted scimitar.

Aziz said, "Roman dogs!"

There was such hatred behind his words; a deep pain resonated within the tones. I watched my leader from the darkness for just a breath and then quickly moved closer. I used the dark like a cloak but the further I went into the room, the more my instincts came alive to alert me that something was amiss.

Clavius and Fortus turned to face Aziz. Fortus raised his hands high and wide and said, "Our guests have finally arrived."

I froze at that statement. He knew we were coming! This was a trap! But how? We had not seen anyone. Soldiers, by virtue of their defensive armor, weren't able to hide in plain sight. I thought, *"He must be bluffing."* I could see that Aziz thought the same. He drew out his blade, not acknowledging Fortus' words. "You have butchered, enslaved, and raped my people." Aziz boldly announced his list of offenses.

Fortus chuckled and looked at Clavius who joined in. Aziz pointed his blade toward them as he continued to walk. Usama and Mas'ud entered. I spotted Gez making his way closer, still hiding behind the pillars. Scanning the upper areas, I saw no balconies for warriors to lie in wait. No movement except the shadows that shifted as the light directed.

It was then that I noticed it, though *it* was not my first time. The creature's eyes glinted in the darkness midway up along the wall, but there was nothing for it to stand upon; it hovered in the air. It was the eyes that revealed exactly what this unearthly thing was.

As soon as I saw it, or perhaps as soon as I was allowed to see, it descended to the ground and landed in front of Aziz. It was the legendary Demon of Ghasa. I stood in shock as the man… no, beast… no, demon, stared intently at Aziz. Aziz spun with his blade, coming around to lop off its head but the creature moved faster than any man. It grabbed hold of Aziz' sword hand, plunging its hand through the chest of Aziz. Blood spewed out and dripped off of the demon's arm as it held Aziz off the floor. The demon retracted its hand and within its grasp was the beating heart of my leader; the heart of another father figure, fallen before my eyes.

"No!" Usama yelled and charged with his bare hands. The demon did not move, but let Usama's strike hit it squarely in the face. Its head turned, but whipped back. It snarled at Usama. Or was it smiling? With its free hand, it ripped the throat out of Usama. He fell to his knees clutching his neck, then fell, face first. His body twitched as his life faded.

Clavius and Fortus stepped back to avoid the blood that pooled on the ground. Mas'ud charged with his two blades, weaving them back and forth, diagonally, and up and down, twirling his body and kicking in the air. The movements he performed were flawless. Many men had fallen to his skill over the years. Except on this night. I heard the buzzing of insects. Mas'ud's blades struck what would appear to be a fatal blow, but the demon burst into thousands of flies and then reformulated back into a man, now standing behind Mas'ud. The demon grabbed his head with both hands and ripped it off. A geyser of blood shot out and splashed onto the ground.

All I remember after this was many of The Forty streaming in from other doors, stairs, and windows. The creature spewed death blows to each one of them as they came at him. The carnage was beyond anything I could ever have imagined.

I hid in the shadow, silently praying to any god that would hear to protect me. Sweat droplets trickled down my forehead and dribbled into my beard. I glanced over and saw Gez clutched at the base of the pillar, curled into a ball with his eyes closed.

Sounds of weapons clashing against the ground, screams of dying men, and the buzzing of the flies echoed around me. I clutched my ears in horror as I stared into the open eyes of Aziz looking at me. His heart was close by, still faintly beating. *I lost it all, again. My family, my father, all gone.*

"You can come out, my children," Clavius' voice echoed around me. "We saved the best for last."

I came out of my trance and looked from behind my stone shield. The nightmare was still happening. Around the room was a sea of body pieces and the once white stone was now colored in red. Clavius and Fortus stood in the far back. Clavius held one hand over his mouth and nose; his face sickened at the sight of the gore before him. The demon was gone. No, it was hiding, waiting to unleash its fury upon me and my brother.

"Come out now!" Fortus demanded.

I stepped fully out into the light, trembling. My eyes darted around the room, looking frantically to see where it waited to lunge at me. I looked for Gez in fear that he had been taken, but he remained where he was.

"Go and fetch your brother," Clavius said.

I mechanically stumbled over and helped Gez to his feet, pulling him out into the open with me. We clung to one another, our eyes trying to avoid looking at the grotesque scene before us.

I whispered to Gez, "I'm sorry."

Gez looked at me and we knew that we were about to die. Roman soldiers grabbed us from behind. Clavius skirted around the edge of the room to bypass the bloodbath. Fortus did the same until they both stood in front of us.

"It is so good to finally be reunited," Fortus said.

"Let us kill them and be done with this night's festivities," Clavius said. Despite his victory, he was still shaken by the sight of it all.

"We promised Pontius Pilate to share in the spoils, did we not? No, these two are meant for greater things, especially this one," he gazed at me. "This one has lived a lie his entire life. He was saved for what is to befall him in Jerusalem." Fortus turned toward Clavius, "Did you know that this one," he pointed at me, "believes he is this one's brother?" Fortus grabbed the hair of Gestas and spun him around. He held him from behind and I was now looking into my brother's eyes. The Roman commander continued to talk, "Isn't that right, Gestas? Does he know the truth yet?"

Whatever Fortus was saying caused Gez to look at me in fear. Deep in his eyes, I caught a glint that something that had been hidden was slowly being dug up from the depths of where it was buried. A deep, dark secret.

"You never told him? How interesting."

"What do you speak about?" I asked.

"Dismas, Dismas, Dismas." His tone mocked me. "I thought you smarter after sixteen years of your pitiful life. Come on now, you can't tell me you didn't know something was off about your *so-called* family? Just look at your imposter brother."

He pushed Gez closer to me. I wanted to step back but the Roman guard held me in place. My nose almost touched Gez.

Fortus continued, "I was there when it happened. When the strange doctor from Hippus suddenly knocked at the home of the

Karpos family. I was there that rainy night when they let him in, fed him, and heard his tale. I was there when he handed over the baby, fighting for his life, to Dora Karpos, when they said they would take this child as their own and raise him as their son. I was there when their crippled two-year-old hobbled out from the hallway and met this baby for the first time."

"How is that possible?" Clavius spoke.

Fortus turned his attention to him, "Clavius, isn't it apparent that the demon and I are one? It shows me things. Great things. It even showed me this night. How, you might ask? Well, for whatever reason, I must thank this one," he said, pointing to me. "For it is through his eyes that I have gained knowledge from the demon. They are connected. Father and son."

Each word pierced me as images flooded my mind. My past unraveled right before me. I couldn't fight against this revelation because deep down, I knew it to be true. I had never spoken the thoughts aloud, but had always known that I had never belonged.

Gestas was pleading for forgiveness through his eyes. A fire began to burn inside me but all the while I wanted to know who my real father was. Who was my family and why did they abandon me?

"That is impossible, Fortus," Clavius said.

"Oh, but this is a reunion night of families," Fortus responded. He leaned closer and whispered, "Clavius now has his nephew, and you, my dear Dismas, have your father."

I looked at him, still not wanting to believe this truth. "Yes," he said. "You know of whom I speak." He grinned evilly.

I felt the soldier holding me in place release his grip. Fortus' eyes fixed on something behind me. Fear soured his face as he backed away bowing low. Gestas cowered away as well.

I heard the low sound of buzzing flies and I slowly turned around. There in the shadows was the gaunt demon-man staring at me. Blood dripped from head to toe over his naked body. His eyes stood out against the gore. Oh, the eyes. Yes, these eyes confirmed the story. I was looking at a mirror image of my own. This demon-man was my father and I was his child. He brought up his bloody hand, the same one that had held Aziz' heart, and caressed my cheek.

My father spoke. His voice was deep and reverberated loudly, "My son."

CHAPTER 23
A LONELY ROAD

-DISMAS-

THE ENDLESS RATTLE of the chains against the bars resounded in my ears. Wooden wheels lurched, vibrated, and wobbled along the dirt road. Dust covered Gestas and me, now shackled inside a stifling wooden box; a Roman slave cart bound for Jerusalem. Two soldiers sat in the front of the wagon leading the horses while a dozen more soldiers brought up the rear on horseback.

"How long?" I said.

"Six years." His voice was calm and he stared intently at me, letting me know he wasn't afraid of the forthcoming questions.

"Why didn't you tell me?"

"What would you have done? Would you have done anything differently?"

I instinctively wanted to say, *"I would have said something,"* but I knew he was right. *"What would I have done?"*

Gez said, "Father told me the truth that day he gifted you the figurine. He gave me the choice. He told me that I could push you away or I could embrace you."

"What are you talking about?"

"I loved you like my own blood. We all did. The truth of who your real father was didn't change that. If I had told you, it would have pushed you away."

"What does it matter now? Look at us," I said, lifting my chains.

"Father said—" Gez started.

"I don't care."

"Father said when what you see before you doesn't look promising, then you must change the course."

"If you haven't noticed, we are cursed."

Gestas smiled mischievously, which caused me to squint at him in contemplation. What was he up to? He slowly looked at his left shackle, subtly letting me know he had picked the lock. All I could think was, *"He was going to get himself killed."* Here we were, chained inside a cage, so what would he be able to do with his hands free? The Romans could easily take him captive. Or just kill him. Maybe it would be for the best. Maybe I should just inform the soldiers now myself. I held my tongue and watched as Gez worked to release his second lock. Within seconds, he had it open.

I could see soldiers sporadically through the small iron window to my left. They were spread apart enough to let the majority of the dust being kicked up from the cart to blow by them.

Gez began to laugh hysterically. It was a god-awful noise of cackling and giggling. He was crazed and without fear.

"Be quiet!" A soldier cried out from the wagon.

Gez increased his volume.

"I said, shut up!" A clang of metal on metal rang out as the Roman hit his baton against the frame. It was a clear warning of what would happen if he continued.

Gez's volume was almost at a scream. I was mesmerized as I watched him play this ridiculous act out. His frizzy hair and beard, cracked lips, and dried blood from a superficial wound on his head added to the spectacle. He was actually convincing me that he was not in his right mind any longer. I slowly pulled my legs in tighter just to gain some distance from him.

A soldier rode his horse alongside to peer inside our cage. Gez put his face close to the soldier and rolled his eyes back inside his head. The warrior lurched away in fear and then sped up to the front of the wagon.

The wheels slowed and then stopped.

"What the hell is going on back here?" the Roman enslaver said, as he hopped down and came around to look inside.

Again, Gez lunged forward toward the soldier with his eyes rolled back, cackling like a crazy man in a high pitch.

"Whoa," he responded and backed away. He laughed, "Oh, you think you can pretend to be the legendary Demon of Ghasa?" He pointed at his comrades, "Hey, boys, look, we have a demon-child." Several began to chuckle as the tension eased.

Someone in the back chimed, "I think Cosca is scared."

This caused a raucous roar. "Is that so, Cosca?" the slave captain said while hitting his baton against the frame. "You a little scared, Cosca? Hey boys, I think we should initiate him now, whad'ya say?"

Several of them nodded with bright grins.

A young soldier clopped forward on his horse, more than a little nervous. Shaking, he said, "What do I do?"

All of them laughed. The slave captain said, "Well, Cosca, why don't you shut this demon-child up. Our ears are bleeding because of his incessant cackling."

More laughs. Cosca dismounted. Another soldier held the reins of his horse with a taunting sneer.

"Go on Cosca. Shut that thing up!" another warrior called.

"Please, just kill it already," another said.

Gez was now frantically pulling at the barred window. All the while his shackles appeared to be binding his wrists. What was he doing? It really was like he was possessed. He had never acted like this before.

He stopped cackling and started growling like a wild animal.

"Ben, give Cosca your baton," another yelled.

Ben nodded and then handed his weapon to Cosca who timidly took it. Cosca's eyes never veered from Gez.

"Come on, get on with it!" Ben yelled. More chuckles from the others.

Cosca slid one boot over, then another. He held the baton tightly while he went to unlock the back.

"Hurry it up Cosca. It's not like you have to chase the boy down." Another burst of hearty laughter from the ranks.

Gez bit the metal bar from the window and continued to growl. Cosca hit the window with the baton and Gez backed away still growling. Gaining confidence from Gez's retreat, the timid soldier, who appeared to be the same age as us, smiled at the others. He quickly unlocked the back with a cocky confidence. He clearly had something to prove to the others.

Cosca held the baton out in front of him and looked inside the cage. The shadows inside played with him. He spotted me curled up in the back, but didn't see Gestas. Fear suddenly gripped Cosca. He turned to say, "He's gone."

Gez leaped out of the confines, tackled the young soldier, and bit off his ear. Blood spewed and Gez spat the flesh from his mouth. He sat on top of Cosca and roared. His rolled his eyes back inside his head.

"It's another demon!" a soldier cried out.

Panic ensued. Horses reared, while men scrambled in multiple directions. Some fell off animals that were spooked. These grown men, warriors of Rome, fled like children afraid of the dark. It was apparent that the Demons of Ghasa had caused great fear in this region.

"It broke the chains!" another yelled.

"Get out of here!"

Gez went into a frenzy and pummeled the back of Cosca's skull with the baton until it caved in like a watermelon. Blood splashed over him.

Gestas turned abruptly, blood dripping from his body and the baton, and gazed at the captain, the one they called Ben. His eyes were fixated on the slave captain. Ben was in shock and started to back away. With a screech, Gez lunged and slammed into the heavier set man. He didn't knock him over but it did cause him to stumble. He ran away with the others.

Gez looked around, yelling triumphantly. Blood and spit flew from his mouth. He popped his head inside the cage and said, "Are you ready, my brother?"

He didn't wait for my response, which was good since I had none. My shackles fell away as he picked them easily with tools he had somehow hidden from the guards.

"Come on. We will take the horses."

I stepped out from the stifling wooden box into the fresh air. Dust clouds from the fleeing Romans billowed behind them.

"They will be back, brother. Come on. We need to ride deep into the desert."

Gez released the cart horses as he spoke. I slowly walked over and helped mechanically.

"Fear is a powerful weapon," Gez said. "Apparently, your father is greatly feared." He smiled.

His smile caused something inside of me to stir awake. Gez had changed somehow right before my eyes. It was some kind of freedom.

Not physical, but emotional. I had been living a lie, but Gestas had been carrying it for six years. He was free of it now. The truth was out.

I said to him, "It must have been a lonely road, my brother."

Gez suddenly stopped and looked hard at me. His eyes spoke volumes.

"You are my brother," I said.

He nodded and said, "Come on, Diz. Those soldiers will regroup and come back soon. We need to be far gone by then."

I began to untie the horse in earnest, but felt a tinge of joy begin to well up inside. "You almost convinced me you were a demon."

He laughed, "Well, that was the point, wasn't it?" He pulled the horse over to the dead body and looted the Roman of his valuables. A coin pouch, a dagger, and boots. "I think they will fit."

There were some water skins and dried rations next to where the captain Ben had sat. Taking it all, we rode swiftly into the desert hills. We had not been in this area before. We were on the outskirts of The Servants' territory.

"Where do you think we are?" I shouted over the sound of the galloping hooves.

"I heard one of the Romans say Gadara."

"Gadara?"

"Let's head south, little brother."

"Why south?" I asked.

"Why not? We are free! We can do whatever we like!"

"Yes, we were free for now," I thought. I didn't think about what was ahead, staying in the moment with Gestas. Right now, we *were* free.

Hours passed and we found ourselves somewhere in the hills. We found a small area of rocks to hide in. There would be no fire, but we were too tired to make one even if we had been able to. It was a calm, starry night. I fell into a deep sleep. No dreams, no nightmares, just sleep.

In the early morning, my eyes fluttered open. I gazed up at the sky, watching it change from orange to blue, when suddenly a face blocked my view. It was a face I will never forget. A face I would come to know very well for the next few years.

He was a beast of a man, hair on his back like a carpet, a scar over his left eye from brow to cheek, dark brown beard and brown curly hair. The curls were big and bold, like the man. He was also very Jewish.

This man loomed over me and said, "Good morning, sunshine! I'm Barabbas! It appears that God wanted us to meet."

CHAPTER 24
A NEW ROAD

-DISMAS-

BARABBAS WAS EXCEEDINGLY jovial and very loud. His laugh was an infectious, deep bellow. I wanted to laugh along with him, even if I didn't know what he was laughing about. Admittedly, his personality was overbearing at times. His eyes, a rich almond color, exuded warmth, but I often felt like he was peering into the depths of my soul.

Gez conversed with him, "So you came out here to pray?"

"Yes, to beseech God."

"You come out here, to this place, to see God?" Gez looked over at me with concern. We had seen these Jewish zealots before; worked alongside them, lived with them.

"Of course."

"And this god speaks to you?"

"Ah, very much so."

"And what did he say to you?" I asked.

"He instructed me to climb to this area and when I did, you were here. My God is a very sneaky god. He brings people into my path for a reason."

"What is the reason?"

"Well, that is for us to find out. A very wise man once said, "It is the glory of God to conceal a matter; to search out a matter is the glory of kings.'"

"Are you a king, then?" Gez questioned.

Barabbas' eyebrows shot up, "You focus on the individual words when you should focus on the heart of the message. God's ways are not ours. I don't presume to have all the answers, but continuously search them out with His guidance." Barabbas looked up into the sky referring to his God in the heavens.

"Enough of me," Barabbas said. "Where do you hail from? Perhaps my answers lie within your story."

I quickly said, "We are just young Greeks trying to find our way." I looked over at Gez and finished, "We don't have a story."

"Ah, I see. Young Greeks trying to find your way. How interesting."

"Why is that interesting?"

"Well, if you have no story, then you are in search of one. Perhaps your story starts now."

Gez smiled and nodded, "Yes, our story starts now. I like that."

"Then it is settled," he stated loudly as he stood up and clapped his hands together with a broad smile.

My brother and I exchanged a confused glance. I said, "What's settled?"

Barabbas bellowed another hearty laugh, "You are to come with me. God brought me here in order to bring you back."

"Bring us back where?"

"South, to Perea."

Gez said, "I just told Diz the other day that we should go south."

"Well then, it's confirmation. Let us be off and in a day or two you will meet my family."

My brother and I really didn't have a choice. We considered ourselves lucky to find a guide through the wilderness. This Barabbas was a bear of a man, not only in resemblance to the animal, but in personality. His voice echoed for miles and, I'm sure, alerted every bandit, Roman sentry, and creature alike. He talked a lot during our travel. We answered his questions simply, which was motivation for him to talk even more! Of course, this Jewish zealot spoke often of God and also spoke of a Messiah, but we were very accustomed to hearing about both when we were in Capernaum with the Zebedee family. Surely they are a strange people to believe so strongly in this person they call the Messiah. Apparently, he will be sent by God to rescue them from the hands of those who persecute them. It wasn't the first time we had heard, *"The Romans time is coming to an end. Just wait and see. The Messiah is coming."*

Well, when this so-called representative of God shows up, I would surely like to meet him. I just wish they would all stop talking about it. It's always "Messiah this and Messiah that." I do have to say though, out of all the cultures I have seen, this one was the most peculiar. Peculiar in that they have such a deep belief. It is something they live and breathe daily. We Greeks and the Romans, however, run to our many gods to seek answers. If one god doesn't suit our needs then we find or make up another. There is a god for everything. These Jews, they exude their religion. Though they seem arrogant when I'm around them, I am somewhat intrigued by their beliefs. At least, I'm fascinated with the stories.

Barabbas blared, as we looked down into the valley below us, "Welcome to my home! The Lord has blessed me greatly!"

We looked in awe, for indeed Barabbas was blessed. A few buildings, smoke spiraling up from chimneys, were nestled at the base of the valley along a stream of fresh water. The hills were green with rugged looking boulders dotting the landscape. Trees of various kinds, from olive to palm, were more abundant in this part of the land. Many fenced stalls surrounded the dwellings, where men and women were taking care of the livestock. Sheep, goats, horses, and chickens abounded, as well as several domesticated dogs who barked at Barabbas' loud welcome echoing above.

We were greeted by everyone with friendly smiles and excited waves. Each of them embraced Barabbas and said how much they had missed him. There were ten Jewish men and half a dozen women in the community, from what we had seen thus far.

"All of these people live here?" I asked.

"Yes, this is our home. We live off the land and away from society. Come, come, we shall rest and clean ourselves before introducing you to everyone."

Barabbas led us into the largest home. Three smaller houses surrounded it. A robust woman in both breast and backside came out of the front door, wiping her hands on a towel. She beamed at the large bear walking before us.

"Ah, my bride. I missed you," Barabbas rumbled and his arms flung wide to scoop her up.

"My husband has returned."

They hugged and kissed before separating. She made eye contact with us and said, "Who are our guests, Barabbas?"

"Ah, these are gifts from the Lord."

"Gifts, you say? Then we shall prepare a meal to receive them." She looked at her husband and asked with concern, "Have you spoken to Mendel?"

"No, we just arrived and have not seen him. What is the matter?"

"Best to speak with him directly. I stay out of things that don't concern me for I have my own battles to wage in a land called *'the kitchen'*."

Barabbas swept her off of her feet again and laughed heartily, "And indeed a land where you are always victorious!"

"Put me down, my love. You know that I'm afraid of heights."

They both laughed as we stared in amazement at these two larger-than-life personalities.

"I said, put me down," she laughed.

"As you wish." He walked her to the front door and set her down, but not before giving her a passionate kiss.

I raised my eyebrow as I looked over at Gez with a smirk.

Gez said, "Should we wash by the stream?"

She broke away and quickly said, "Nonsense, don't you mind this 'sweet talker'. Now come in and get yourself settled. I have a private room prepared for such times as this when my husband brings surprise guests. God says to always be ready."

"He does?" I said.

She stopped, wrinkled her brow and squinted hard at me for a long moment and there was an accompanying awkward silence. Changing the subject, she said, "Stew. Yes, stew with a hint of...garlic is your favorite." She turned around and headed back toward the kitchen. "It will be ready before long."

I looked at Gez in shock, "How did she know?"

Gez shrugged his shoulders. Barabbas laughed as he ushered us inside his home.

I took a few steps but was completely dumbfounded. My mother made stew and it was my favorite. How did this woman take one look at me and know? It was as if she read my thoughts, and I was not even thinking of food.

I turned and looked out the front window around the area. The sun was setting. Workers were getting the animals settled and fed. Oil lamps were ignited inside the surrounding homes and the smell of baked bread mixed with farm animal stench permeated the air. There was a slight breeze that washed over me. I noticed the temperature had changed drastically in the shadow of the hills.

All I could think about was that we *were* embarking on a new story. We were in a new land, with new people, traveling a new road. But how long before it would all be taken away from us? Suddenly, inside my mind, I saw the once quaint village before me, burning. The villagers and livestock all dead and my father, the Demon, standing over them looking at me. Then the vision ended.

Gez grabbed my shoulder from behind, "You all right?"

"Just thinking, is all."

Gez paused, "This is a different place."

I faced my brother, "And we are different people, now."

Gez nodded, holding eye contact for an extended moment.

Barabbas' wife called for us to come eat. Gez went first and I took one more look outside before closing the door. I thought I saw my father, far off by one of the homes, staring at me. Then he was gone. My nightmares were no longer when I sleep. They were now my reality.

CHAPTER 25
THE STRANGER

-DISMAS-

THE CROW OF the rooster awakened me. I turned to find Gez still sleeping so I nudged him awake.

"What is it?"

"Get up."

"Why, what's wrong?"

"Nothing."

"Then why are you waking me, you idiot?"

"'Cause I'm not going out there alone."

Gez chuckled, "You're afraid of Gaddi?"

"Well, yeah. She wouldn't stop hugging us last night."

"Ah, Zebedee and Salome hugged a lot also. It's just what these people do."

"Get up, brother. We do this together, remember?"

"Fine, I'm up. You're ridiculous, but at least I smell some good food."

I didn't realize how much I had missed home cooking. I was hungry, but didn't want to venture out into the kitchen area alone. Gaddi tended to ask a lot of questions and I was not up to entertaining her this morning.

Someone was talking, but it wasn't Barabbas. As we walked the short hall to the open kitchen area, we saw him sitting at the table with someone we had not met. A short man with a properly trimmed beard no longer than a finger's length. Gaddi was stirring the breakfast inside an iron pot.

"Ah, our company has awakened," she said loudly upon spotting us.

Barabbas stood to greet us, just as loudly, "My Greek brothers, good morning!"

We smiled slightly and were ushered toward the table to join them.

Barabbas said, "This is my dearest friend, Mendel. Mendel, these are the two that God sent me out to fetch. This is Gestas and this is Dismas. They are brothers."

"Well met," Mendel responded with a nod. He looked back at Barabbas as Gaddi brought two bowls filled with some kind of morning soup concoction.

Mendel said, "So, what do you make of it?"

"Mmmm, it is something we need to pray about. This stranger you speak of says what again? You said that he repeats something."

"Yes, he simply yells whether there are people around or not, 'Prepare the way'."

"And what does he look like?"

"I didn't see him up close. His voice travels like yours but the wind carries it even further. There is something different about this one."

"If I had a shekel every time I heard that, then I would be a rich man, Mendel."

"No, this could be the—"

"Ah, don't say it, Mendel. We have gone here and there waiting for him, searching for him, even promoting his arrival."

"The others were a mockery of the faith."

"Mendel, listen my friend, this man that is yelling 'prepare the way' and says nothing else doesn't lend himself well to being a Messiah."

I jerked up from sipping my soup and interjected, "Messiah? You believe this man is him?"

"No, we are just discussing how it is *not* him, right Mendel?"

"Yes, but you need to hear him for yourself. You need to see him with your own eyes and then judge."

"We shall see. I just got home and want to spend my time with friends and family before chasing more would-be Messiahs. It seems these days everyone is the Messiah."

Mendel slurped his last bit out of the bowl and stood. "I must be going. We had a little trouble yesterday in town that I must attend to."

"Trouble?" Barabbas responded.

"Ah, it's nothing. Gavin was in fine form with young Asher in the market. Nothing I can't handle."

"You watch yourself around that Gavin. He always has something to prove so let's not provoke him to prove anything with us."

"Agreed. May the Lord bless you."

"And you also, my friend."

We waved goodbye and waited on Barabbas to share more of what was going on with this stranger, but he did not. Just yesterday we could not shut him up but this morning he was deep in thought. We slurped our delicious breakfast while keeping an eye on him. He stared at nothing in particular, while eating mechanically. Whatever he was thinking weighed heavily on his mind. Gaddi was also peculiarly quiet as she moved about in the kitchen cooking, cleaning, and attending.

I said tentatively, "I'd like to see this stranger."

Barabbas turned to me. Gez froze. "Is that so? Gaddi!" he bellowed in a sudden shift, "we will be visiting this stranger in the wilderness that Mendel spoke of."

She stopped as she wiped her hands clean and smiled softly. Not a word came out of her mouth, still, there was something in her look that I couldn't quite place. What was she thinking? Perhaps she was attempting to read my mind again. I waited but she said nothing.

Barabbas said, "God is speaking to me through you both."

"What is he saying?" Gez asked.

"Your story is unfolding, but we need to continue to walk it out. Dismas is interested in this man yelling God knows what for who knows who to hear. Perhaps God is instructing us. We must be open to his leading."

"I don't know what you mean," Gez said.

Barabbas smiled, "Not to worry. Today we explore. Come, let us get ready. The Jordan River is not far."

Days earlier, we were part of an elite group called The Servants. Now we are here in this land to the south of our home with these strange people. Now that I think about it, where is home? Home was wherever we went and that appeared to be here, for now. My mind shifted back to this stranger at the Jordan. Could he be this mysterious Messiah the Jews speak often about? What was a Messiah anyway? My curiosity was getting the better of me but what else was there to do? I had no chores to attend to. I could only say that there was a compelling inside me to see this man at the river.

It was a cloudy morning, a foretelling of rain to come. Our travels took us down the mountain to what Gez and I quickly discerned to be a not-well-traveled path. Barabbas' home was definitely out of the way of any settlements.

The trees became thicker the closer we came to the base of the mountains. We could see the Jordan River flowing down from the Sea of Galilee into the Dead Sea. We finally came to the sandy banks of the water where we traversed a wooden bridge with rope railings. The river flowed smoothly in this area and I could see rocks of varying sizes below the surface.

"Just beyond is the town called Aenon. Come," Barabbas said over his shoulder.

This town was not a place we had ever been before and yet the ambiance of it was the same as what we had experienced. There was a strong Jewish presence, mixed with Arabs, Assyrians, and Samaritans. The structures looked different. They were rounder on the edges than the squarish look of buildings in Capernaum. The stone was different, darker, with colors ranging from light brown to rich mud hues.

What caught my attention the most were the Roman soldiers. Gez and I both kept our heads down as if we would be recognized. Our sudden departure from these occupiers just days ago was still fresh in our minds. They were our enemy and being around them made us uneasy.

Uneasy enough for Barabbas to notice as he took hold of my arm and whispered, "Steady now, boy. There is no reason for alarm."

The large man then broke away, spread his arms wide, and loudly greeted a commoner in the distance. What they spoke of, I did not know. Gez and I exchanged glances and continued to keep our heads down, covered by our hoods. We meandered to a building, leaning against it while Barabbas socialized with not one, but several people at a time. He drew them in, and from what I could tell, he was catching up with the happenings in town. His presence was like that of the town governor. He received respect and waves from passersby. Every now and then, Barabbas would glance in our direction.

Eventually, our guide waved for us to follow him and we paraded down the main road into the marketplace. If there was one common denominator for every town, it would be the marketplace. This is what makes the world move forward; commerce. Buying and selling brought wealth into towns and those who mastered this lived amongst royalty. Many would try to navigate the intricate web but only a few would come out valiant. Regardless, no one walked away without scars, for the market was a battlefield. These were valiant warriors skilled with their mouth and the knowledge to use their skills to perfection.

"Come," Barabbas said. "We will meet Mendel to take us to the stranger. He waits for us on the north side."

I noticed quite a few people around for such a small town. Was there some kind of festival happening? None that I could tell, but something was drawing them.

Mendel, Barabbas' friend, wore standard clothing for the area and in all respects blended in as a normal citizen from the region.

He greeted us, "Well met, again. Barabbas, thank you for coming. This is something you need to see."

"Why so many people?" I asked.

"You see, Barabbas. Even this one notices the large crowds. Why, you ask? Well, it is because of the stranger. More come out each day."

"More? But why?"

"No words to describe it. Come, come. You must see for yourself. It is not far."

"Lead on, Mendel," Barabbas said.

We were out of the town and walking along the wide, dirt road. More people were coming in caravans from neighboring towns. Oxen-driven carts kicked up dust as they rolled along. We walked ten minutes, came to a small ridge around a bend, and there it was. I had never seen anything like it.

Hundreds of people were lined up along the roadside. Hundreds more were scattered around the sandy embankments, where pools of water stagnated in pockets cut off from the flowing Jordan. The beach was extensive, running hundreds of feet on both sides of the river. During the rains, the water pooled in these areas and eventually dried up over time. Smaller streams, broken from the main river, flowed calmly into channels along the edges.

In one of the channels stood a man in a loincloth waist deep in water. His hair was wild and he had a beard to match. His skin was darkened by the sun and his eyes were brilliant, even from our vantage point.

I watched in awe as two men took off their clothes, sandals, and rushed toward the stranger. Water splashed around them. They fell to their knees with their shoulders just above the water. I could not see clearly, but the stranger placed his hands on both as he stood between them, plunging their heads under water.

His voice resounded all around us, "Be cleansed, dear brothers."

They burst out from under the water with unconcealed joy upon their faces. A joy I had never seen before. They hugged one another and then walked back to shore to collect their belongings.

Gez and I looked at each other.

Mendel whispered to Barabbas, "See. What did I tell you? There is something different about this one. Look at the crowds."

"Yes," Barabbas said reservedly, "I see the crowds. Let's get a better view of the happenings. Lead on."

Mendel cut through the people and we followed. We now stood along the sandy embankment five men deep. So many people and all I could think was, *Why? What are they doing? What is it about this single man who bathes men openly in the Jordan that is attracting these crowds?* My questions soon increased, for the stranger spoke brazenly to the gathered crowd.

"Prepare the way for the Lord, make straight paths for him. Every valley shall be filled in, every mountain and hill made low. The crooked roads shall become straight, the rough ways smooth. And all people will see God's salvation."

Mendel whispered, "This is what he repeats day in and day out."

The bizarre stranger thrashed the water around him, splashing and yelling, then calmed. Water was trickling down his face and beard as his eyes raked across the patrons watching him.

He said, "You brood of vipers! Who warned you to flee from the coming wrath? Produce fruit in keeping with repentance. And do not begin to say to yourselves, 'We have Abraham as our father.' For I tell you that out of these stones God can raise up children for Abraham. The axe is already at the root of the trees, and every tree that does not produce good fruit will be cut down and thrown into the fire."

This elicited much murmuring from the people. I paid attention to Barabbas as he stroked his beard and watched in deep contemplation.

Mendel said, "What do you think, Barabbas?"

"He quotes Scripture. It is from the prophet Isaiah. He also speaks with authority."

"Now do you believe me?"

"It was never about whether I believed you, Mendel. Now we wait and see what happens. The time ahead will reveal much."

People along the edges, closest to the man calling out from the water, yelled back, "What shall we do then?"

He responded with conviction, "Anyone who has two shirts

should share with the one who has none, and anyone who has food should do the same."

More people came out into the water and knelt before him. Each was submerged and blessed by the wild man of God. It was at this time that I started looking at the people more closely. These were men of every status. Rich and poor alike stood side-by-side, commoners and soldiers, tax collectors and brick layers. It mattered not what they did. This stranger had somehow brought them each out of their world and invited them into a new one. I had no idea what this new world was. But those who did, took the plunge to receive a blessing from this apparent holy man.

A tax collector stumbled out into the water and tripped over a rock. He splashed around in panic but kept his eyes upon the stranger.

"Please. I beg of you. Bless me," he said.

The wild man of God placed his hand on the man's head and shoved him down into the water. He held him down a little longer than the others and then released him. He came up for air, screaming. Wait, not screaming... laughing, with that unusual joy, the likes of which I had never seen, and certainly never experienced.

The tax collector clutched at the wild man and said, "Teacher, what shall I do?"

"Don't collect any more than you are required to," he told him.

He sloshed to the shore and left with a smile from ear to ear. He was a tax collector. I knew that whatever this stranger imparted to him would subside at the first sight of a denarii. If he didn't rob another man again, then that would truly be a miracle.

"I've seen enough," Barabbas said.

Mendel began to make his way through the crowd and we followed. We stopped, however, when someone yelled out, "Are you the Messiah?"

Not a sound was heard. I think the river even stopped flowing. This was the question that weighed heavily on everyone's heart. It was the question no one was willing to ask openly. Everyone hoped this man would say 'yes'.

No one was prepared for what he did say. "I baptize you with water. But one who is more powerful than I will come, the straps of whose sandals I am not worthy to untie. He will baptize you with the Holy Spirit and fire. His winnowing fork is in his hand to clear his threshing floor and to gather the wheat into his barn, but he will burn up the chaff with unquenchable fire."

All the way back to Barabbas' home, all I could think of was the words the stranger spoke, *"Someone was coming more powerful than him."*

There was only one question to be answered after that and that was, *"Who was coming?"*

CHAPTER 26
THE SECRET MEETING

-DISMAS-

WEEKS PASSED. GEZ and I worked Barabbas' homestead, cleaning and feeding the animals. It brought us back to when we were with Father taking care of the pig herds. Mendel would stop in occasionally, keeping us up to date about the stranger. He found out his name was John. Many had termed him 'John the Baptist'.

Gez and I had not been idle during our free time while taking care of our current residence. We'd done some of our own investigating. Both of us thought it suspicious that there was no actual farming and Barabbas' people did not slaughter the animals for food. The question was where were they getting food and how were they paying for it?

It didn't take long to discover that Mendel handled the business side of things for Barabbas. Mendel made purchases in Aenon and brought the items to the base of the Beth Shan Valley. We would pick up the supplies and haul them back through the narrow pathways. This was done weekly.

But where was the money coming from to pay for all of this? We had first thought that Barabbas was secretly rich, but there was no money to be found. I mean nothing. Not a shekel. Believe me, we searched high and low. We also watched Barabbas and his wife, Gaddi, to see if there was an exchange of any kind, but nothing. So, how then? Well, this took a little more investigating. Since Mendel was the businessman for Barabbas, then Mendel must be the one fronting the money. One day, we followed him into Aenon where we watched him haggle in the marketplace. Every item he purchased, he stored on a cart pushed by a young boy, early teens. This cart was brought to a Jewish temple. A temple? Why?

Mendel left the cart as if it was a donation, walking away. A day later, we were beckoned again from the homestead to pick up the shipment at the base of the valley. This seemed more strange to us than the stranger calling out in the wilderness for people to be baptized. It now became our mission to find out what was really going on. Barabbas was hiding something and it was in our nature to find out what it was.

A couple of days later, we were at breakfast with Gaddi and Barabbas. Despite his secret, we thought him to be a very kind man that truly loved everyone he came into contact with. He was also very much in love with his wife. That day, their conversation at the table caused Gez and I to take notice. It was as if they were trying to talk secretly in front of us.

Barabbas said awkwardly, "Gaddi, I have an appointment with the town physician this evening."

"Oh, is that so? Should I come with you this time or is it something minor?"

"The physician says nothing to worry about."

"Well then, be safe and I will see you when you return," Gaddi said without a hint of concern.

When Gez and I were alone outside we talked it over.

"What did you make of that?" I said.

"It seemed very cryptic to me. Gaddi and Barabbas talk openly all the time and she didn't even ask what the problem was," Gez stated.

"Maybe it is something recurring and they both know what it is without saying."

"Perhaps, but it seemed very odd, like they were speaking in code."

"When did the physician speak with him, I wonder? He made no mention of seeing a doctor earlier and hasn't left the homestead for weeks."

"Well, you were wondering what to do tonight. I think we now know."

I smiled in agreement as I patted his shoulder. We walked to the horse stables to clean and feed the steeds we had commandeered from the Romans.

"Gez," I said.

"Yes."

I stopped walking and said, "What are we doing?"

Gez stopped and looked back at me. "We are going to the stables."

"No," I stepped toward him. "I mean, what are we doing here? Is this it for us?"

Gez narrowed his eyes, "Little brother, we have been through much but by no means is this it. I'm trying to figure out our next move. Something is coming. I can feel it."

"You're right."

"I'm always right. Just be patient and stay ready."

I smiled and said, "You know me. I'm always ready."

"I know. That is why I haven't replaced you." Gez quickly wrapped his arm around my neck and brought me under his armpit.

I twisted out, maneuvering my left foot to trip him backwards where we both fell to the ground. Wrestling was something we had not done for quite awhile. We both laughed through grunts of pain as each of us got the upper hand at some part of the match. As always, it ended with me grappling Gestas' bad leg and twisting it to cause him to give up. He tried to rub the pain away as I laughed. Then Gez joined me laughing, sitting on the grassy field outside the stables. My brother had formed a strange cackling, high-pitched laugh that caused me to wince. It was truly horrible and the horses inside the stable began to kick and whinny.

"Even the horses protest," I said as I got up and walked away. I looked back at him as he was still rolling on the ground holding his stomach. "I hate your crazy demon laugh. It's stupid."

This just caused him to get louder. I shook my head and walked over to calm the horses.

After dinner, we retired to our room, then snuck out to wait. Barabbas left just after sundown. The half-moon shone its milky-white light and the stars twinkled in the darkened sky. The night was our time. Gez and I easily followed the lumbering hulk of a man who seemed to have no concern that anyone might see him. If this was a secret meeting, he sure wasn't acting like it.

We entered the town of Aenon once again. But this time, under the veil of darkness. The first thing we noticed was that there were fewer people. John the Baptist moved to locations up and down the

Jordan River and the droves of people moved with him. Towns near the wild man would swell during his baptisms.

Barabbas finally confirmed our suspicions. He was not meeting a physician. He ducked down an alleyway that took him behind the Jewish temple. It was the same temple where Mendel dropped off the cart of food each week.

I pointed to an open doorway toward the front. Gez moved in the direction. Torches burned on the outside sconces, creating wonderful shadows for me to hide in. My brother was somewhat skilled at sneaking around, but I had mastered it. I found it funny that I used to be afraid of the dark and now it was my playground.

This temple was small, only fifteen cubits by twenty cubits inside with a vaulted ceiling ten cubits high. A stone altar with ornate carvings was prominent at the far end, where we assumed the Jewish Rabbis performed their rituals and taught the people the ways of Yahweh.

Just then Barabbas' voice echoed in our ears, but despite the open space, it was too muffled for us to discern the words spoken. We waited outside the doorway hidden in the shadows. Candles and torches were lit throughout the mud-colored building.

A hooded individual whisked by us and entered hastily. I could hear more shuffling around the front of the temple and pointed for Gez to check it out. He hobbled to another pillar and peeked around. He quickly pulled back and then indicated there were two others guarding the entrance. Gez remained there to keep an eye on them while I refocused on the clandestine meeting inside.

After getting myself into a better position, I saw another guard dressed in black exit. The real conversation had just begun. Barabbas said, "Shalom, my brother."

The cloaked man pulled the hood back and responded, "Shalom." His voice was very controlled and soft-spoken. In the light, I could see patches of gray hair. His beard was long and also gray. He instructed Barabbas to sit on a nearby stone bench then sat next to him, angling himself appropriately. It was the way he was sitting, so proper, back straight, knees close together that caught my attention. There was nothing casual about this man's posture. It revealed a level of etiquette not found in the common man.

"How is my sister?" the mysterious man asked.

"She is well. Waiting for her husband to return. You didn't call this meeting to inquire about Gaddi. What is going on?"

"Gaddi. Such a strange name for my ears to hear. I pray for my eyes to one day see her again."

"It is her prayer, as well. What troubles you?"

"Barabbas, these are troubling times. I fear the dormant beast has been awakened."

"What riddle do you speak, Joseph? We have been in more troubling times than this."

"No, you have no idea. I'm afraid something has stirred the cage of the lion and if we don't figure out a way to feed it, then it will attack its keeper."

"More riddles, Joseph. Come now, the Romans are still in their cage."

"No!" Joseph stood quickly, turning away, and began to stroke the length of his beard. He turned back to face Barabbas. "No. This man they call John the Baptist is causing all of Jerusalem and the Roman legion to be awakened."

"One man? Please. You exaggerate."

"Exaggerate? Barabbas," he scoffed in contempt, "you have no idea of the pressure I am under. The Sanhedrin squabble over the smallest nuance of meaning in the Scriptures and want me to agree with their every interpretation to elevate their own status. Truly, there are days I wish I was just a student again."

"I am still not sure what you require of me in regards to these political issues. Your sister is safe. No one knows about us, not even my closest aide, Mendel."

"I have no one to talk with about such matters in Jerusalem. Spies are everywhere and the Romans watch my every step. This man baptizing people in the Jordan River, what is he all about?"

"Just another man, Joseph. He is making a lot of noise, but it is just noise."

"I wish it were so, Barabbas. He preaches that someone powerful is coming. It is this single message that is pricking the ears of the religious leaders and has already begun to be talked about by leaders of Rome. Pontius Pilate even speaks of him now. This is not good. Not good for any of us, especially me." Joseph began to pace back and forth in front of Barabbas who remained seated.

"It's another false Messiah."

"No, this has nothing to do with whether the message is false or not. This man is gaining attention. Serious attention." Joseph paused and then said, "I have spent years with my father-in-law, Ananius, lulling the beast to sleep. But John the Baptist is awakening that giant and I'm afraid I don't have a young King David to throw a stone at it."

Barabbas laughed, "Your speech is so poetic, my brother."

"Be serious."

"Serious? Well, what would you have me do? Drown John the Baptist?" Barabbas laughed, but it slowly died out when he saw Joseph actually seriously considering the idea. "You are foolish," Barabbas countered.

"Foolish, Barabbas, is the fact that hundreds are saying he is Elijah, and hundreds more are saying he is the Messiah. *That* is foolish. Now Rome is taking notice and will strike us all down if they feel that we cannot quiet the situation."

"What do you propose I do, Joseph? You are the great Caiaphas, the High Priest. I have no power."

"You think of me as all-powerful but I am a mere puppet for the Sanhedrin. There lies the true power, and it sways constantly from one Sanhedrin faction to another. I am indeed caught in the middle."

"Again, I ask, what would you like for me to do?"

"I do not know. I came to see what you had to say or maybe just to hear myself talk out loud."

Barabbas leaned his head back and looked up at the ceiling mural. "There is little I can do while still maintaining the safety of my wife."

"Gavriella is quite capable of handling herself if you are needed elsewhere."

Barabbas cocked his head, "Oh, is that so? Gaddi can take care of herself? That wasn't the arrangement. We came here to hide in order to protect you. The Romans believe they have leverage over you with your wife. We will continue to let them think that. They have no idea about your sister and I want to keep it that way."

"As do I, Barabbas. But if we cannot quiet this man, then I fear it won't matter. Rome only tolerates the Jews as long as we remain under control, but a man baptizing hundreds, while proclaiming someone greater is coming, only brings suspicion and alarm."

"Rome doesn't scare that easily, Joseph. I think you are overreacting."

"Overreacting? You do not understand the superstition these Romans condemn themselves to. They believe in everything. Why? Fear is why. They fear everything and thus look for anything out of the ordinary so they can squash it before their fears are realized. They do not know anything about our God, the true God, and a single man crying out in the wilderness that someone more powerful is coming is already alarming them. Pontius Pilate comes to me to appease his fears. Can you imagine? This is a Roman leader and he fears such things as this."

"I had no idea."

"Barabbas, there has to be a way to speak to this John. Perhaps buy him off or have him arrested."

"I have seen his kind. Money won't dwindle his zeal. He lives off of locusts and honey, from what Mendel tells me. No, money won't work. I fear arresting him won't work either."

There was a long pause. Joseph continued to pace and stroke his beard. Barabbas leaned his head back once again.

There was a long silence. My mind raced but a succinct idea had formulated during their conversation. I don't know what came over me. I brazenly walked into the room and said with all confidence, "Bandits."

Startled, Joseph turned and Barabbas stood quicker than I thought possible for such a large man. Joseph Caiaphas was about to call for his guards but stopped when Barabbas spoke.

"Dismas?" Barabbas' eyes narrowed. "What are you doing here?"

"Who is this, Barabbas?"

"My name is Dismas and the answer to your dilemma is simple. Bandits."

Joseph stepped toward me and said, "I can have you killed for speaking to me plainly, as you are. Wait. You are not Jewish."

"No, I'm Greek. But I know how to wield that stone and knock your giant back to sleep. Are you interested or not?"

"Do you know who I am?" Joseph asked.

"Someone afraid. You are Barabbas' brother-in-law and I want to help. That is all that matters to me."

"Barabbas," Joseph said, "Who is this Greek boy?"

"God led me to him out in the mountains. I found him and his brother on one of my fasts. I've been waiting to see how their story would unfold. And right now I'm not caring much for it."

"And what is their story saying to you, Barabbas?" Joseph asked.

Barabbas sighed, "Tell us Dismas, I'm interested to hear what you know of banditry?"

"I know a great deal and so does my brother, Gestas."

"You are just a boy. What would you know of the politics of Rome?" Joseph questioned.

"I don't know politics but I do know Romans. They fall over just like any man as long as you give them a good push."

"And how do you plan on pushing them?" Joseph said, intrigued.

"John the Baptist isn't the problem. He is the solution," I said.

Barabbas scoffed, but Joseph interrupted Barabbas' lack of confidence, "Let him continue."

"Hear me, if Rome is the giant, then we need to distract this giant away from what attracted it in the first place."

"What are you saying?" Barabbas said.

"I'm saying that Roman soldiers have been summoned to bring order to the throngs of people following John the Baptist. If we raid caravans throughout the region, never striking the same way, and always in different locations, this will cause the Romans to be distracted, paying John no matter. After all, he is but a single man yelling in the wilderness. The soldiers would have to turn their attention toward the bandit raids."

Barabbas barked at the absurdity, "What bandits? Who is going to lead something like that? This area is completely controlled by Rome and they care little about the outskirts."

"Not true. They care about *everything*, Barabbas. Rome wants to control everything and, if something is out of their control, they will step in. This is how we lure the giant away and back into its cage."

Joseph stared at me for a long moment. I could see him contemplating the strategy while at the same time trying to figure me out.

"It's an absurd idea," Barabbas said.

Joseph quickly responded, "It might just work."

Barabbas turned to face his brother-in-law, "You can't be serious!"

Joseph looked hard at me, "What would you need?"

"You will supply us the money to pay the people we hire. Gestas and I will do the rest."

"Hire?" Barabbas laughed, "What are you talking about?"

I looked at him, "Suffice it to say, Barabbas, there are many things you don't know about people, especially those under the weight of Roman taxes."

"And you do?"

"Gestas and I will find them. We know what to look for and where to look. We will start attacking caravans along the roads, taking all their valuables. These victims voices will carry weight with the Romans, pushing them to do something. This will take their focus away from John the Baptist." I paused, "It will work. Trust me."

Joseph stared a long while at me, but I didn't back down. I knew this was what we were supposed to do. This was what we were trained for. Not only were we helping Barabbas and his wife but this would help Gestas and me in carrying out our revenge against the Romans.

"You say you need funds. If I were to supply you, how fast could you start this business venture you are proposing?"

"Immediately."

Joseph turned to Barabbas. The big man scoffed, "This is crazy." Barabbas pointed his meaty finger in Joseph's chest, "*You* are crazy."

"Indeed I am. It seems our God has provided us an answer through our Greek friends and," Joseph pushed his skinny finger in Barabbas' chest, "I want you to lead it."

"Me?"

"Yes. Let Dismas be your eyes, along with his brother. They will report to you while you remain unattached, so you can still protect Gavriella." Joseph pulled out a leather purse and tossed it to me.

I caught it and felt the weight of the money inside. I untied it quickly to peer in and saw the glint of silver. Not showing my excitement, I looked up at Joseph, "This is a good start. We will require this monthly."

"Monthly?" Joseph squawked in surprise.

"Yes, monthly. Your giant won't see what's coming."

"How do I know that you and your brother won't just take off with the money?"

"It will require a little faith. You do have faith, don't you?"

"Don't mock me, boy."

Barabbas stepped in, "This one is loyal. I have seen it first-hand."

"Just don't fail me, Barabbas. This is for all our sakes. May the Lord our God bless us." Joseph pulled his hood back over his head. "Barabbas?"

"Yes."

He didn't say anything but there was something about his look. He was pleading with Barabbas to help him. This man of importance feared what was ahead. I planned on using that fear to fund Gestas and me. This was our time. I caught sight of my brother in the recesses of the shadows and saw him nod slightly at me. He had heard everything and understood that our life's purpose had just unfolded before us.

The money was good, but what was better was the pain we would inflict on the Romans. Yes, we would make them suffer a hundred-fold compared to the suffering they had brought upon us. As long as we could keep them occupied away from John the Baptist, the money would flow. Soon, the flow of Roman blood would be even greater.

CHAPTER 27
SHIFTING SAND

TWO YEARS FROM THE CROSS
-DISMAS-

I T HAD BEEN many months since that fateful meeting and many things had changed. Our relationship with Barabbas and Gaddi being the most dramatic. Barabbas explained to us very forcefully after we met his brother-in-law, Joseph Caiaphas, that Joseph was the High Priest of Jerusalem and of the entire region. I was uncertain as to how much importance that position carried but I knew he was definitely someone who had great influence. We now knew Barabbas was hiding in this valley in order to protect Gaddi. Since we knew their secret, it gave them comfort to be able to talk openly, for they had carried this burden for quite some time.

I remember Barabbas' words to us. His voice, very serious to the point of threatening, *"Don't do anything foolish, for what you do affects Gaddi. And I won't have her hurt in any way. Do you understand?"*

Gaddi was Barabbas' concern. The Romans were ours. Someday, those priorities would pull us apart.

Gez and I were not much for politics but being with Aziz and The Servants taught us that knowledge was power. In the political arena, that was the weapon. Gaddi, being his sister, posed a great threat to Joseph Caiaphas directly, for if the Romans and Sanhedrin knew about her, then they would manipulate the High Priest to do their will. Joseph would most likely lose his sister as she would most assuredly be taken as a hostage.

Joseph had foreseen this danger and hired Barabbas to escape with her and protect her. Over time, Barabbas and Gaddi fell in love and married. As with all secrets, however, they were bound to eventually be found out.

Our bandit raids started a month after the secret meeting with Caiaphas. We hired a handful of locals through our subtle inquiries around the marketplace. We were well aware that the marketplace was not only a place where food and essential items were sold, but where information could be bought. With that knowledge, we were able to find those who were highly motivated against the Romans.

Gestas and I envisioned that our bandit brigade would eventually lead to open rebellion against the Roman invaders. Barabbas, along with Mendel, had us focus only on caravans and making sure John the Baptist was no longer the primary focal point of the local Roman soldiers.

The trick was to keep our band moving up and down the Jordan River region, never creating a pattern. Of course, Barabbas was never with us on our raids. He was well known and his boisterous personality would have easily left a memory wherever he traveled, especially with the people he knew. Barabbas stayed behind the scenes while my brother and I were in the forefront. No one knew who we were. Two Greeks showing up unannounced, causing trouble in Perea wouldn't trace back to our friend. Joseph Caiaphas supplied money to our troops and we supplied the raids. We would then bring the stolen loot back through Mendel's contacts. Not all of it, however, found its way back to Barabbas. Gez and I would skim what we needed and even give out bonuses to the men to keep them loyal and happy. We knew the ways of banditry and caravan raids were easy work for us.

Barabbas instructed us not to kill anyone. but we were allowed to rough them up a bit. Our intentions weren't to kill innocent citizens. Our intentions were on the Romans.

The raids went according to plan. Everything was working. Rome was fully focused on capturing these criminals. At the same time, other groups of bandits rose up, adding to the distraction. There was no shortage of people to recruit as long as John the Baptist kept doing his part. And he did, until…

Yes, until that day, that strange day when everything changed.

Like scaling a dune as the wind shifts the sand, we had to stay ahead of the break or the avalanche would swallow us.

John had been calling out in the wilderness 'prepare the way' and 'someone more powerful than I is coming'. And on this day, someone *did* come.

We were not there to witness what happened, but we most definitely heard about it. I remembered the young boy of fourteen telling us what he saw. *"This man they call Jesus approached John in the water. I heard a voice like the sound of rushing water, but didn't understand what or who was speaking."* The most unusual part of the story was what he saw next. *"Then it happened,"* the boy continued. *"It was like a dove coming from the sky toward Jesus and then it disappeared."* I thought this had to be a false testimony. Gestas said it was only a false testimony if one person said it, but when dozens more reported similar stories, then it had to have been true.

I've seen demons face to face, so a bird appearing and disappearing didn't cause me any surprise. But suddenly, as fast as this Jesus came to meet John, he went off into the desert alone and wasn't seen for forty days, from what I was told. *"What was he doing out there all alone?"*

They said Jesus came from a small town called Nazareth, someplace I am not familiar with. All I have learned has come from passersby or bandit raids. We have not encountered this Jesus of Nazareth firsthand. They said people were being healed. When I say healed, I mean completely. One moment they had a broken arm or leg and the next they didn't. The reports came to us in a constant stream.

I personally witnessed something that I have not even told Gestas about. On one of our raids, there was a blind man. I remember him well only because his eyes were not only blind, but rotted out. He wore a bandage over his sockets. There have been many horrors I've seen in my life, but when I removed the bandage out of pure curiosity to verify his blindness, what I saw was indeed of nightmares. His flesh was black around the edges. A yellowish pus seeped out at the base, but it was the dark cavity that caused me to wince. I quickly fumbled to put back his bandage. The old man said to me, *"Thank you for your kindness."* My kindness? What was he talking about? I rejected him. I felt sorry for him. I had hoped to never see him again.

Months later, I heard this man's voice from one of the carts we were offloading during our raid. *"Thank you for your kindness,"* he said to one of my men. I walked over to confirm and it was the same man, but...he had eyes. It was impossible.

I asked the old man, *"Where did your group come from?"*

He smiled, his brown eyes sparkling with joy, *"Oh, we came from Galilee. This is my family."* He pointed to the group of people we had tied up. Before I could ask, the man said out loud what I knew in my heart had happened. *"Jesus healed me."*

It knocked the breath out of me. This man wasn't just blind, he'd had no eyes. Not only had he not had eyes, but the place where his eyes should have been was decayed and rotting. I couldn't speak and walked away. I told no one, burying the memory.

Once this Jesus came into the picture, John the Baptist slowly faded. Eventually, he was arrested and hauled away to prison by the orders of Herod Antipas, the Tetrarch over Galilee and Perea. This caused a political problem in the region, for the crowds continued to grow, first with John the Baptist, and even more now, with Jesus of Nazareth. Herod, we surmised, felt that freeing John might lead to rebellion, but to murder him might incite one, so John currently remains in prison where he cannot share his doctrine openly with the people any longer.

Our bandit brigade enlarged and grew in power as time continued. We broke into multiple groups and were following the ways of The Servants we had trained under. Gez and I became famous amongst our own, as we led everyone in many victories, sharing the spoils. We started pulling out the elite ones and formed a new group, a group that sought more than raids. This group wanted Roman blood to be spilled. That time had finally come. This was a secret group that Barabbas knew nothing of and we paid these men even more than the others to keep it that way. Each of the men, hand-picked by us, had experienced a great loss at the hands of the Romans.

The time we lived in became much more complicated once Jesus of Nazareth showed up. There was a strange feeling in the air. Gez and I sensed it, but couldn't fully grasp what it was about this single man that was healing people in the region. The word Messiah was on everyone's lips. All eyes, from Jerusalem to Capernaum and beyond, were now turned toward Jesus. Could he truly be this Messiah the Jews had been waiting for? Could he be the one to lead a rebellion against the Romans? The number of his followers increased daily. It was only a matter of time before Rome would be moved to action.

The words of Aziz came to me, *"I'm against my brother. My brother and I are against our cousin. Our cousin and I are against the stranger."*

We were patient and knew one of these days we would meet this miracle man.

If this Messiah rose to strike against the Romans, then we would ride beside him into battle; cousins and strangers united. But for now, we would watch and strike at the time of our choosing. A great shift in the sands was occurring. Rome's days were numbered.

PART III
THE MESSIAH

CHAPTER 28
HE'S COMING!

TEN MONTHS FROM THE CROSS
-NESTOR AND JESUS-

"HE'S COMING! No, no, no, no! This isn't his time. Not his time. It's our time, not his time. What are we going to do? Yes, what to do, what to do?"

It was a cloudless, starlit night. The air was brisk and the wind gave a low howl outside the cave entrance. An unclothed man perched like an animal on top of a large rock outcropping began to scream, thrashing his arms at something further out in the darkness, something unseen.

Small waves lapped onto the shore. Reflected moonlight created a shimmering mystical atmosphere. The gangly man threw stones out into the sea, yelling and screaming unintelligible words. After several minutes of rampaging, he settled, taking heaves of air into his lungs. Froth built up around his cracked lips. Dried blood and dirt plastered his face and melded into his gnarled beard where several patches had been torn out. His eyes glared red, casting the appearance of a wild animal...or perhaps a demon of sorts.

A second naked man, shorter and more haggard, scuttled out on his hands and feet like a beast. He stood and howled a sound wicked and unearthly, a sound unlike any beast ever heard by men. He stopped and looked at the first man, "It will not...not, not, stop...

him, him." His speech was slurred and a string of drool fell from his dirt-encrusted mouth before being captured by his frizzy beard. Twigs and debris were tangled inside his dark brown hair.

"You will not have us! Not ever! I curse thee!" the first man yelled toward the sea.

As if summoned, clouds began to form and billow out with a fury. The enraged man screeched toward the strange unfolding weather. The ground underfoot began to shake and stones slid off one another, clattering nearby. It wasn't an earthquake; rather a supernatural force resonating from the crazed being. A crack of lightning resounded. Clouds darkened and spewed out toward the sea like a beast in search of its prey. This storm was not like any other. This storm was on assignment and violently lashed out without relent. Wind screeched over the surface, and the once small waves grew into violent creatures ready to swallow all in their wake.

A hideous cackle echoed as the man stood fully upright on top of the boulder and beat his chest with the rock he held in his clenched fist.

"I curse thee! Go from here! It is not your time!" Dirty fingernails, some broken and jagged, others long and deformed, scratched at his bare chest. "It's his eyes, they see me. No, go away. Do not look upon me. NO!" He howled into the air and shouted curses toward the stormy sky. Another crack of lightning lit up the area as the bolt struck the edge of the shoreline nearby. Rain began to pour down in unprecedented torrents. The ground could not contain the deluge and the water flooded down the rocky hillside bringing mud and debris with it.

The two men, drenched, but undaunted by the elements, whooped and hollered and danced in a maniacal frenzy. They scooped up the mud that pooled at their feet and smeared it over their bodies and faces. The torrent continually washed it away. They matted their hair with the mud and streaks of watery dirt ran down their naked bodies. Their eyes glowed a supernatural red and they gnashed their teeth making a hideous grinding sound. An hour passed and they both settled just inside the opening of the small cave. The shorter man scooped mud and began to eat it. It sloshed back out of his mouth each time he chomped down. They were both preoccupied with the result of the storm, their eyes transfixed on the darkened, thrashing sea.

Suddenly, the storm ceased. It was swallowed up in an instant and the moonlight shone clear and bright. The men stumbled out from the cave in awe. The tall one spoke, "Our end is in sight."

"No, no. Say, say, say it is...not, not so."

"Many of us have fallen. His eyes are upon us. There is no escape." He paused and finished, "It is not his time." He spat onto the ground, some of it catching in the coarse hairs of his patchy beard. The shorter man scurried back inside the cave, mumbling words in his wake.

A hundred yards from the shoreline, a boat approached as the sun began to rise. Men acquainted with the workings of the vessel moved about on board, but one man watched and sat still at the stern. These were the eyes that had been watching him from the beginning and they brought him great fear. He knew that his dominance over the region was coming to an end. So many souls left to harvest, but his reign of terror was about to be cut short. The spiritual walls and fortifications had been besieged and broken down. Now the conqueror approached to gloat over the former master of this region, the caretaker of the lost souls, the tormentor of dreams, the dasher of destinies.

Pigs squealed far off and drew the scarred-faced man to look in that direction. Herdsman shepherded the thousands of swine in a far-off pasture high above the sea. The green grass and colorful weed flowers that bloomed there were disintegrated under the hooves of so many swine, especially after the recent rainfall. The ground quickly became a slick, muddy hillside.

Voices below pulled the demon's attention back to the boat as the strangers slid ashore on the pebbled beach. Their words carried easily to his ears. "What is this place?" one asked. Another answered, "It looks to be a burial site for the Gentiles." They pulled the boat deeper onto the sand and rocks to ensure it would stay lodged. Then the twelve men waited for the final passenger to disembark.

Both of the crazed, demon-eyed men lurched and sprinted to the bottom to meet the new arrivals. The crew of the boat saw and heard them coming. The sounds from the demons were feral. The one who sat still at the stern held up his hand, signaling to the group to remain steadfast. All of them froze, waiting in anticipation.

The two wild men slid to their knees before him. One cried out in a loud voice, louder than that of a normal man, "What have you to do with us, Jesus, Son of the Most High God? I adjure you by God not to torment us before the time."

Jesus, undaunted, simply asked him, "What is your name?"

He replied, "My name is Legion, for we are many. I beg of you not to send us away from this country. Send us to the pigs; let us enter them."

Jesus looked over at the swine, then looked back at Legion and said, "Go."

Immediately, as he gave this command, the unclean spirits inside the two men left. High-pitched screeching caused Jesus' followers to wince and cover their ears in pain. Buzzing like that of a swarm of bees resounded, though no insects were seen. The cacophony of demonic noises faded as they left the area and hurled themselves toward the herd of pigs. The normal grunting and feeding sounds changed to agonizing squeals as the swine were overtaken and indwelt by the demons. The herdsmen shifted uncomfortably, not understanding what was happening. They tried to control the pigs nearest them, but it was futile. Within moments they all stampeded away toward the steep embankment leading to the sea. Some were convulsing, others were bleeding from their eyes. All of them moved at a crazed, fanatical pace down the hill. Scores of them flung their bodies over the edge, plummeting to their deaths in the water below. More and more followed recklessly, throwing themselves over. The first group hit the water hard, skin slapping loudly against the surface. The ones that followed landed on top of one another. Bones broke, flesh tore, blood spewed, and the water turned red as the gore escalated and then came to an end. Some pigs remained on the hill but they were either trampled to death or killed by the severity of their sudden seizures. A few still twitched as their pink tongues hung loosely from their mouths. A grotesque steam rose from the mass of bodies. The tide began to slowly separate them and pull them farther apart to drift away like pieces of wood caught in the ebb and flow.

The herdsmen, roughly ten men, stood in shock and horror. They looked down from their high point at Jesus and the disciples and then ran away in fear.

Only the small lapping waves of the shore could be heard. The two naked men were curled up on the ground, side by side, shivering. Both of the men slowly looked at Jesus, then to the disciples who gathered around them. Several open wounds on the two men's bodies closed shut before the disciple's eyes.

Jesus said, "Let us clothe and feed these men."

Without a word, a few of his disciples pulled out extra clothing while others began to pick up loose driftwood for the fire.

"John," Jesus called.

"Yes."

"See that they are bathed."

He nodded, then approached the gaunt men, helping them to their feet and guiding them into the water. The formerly-possessed men were still in shock and uncertain of their surroundings and their new circumstances. They had apparently been lost for quite some time.

Hours passed. The two sane men ate cooked fish and broke bread with Jesus and his followers. The disciples shared stories and laughed as the two men listened and continued to gather themselves in mind and body after being separated for so long with demons in control.

One of the disciples, the one with a deep voice, said, "Now I know why our Master had us purchase extra clothing. I'm always afraid to question 'why' these days." This statement caused a raucous laughter; even Jesus chuckled. Midway through their laughter, John pointed above them to the top of the rocky hill and said, "Peter." The deep-voiced man quickly looked to where he pointed, as did the others.

A large gathering of people had gathered and looked down at them. Several of the herdsmen were at the front. Judging by the movement of their arms, it was apparent that they were sharing what had transpired earlier. Then a large part of the crowd broke off and descended, while others remained. Their steps were bold toward the group around the beach fire, indicating an imminent confrontation.

A man in noble attire, a white robe with a beige cloak, led the charge and said loudly, "What is the meaning of all this?" He stopped ten steps away, followed by at least twenty other people who began to murmur when they saw the demon-possessed men now clean, clothed, and appearing to be of sound mind. The nobleman also noticed and instantly shifted from authoritative to fearful.

A herdsman whispered, "These men showed up and spoke to the crazed ones. Suddenly my pigs spooked and killed themselves. It was them, Galenus, I swear it upon the Goddess of Luck."

Galenus, nearly forty years of age with a larger than normal stomach, looked out at the massive carnage of pigs floating in the water. Then his eyes fell upon the two demon-possessed men. "How is this possible? Do you know what you have done?"

Neither Jesus nor the disciples responded. Galenus was flustered and unable to form a complete sentence. His breaths became short and his face red as he stammered, "What, how...I don't. What can... this is..."

Peter boldly spoke, "We have done nothing wrong. Jesus banished the demons who have been tormenting these men."

Galenus held up his hand, wincing at Peter's statement. Closing his eyes, not wishing to hear anything further, he said, "I beg of you, please depart." He opened his eyes and looked directly at Jesus, "I don't understand what has happened, nor do I care to hear your side of the story, foreigners. But I demand that you depart from here immediately."

More people gathered at the top of the hillside, including Roman soldiers. Jesus looked around at all the people, nodded his head slightly in satisfaction and then turned toward his disciples, "Let us go then."

"Yes, Rabbi," Peter responded.

They quickly gathered their belongings in silence. Jesus was helped into the boat and one of the once demon-possessed men rushed toward him, falling to his knees, "Please take me with you. I wish to follow you all the days of my life."

Jesus humbly smiled, slowly looking at all the people gathered, and said, "Go home to your friends and family and tell them how much the Lord has done for you, and how he has had mercy on you."

With that, the disciples shoved the boat out into the sea and climbed aboard. Jesus kept his gaze upon the man. There was much power emanating from Jesus and an internal glow that rivaled the sun. The man was astonished at what he was seeing. Smiling, he looked around, but no one else appeared to notice. He attempted to look at Jesus again, but the brightness blinded him, causing him to hold up his hand to try to shield it.

He pushed himself up to stand and then turned toward the crowd. With boldness in his voice, he announced, "My name is Nestor and this is Philos. Today we were saved by God. The God of Jesus, the very one you sent away. You are all witnesses of this miracle that no other god in our land has ever done."

The disciples heard Nestor and were stirred with joy. They knew the assignment had been completed. Only afterward could they understand. The mission had always been these two Gentiles in the land of the Gerasenes.

They heard Nestor continue, "You know it to be true. You saw the chains we were in, these very chains!" He held up his arms and the old rusted links dangled from the shackles. "The chains that no normal man could break," he continued, "and you saw the immense strength we had that overcame the mightiest of men. You feared us and left us alone to rot in the tombs and caves, but now we stand before you of sound mind once again." Nestor pointed back to the boat, "Jesus set us free!"

Nestor began to walk through the crowd and continued to speak out, while Philos stayed close behind him. Many began to follow Nestor and Philos. Others stood in awe, breaking off into conversations, trying to digest this extraordinary event. Roman soldiers clustered nearby, leaning on their spears and watched the two formerly-possessed men closely. They were uncertain themselves as to what to say about this and how to present it to their commanding officer, Fortus.

Something had happened, something very strange, and they all marveled at it.

PART IV
NESTOR

CHAPTER 29
AWAKENED

TEN MONTHS FROM THE CROSS
-NESTOR-

TEARS STREAMED DOWN my face as I stood in the doorway of my old home. It was now a shell, burnt out and dilapidated. This very day we were released from our demonic prison by a man named Jesus. With but a single word, this man filled with deific authority, banished the demons. Jesus exuded a power that was foreign to us. Philos and I experienced this power when a great light came into our dark cell. My mind tried to shield the light but as it consumed me, no, as it consumed the darkness around me, we were suddenly jarred back to reality, returned to normal.

I remember color coming into view. Color so vibrant, like nothing I had ever seen before. Even the dull colors of sand and rock came to life. Yet here we stood, our bodies feeling much like our home—a shell. Fragmented memories flooded into my mind as I took each step, making my way to the back bedroom. I could barely walk. I felt like I was dragging a boulder behind me.

The bedroom, now an exposed area with felled walls and rubble underfoot, was the last place I had seen my Vena and the last time I had held my son. The realization of the magnitude of what I had lost in this very place began to overcome me. My bottom lip quivered. My son, also dead, was a memory that crushed my heart. Standing in this area, recalling all that happened, overwhelmed me so much that I fell to my knees crying.

Philos quickly dropped down to my side, "I'm sorry, Nestor."

All I could do was grab onto him and wail. The full force of my grief came forth in a crushing torrent of bitter emotion.

"Why?" I sobbed. My voice was muffled, buried in my friend's shoulder, while I clutched Philos' robe.

Philos cried with me. After awhile, our tears stopped. We parted, sitting against the wall in the silence that embraced us.

Philos broke the silence, pain in his voice, "It was my fault, Nestor. I'm the one to blame."

I looked at him, "What do you speak of?"

"If I hadn't told you about the witch-doctor, then perhaps Vena would still be with us. I failed you and I failed her. I was the one that brought Legion upon us. You have every right to send me away."

I contemplated his words. This was something I had wrestled with inside the dark cell we had been trapped within. I looked at my friend for a long moment before speaking. "It is strange," I responded.

Philos looked at me quizzically.

"If I were to ask someone what darkness is to them, they might say when they close their eyes. You and I, at one point in our life, might have agreed, but no longer, for we have been someplace much darker than just the closing of our eyes. We have been to the birthplace of darkness itself. Both of us experienced the darkest of dark and, every second, all I could think about was how I had failed my wife, my son, my friend, my very life. And now, here in this place, in a future I never imagined, you of all people, confess your shame to me."

Philos remained silent as we stared at each other.

"No one can understand what we have endured, where we have been, what we have seen. You are the only one that would understand it when I say the darkness we were in was beyond any darkness known to this natural world." My eyes squinted as the intensity of my words flowed, "No one would know this but *you* because *you* were there with me. You suffered with me, Philos. There is no worse punishment for the choices we *both* made than what we have already endured."

Philos, on the verge of tears, said, "Nestor, but...your family. I played a part in—"

I took hold of his robe and brought him forcefully to my face. He averted my gaze. "Look at me!" I demanded. He slowly brought his eyes to mine.

My tears welled, "Listen. It was not your fault, Philos. I don't blame you. Nor shall I ever blame you."

Philos crumbled in my arms and I held him tightly as he cried.

We finally released each other and sat against the broken wall, staring blankly into the dusky sky. The pink and orange clouds spattered across the expansive palette.

"Do you remember anything?" I said softly. "I mean, do you remember anything that Legion did while we were imprisoned?"

"Some. It's fragmented. Hard to discern if it is a memory or just my imagination."

I nodded in agreement, "The memories are covered in a fog and sometimes I see glimpses and wonder the same, whether they are real or not. Even now I feel like I'm in a dream."

"Yes," Philos said, "It is the same for me."

We remained quiet for a long stretch of time as we both contemplated where we were this very moment. Eventually, exhaustion overcame us and we fell asleep.

I was startled awake by a lizard scurrying through the rubble next to me. Realizing what it was, I ignored it. My eyes adjusted to the morning light as I looked around. Philos was curled in the corner and did not wake from my movement. I stood, my eyes slowly taking in the ash and debris left behind. I knelt down and dipped my hand into the fine sediment and let it sift through my fingers. The broken rusty chains, still latched around my wrists, weighed heavy. *"How long have we been away?"* I wondered.

My eyes wandered from the chains to my hands and arms. The scars were healing faster than normal, I thought. Without warning, my mind flashed to me holding a sharp-edged stone and slicing across my forearm. Blood trickled out of the exposed flesh. I cut myself again and again. The warmth of my own blood covered my arm as I held it up. The horrific memory suddenly ended. I was back in the burnt out room where I lost everything. Fear overtook me. I scuttled backwards and fell to the ground. Philos was staring at me.

"Are you alright?" He asked as he sat up.

"I lost everything," was all I could say, clutching my shins to pull my legs closer to my chest.

Philos chose not to answer. Perhaps he had no answer.

"Why am I still alive, Philos? What does any of this matter? This life? This world? Why?"

"I don't have the answers, my friend."

Several minutes passed before I took a deep breath and said, "I'm afraid to sleep and now it appears I should fear the day as well. The memories of our past haunt me."

Philos grew more concerned and asked once again, "Are you all right?"

I responded, "I want to tell you so, but…"

"You don't have to explain. I apologize for even asking. Neither of us is all right."

Philos stood and stretched his muscles. I heard his spine crack as he slowly moved about and I watched his face strain a bit as he loosened the tightness in his body.

"Discomfort in my physical body was far from my mind while we were overtaken. Like you, I feel old," I said.

Philos responded, "Our minds were cut off from our body. Legion controlled the physical while at the same time caging our minds."

I looked long and hard at my friend.

Philos said, "What is wrong? Why do you look at me this way?"

"Why, Philos?"

"Why, what?"

"Why did Jesus send us away? Why would he tell us to come back here?"

He sighed, "I don't know. This is something that I have been wrestling with myself. Jesus said very little to us on the beach while we adjusted. I do want to know, however, what he whispered to you, before the crowds came to disband us?"

"Whisper?"

"Yes, he said something to you. I watched your face contemplating his words."

I slowly nodded, pulling on the memory. "It was odd. Jesus simply said, 'I like skipping rocks on the Sea of Galilee.' That was it, then the crowd came."

"Skipping rocks?"

I asked Philos, "Do you remember Jesus saying anything else? Everything is so distant in my mind even though it was only yesterday."

"His followers spoke most of the time, not to us, but just in general, around the fire. The one called John checked on us most often. I remember Jesus being with us, but no words." Philos slowed his speech, "I do remember though…"

"What?"

He looked at me, "It was his touch. I remember him touching my shoulder and in that simple grasp it felt like…"

"Like what?"

"I don't know. It is difficult to explain. It was like in that moment he was telling me it was all right. There was a sensation in his touch that brought a strange warmth, like the embrace of a father to a son. I don't know if that makes sense."

I picked up a small, loose stone and sighed, "Nothing makes sense, Philos."

I paused and then asked, "What are we going to do?"

"I don't know, my friend."

I tossed the rock to the side in frustration, "It feels like I'm missing something. I don't know what it is."

"How so?"

"All I can think of is that I lost them, Philos. I lost Vena and Dismas. There is nothing but pain that remains in this place. Why would he send us back here and not let us go with him and leave this place behind?"

"I have no answers, but what I do know is that we were lost, if not dead ourselves, and now we are alive and here."

"But why? Why now? What can we do with such a great loss as this? My wife and my son are gone."

Nothing was said as we stood there in our burned down, exposed home.

Philos said plainly, "We fight."

I looked at him and I saw a glint in his eye.

He said again, "We fight."

"What is it we are fighting?"

"Jesus came to us for a reason. Let us search out what our fight is against, for surely we were once without hope, but now we find ourselves here poised for whatever lies ahead."

"But where do we go, Philos?"

"Did not Jesus instruct you to go and tell your friends and family about what he had done?"

"I have no friends and I have no family."

Philos said sharply, "Am I not your friend?"

Nestor responded, "You want me to tell you about Jesus?"

"No, I want us to tell others about him. We need to. I need to." Philos stared at me. "I'm compelled to, Nestor. I don't have the answers. There is nothing for us in this place," he swung his arms and looked around. "Our lives are his now for he has given us life again. Perhaps our fight is against the demons set loose in this world."

I chuckled, "Are we now able to see demons, Philos? No. So what are you saying exactly?"

"I'm saying we tell the people the truth about what has happened and let the will of the Jewish God direct our path wherever that may lead us."

"I don't know. I need time, Philos."

"Look around you, Nestor. Time spent here will not help you move forward."

I looked at Philos, "Maybe I don't want to move forward."

"Come. Jesus' disciple, Judas, gave me money before we left the beach. Let us rest in a real bed and eat real food this night."

He started to walk out but stopped and looked back.

My gaze fell to the ground, "I need more time."

"I know. Let's get food in our stomachs and be in a real bed."

"No, I…I just need…"

"More time, I know. I will not pressure you."

"No," I looked at Philos sternly, "I need time alone."

Philos stared at me for a long moment, "Oh, I see."

I stepped toward him but he retracted and said, "I will make arrangements in town. You can find me when you are ready." Philos departed.

It was a different time, an unknown time, and yet I was brought back to this familiar place. I couldn't walk away. I closed my eyes and let my imagination take me back to my wife. I watched Vena in the kitchen getting the bread ready to be baked. She looked up at me and smiled. She was talking to me but I couldn't hear her, just saw her pink lips moving. There was so much joy on her face and the light of the sun coming into the house made her look all the more angelic.

The sweet memory slowly fell apart when the surreal images of Vena transformed into those of her covered in blood. Her smile faded. Her blood-drenched hair was matted against her face and skin. She reached out to me. No, pointed at me. I heard her voice inside my mind so clearly; it was as if she stood there in front of me. *It's your fault.*

My eyes shot open and I gasped for air. I clutched at my chest, grabbing my robe, and slumped to the ground in defeat. She was right. *It was my fault. It was all my fault.*

The ground under me was cold and hard as I lay upon it, tears streaming down my face. The bleak room with its moldy, black and gray rock represented my very soul. Jesus brought me out of darkness, but for what?

I couldn't close my eyes because the horrors of what Legion had done haunted me. But keeping my eyes open only reminded me of my loss. I stared blankly at the toppled stones and ash-colored dirt for several minutes.

My eye caught something in the corner of the room. It was a small desert flower sprouting out of the ash and debris. I stood and walked over to get a better look. Its pink petals fluttered lightly from the cool morning breeze as I knelt to inspect it.

This wasn't just any flower. It was Vena's favorite. It was here, in this place, at this time. I looked around and did not see any other, only this one. These flowers grow all around Galilee in the crevasses of the rocks. Vena and I would walk the hills together and I would eventually sit and watch her pick them. She would smell each one, look back at me watching her, and smile.

This was impossible. This desert flower was not in season. I closed my eyes and smelled its fragrance. I smelled my Vena.

Placing my hand upon the ground, I whispered, "Goodbye, my love. I pray the God of the impossible rescued you in your final moments and you now reside in the palaces of heaven. Forgive your husband for failing you. I carry your heart with me and pray that God never takes that away. I also carry the burden of the loss of our son. Let that not be yours to carry any longer, my love. It is time for you to rest and be at peace. God, the true God, has given me the strength to stand again. And though I don't understand what it is he wants me to do, I trust him. He now leads me and I pray he leads me somehow back to you. Give my love to Dismas and let him know that I love him and will never stop thinking of him all the days that I am allowed to breathe."

My tears dripped onto the flower and the dirt. Deep down I felt a shift within me. There was a release of pain, replaced by a need to figure out why I was here. *I don't know who I am or my purpose, but something inside me wants to fight,* I thought. Perhaps this simple flower, miraculously birthed in this place, was a message from Vena to move forward. Just like me, it symbolized that in all this destruction, this darkness, a flower could still bloom.

Philos and I had lost our way and now, for whatever reason, God had given us a second chance. An unknown future now loomed before us, but this calling on our lives was greater than even the unknown.

I stood, taking a deep breath, and walked out. I knew that I would never return here again.

Stepping outside, I saw Philos leaning against the wall on the opposite side of the street.

He said, "I couldn't leave you behind."

I walked up to him without a word.

"What is it?" Philos asked.

"You were right, my friend. It is time to fight."

CHAPTER 30
HOW LONG HAS IT BEEN?
-NESTOR-

THE GOLDEN HUE of morning splashed across Hippus. Roman-Greek buildings absorbed the color spray and faded yellow bricks suddenly sparked to life. It was a peaceful walk back into the town. Our former home, along with several others around, were now abandoned. Superstition, after the death of Vena and my son, Dismas, had caused many to flee the area and rebuild elsewhere.

Many people we walked by stopped what they were doing and stared at us in disbelief. Others who didn't know what happened were soon told. Word spread quickly. I turned around periodically to see dozens following us with more joining in as we continued through town. Hearing the chains, rattling at my wrists, suddenly brought me shame and I pulled the shackles in closer to hide them.

Philos said, "Should we say something?"

"What do we say?"

He said, "I need to say something."

"Wait," I grabbed his arm, "What are you going to say?"

"The truth."

Philos turned and before he spoke, a man and his wife rushed up to us and fell to their knees crying. The man was older with graying hair and prominent wrinkles around his eyes. His wife, adorned in a head covering made of thin white silk, kept her head bowed. He looked up at us, tears in his brown eyes. He clasped his hands together and said, "We see the glory of God about you. We beg of you to bless us."

Philos and I exchanged glances. I looked back at the older man and said, "You see the glory of God around us?"

"Yes," he responded. "The God of Abraham, Isaac, and Jacob has touched you. I am Jewish and my wife is Greek. We live here in Hippus. Please bless us."

I said, "We are not holy men. We lived in caves under the control of demons and Jesus cast them from us with just a word. We stand before you today because of his power."

My voice became louder as I spoke. Something came over me. "Hear us, citizens of Hippus!" I shouted. "We are nobody special. Jesus rescued us from darkness. It is he you should seek. Not us."

I finished and, one by one, people from the crowd of thirty or so began to push through and walk toward us. Each of them knelt on the ground to ask for forgiveness. Some wept bitterly and others remained silent, waiting in anticipation for us to do something.

I pulled Philos and we walked away. Most of the people remained on the ground, pleading with us to come back. Others in the crowd stared, while some began to follow us.

The same Jewish man with gray hair ran to our side and walked beside us. He grabbed the chain that dangled at my side and kissed it, "Thank you, thank you," he repeated.

Embarrassed, I pulled the chain away from him.

He said, "Forgive me, holy men of God. My wife and I would like to invite you to our home. We have food and extra beds. Bless our home, please."

"We have other—."

Philos quickly stepped in front of me causing me to stop abruptly and said, "Yes, we have *other* matters to attend to but we will graciously accept your offer."

Philos looked at me, demanding with his eyes that I also agree.

"Yes, thank you," I relented.

Philos said, "We appreciate your hospitality. What is your name?"

He was delightfully shocked and said, "My name is Baruch and this is my wife, Apphia. We are honored. Come, come, this way."

Baruch took us to a large home, much more like a palace. He had private guards to hold back the crowd that followed as we entered the pillared home. Marble floors with large mosaics filled the space. It was at this time that I noticed the expensive clothing he and his wife wore. My mouth dropped in awe as my mind wrestled with my thoughts. Just yesterday, I was in prison. Today, I stood in a palace.

"And what kind of work do you do?" Philos asked.

"Ahhh, I am a government representative sent from Jerusalem to advocate peace between Jews and Greeks, and of course Rome."

I had no response. Baruch saw my confusion.

"Well, you see, the Roman government likes to keep peace between the different groups, while at the same time incorporating Roman law and culture into regions and so, you see—."

His wife came alongside him and said, "Baruch, our guests are tired. Let me show them to their room and get them settled. We can talk politics later, once they have rested."

"Ah, yes of course. Thank you, my wife. You are so good to keep me focused. I would ramble till the morning."

"Yes, I know." She smiled lovingly. "Follow me. Your room is upstairs. I will have someone bring you food. Across from your room is a private bath for your use."

As we followed Apphia, I said, "Thank you for your hospitality."

"It is a great honor to have you here." We continued up the stairs. I was caught up in the extravagance of their dwelling when Apphia said, "I will make arrangements to have your chains removed. If that is all right with you?"

Philos and I exchanged looks, stunned at the thought of being free of them. In some strange way, they were part of us, but in order for us to move forward, it was time for the shackles to be removed. We nodded our appreciation.

A little while later, I stood naked in front of the bath, steam rising from the water, staring at the chains on my wrists. I had carried these iron links for so long. *"If they are removed, will I forget who I was?"* Maybe the nightmares would be expelled. I looked at them for a long time.

The sunken white marble bath had steps leading to the water. I noticed my reflection and saw the chains dangling a foot in length from my wrists. I slowly brought my hands down to my side and watched the image of the metal links disappear. A question suddenly came to my mind, *"Would my wife want me to be in shackles?"* I could hear her voice inside my mind in response to my question, *"Husband, be free."*

I slowly stepped into the water. Tears of pain, sorrow, and joy, streamed down my face. The warm water covered me as I submerged my entire body. My face felt cooler as I came up for air. Resting my head back with my eyes closed, I was filled with a peace that I had never felt before. Still, no amount of peace could fill that part of my heart that ached because of the loss of my family.

I replayed the words of Jesus on the shore that morning. Everything in me longed to go with him. To leave his side felt like being torn away from the very source of life itself. At least that is how I could best describe it. But no, Jesus humbly smiled and said, *"Go home to your friends and family and tell them how much the Lord has done for you, and how he has had mercy on you."*

Go home. *What* home?

To my friends. What *friends* were there, other than Philos?

To my family. My family. Oh, *my* family. I desperately wanted my family.

As I rested, eyes still closed, a sudden flash of me holding my son burst into my mind. It came upon me so profoundly that I shot up out of the water, my eyes wide and my chest heaving. The vision continued with my eyes open and I saw a doctor taking my child away. Then the vision ended and the room came back into view.

The words fell from my lips, "My son was taken."

What had just happened to me? The vision seemed so real, like I was actually there with my son. The physician. He took my son away. He took him. Wait! *"Could my son possibly be alive?"*

I jumped out of the bath, fumbled to open the door, then called out, "How long has it been?" My voice echoed through the marble home. I walked out dripping wet, almost slipping to the ground on the shiny marble floors several times. Again I called, "How long has it been?"

A servant woman came through a door to my left and screamed, dropping a tray of food and drink, startled. I looked down and realized that I was naked. She slammed the door, leaving her tray with the broken crockery where it lay. I banged on the door, more concerned with getting the answer to my question than with my state of undress. I *had* to know.

Philos came out of our room to investigate and saw me. "What are you doing, Nestor?"

"How long has it been?"

"How long?

"Yes, how long have we been away?"

Philos took off his robe and covered me. He was now in his loincloth.

Baruch and Apphia raced up the stairs with a bodyguard. "What is the meaning of this?" Baruch blustered.

"Oh, my," Apphia said, diverting her eyes away in embarrassment. She called for a servant.

The woman who had slammed the door opened it a crack and peeked out.

"Get a blanket!" Apphia ordered.

"How long has it been?" I began to cry. My knees hit the hard marble stone but I didn't feel any pain.

"What do you mean?" Baruch asked.

"How long?" I pleaded.

Philos interpreted, "He needs to know how long we were gone. How long were we in the tombs?"

"You don't know?"

"No, we don't."

"How long?" I whispered.

Baruch softly said, "Nineteen. You have been gone for nineteen years."

"My son." I fixated my eyes on nothing at the realization of so many years lost.

"He's gone, Nestor. Let him go."

"No, Philos." I stood and grabbed him. "God awakened me with a vision." My tears stopped flowing and my resolve slowly returned. "God awakened me."

"What are you saying, my friend?"

"The doctor. I remember. I saw him." I placed my hands on either side of Philos' face, "The doctor took Dismas away. My son could still be alive!"

CHAPTER 31
THE SEARCH BEGINS

-NESTOR-

Baruch and Apphia were gracious hosts. In the weeks following our arrival, we used the time to get ourselves in order, cleaned up, and well-nourished for what lay before us. What exactly that was, neither of us knew. But knowing my Dismas was out there somewhere consumed my every thought.

I looked over to the desk and saw the shackles and chains that were part of me for nineteen years. My wrists were no longer bound and the many scars on my arms continued to fade. I was free. Baruch wanted to throw them away, Philos agreed, but I wanted mine. I don't know why. Perhaps to remind me of where I had been and what God had done for me. I scooped up the links in my hands and said, "Vena, I am free now." Deep down, however, I found myself thinking, *"Are you truly free?"* Physically, yes, but not from my own mind. *"Not until I find my son,"* I thought. After placing the chains inside my travel bag, I walked to the window overlooking the grounds.

Philos went outside periodically to speak to the people who gathered at the gate of Baruch's home. I watched from the window above, seeing the impact his words had on them. They turned, one by one, toward the one true God; the God of Abraham, Isaac, and Jacob. Baruch and Apphia had given us basic knowledge of the Jewish God through our conversations these last weeks. Greeks, once absorbed by the intricate web of deities, each came to bow before the King of all gods.

My eyes locked onto one of the patrons. A woman, holding her baby, edging forward to receive a blessing from Philos. The baby was wrapped in cloth with his or her face barely exposed. My imagination transformed the scene to be Vena holding our child. I caught myself smiling at the thought.

A knock at my door jarred me back to reality.

"Yes," I called.

A muffled voice responded. It was one of the servant girls, "Master Baruch awaits you downstairs."

"All right. Thank you. I will be there shortly."

I turned back to look down at Philos ministering to the small crowd. Some of them were people we had already blessed but they wanted more. Some had questions. They wanted to be taught the ways of the Jewish God. We, however, were not rabbis, and there was no Jewish temple to send them to. My eyes slowly diverted to the Sea of Galilee. The city of Hippus, situated on a high peak hundreds of feet above, overlooked the sea. I saw the small fishing boats out in the water and the docks that harbored them. The sun glistening, conjured up a mental image of sparkling diamonds moving in the palm of God's mighty hand.

I descended the marble staircase, noting the rich brown veins running through the polished rock. The stone railing had a rough texture against my palm, yet still elegant in design with its flowery carvings. Baruch stood in the center of a tiled mural of the sun positioned in the entryway of his luxurious home. He was speaking to one of the guards. Baruch motioned him away once he saw me coming.

Baruch smiled broadly, "Ah, it is a blessing to have you here, Holy Man of God."

He liked to call me this name even though I had repeatedly told him not to. I sighed and didn't correct him.

"I have news for you," he continued.

I quickly made my way down the stairs, bypassing several steps. "News? My son?"

"Perhaps."

"What is it?" I asked excitedly.

"Well, it has been nineteen years so getting information is quite a challenge. The doctor you mentioned, you did not get his name, correct?"

"Yes, that is correct. It was someone that lived in our community and he came to help us when Vena was having difficulties and experiencing early labor. I never got his name."

"This is as I thought. So, I had someone look at the magistrate's records. Unfortunately, there was no documentation at the time to monitor a citizens act of service to the community *but*," he paused.

"But what?"

"The magistrate had a friend in your area at that time who was a doctor. He moved soon after the demons came about. He could be the one who helped you, but no one truly knows."

"Did the magistrate know where he moved?"

"The last he heard, it was a town not too far away, called Dion. It is a two-day walk."

"Good. Philos and I will leave immediately."

"Wait, let me send one of my men with you."

"No, Baruch, that is not necessary. God is on our side. He set us free and he will show us the way and protect us."

"Yes, of course he will. I apologize for my lack of faith in him."

I looked appreciatively at Baruch and said, "Don't be sorry. Be thankful. The Messiah has come and soon things will change for everyone."

"Yes, yes. Jesus of Nazareth. We are hearing good reports from the region. Miracles abound around him. Our prayers are that he will come to Decapolis."

I smiled and grabbed hold of his shoulder in acknowledgment of his prayer. Just then Philos entered.

Rushing to him in excitement, I said, "I have great news, Philos."

"Good morning. What is it?"

"Baruch found the doctor."

"Maybe," Baruch quickly corrected.

"No, it's him. It has to be. Come, we leave now."

"Now? But where are we going?"

"To Dion."

I opened the front door to see the great crowd still out there, hands lunging toward me. People were reaching to be helped by us, shouting, "Bless me." I shut the door and turned around, catching the eye of Philos. I simply had no capacity to bless anyone for my heart was solely on Dismas.

Baruch said, "There is a back way. But please, before you leave, I will have my servants wrap food for your travel and blankets to keep you warm during the night."

Baruch clapped his hands twice. A servant standing close by turned quickly and ran to prepare the items.

"Come, this way." We followed Baruch and as we reached the back door, the same servant had in hand a satchel of food and blankets. I smiled as she handed me the bag. Her eyes remained diverted as she bowed slightly.

Baruch pointed to walking staffs leaning against the building.

"Thank you, Baruch, for everything," I said as I grabbed one.

"It is my pleasure, Holy Man of God."

We smiled and were off, with hoods shielding our faces and walking staffs in our hands. We were two followers of Jesus pursuing something that, to most, would seem to be impossible. But hadn't our transformation just weeks earlier been considered impossible? Nothing, absolutely nothing, was impossible for God, and I anchored my hope and faith in that reality. Our testimony bore witness to it and demolished any doubt.

"Slow down, my friend," Philos said.

I snapped back to my surroundings and stopped to look at him. "My apologies. I was lost in thought."

"Yes, I know. I've been asking you questions for the last mile."

"Forgive me, Philos. I—."

"It's okay, my friend. I am with you. But let's do this together. I would hate to enter the next city *alone.*"

We both chuckled. I sat on a nearby rock under a thicket of trees. Philos joined me and pulled out the small sack he carried.

"Let's see what Baruch graciously provided. Ah, we have some dried meat, nuts, and...and I don't know what this is but I'm sure it's good. Here, you try it."

I smiled and took the food. It was a type of dried fruit that had a pleasant taste I couldn't quite discern. Philos watched me carefully to see if I was going to gag. I gave him a nod of approval, "You will definitely like this, whatever it is."

That was all he needed to hear before taking a bite, which elicited moans of enjoyment. "This is wonderful," he said. "Why is food so much better now than before? It's like I am tasting everything for the first time."

"Well, we were gone for quite a long time. I remember the taste of blood constantly in my mouth during our imprisonment."

"Yes, I guess so," Philos said. I could see the memory of the blood made him uncomfortable.

I changed the subject, "Come, let us continue on." I took a swig of water from the skin and handed it to Philos. He took a sip, capped it, and then we were back on the road with many miles still ahead of us.

Mile after mile came and went. We inquired from passersby how far we were from Dion. With that information, we estimated that we could press on and enter the town late that night.

I could feel Philos wanting to ask me to slow down, but he never said a word, keeping pace with me. I was anxious to get closer and to be able to search for the doctor at first light.

Faint lights in the distance alerted us to the city of Dion. The moon was barely visible behind the dense cloud cover blocking its light.

Roman guards greeted us at the gated entry. "What's your business?"

"Our apologies, we have come from Hippus."

"Why so late? You know there are bandits along the road don't you?"

I looked at Philos, who shrugged. I turned back to the guards and said, "We did not."

Another guard said, "No one travels at night. Everyone in the region knows that. We are on the outskirts, and most who dare to travel at dark are robbed of all their belongings, or worse. What is your business here?"

"My name is Nestor and this is Philos. We are looking for someone."

"Who?"

"A doctor who moved here many years ago."

"Are you sick?" He took a step backward and looked at me with suspicion. "Remove your hoods," he suddenly commanded.

We did as instructed. "We meant no disrespect. We traveled all day and only wish to find shelter for the night so we can start fresh in the morning."

He looked at us, squinting his eyes. "Show us your arms."

"Why, might I ask?" We did as he said. The guards scrutinized our arms. One was holding a torch, while two others looked closely at our fading scars and the white rings on our wrists where the light of the sun had not weathered because of our shackles.

"Been reports of lepers and we don't want their kind here." He looked back at his comrades, "They are clear."

The older guard responded, "Well, let them through, you idiot."

"You may enter. Welcome to Dion."

"Thank you, and may God bless you."

We began to walk through when the guard suddenly said, "In the name of what god do you bless us? We worship Dusares, chief pantheon god equal to Zeus. We only accept blessings from him."

I looked at Philos and then back to the soldier. He was older than the others. Heavier, his chin was profoundly squared and covered with thick stubble, gray in patches.

Philos calmly said, "We bless you with the Jewish God of Abraham, Isaac, and Jacob. God has sent us the Messiah and his name is Jesus of Nazareth."

One of the younger guards spouted, "I have heard of this Jesus, Captain."

"Where?"

"I came through Capernaum and was stationed there but a month ago. We had seen the great crowds that follow this Jesus. And…," he paused.

"And what, Antonius?"

"And we saw things."

"What things?"

"There were reports that this Jesus of Nazareth could heal the sick."

"That is absurd."

"No," Antonius said defiantly. It appeared that this young boy, probably the same age as my son, had been affected by what he had seen. "No, it's true. We had passed one of those lepers one day on the side of the road. I remember looking at this poor soul who was going to die. I looked into his eyes and saw the hopelessness he carried. I saw the rotting flesh falling off his face. His soul longed to be set free. If I could have, I would have run him through myself to relieve him of his pain. I would not go near him or break rank from our march, but I remember."

"What happened?" I asked.

The young guard looked at me and said, "I saw the same man days later walking past us as we marched. He saw me and smiled. I saw life in him. The leprosy had vanished. He had all new skin but it was his eyes that confirmed to me that it was the same man."

"You are certain?" another guard asked, visibly moved by the testimony.

"Yes. It was him."

The older one said skeptically, "How do you know it was the same Jesus?"

"The man who was healed was yelling excitedly that Jesus had healed him. He claimed that Jesus was the Messiah."

It was silent for several seconds. Philos stepped forward and said, "There is another story."

Everyone turned to look at Philos.

"Jesus of Nazareth sailed across the Sea of Galilee to land on the shore of the Gerasenes. He was in search of two men who were possessed by demons."

I saw how the mention of demons affected the guards. They shifted uncomfortably, looking at one another.

Philos continued, "These demons knew Jesus and ran toward him begging for mercy. They called Jesus the Son of God and asked to be cast into a nearby herd of pigs. With but a word, Jesus said, "Go," and they went. His disciples clothed the men who were now free from the demons. They fed them, and Jesus, the Son of God, sent the men back to their town to tell of all that the Lord had done."

"How do you know this story?" the captain asked.

Philos looked at him long and hard before saying, "We are those two men."

The soldiers took a step back and grabbed the hilt of their weapons. They were visibly afraid.

Philos stepped forward with his hands out, "You asked which god we bless you with. We have been set free by a loving God, by the Son of God. His name is Jesus. It is through his name that we bless you."

Antonius, the younger soldier, edged forward while the others looked at him incredulously.

"What are you doing?" the captain asked.

"I have to. I have seen with my eyes and I cannot deny it. This god of the Jews is like nothing I have ever seen." With that, he turned and fell to his knees, "Bless me, holy men of God."

I watched the captain. Something was happening inside of him. He was battling something in his mind. I don't know why, but I pressed him.

"You have seen much over your years, have you not?" I asked.

His eyes darted to mine and then to his men, then back again.

"We were lost to demons but now we stand before you today."

He stuttered, "It is not possible."

"Nothing is impossible with God."

"You don't understand. I have seen much. I have...done much."

I pressed in, "What is it that holds you?"

His eyes continued to dart back and forth between me and his men.

"What is it?" I asked again.

He burst out, "I didn't want to kill those children!"

We had not expected to hear such a claim come from him. I looked at Philos in shock. His eyes were wide as well.

The captain fell to his knees. His hands were out, fingers contorted like a statue, unmoving, as tears began to stream down his face. "I didn't want to. I had to follow orders."

I was uncertain as to what to do next. What should I say?

He slowly lifted his hands, looked at his palms, and said, "The blood on my hands. I am eternally damned."

"No," I said and fell to my knees in front of him, grabbing his hands. "No, that is not true. God took the demons from us. God healed that leper. God can heal you also."

"I murdered those children. Don't you understand? Their blood is on my hands. What god can heal that?" He stood, turned, and walked back into the dark night. We could hear the captain from the darkness that swallowed him, "There is no god that can take this blood from my hands."

I had no words. One man received God and the man next to him would not. Two other soldiers stood by watching everything unfold until finally turning to follow their captain back to their post.

It was hard for me to fathom the depth of God's forgiveness. I couldn't know each man's heart, each man's experience, each man's journey. A soldier required to do a horrible act in the name of their commander. A father who abandons his son. This world would certainly condemn both. This world brings judgment and condemnation. The God of the Jews brings mercy and forgiveness. And for this, I am forever grateful.

On this strange night, we witnessed the power of choice that is set before all men. Light or darkness. Life or death. There is no in-between and it is a choice that every man must face. There is no exception.

My thoughts for my son were now stronger than ever. *"I WILL find you, Dismas. I know in my heart that one day we will be face-to-face; father and son. I swear it."*

CHAPTER 32
THE DOCTOR

-NESTOR-

PHILOS AND I made our way into town. Being that it was very early and still dark, we eventually settled behind a merchant cart in the dark streets of Dion. It was early morning, too early yet to inquire about where to stay. Our spirits were high until the break of sunlight first appeared and Philos was stung by a scorpion while folding our blankets. This yellow scorpion, five-striped and smooth-tailed, was indigenous in the region. It could be deadly to children and the aged, bringing great pain. Even the healthiest of men have fallen to the grave because of this deadly arachnida.

Philos yelled in great pain, thus alerting the owner of the cart in the adjacent home. A gaunt man, still in his night robe opened the door and peered out at us.

"What is the matter?" he asked with concern.

"Deathstalker! We need a physician!"

"Oh! I-I-I…"

"Do you know of one? We just arrived in town."

"There are several but I only know of one who can cure that kind of sting."

"Take us!" I commanded anxiously.

He went back inside but soon came back with his cloak wrapped around him. Philos' olive complexion was turning white. "Can you stand?" I asked him.

Philos didn't answer. Instead, he tried to stand, but wobbled. The stranger and I caught him. Together, Philos leaning between us, we led him through the narrow streets of Dion, oblivious to the scope of this large town. We passed a contingent of Roman soldiers and I surmised this was a military town of some importance.

We crossed a stone bridge that spanned a fast-moving river and then went through another gate leading outside Dion. More guards watched as we ushered Philos, still clinging to our shoulders, out of the town. They did not say a word as they looked on intently.

"Where are you taking us?" I asked the stranger. The merchant's breath was labored as Philos' feet slowed the further we went, putting more pressure on us.

"It's not far. Samuel lives outside the town. He keeps to himself but he will help."

I couldn't argue, silently praying for my friend, gripped by the poison running through his body. His leg muscles spasmed and tightened. We were ultimately forced to drag Philos along the rocky shale, over the desert shrubs sprouting up from cracked stone. The merchant and I hiked for close to an hour to find the doctor. Sweat dripped down my face and my legs were ready to give out.

The stranger's labored voice said, "We are here."

Philos' head slumped to my shoulder and I could feel his entire body go limp, causing the merchant and me to carry the additional weight. My adrenaline would not let me slow down.

"Just a little further, Philos. Stay with me." This was my lifelong friend and I would not lose him also. Not to anything.

We came around a bend into a spectacular view of the valley looking east—golden dunes as far as I could see. Desert flowers of all colors bloomed along the cliff walls with clusters of green olive trees throughout. There was a single dwelling along a small plateau that blended into the rock wall. The home was dark, but brightened by colorful plants growing inside pots and wooden boxes placed around the dwelling. I could smell the fire burning and saw a small amount of smoke coming from the roof.

"Samuel!" the man called. "Sam, help!"

Suddenly an older man with gray hair and beard appeared in the doorway, wiping his hands with a rag. His eyes squinted to search out the source of the one calling his name.

"Rue? Is that you?"

"Yes, my friend, it is I. This man was stung by a Deathstalker and needs your attention."

"Bring him inside. Quickly." His voice was firm and without panic.

There was a single bed in the corner of the small room. Samuel pointed and we rested Philos on it. I realized that Philos was sweating more than I was. The old man edged closer to get a better look. He stood and pulled the leather drape away from the window to allow more light. He placed his hand on Philos' forehead, then knelt lower, placing his ear to his chest, listening to his heart for several beats.

The doctor looked up at us. "The yellow scorpion has taken many lives but will not take this one today."

I let out my breath and said, "He will live, then?"

"That is what I said. Now, I need to give him some herbal medicine to reduce the fever and I have some other remedies to extract the poison from his system. He will need to rest a full day though."

"Whatever you need. How can I help?"

"Just stay out of my way," he said, now set on the task.

Rue and I moved away and watched the physician gather what he needed, mix medicinals, pour boiling water into a cup and mix some more. Finally, he lifted Philos' head and gave him a sip of the medicine. Sam then formed a paste and placed it directly on the sting on Philos' wrist, then wrapped a bandage around it. I spotted Samuel taking notice of the scars on Philos' arm.

He caught me looking at him and said, "There. Now he must rest."

The merchant and I sat on the floor as there were no chairs in this hovel. There was a stove, a few cooking pots, various items a physician would use, and a bed.

"Rue, how long has it been?" Samuel asked.

"Months, I'd say."

They quickly embraced.

Rue retracted and said, "I'm sorry for the intrusion, but these men were outside my home when this one was stung. You are the only one who has dealt with such things, so I brought him here. My apologies."

"Oh, no apologies necessary. I was just thinking how I wished to have some company and then you arrived. So, do your friends have names?"

"I just met them. In light of the situation, we never exchanged names."

"Oh, so these men *were* literally outside your home. I thought you knew them."

I stood and said, "My name is Nestor and this is my friend Philos."

Sam's eyes suddenly widened and he took a step back as if seeing a ghost.

"What is it?" Rue asked.

It was then, in response to Samuel's startled reaction that I recognized the man who helped attempt to bring my son into the world. Older and grayer, this Samuel was the doctor from that night nineteen years ago. My eyes began to tear up.

"How is this possible?" Sam whispered.

I said simply, "God has intervened."

"I recognize your eyes. It truly *is* you."

"Where is my son?"

"Your son? I know not."

"What happened to him? You must know something."

He sighed and then said, "Come. Let's talk outside while your friend rests. I will explain all that I know and you will do the same."

We sat on a makeshift stone bench that ran along the front of the home, overlooking the valley.

"This is where I spend my time, looking upon the beauty of this land. But today, I feel like I'm dreaming to see you here and in sound mind, Nestor."

"In reality, I feel the same."

"That time was beyond anything I had ever seen. You transformed into something that was...no longer you. I don't know how to describe it."

"Philos and I were overtaken by demons."

Rue and Sam exchanged a quick glance. Sam said, "You say it so casually. These are things mere men do not speak of."

"I know, but it is what happened."

"It was because of the witch doctor your friend brought back," Sam concluded.

"Yes, we believe so."

"No, I know so. She became well-known for her sorcery after your encounter. I fled Hippus with my wife after that event. I have been here ever since. My wife died two years ago right on this spot and I built my home here."

"I'm sorry," unable to focus on his personal loss. "I need to know. What of my son? Where did you take him?"

Again, Samuel exchanged a look with his friend, Rue. Sam took a deep breath, preparing to recall that morning, exhaled, and said, "After the Romans took you away, my wife and I took your son to friends of ours in a small town called Gergesa. A few miles away from Hippus."

"Yes, I know of it. Uh, pig farms or something."

"That's right. I took him to the owner of those farms. His name is Karpos. Karpos Sedontin, a Greek family. He and his wife, Dora, took your son in as their own. They already had a crippled two-year-old boy. They never asked about where your son came from and I never told them."

"Do you know if he still lives?"

"That was the last I saw of him. We moved away the next day. Staying weighed too heavily on our hearts and minds. It is hard to undo the horror of what my wife and I saw that night. Yet here you are standing before me." Sam looked at me from head to feet, gesturing with his hands. "What... how is this possible?"

I cleared my throat, looked out over the valley, and said, "A few days ago, Philos and I headed to Dion to search for a doctor who might have known what happened to my son. We then found a place to rest for a few hours beside a merchant cart in the street, where Philos was stung and poisoned. Then the man who owns the cart told us he knew of only one person who could help and he led us to this remote place. Philos and I were greatly worn and desperate, but you and Rue helped us. And then we find that you were the doctor we sought from the beginning. It is a miracle, don't you think?" I looked at Sam.

"What are you saying, Nestor?"

"What am I saying? I'm saying it is a miracle from God. He orchestrates the heavens and the earth and all the inhabitants from the beginning, up to now and beyond. The more my journey unfolds, the more I see his work." I looked back to the valley, "I know that my son is still alive. Do you know what name they gave him?"

"I kept the same name you told me if it was to be a boy. You wanted that name specifically and instructed me not to reveal it to your wife until you told her after the birth. I told Karpos and Dora that his name is Dismas. I remember Dora's face brightened when I said the name but I do not know for certain if they kept it."

"Dismas," I whispered.

"How did you escape the demons?"

"I didn't escape. Philos and I were set free."

I looked at Rue and the doctor, who were confused by my statement. I smiled and said, "A man by the name of Jesus came and set us free."

Sam, puzzled, responded, "A man?"

"Not just a man. God had sent Jesus to us. With a word he sent the demons away."

Samuel said, "I have not heard of this Jesus."

"I have," Rue responded. "He came from a town called Nazareth and reports of miracles have trickled in from many travelers. To be honest, I didn't believe, until now."

Just then I heard a familiar voice, "Nestor, are you ready to find your son?"

We looked to see Philos standing outside the home. It had been less than a few hours since the doctor administered the medicine. The fever was gone, his face was normal, and he stood strong.

Sam said, "What is happening? You should not be standing."

"Yet, here I am, kind doctor."

Rue said emphatically, "It's a miracle! It truly is a miracle!"

Samuel was partially smiling, but clearly shocked as his friend grabbed his arm and shook it with excitement.

Rue said, "Tell us all you know about this Jesus. What I have heard and now have seen! I must know the message he speaks."

I said, "We have heard that he heals the sick and we know firsthand he sends demons to flight with a single word. It is said he is the Messiah."

Rue said, "I will travel back to Hippus with you, for I plan on finding this Jesus of Nazareth and encountering him face-to-face. When I find him and he blesses me, I will bring his blessing back to Dion."

I smiled, looked at Philos, who was also smiling. What God was doing in and through us was unbelievable. Baruch and Apphia, the crowds, a Roman soldier, and now a businessman and physician in the far reaches of Decapolis.

Getting to the small town of Gergesa loomed before anything else. My son, Dismas, was there. After nineteen years he would finally meet his father.

CHAPTER 33
AN EMPTY HOME

-NESTOR-

WE ROLLED INTO Hippus on carts pulled by horses. Rue had a large business importing high quality carpets from his native land, Arabia. He had many contacts in the far regions. We rode up to the entrance of Baruch's palace and, upon recognizing us, his personal guards opened the gates.

Baruch rushed out to greet us, "Welcome back, holy men of God."

Smiling, I said, "It is good to see you. Let me introduce you to our new friend—"

Before I could say anything Baruch broke away, arms open wide, a joyful smile upon his face, and greeted Rue excitedly, "My friend! How is this possible?"

"Baruch, you know of these men?" Rue asked surprised.

"Yes, of course. I know every man." They both laughed heartily.

"Nestor, Nestor," Rue said, "this man truly does know everyone. He is one of the best I have encountered when it comes to business. Shrewd mind, big heart."

"Ah, you are too kind, Rue. Nestor, this man, oh, this man, how can I say it without weeping? This man, he knows what to say and when to say it. He brought me great comfort during a painful time in my life."

"It is you who are too kind, Baruch. Where is your wife? I must see that she is well-taken care of and, if not, then I will take her from you."

They both laughed and Baruch said, "Come in, come in. We will find her and have her give you the report firsthand. I must hear about how your meeting with Nestor and Philos came to be. This is a spectacular day."

Philos and I watched the two friends walk away, oblivious to the fact that Philos and I were not following them. I yelled out to get Baruch's attention. They stopped and turned around confused that we were still standing where they had left us. "What is the matter?" Baruch asked.

"Philos and I are going to Gergesa."

"Yes, but now? It is time to eat and hear stories. Gergesa will be there in the morning just the same."

"I'm afraid I can't wait—my son—I need to find him."

Baruch nodded, as did Rue. "We will pray for your travel and for your journey to find your son."

"Thank you," I said, giving a slight bow.

"One other thing, holy men. These people that continue to come daily, they need someone to teach them the Jewish ways of God. Might you spend some time teaching them upon your return with your son?"

"Baruch, we are Greeks. You are the Jew. Is there not someone you know that you can call upon to assist? Our knowledge is but testimony deep and we look forward to learning, as well."

"Ah, yes, of course. I will look into it. There is a rabbi in Capernaum I could possibly call upon."

Rue said, "This is a good idea. I plan on traveling to Capernaum in hopes of seeing this Jesus of Nazareth. Let us travel together, my friend."

"Wonderful! Let us make our plan over a meal." Baruch and Rue entered the home.

With that, Philos and I left on foot and began the second leg of our journey. Gergesa, also known as Ghasa to the locals, was not far from Hippus, only a few miles. We were able to move fast and leave behind a small crowd of people who tried to follow us. They would eventually catch up in Ghasa, but we hoped to find Karpos and his family beforehand and avoid any further delay. *His family?* I thought. It was odd that I thought in that manner. Dismas was not his family but I came to be thankful to Karpos for taking care of my son. For treating Dismas as his own.

A few hundred people resided there. Most worked the swine farms or the marketplace, sometimes both. Less than a mile away from Ghasa was where Philos and I were under the control of the demon, Legion, for the last nineteen years. I felt a little uneasy at first but settled myself by keeping my mind focused on finding my boy. My search for Dismas anchored me. I fear that, without this pursuit, I would fall victim to the darkness once again. It was like it was dormant in the back of my mind, a dark assailant waiting to strike with its blade called 'Shame'.

Philos gently grabbed my shoulder, jarring me from my thought. "Dismas will be there," he said.

I nodded, grateful for his encouragement.

It was late afternoon when we entered the town. The marketplace appeared to be closing down but the activity was overridden by a heavy somberness permeating the area. Something had happened that seemed to have dramatically affected the people. Their faces were serious, devoid of joy.

I approached a young man closing up his makeshift cart filled with silks of all colors. His beard was short and I wasn't sure what lineage he was when he turned to face me. His eyebrows were sharply defined and the right brow spiked as he contemplated who we might be.

"Shop is closed," he said definitively.

"My apologies. We are in search of the Karpos family."

"Karpos?" his head tilted slightly to the left. "I have only been here for a few weeks."

"We are sorry for intruding," I began to back away with a slight bow.

"Do you know that he is dead?" the tall, thin merchant responded.

I stopped and looked at Philos with concern.

"What do you speak of?"

"This Karpos you are looking for. He is dead."

"I thought you didn't know of him?" Philos interjected.

"I never said that." This man's voice was sharp. Every syllable pronounced with an edge.

"Tell us what you know, for we were hopeful to find him. What about his wife?"

"That I don't know. I can tell you that Karpos was the former owner of Ghasa farms."

"Former? Well, who owns it now?"

"I believe his name is Clavius."

"Clavius," I slowly repeated. "Do you know where he resides?"

"I've not seen him personally but I believe Aetolos would be able to assist you with more information." He pointed down the tight street that meandered through the small town and indicated an older gentleman of about forty years.

Philos said, "Good day to you and may God bless you."

We hurried to the man. He spotted us approaching him hastily and stood his ground waiting for our apparent assault. Before we spoke, he raised his hands and closed his eyes, "Your complaints of faulty craftmanship are no good here. My son has done incredible work for many, from the Pashas in Arabia to the Roman elite in Jerusalem. Turn around before I call the guards."

"We are not here to complain."

He looked at us a bit puzzled and said, "You're not?"

"No, we were told you know who Clavius is and where we can find him."

"Clavius?" His eyes darted left and right.

"Yes, do you know him?"

"Have we met before?" He looked right at me with a strange look on his face.

I looked over at Philos and then turned to him and said, "I don't believe so."

"Your face and your eyes. They look familiar."

Philos said, "Clavius? We must find him."

He broke away from me to look at Philos, "Why are you looking for him?"

"He might have information as to where my son is."

Aetolos looked at me again, long and hard, squinting his eyes. *"What did he see? Had this man seen my son and perhaps recognized similarities?"*

"Do you know?" Philos asked.

"He left his home weeks ago, once the farm fell."

"The farm we are not concerned with. What of Clavius?"

"No farm, no money. No money, no Clavius. Now do you understand?"

I looked around the marketplace and finally noticed that people were scarce. Cart owners were closing early while it was still light.

"Does the marketplace close early on these days?"

"Early? No, these poor souls are leaving."

"Leaving? What do you mean?"

"Leaving, as in not coming back. Moving on. Without the farm, there is no town. Ghasa is dying."

"Karpos. What do you know of him?" I asked.

"Karpos? Who are you? Why do you speak of the dead?"

"What of his wife? Is she still here?" I pleaded.

He scoffed and shook his head in unbelief, "You know nothing, strangers. These are hard times. Best to leave the Karpos family alone. There is no one left." He turned away.

I grabbed him. "You know something and all we ask is for simple information." Our faces were close together as I clutched his tunic in desperation.

"Let go of me!" he yelled while trying to pry my hands away.

I did, realizing my anger had gotten the best of me. "My apologies. I just need to find them."

"Find them? Okay, you want to know where his wife is? I will take you to her. Come."

I looked at Philos and then we both chased after the man, who walked hastily. We headed toward the Sea of Galilee, to a small homestead in the distance overlooking the sea. To the right was farmland with larger corrals, now empty. The smell of manure strengthened. It was not a fresh smell, but stagnant, old, and rotting.

As we approached, I noticed the home was in disrepair. Broken pots littered the ground near a window that held a shredded dirty cloth waving gently. The front door was broken and laid on the ground partly perched against the structure where it fell. A dining table with broken legs and chairs were piled outside. There was an overwhelming feeling of emptiness. It was abandoned.

"There is no one here," I said.

Aetolos turned and said, "Oh, there is someone. The wife of Karpos." He kept walking toward the back of the home, around the side.

The man brought us directly to a grave. "Here she is. Dora. Wife of Karpos. You go ahead and let her know what you need." He then stormed off back the way he came.

He stopped and yelled, "She might have difficulty talking to you since the Romans slit her throat for all to see."

Philos and I stared at the grave. I fell to my knees and wept. The Karpos family was dead, along with my hopes of locating Dismas.

Through tears and with a strained voice I said, "What about my son? What about my son?"

Philos knelt down and comforted me. "We will find him, Nestor."

Something crashed inside the home. It caused us both to quickly stand. We heard someone inside moving about. "Who goes there?" Philos called.

Another crash, like a chair toppling over, then sandals sliding across a stone floor. We made our way to the front of the house and approached through the open doorway. It was dark inside with the diminishing sunlight casting eerie shadows.

Philos called again, "Come out!"

"You stay away!" a voice responded.

I walked further inside the home. It was in shambles. The few remaining furnishings were thrown about. It was bare, with only remnants of the life once lived within these walls. We heard more movement in the bedroom to our left. The curtained divider waved gently back and forth in the slight breeze that came funneling through.

"We come in peace," I said.

"Stay away!"

I slowly entered the dark chamber. Dim light came from a half-draped window. The soft wind fluttered the fabric gently. A shadow of a man lay crumpled on the ground, entangled in the legs of a chair. He tensed as he saw me enter.

"I killed them. I killed them all," the man whispered in the dark.

"We mean you no harm. We came to look for the family that lived here," I said softly, with my hands out in a display of peace.

"Everyone is gone," he said.

His leg was wrapped between the crossbars of the bottom of the chair. Tentative, I edged my way closer and reached out to assist him.

He kicked violently, "Keep away from me!" The chair broke, freeing his leg. He pushed himself to the back wall and brought his knees up to his chest, clutching them tightly.

Philos pulled the drape off the window causing more light to flood into the room.

"No!" he said in reaction. His emotional state changed like the tide. Mumbling, he said, "I'm sorry, so, so, sorry. Please forgive me. I..."

"It's okay. We only want to help," I tried to appease.

The shadow was still cast over his face, but I could see that his clothes were dirty. The brambles caught throughout his robe indicated that he had been out in the open for some time.

"Who are you?" Philos asked.

"I'm nobody, now. Just leave me be."

"We can get you food and water," Philos came closer.

"Just leave me alone! Just...kill me already!"

"Kill you?" I said. "We are not here to kill you."

"But, why? You are them. That is what you do."

"We are who?"

He began to laugh or cry or perhaps both and then he said, "You play with me."

Philos looked at me and whispered, "He called us 'them'. I think he recognizes who we were before."

"Could it be?" This man must have known us somehow as the demon men who lived in the tombs. If only I could see his face more clearly.

"We are free now. We are no longer possessed," I said.

"You lie! You killed my pigs and now have come for me."

"Are you the owner of the farm?"

"Owner," he chuckled. "I own nothing, not even my heart. I beg of you to rip it out of me like the others."

"You don't understand. We are no longer those monsters. Jesus of Nazareth set us free."

"If you won't kill me, then go away and let me be."

I looked at Philos and shrugged, not knowing what to say or how to get through to this man. He was filled with so much sorrow. What pain had we caused this soul? No, not us, but the demons named Legion.

"We can help to restore the farm again, somehow," I said, not truly understanding why I said it, for we had no money.

"Get out!" the man yelled with all his strength. He leaned forward, his face entered the full sunlight. Veins strained and protruded along his neck. His cracked lips were slightly bleeding. I *had* seen this face before. Images flashed inside my mind. Horrific images. I heard Legion's voice as the memory flooded in, *"I will kill them. All of them."* Then I saw the face of a desert nomad, his eyes wide in horror, my arm through his body. In my grip I held this nomad's heart. It beat in my hand, as blood sloshed off of me. I saw so much blood. Then the vision went away just as quickly as it had come. I gasped for air as I came out of the trance.

This familiar-faced man lunged at me, tackling me to the ground. I smelled the alcohol on his breath as he snarled at me in rage. "Kill me!" he yelled. "Just kill me!"

His hands clutched my throat. As he squeezed, all I could do was look into his rage-filled eyes. I had done this to him. Not me, but this flesh I live in. It had been used to hurt people, many people, including this man. I couldn't put all the pieces together of who this person was, but perhaps it was justified for him to take my life in order for him to feel some kind of relief. Perhaps my death would transform this man's heart. I didn't resist. I laid there with him atop me, crushing my windpipe. I felt my body slowly shutting down.

The darkness lying in wait in the recesses of my mind began to flow over my consciousness. There was nothing but death in this place. My son was not here. I no longer wanted to be here either.

Philos wrapped his arm around the man's neck and yanked him off me. I felt air suddenly enter my lungs and gasped for breath. There was a crash as both men dropped to the ground. Then it was still. Philos had twisted the man backwards and landed on top of him. My friend slowly pulled away and stood, but the man wasn't moving.

"Philos?" I could barely speak. My throat throbbed in pain as I tried to massage it.

"I only pulled him free from you."

"Check to see if he is okay," I managed to say, sitting up and trying to catch my breath.

Philos knelt and slowly rolled the man over. He gasped when he saw the blood pooling underneath. One of the broken pieces of the chair had stabbed him in the stomach and was embedded deep.

"Philos!" I said.

I scrambled to the stranger's side and we looked the wound over together. We knew there was nothing we could do as we helplessly watched blood gush out of the sides of the wooden stake. The man was gurgling and looking at us while concentrating on his final breaths.

"Please, God. Don't let this man die," I said.

The man was trying to say something and I leaned down to hear him.

Under shallow breath, I heard him say, "Dis...mas. I did...n't know." He exhaled one final breath and died.

There was nothing but silence for a few moments. I closed his eyelids, then looked at Philos.

"I'm sorry, Nestor. I didn't mean—"

"It's not your fault, Philos." I was in shock myself.

"What happened? Who was that man?" Philos questioned.

"I don't know," I said, having fallen into a stupor.

Several minutes elapsed before Philos finally said, "Come, we will bury this man and pray for his soul."

Hours passed as we sat at the foot of the grave next to Karpos' wife in the dark of night. We prayed and then sat in silence.

I finally said, "He knew my son."

"How do you know?"

"In his final words, he said "Dismas" but he also said he didn't know."

"Didn't know what?"

"That is a mystery. But he said my son's name. He said, 'Dismas.'"

More silence passed before I asked Philos, "What are we to do next?"

"God will show us, Nestor. We must believe."

"What happened here, Philos? I mean, what did the people who lived here go through? It seems that there was a great deal of pain and suffering. Yet there was once a family here raising children, raising my son. What happened to bring this home and this family to such devastation?"

"I don't know, Nestor." Philos stood. "But tomorrow could be the day."

There was something in my friend's voice. Something that was different. I heard hope.

"The day for what?" I asked him.

"It could be the day we find your son. We can't give up. We suffered at the hand of Legion for almost two decades and now we are here. We don't know what each day brings, but as each day ends, we must have hope that tomorrow could be the day."

His words penetrated my heart. Those five little words brought nourishment to my soul. I took a deep breath of the cool desert air. Looking at my friend and seeing the glint in his eye under the moonlight, I said, "Tomorrow could be the day."

CHAPTER 34
LOST AND FOUND

-NESTOR-

I AWOKE JUST BEFORE sunrise. We slept in the Karpos home, making do with what little we had, yet we felt like kings in our spirits. The mere thought of having come so far from where we had been brought us renewed energy and strength. Once we were controlled by demons and now, we were of sound mind and in search of Dismas.

My mind wandered. I realized that where I slept was where the children once slept. Could we actually be in the same house where Dismas played and learned and was cared for when he was five and ten years old? Or even a couple of years ago? I know that Dismas walked here. This was where he was raised. This was where he was loved. This was where he was fed and clothed. I was so thankful for this place and this family that I never knew. I pray that Karpos and his wife Dora were known amongst the people to be of good rapport.

"You can't sleep either?" Philos said.

"Dismas was here. This is the place God provided for him while I was gone for so long."

"It's strange to think about it in that way."

"My hope, Philos, is that we can find him and that he will tell us stories of his youth. It would fill my heart to hear of his exploits, good or bad."

"I'm sure it has been a grand adventure, one worthy to be told."

"I long to be a part of his story, Philos. I long for my son to know me and to let him know that God blessed him with two fathers."

We laid in silence for another hour and watched the sunlight begin to trickle in through the window. Smiling, I rose and said, "Today could be the day."

Philos got up also, echoing my words. We gathered our belongings, heading outside and handing one another food to eat as we walked.

"So, where to?" Philos asked.

"Come with me. I can't explain it."

We walked in the direction of the Sea of Galilee along a narrow trail.

Philos said behind me, "Nestor? Where are you taking us?"

"I dare not say, just trust me."

Philos followed, quickly understanding that I was taking him to the very place he thought he would never see again. I, too, had thought that, but there was something inside of me pulling me back to our prison cell of nineteen years.

"Why here?"

"Not certain, my friend," I said, as I kicked some loose rocks at the foot of the cave opening.

Philos said, "I find it strange being here. I know every detail of this area and yet it feels like a distant memory, not a recent reality."

I looked out onto the Sea of Galilee. I closed my eyes, slowly listening to the seabirds and the water lapping against the pebbled shore. I opened my eyes and began walking down the steep incline toward the water. Philos followed without a word. Within minutes we stood twenty feet from the shore.

I saw the remains of the campfire where Jesus and his disciples had shared their food with us. Replaying these memories over in my mind disrupted the horrific memories that attempted to infiltrate my thoughts. I sat down to rest on a large rock and let the memory of our encounter with Jesus wash over me.

No words were shared. They were unnecessary. We both began to pick up small rocks and toss them toward the sea. They clattered on the shoreline and then splashed as they hit the water.

"I wonder, Philos, if Dismas ever found out that I was his father."

"Well, I look forward to asking him."

I looked over and gave him a slight smile, acknowledging his optimism. We would soon find Dismas.

"I *wonder*, Nestor, what Jesus is doing right now? He is somewhere out there."

I chuckled, recalling what Jesus had whispered to me at this very spot.

"Why are you laughing?"

"Jesus is probably skipping rocks on the water." I looked at Philos with a grin.

Philos smiled, "Perhaps so."

"Once we find Dismas, we will go to him together and follow in his steps. I will introduce my son to him."

"Yes, that will be a glorious moment. One that I will dream of as well."

We continued to throw rocks, one after another. The lull of the small waves washing ashore, the rhythm of the rattling stones rolling back and forth in the water, and the peaceful companionship of my longtime friend, soothed my mind.

"Can you believe we are here in this place and of sound mind?" Philos asked.

I chuckled, "No, my friend. It is too daunting to think of. That God would save us is unfathomable to my mind."

"It makes me wonder about others Jesus has set free. The Jews believe he is the Messiah that will bring freedom from the oppression caused by the Romans. What do you say? Do you think he will raise an army and march into battle?"

"I don't know. With a word he commands demons. I have no doubt that, with but a word, he could subdue the Romans."

"Yes, truly, truly."

We continued to throw rocks, mindlessly reaching down, grabbing and tossing, and then my hand felt something partially buried in the dirt that was softer, unlike stone. Curiously, I peered down. What I saw provoked me to dig the rest of it out.

Philos joked, "Did you find some silver?"

"I don't know." I pulled out a piece of wood half the size of my hand. I rubbed the dirt and sand away with my fingers the best I could before using my robe. After several seconds of wiping, I unwrapped it from my garment to see a lion figurine made of wood. Three of its legs and its tale had chipped off, but it was still easy to discern what it was. My finger slowly followed the scratch down the center of the body.

I whispered, "I did this."

"What are you talking about? You made this figure?"

"No, this scratch, I remember doing that."

"Where did it come from?"

I searched deep into my memory and sudden images of a young boy, about ten years of age, came into my vision. The boy had stood on this very shoreline. The images were sporadic and each flash revealed more of the story.

Flash. A boy backing away.

Flash. Boy swimming away.

Flash. I picked up the figure left behind at the edge of the water.

Flash. I scratched it with my fingernail. *Flash.*

"Nestor!" Philos was calling to me as I came back to reality. "Nestor! I'm here, I'm here!" Philos was patting my shoulders, bringing me reassurance. "What happened? You were in a trance and began to shake like you had a fever."

I jumped up, "I saw him, Philos! He was here!"

"Who?" Philos stood.

"He was here, Philos. This was his," I held it up to show him. "This belonged to Dismas."

"How can you be certain?"

I said more forcefully, "This was his."

"Okay, it was his, my friend. It was his," he said softly, trying to calm me down.

I sat and gazed upon the treasure I held in my hands. I examined it from all angles. I wanted to know this piece inside and out, every nuance of its carving, every crack, and scratch. *"Had my son carved this?"* I gazed longingly at all the worn edges, the intricacies, the imperfections. My son had owned this item, and God had brought me here to find it.

"Philos, another piece to our puzzle has been found. Another piece of my son's story has unfolded by the grace of God."

God's goodness overwhelmed me. I grabbed Philos and wept in his arms. Moments later, a realization came over me. I pushed back and said, "This means that Dismas saw me. He saw his real father, Philos. What should I do when I see him? I am ashamed of what I became."

"Don't be troubled by that. It was not your fault. You will be reunited with him and be able to tell him the truth. God rescued us. That is all that matters."

A loud voice called from above, behind us, "There you are! Hope I'm not intruding but I had to see this with my own eyes!"

A tall man with black and gray-peppered hair stood on the nearest rise. He had the familiar beige tunic wrapped in the Greek fashion with a dagger sheathed at his side. He smiled, and even in the distance, we could see his big bright teeth.

"My name is Max and I'm the best tracker in the region."

CHAPTER 35
THE WEIGHT

-NESTOR-

"So, you are the legendary Demons of Ghasa," Max said in a loud, boisterous voice. "I had heard of this miracle and came from Tiberias to see for myself. May I approach?"

I looked over at Philos and he shrugged. Before we could reply, the man boldly took the remaining steps down the path to stand in front of us. His eyes bore into mine.

"You look like him, just older."

I couldn't believe what I just heard. This man had seen Dismas. I could barely get the words out of my mouth, "You have seen my son."

"Yes, led him back home after his stint in Capernaum. Must have been over five years ago now."

"Do you know where he is?" I pleaded.

"Can't say that I do but for a price, I can help. I am the best tracker in the region."

"We have no money!" Philos said indignantly.

"That isn't the first time I've heard that. People always seem to find a way. Listen, I found your son before and I can find him again. I found you, didn't I?"

"Yes, how did you?"

"Well, you two leave a trail that my blind grandmother could follow, and oh, did I mention she has no legs?" He laughed heartily. "You two have made a name for yourselves, that is for certain."

"What do you speak of?"

"You have turned this entire area upside down. Between the pigs jumping off the cliff and this miracle with you two, Decapolis is spinning. Don't you realize what you brought to this area before your miraculous change?"

Philos and I shook our heads slowly.

"No, I take it you don't. You, or should I say the demons once within you, brought a strange stability to the region; stability motivated by fear. The demons controlled the Romans and now the Roman hive is confused. Once the hive comes to their senses, the area would have been better off if you two were still possessed and *here*," Max said, raising his arms out wide and swinging them as he looked around the area. "Now, I realize that this Jesus of Nazareth somehow released you from your imprisonment as the people have testified. I must confess he is building quite a name for himself across the land, but the Romans will be sure to strike him down soon enough."

I said, "Jesus will not be struck down. He commands demons and he will command the Romans."

Max paused and looked us over for a second, "Hmm, we shall see. I haven't quite figured him out just yet, but I do know the Romans will strike. That is for certain. Now, let's talk about your son, and how I can be of service to you. I have a feeling you won't let this opportunity pass by. You will find a way to pay me."

"I believe God will make a way for us," I said.

"That's the spirit!" Max slapped my shoulder. "God always makes a way. If I had customers with half your faith, I would be better off."

"You make no sense," Philos said.

"I make perfect sense. I provide a service, and you pay. Now, your god *has* provided a way, and that is me." Max placed his right hand on his chest, flaring his big bright teeth. "Doesn't your god align stars and moon or something like that? Suppose I am the moon and you are the stars; well, we are aligning, don't you think?"

My brows furrowed as I contemplated Max's interpretation of the situation, but he didn't relent. "Now, what say we map out a plan that we both agree to and get on with the search for your son."

I looked at Philos who stared back at me silently pleading, *"Don't do it."* But I had to see what this was all about. Perhaps God *had* brought this Max into our path for a reason.

I took a deep breath, let it out slowly, and said, "All right, what is your price, tracker?"

"I knew you were a reasonable man. Now, this is what I propose. One silver piece—"

"A silver? Are you crazy?" Philos snapped.

"As I was saying, one silver piece to start." He let it hang in the air as he glared at Philos, then continued, "One to start and, upon locating Dismas, two more."

"Three?" Philos exclaimed. He turned to me, "Come, Nestor. Let's go."

Max held out his arms and smiled broadly, those giant white teeth of his glinting in the sun, "Remember, I found him before. I can do it again."

Philos said, "Yes, but what you ask for is several months' wages. We do not work yet, and have neither the way, nor the time to build up such an amount."

"Hmm, are you not working?" Max asked. "You seem to be working for your god, are you not?"

"That is different. He doesn't pay us."

"I believe your god will make a way." He turned to me and continued, "Don't you think so?"

I looked at Philos, then back to Max and nodded agreement. God would have to make a way.

I said, "This is quite a toll. One we need to pray about and wait for the Lord to provide. Come back to Hippus in a couple of days to give us time. We will give you a report as to where we stand."

Max stared at me for a long second, then startled me when he flung out his arms in a grand gesture, announcing with obvious glee, "I look forward to working with you."

Philos and I left Max behind, heading back to Hippus. I stopped at the top of the hill, taking in one more view of the area. Looking back down the hillside, I saw Max staring out into the sea. He had not budged from where we left him and I wondered what he was thinking. That strange boisterous man had found my son five years earlier. I prayed all the way back to Hippus for God to grant us the funds to have him find my boy again.

We entered Baruch's palace after quickly blessing the people lined up outside the gate. Roman guards were now stationed outside, watching over the people who consistently gathered. I couldn't help but fear these soldiers in some way. I knew these oppressors could strike at any moment with no grounds, other than to show their strength and control.

Baruch welcomed us in and asked us to join him and Rue, his Arabian friend we had met in Dion. "Come, come. We are discussing our plans for Capernaum."

We entered and sat on plush pillows in a cozy antechamber, adjacent to the main entry.

"When do you leave?" Philos asked.

"We leave tomorrow. Rumors of Jesus' exploits continue to come in daily. We cannot delay any longer. We also have business dealings to take care of."

"I apologize," I started.

"What for?" Baruch said.

"I need to ask a favor before you leave."

"Anything."

I looked at Philos. His visage begged me not to do it, but I was determined. I looked back to Baruch. "I wish to hire a tracker to find my son, but he asks for money up front, and money upon delivery."

I saw Baruch's eyes narrow a bit and then he said, "How much?"

With a long pause, "One silver now and two upon finding Dismas."

"Three silver pieces? Well, that is quite a bit of money, don't you think? Who is this tracker, might I ask?"

"His name is Max."

With a furrowed brow, he grimaced. Baruch knew of him; that was for sure.

"This Max, yes, he is a good tracker, but his ways are not always kind ways. You see, he does whatever it takes to find whoever it is he's seeking. Is this something you want to carry upon your shoulders? I could suggest other reputable trackers who also charge less."

"This one found my son before, and he knows Dismas already. I know I don't have the say, for I am asking that this money be given to me, so the final choice is yours."

"Given?" Baruch scoffed. "No, I think not. I will not give you the money, but I am willing to work out a deal with you. My friend Rue and I have been talking. I want to build a Jewish temple here in Hippus, and perhaps in other towns of Decapolis as well. I will be talking to a rabbi in Capernaum. I will also seek an audience with Rabbi Jesus to have him visit Decapolis in order to promote the temple building project. If I can obtain his blessing in front of the

Sanhedrin, then the funding will come. In return for the money, I will require you and Philos to stay here in Hippus for a few months to oversee the construction and to teach the people the skills they will need to complete the project,

I started to protest but Baruch held up his hand, "I will give you the silver piece now to pay your tracker to begin his mission so that no time is wasted, but you must agree to stay for three months. Do we have a deal?"

"What if Max returns sooner with word of my son's location? What then?"

"If that occurs, Nestor, then know that I will rush you personally to his side without delay. My heart, along with the rest of us here, is to see you reunited with your son."

I looked at my dear friend Philos, registering the warning in his eyes. Was this the way? Is this what God wanted? I knew not. But I had to believe that God was with me. The burden of promising to stay for three months without searching for Dismas with Max weighed heavily upon my heart. But the burden of letting the tracker go, the very one who had searched and found my son before, also greatly pained me. I wanted to be there when Max found Dismas. Baruch's deal sat before me. All eyes waited for my decision. I had been trapped for nineteen years. Could I handle being trapped for three more months?

I looked at Baruch and said, "Agreed."

CHAPTER 36
BROKEN SILENCE

SEVEN MONTHS FROM THE CROSS
-NESTOR-

IT HAD BEEN over a month since Baruch and Rue departed for Capernaum and Max went off in search of Dismas. I remember Max' face when I delivered him the silver piece the same day I agreed to the deal with Baruch. He said, *"You are full of surprises."* With his bright smile and big teeth, *"What did I tell you, God always finds a way."*

Philos and I had been overseeing the operation of building the synagogue here in Hippus. We ensured payments to workers and taxes to the Roman magistrate. We were still months away from completion, and I dreamed of having my son by my side upon its finish. Baruch began construction just before leaving and went with hopes of having Jesus of Nazareth come and bless the temple. This would bring more investors. Baruch was a businessman through and through.

Part of the deal I had made with Baruch was to teach the people about the Jewish God, but I had little knowledge myself. A week after Baruch left, a rabbi from Capernaum showed up at our doorstep. His name was Rabbi Shem. Philos and I came to find out he had been overlooked by the Sadducee elite, governed by the High Priest named Caiaphas. In his words, *"Their minds preach God but their hearts are not to be desired.*" Rabbi Shem spoke vehemently against the politics of Jerusalem and the leadership within, calling them "spawns of chaos".

I laughed inside, remembering Rabbi Shem muttering under his breath, *"They are spawns of chaos, Lord. You say to pray blessings upon my enemies. My mind is reluctant but my heart does your will. Bless them."*

This teacher of the law also had little patience for people, especially Greeks. Including Philos and me. More people of Jewish descent came daily to learn in an open forum. They gathered just outside of town at a location called 'the Gathering Place'; *Kanas* in Hebrew. We had initially started meeting outside Baruch's home, but the Romans didn't want large numbers of people blocking the street. They soon ushered us to an open field next to where the new synagogue was being built.

Over the month I had grown weary, my patience thin. Philos continued to give me strength with his ever present positive attitude. I thanked God daily for my friend, right after I asked for forgiveness, which became a daily ritual.

Rabbi Shem would teach us the Law of God daily and I was eager to learn his ways. Each day brought me new revelation and understanding, but also more questions. Rabbi Shem was not the most patient man, often saying, *"You ask too much when you should be listening."*

My thoughts would wander when he taught about what behaviors the Law deemed unacceptable in the eyes of God. Though I tried, I was entirely unable to live up to those standards. I could only think that there was something wrong with me. All my heart wanted to do was tell people about the love of God and yet all of these laws that I learned became, dare I think it, *shackles.* I found myself watching every step I took in light of these laws and missing the person that stood in front of me. I confessed my thoughts to Philos nightly and we talked through our questions together.

Shipments of farm animals began to come to Hippus, in an attempt to keep up with the demand for sacrificial offerings to the Jewish God. More and more people turned away from their gods daily and came to be blessed by the true God. With the increase of animals came the increase of businesses, and along with that, the increase of tax collectors.

There was no word from Max the Tracker. With each passing day, my anticipation was being replaced with bitterness and depression.

Baruch and Rue finally returned after six weeks. Their carts were full of goods of all kinds. Apphia rushed to her husband, causing Rue to smile and give a single clap at the reunion. I believe Rue had a sincere desire to see his friend's wife taken care of. There was a deep bond between the three of them.

With his arms opened high and wide, Baruch said, "My dear holy men of God, it is good to see you. We have much to tell. Come, let us feast and celebrate our return."

Since living with Baruch, I also noticed that food was a central focus for him. Anytime he could find evidence of something to celebrate he would throw a party for the occasion. *"The sun was shining brighter than yesterday, let us celebrate,"* or *"I am happier than the day before, let us feast."* Baruch was a good man that treated everyone fairly, including his slaves. He would also have celebrations to honor them, though he did not attend them himself.

Philos and I cleaned up and came down the stairs to the dining area where Baruch, Apphia, Rue, and Rabbi Shem greeted us.

We sat and Baruch spoke immediately, "How are things going with the building project?"

"Well," I said, "there seems to be a new tax every time I turn around. Four men were injured when the eastern wall collapsed. Brick production slowed due to bandit raids in the south, and Commander Fortus won't acknowledge the plight his soldiers cause our workers. They harass them each day and, in one case, arrested one of our foremen. There is also the—"

"I should say that I'm wondering what a bad day looks like," Baruch interrupted and caused the others to chuckle at the table.

"This isn't funny, Baruch, I've—"

He held up his hands, "Please, Nestor, I understand." Waiting a moment, he continued, "I will be here to handle these things moving forward. I don't dismiss the matters that concern you, but from what I, I mean, from what *we* have seen of late and will tell you now, our perspective on things has changed."

"Perspective? What do you speak of?"

"Jesus. I speak of Jesus of Nazareth." Baruch looked at Rue and they smiled. His gaze came back to Philos and me. He took a deep breath and exhaled. "Rue and I have seen Jesus do mighty things with our own eyes; things that are beyond belief."

Philos quickly said, "What things?"

Baruch let out a breath, "Where to begin?" He looked at Rue first and then started his story, "When we entered Capernaum, we passed many people who spoke of a great miracle that took place when thousands were gathered for days to hear Jesus speak. They were far from the city and the people say that he fed them all with but a small amount of fish and bread. They said thousands upon thousands sat in family groups all over the fields. It would take hundreds of carts of food to feed such a crowd and yet Jesus prayed to God and the food multiplied right before their eyes."

Rue said, "I could not believe such a claim."

"Nor could I," Baruch continued, "then it happened."

"What happened?" I asked, now very intrigued. My desire to be with Jesus equaled my desire to be with Dismas.

"Jesus is what happened. He came to Capernaum. I have never seen so many people follow a man like that. It was truly incredible to witness such a thing. We couldn't get close, but people spoke of the many miracles that he had performed. We first heard him at the synagogue, where he taught something very difficult to understand."

"What did he say?"

"He said that he was the bread of life and that he would give this bread to the world. He went on to say how his flesh was real food and his blood was real drink. This one thing he taught caused a lot of rumbling amongst the people. At first, Rue and I thought he was joking, but he was not. He spoke with authority and confidence, like no other we have ever heard."

"Baruch, get to the one part," Rue insisted.

"Yes, yes, I was just getting to that. So that was the most difficult thing about our trip and made us question Jesus truly being the Messiah. Perhaps Rabbi Shem can help us with Jesus' teaching of eating flesh and drinking blood, but what happened next defies logic. It was truly remarkable."

Baruch settled in and lowered his voice. We waited in anticipation. "Jesus vanished. We woke the next day and he and his disciples were gone."

"What do you mean gone? He couldn't have just disappeared," Philos questioned.

"Vanished," Baruch whispered, eyes wide. "Thousands of people milled about looking for him in synagogues or out in the countryside. He was nowhere to be found. That was when we decided to conduct some needed business. A few days later we went to Bethsaida, a smaller town several miles away. It was then, as we were arriving, that we spotted Jesus outside the town, leading an old man. A small crowd of people were following behind, so Rue and I headed over to join them. The old man was completely blind."

"How could you tell, Baruch?" Apphia asked.

"Oh, my sweet bride, this man's eyes were white with the fog of blindness. A rickety old man, but Jesus gently guided him out away from the town. Then Jesus stopped and stood directly in front of the man. There wasn't a sound, as everyone watched what was happening. I was completely mesmerized. What happened next was truly unbelievable." Baruch shook his head and looked at Rue, who nodded his head in agreement.

"Come on, tell us," Rabbi Shem said.

"I'm getting there. Jesus spit into his own hands and rubbed them on the eyes of the man. He spit. Can you believe it? Yes, spit. Unbelievable, but wait. Jesus asked, "Do you see anything?" and the man responded after looking around, "I see people; they look like trees walking around." This same man just moments before couldn't see a thing and now he saw images! Incredible!"

"But he only saw people that looked like trees," Philos said.

"Ha! You of little faith! A blind man seeing something, anything, is amazing, but, Jesus wasn't finished. He rubbed the man's eyes again and asked the man to look around once more. The blind man could then see perfectly clear! He started pointing to people he knew. The fog of blindness over his eyes cleared away, leaving them a crystal blue. It was as if he received new eyes. It was a miracle, was it not, Rue?"

"Indeed, my friend. I have never seen anything like it; that is for certain."

"Rue and I are still shaken by what we witnessed. It was truly amazing. This Jesus could be the Messiah."

Baruch sat back, emotionally exhausted from reliving the event with us. He had seen a miracle firsthand. Apphia comforted her husband and Rue sat there in silence staring blankly at his tea in front of him.

I said, "Did you go with Jesus further?"

Baruch refocused on me and said, "No, he went on to Caesarea Phillippi to the far north. We thought perhaps he would come back through Capernaum but many weeks had passed and our business had been concluded, so we came home."

Food was brought in by the servants and we ate, but I found myself resisting interaction in the conversations. Mixed thoughts raced through my mind and heart. Finding my son consumed me.

Yet everything I had just heard pulled my spirit to follow the Messiah, whatever the cost. I looked around the table and watched my friends interacting with one another, while I felt detached. I was sitting and eating while my son was lost and alone.

"What was Dismas doing? Where could he be at this very moment? He was somewhere out there and I was stuck waiting. Where was Max? Where was this supposed great tracker? Perhaps he found my son and was on his way back to inform me and collect his money? On the other hand, perhaps he traveled far away, living off the silver coin he'd already received, with no intention of returning." Oh, my mind, what anxious, tortuous thoughts rattled around inside my head.

I got up from the table and slowly walked away.

"Nestor?" Baruch called.

I didn't turn around.

"Nestor? Are you alright?" he said again.

I heard Philos answer on my behalf, "The weight of Dismas and no word from Max has become a distraction of late, more so than ever. Let him go."

I could feel everyone watching me but I did not turn around. I just needed to get out. I loved these people, yet my heart was not there with them in celebration. My heart was weak. The torturous silence of not knowing where Dismas was needed to break before I did.

CHAPTER 37
TIME'S UP

FOUR MONTHS FROM THE CROSS
-NESTOR-

I HELD THE LION figurine in my hand, rolling it around slowly to look at each imperfection. This simple item, a wood sculpture, kept me connected to Dismas with a strange, yet very real sense that he once owned it. Possibly carved it himself.

I looked out over the Sea of Galilee and watched the white caps of the disrupted water spark in random locations. It was too rough for fisherman during the winter storms. The wind buffeted me from behind, then raced down the hill and out over the sea. Stormy skies formed and I could see rain falling from various pockets of clouds. This weather reminded me of how I felt. One moment I was at peace and the next, my mind became a storm of frustration, anger, and worry. During those times, I couldn't stand having anyone around me. I felt alone amid a crowd.

We had just reached the three-month deadline in the agreement I had made with Baruch. But there were months still remaining before the synagogue would be ready. Other Jews had come and didn't want Rabbi Shem teaching outsiders such as the Greeks, or heaven forbid, a Samaritan. This caused great contention in Hippus. For now, the Romans stayed out of it, but even I could tell there was uneasiness with the guards. Philos and I were watched and in some circumstances followed. Even now, behind me, there were two soldiers just around the bend out of sight.

This was my spot, a mile from the Karpos home, overlooking the sea, and I knew it well. This is where the pigs, infested with the demons that had once afflicted Philos and me, plunged to their deaths.

I could hear the water from the stream falling down through a patch of dark rock. Someone had attempted to block the opening with smaller rocks but the water still flowed. Perhaps Karpos had the rocks installed in order to protect the children from falling through. Whatever happened, it wasn't by natural means.

This place brought me comfort as I imagined my son playing in the open fields or standing on the highest rock overlooking Galilee.

"Where are you, Dismas?" I whispered.

I thought the howling wind had responded when I heard my name from afar. Turning around, it was the man I had prayed to see much sooner. His arms flung out wide as he flared his big bright teeth. Still, I was shocked to see him at all. I had almost lost hope.

I immediately stood and watched Max and Philos approach.

I said half-heartedly, "I thought you weren't coming back."

"Oh, it is good to see you too, Nestor. I see that you have been busy while I've been away."

"Just tell me."

"Tell you what?"

I was about to respond in anger, but Max smiled cheerfully and held up his hands, "Yes, yes, of course you want to know, and I will tell you."

I looked at Philos, "Did he tell you?"

"No, he asked to speak to you directly. I brought him to you and didn't press him."

"My business is with you, Nestor. You hired me."

"I don't have the two silver coins but I am good for it. Baruch promised as much."

"I understand. Well…"

"Did you find him or not?"

"Yes and no."

I was perplexed, "What do you mean?"

"Upon receiving the two silver pieces, I will tell you all."

I lunged for Max and grabbed his tunic, tightening it in my grip, "Tell me now!"

Max didn't flinch. He was a taller man than I, holding his ground from my feeble attempt at strong-arming him. He smiled with his large bright teeth as rain began to fall upon us. My anger turned to tears and I let him go. "Why won't you tell me?" I fell to the ground, unable to hold myself up. Philos was quickly by my side.

He yelled at Max, "Do not torture him! We are men of our word, but hear me, Max, if your information is not substantial enough to locate Dismas, then payment will be forfeited."

Max leaned against the black rock and brought his cloak in closer to himself. "Do you remember me saying that your God would provide a way?"

I continued to cry under my hood and watched the drops of rain fall along the edge of the seam, melding with my tears.

Max continued, "My reputation to remain the best tracker in the land is important. In order for me to keep that reputation, I only require that you tell others, if asked, that I found your son and gave you the location."

"Tell us what you know, Max, and then we will decide the next course of action," Philos said.

"The times are changing," Max started. "Your son has vanished. He was captured by the Romans, but escaped while traveling to Jerusalem."

I looked up and said, "Jerusalem?" I stood, Philos helped me up. "Where could he have gone? How did he escape?"

"Your son is a clever one. He used his association with you, as a man plagued by demons, to invoke fear in the soldiers who were transporting them. They even killed one soldier."

"Dear God Almighty," Philos said. "Killed?"

"Yes, Gestas, the crippled boy of Karpos, somehow got out of his chains and attacked a nearby soldier so ferociously that everyone thought he was possessed. Romans can be very superstitious, and fear is a powerful tool against them. Gestas and Dismas rode off with two horses, food, supplies, and weapons."

Philos asked, "Who is Gestas?"

"Oh, that is the true son of Karpos and Dismas' brother in all respects."

Being more concerned with their whereabouts, I quickly said, "Where did they go? The horses, perhaps, could be tracked."

"Very good, Nestor. I had hoped your son would have sold the horses, but they had not. I checked the nearby hills and towns.

Nothing. I followed the Jordan from the base of the sea to as far as Scythopolis, but found nothing. No one had seen or heard of them."

"That is it? That is all you found?"

"There is one other thing. Before I returned, I heard of an increase in banditry along the roads and countryside."

"What does this have to do with my son? Are you saying he is a bandit?"

"Your son and Gestas are very familiar with this lifestyle. They had been trained by a brutal group of men called The Servants, who reigned in this region for many years. They were bent on destroying the Romans when they had conquered Decapolis. There was an incident, however, years before your encounter with Jesus, that disrupted the band of mercenaries."

"What happened to them?"

"*You* happened to them."

"I don't understand."

"The Demons of Ghasa happened, destroying the hand of The Servants, whose name was Abd al-Aziz. These Servants are still about, but have fled to the Arabian desert. They attack Roman patrols from time to time, but have shifted their focus more to acquiring wealth rather than eliminating Rome."

"Why would my son join such a group?"

"Let me make this plain, Nestor." Max paused a second, "Your son watched Clavius Sedontin and Fortus, the Roman Commander, murder his mother in front of an entire town."

"Murder?"

"Fortus slit her throat after flogging her."

I looked at Philos, concerned. The vendor in Ghasa had taken us to the gravesite, but we did not know that Dismas had watched it take place. This was our first time ever hearing of his past in such detail.

I turned to Max, "What is Clavius' relationship to all of this?"

"He is the brother of Karpos and the man who hired me to find your son the first time. I can't say for certain, but rumor has it he killed his brother and took his wife as his own, along with their children."

"But why?"

"Money. The pig farms were big business in the region. Roman law forbids soldiers from owning businesses. Fortus and the demons were connected with the farms somehow. But this Jesus changed all of that when he set you free. *Everything* changed."

"I just want to find my son, Max. I care nothing of all this."

"You should. It is your son's past. Knowing one's history can be helpful in discovering who they will become."

"So we come back to robbers and thieves," Philos surmised.

"Yes, but due to their history, I have reason to believe I have valuable information to pass along to you. Bandits have increased in the region south of here. Those attacks have been against caravans, merchants and the like. However, there was one incident involving a Roman patrol."

"What does this have to do with Dismas?"

"Dismas and Gestas are no friends of Romans. Based upon their history, they would have every reason to want to see the Romans dead. This particular incident was an attack against the Romans. I canvassed the area, but found no evidence. Nothing."

"What do you mean? What does nothing tell you?"

Max suddenly came alive, giving us his huge, annoying smile, "This is why I'm the best tracker. I know things, have seen things, and know that *nothing* can speak volumes to one who knows what to look for."

"Max, you speak riddles. I just don't understand."

Philos whispered in realization, "The Servants."

Max's eyebrows shot up in surprise. The rain suddenly stopped and a small amount of sunlight shone through. "Yes, The Servants. They are well-trained in hiding themselves. They left no signs behind, and to most were considered ghosts. This brought fear to the Romans. When I came to the place the soldiers were attacked, there was nothing. It was as if ghosts had attacked them. So, if The Servants only reign in the Arabian desert, what does this tell us?"

"Dismas is south," I said.

"Yes, but the south is a vast area to cover. Even I can't track ghosts. Besides, my time was up, and I stand before you with some insight, but not fully knowing." Max continued after a long pause, "I know it's not much, but—"

"It's the best news we have heard in a long time, Max," Philos responded.

I looked at Philos and then to Max.

Philos said, "What is it, Nestor? Are you not pleased?"

"It's overwhelming, Philos. Dismas has seen me as a monster, he watched the woman who raised him murdered, he's become a bandit, and worse, he has killed someone. How can I be his father?"

"How can you not be his father? He needs a father now more than ever. I do know that we have come too far not to see this through. God made the impossible possible when he rescued us." Philos looked at Max and then to me, "Come, we shall settle our arrangement with Max and make our preparations to set out."

We walked briskly back to Hippus in silence.

We entered Baruch's home as I yelled for him, "Baruch! Baruch!"

"Yes, yes, I'm here, what is the matter?" Baruch rushed from the kitchen area, finishing a bite of food. Apphia was right behind him. They saw Max. Baruch and Apphia exchanged a concerned glance. Baruch asked me directly instead of Max, "Did he find him?"

I said, "It's a long story, but in some fashion, yes. Philos and I will be leaving immediately for the south to try and find him. First, however, we need to settle payment with Max."

"Yes, of course. I will handle those matters. Let me also prepare your belongings and travel arrangements. Apphia will get you the necessary supplies." His voice had an urgency that I had not expected.

I had somehow in my spirit thought Baruch was against my leaving, in order that the temple be finished, and would argue with me. But now I realized just how much he had helped us, from the beginning up till today. It was beyond anything I could have imagined. I silently thanked God, then expressed my gratitude to Baruch and Apphia. "Thank you," I said. My eyes teared up.

"It is our pleasure to serve you, great holy men of God."

Months had gone by and Baruch had never stopped calling us this name. I smiled, receiving it. I had grown fond of his name for us. It was a name no longer awkward to hear.

I gently laid my hand on Baruch's shoulder and said, "I bless and thank you, Baruch and Apphia. You have shown nothing but love to Philos and me. Though I don't have much, I give you my fullest blessing and pray it will be enough for now."

I saw tears welling in his eyes, when he said, "Your blessing is all we have ever wanted. Now go and find your son. Apphia and I long to meet this great man. Bring him home."

I nodded agreement, then embraced him. I felt hope rising inside of me like the sun breaking over the horizon. My hands had been working but my heart had been idle for too long. A surge of energy came upon me and the insatiable desire to find Dismas at all costs enveloped me once again. Our next destination was the city of Scythopolis, at the edge of Decapolis.

We were finally leaving; a found father in search of his lost son.

PART V
DISMAS & NESTOR

CHAPTER 38
BARABBAS' FURY

TWO MONTHS FROM THE CROSS
-DISMAS-

GESTAS AND I just finished burying the chest that contained our share of stolen goods from the caravan raids. This was actually our sixth treasure, buried far away from the normal paths of travelers within the Jezreel Valley.

I laid down on top of the fresh dirt, exhausted from digging. Gez plopped beside me. We were in a ravine under the shade of the descending sun, looking up into the sky. Gray clouds were rolling in.

"It's gonna rain again," I said.

"Yep."

"Do you think Barabbas is mad?"

Gez didn't answer right away but he finally said, "Nah, I'm sure he's fine."

"You should have told me."

"Diz, what's the big deal? They were just Romans."

I turned my head to look at him. He met my gaze. We couldn't contain our laughter and we sputtered out uncontrollably. "*Just* Romans!" I laughed.

Gez sat up in exuberance, "Did you see their faces when I jumped out?"

"Yeah, then Tubs tripped and rolled down the hill. We couldn't have planned it any better." I continued to giggle, "They truly had no idea."

We settled back down. I continued replaying yesterday's incident in my mind. I could still feel the blood running over my hand from when I stabbed the Roman soldier. It was just a small patrol we ambushed in retaliation for what they had done to one of our crews. I relished every moment, but my heart still felt empty inside. I wondered if there was any amount of Roman blood that could fill that emptiness. My one motivation, my *only* motivation, was replaying in my mind the brutal murder of our mother. *"Do they not deserve any better?"* I wouldn't stop. I couldn't stop until they were all gone. Every last one of them.

We finished off our hidden burial ground with wild flowers and plants before heading back to our base.

We never stayed in the same location very long; we were constantly on the move. The tent skins blended into the environment. Everything was ready to be loaded and transported at a moment's notice. We had several locations of raiders in the region under our command and, much like we learned from Aziz and The Servants, we had our elite group. It wasn't forty, instead a small unit of ten; Gez and I plus eight others. In the last several months we had only lost one raiding party of twelve men to a Roman patrol that had shown up unexpectedly from Tiberias. None of our men escaped. All were killed by crucifixion. The Roman dogs lined up the wooden crosses along the road leading to Scythopolis to show others what would happen to those stealing from the people.

When we approached, I instantly wished we had stayed awhile longer at our hidden cache. Our lookouts alerted us that Barabbas was waiting in the main tent and wished to see us immediately.

It was time to face our leader, or at least the one who thought he was our leader. Gestas and I always knew it would come to this. Our mission wasn't to loot patrons and become rich, but to raise an army and bring pain to the Roman infiltrators. More and more recruits came in and were trained to plunder caravans in the region. Aziz had always told us that the natural skills embedded inside each person would eventually become known under pressure. Our enlisted men were being formed perfectly.

Barabbas' face told us everything in one word; outrage. But there was something else under all the anger as I looked into his eyes. Something beyond the temper. It was disappointment. This bear of a man loved people. Even though he knew what we did was wrong, somehow he justified what he was doing by giving the stolen goods back to the church and the poor. He was not a man of murder. He was not one of us.

"We can explain," I contested.

Barabbas exploded, "Shut up and listen!"

We quieted immediately, waiting for our reprimand. Barabbas' face was red with anger and his lips were pursed tight as he stood in front of us. "Why? Why would you do this? To me? To Gaddi? To everyone?" He looked about at the others outside the open tent who paused to watch the confrontation.

"It was an accident," Gez lied.

"It now comes to lies? Have I wronged you? Have I not treated you like family? What? What is it that I must do? We agreed to not attack any soldiers. Do you realize what you have done?"

There was no need to answer. Barabbas was just getting warmed up.

"I will tell you what you have done. More Roman soldiers are surely on their way and our operation is now in jeopardy!"

Gestas responded, "I know you are angry."

Barabbas was quickly in Gez' face, "You haven't seen me angry!" Barabbas backed away and said, "Some, if not most, of the people you have brought into this mess have families!"

I jumped in, "Families under the rule of Rome? We call that slavery!"

"You see," Barabbas said, flustered, "This is what I'm talking about. You two have been so hurt by them that all you can see—"

"Is their corpses," Gez interrupted.

Barabbas grabbed a wooden tent pole and bashed it repeatedly into a boulder until the pole splintered in his grasp. He roared with every blow, his chest heaving. When he finally calmed, sweat dripping from his brow, he walked away without another word.

I said mockingly to Gestas, "Now, I think he's angry."

We watched him begin to storm away while trying to contain our laughter. Nobody moved. Suddenly, Barabbas stopped and slowly turned to face us. Gez and I sobered quickly.

He said calmly, "We have another meeting. Mendel will come for you when it is time." Then he was gone, disappearing around the bend.

We both knew this meeting had to be with Joseph Caiaphas.

Nobody knew who we were truly working for. One by one, each of our men gathered around us and knelt down.

Jacob, nicknamed Tubs, said, "We follow you. These Roman dogs will pay for all they have done, with or without Barabbas."

The others nodded wholeheartedly as Gez and I exchanged a glance. This went beyond simple raids now. Caiaphas would soon find out. Barabbas was one thing, but what would the High Priest have to say, or, for that matter, decide to *do* about it? We now had warriors who cared little about banditry. Shedding Roman blood overshadowed our thoughts.

Gez and I retreated from the men to talk the matter over privately.

I said, "We need to attack someone of importance within the Roman elite."

"Agreed, but we have no one on the inside to inform us when that someone will be out and about. I'm more concerned about Barabbas at this point."

"Why, my brother? He is angry but he is a good man."

"We don't have time for good men, Diz. A man who doesn't say what he thinks can be more dangerous than one who does."

"What are you saying?"

"You know what I'm saying."

"Gez, Barabbas will come around. He will be forced to."

"And if he doesn't, are you willing to do what needs to be done?"

I hesitated, "Of course."

"Just to be clear, I'm not talking about keeping his wife's secret from the Romans and those religious zealots, the Sadducees." Gez stared at me hard.

My tone became serious, "I said I would. Whatever it takes."

He then eased up and smiled. "Good. I will inform the men about our next raid." Gez' face softened for just a moment before he said, "Mother and Father would be so proud of you, Dismas." He placed his hands on my shoulders. "I'm proud of you. I'm proud to call you my brother." Then he walked away.

I watched Gestas talking to our men. He glanced back at me, then continued to talk to them. *"He must know that I would do whatever it takes."* My mind shifted to Barabbas. He was caught in the middle of this web. *"Barabbas knew what he was getting into. But could I do what was needed if that time ever came?"* I took a deep breath and exhaled, continuing to watch Gez interact. He gave each of our men their assignment, placing his right hand on a shoulder and instructing the individual what to do. They nodded and then headed out one by one.

I genuinely feared for that bear of a man. I will never forget him overshadowing me on that fateful morning. His words echoed in my mind, *"Good morning, sunshine! I'm Barabbas and it appears that God wanted us to meet."*

He believed in his god and he believed his god brought us together. I couldn't. I wouldn't believe after all that had happened to me. He continues to follow a lie and that lie will get him killed.

"Just stay clear of us, Barabbas. Just stay clear. If your god can hear me, I pray that he keeps you away."

CHAPTER 39
THE HIGH PRIEST

TWO MONTHS FROM THE CROSS
-DISMAS-

WHAT I SAW took my breath away.

Never had I seen such a magnificent city in all my twenty years of life. Jerusalem; the most powerful city in Israel. The Jewish crown and historic burial location of King David. I had heard the stories of this king, who reigned a thousand years ago, from our time with Zebedee and Salome in Capernaum. I feasted on my imagination. At that very moment, in my mind's eye, I was a king entering the city. Those around me were my loyal subjects.

We rode on donkeys, traveling amongst a large caravan. Barabbas was atop his own wagon, directing the donkey who pulled it. Hundreds of people came and went as we descended the road from the Mount of Olives into the valley. We were able to see the city from this great vantage point.

The temple was most prominent, and in several districts there were large building projects in process. Scaffolding and hundreds of laborers looked like a swarm of ants from our perspective distance. The city was a chaotic poem, and I wondered if it had ever truly known silence.

As we came closer, we could see Roman soldiers lining the upper walls watching everyone coming and going. Tax collectors stacked their coins high upon the tables as people paid their way to enter Jerusalem.

Barabbas flashed a parchment at one of the tax collector's supervisors, and we were quickly ushered inside the city. Caiaphas, the High Priest, had summoned us with great urgency. He had called a meeting with the Sanhedrin and wanted us to be there.

I didn't know the politics of this city, but it was clearly the crown jewel of the area, held dear by the Romans. Pontius Pilate was the ruler of Jerusalem while the Tetrarch, Herod Antipas, governed the region to the north, the land we had just come from. Gestas and I had to topple one of these Roman leaders to give the people courage and hope to take on the others. We needed something big to happen. I was thankful to have the opportunity to discuss such a thing with Caiaphas.

The sun was setting, so the torches along the walls of the temple district were lit. We came to the back of what they called "the Gentile area" of the temple. We dismounted from our donkeys. A wooden door nearby opened to us. The door was several inches thick, reinforced with lead. It was apparent that these priests didn't want anyone easily entering their precious temple.

A hooded figure in black robes and a white sash kept his face shielded as we passed him entering the dimly lit corridor. I heard the door close behind us. Several latches and locks reset. Barabbas led the way. It was evident he had been here before. Within a minute, we entered a pillared room with torches along the walls and chairs filled with men adorned in priestly garments. Light reflected off the gold and silver tassels and larger than life head coverings. These were the Sanhedrin, the Supreme Court and legislative body of Israel. Why Caiaphas had them gathered here this night, I did not know.

We entered from above where we could look down upon them. The religious leaders seemed unaware of our presence. There were smooth pillars set every five feet along the stone railing, creating a shadowy walkway in which Gestas and I easily remained hidden.

Barabbas whispered, "You stay here."

We watched the big man walk down the stairs. He was quickly ushered to a corner by two more black-robed men, their faces hidden by large hoods.

I looked around, but did not see Caiaphas. Not yet. I knew he would stand out. He was the High Priest, the one that governed these men.

It was loud in the chamber as they spoke to one another. The sound bounced off the stone walls but I heard keywords such as 'blasphemous', 'change', and of course, 'Jesus'. This single man had caused the commotion and had caused this gathering I was witnessing. I saw and heard about the miracles, but what was their purpose? I heard that he was the Messiah, which means King of the Jews, but where was his kingdom and his army? He wasn't a very good king. He let John the Baptist be beheaded by the Romans. Or perhaps, this Jesus was using John's death to bring more people to his cause. I wasn't quite sure what his cause was and neither did the priests. No, these people were afraid and that was something I could use against them.

Caiaphas entered the room. Instantly, heads bowed and all talking ceased. I watched, noticing several of the leaders didn't appear fond of Caiaphas, but they respected the position. Their subtle glances to one another, with raised brows here and there, spoke volumes to me.

"We must do something, Caiaphas!" one of the Sanhedrin stood. His voice echoed throughout the hall. His plea incited several others to join in.

Caiaphas raised his hands and, without a word, commanded them to silence.

The High Priest said, after lowering his hands, "We are in desperate times. All that we have done to placate the Romans is being disrupted by one man. Let us assemble and make a decision to set things back on course. Now, please sit. Let us conduct ourselves as holy men of God."

The rustling of clothes increased as the priests settled into their seats.

Caiaphas remained standing. Once everyone was seated he said, "Who would like to speak?"

Several hands shot up and Caiaphas pointed to one, "We will hear from Micah, a descendant of the tribe of Reuben. Please address the congregation." Caiaphas sat.

Micah stood and turned to gaze into the crowd of seventy assembled priests, "The Scriptures point to a Messiah and we wait upon the Lord to deliver us once again from the hands of our enemies."

A priest from the crowd yelled, "What are the intentions of your words, Micah?"

"I'm only saying that we should pay attention to this man Jesus of Naz—"

The mention of Jesus' name roused many voices and several priests stood, pointing fingers.

Caiaphas stood and raised his hands to silence the group. "Micah is to be heard!"

"As I was saying, Jesus of Nazareth has done many miracles throughout the land. Are we not to give account?"

Another man stood up and said, "Caiaphas, let me respond."

Caiaphas nodded.

"This Jesus," he said in contempt, "does not follow the Sabbath. He is a lawbreaker and clearly no Messiah."

Dozens of others confessed agreement upon hearing this. Caiaphas silenced them once again.

Micah interjected, "A few days ago I saw a man who had been buried for four days raised back to life by this Jesus of Nazareth. How many of you have raised the dead?"

"You saw it happen? With your own eyes?" Another voice blurted from the crowd.

Micah looked around nervously, "Well, no, not exactly, but—"

It was too late. The group quickly butchered his claim and forced him back to his seat in resignation.

Caiaphas pointed to another person, "You have the floor, Chief Priest Isaac."

This chief priest wore many garments, flaunting his position. He was adorned with colors from head to toe, ranging from a bright yellow-trimmed robe to a rich red linen girdle. He walked stiffly, which I surmised was so that he wouldn't fall over from the awkward weight of the headdress.

He turned to address everyone, "What are we accomplishing? Here is this man performing many signs. If we let him go on like this, many will believe in him, and then the Romans will come and take away both our temple and our nation. Do we not have witness of him blaspheming God?"

Several stood to argue against this point. What he suggested was a death sentence to Jesus. The men standing were clearly *for* this man from Nazareth, though their number was much fewer than those who were against him among the seventy or so assembled.

I watched Caiaphas let the arguing go on for a minute. Then he slowly stood to address them. The act of him standing brought immediate order.

"You know nothing at all!" he yelled. His voice resonated contempt as he continued, "You do not realize that it is better for you that one man die for the people than the whole nation perish."

He let his statement sink in. "The Romans will take everything we hold dear. Do we truly believe this Jesus is the Messiah? I say not. Deep down you want to believe, but you don't *truly* believe. Hear me! We are commissioned by God. Do you not believe that God Almighty would inform us who the Messiah is? Could it really be some carpenter from a village we have never heard of? *We* are the priests that understand the Scriptures beyond any man outside these walls. *We* carry truth and justice! Let us reason. To have one man die, rather than the whole nation, is the correct action to take."

Caiaphas sat down and then said, "We shall vote. Raise your hand if you agree with what I have said."

Many hands shot up quickly, others hesitantly. Only a handful did not raise their hands at all.

Caiaphas said, "Then it is decided."

The ones who did not win stood vehemently, storming out of the room. The meeting was over. Groups of people gathered in pockets to discuss their thoughts privately.

I looked over at Gez, who shrugged, and said, "Once John the Baptist was killed, I knew it was only a matter of time before this Jesus would be also."

I had no argument there. If his plan was to be the King of the Jews, it didn't seem like he was doing it right. Miracles could gather the masses, but they didn't train them for war. The Roman soldiers would slaughter them. But if someone could ignite these millions of people to take on this giant called Rome, then things could shift dramatically. I wanted to make that happen and was hoping Caiaphas would help us do just that. It was now time for *our* meeting.

CHAPTER 40
THE PLAN OF ATTACK

TWO MONTHS FROM THE CROSS
-DISMAS-

I HAD NOT SEEN Caiaphas wear his High Priest robes with all the intricate religious stitchings and details before. Our last meeting was in Aenon years ago where he didn't want to be seen. This time, however, he was dressed in regal attire. The man exuded confidence, when before he was fearful. Caiaphas had let his guard down in Aenon. Now, he would not display such weakness before us. He thought he was in control. We would let him continue to think so.

Caiaphas said, "You have been busy in the north, I have heard. Your raids caused concern among the Romans, and my spies confirmed that both Pontius Pilate and Herod Antipas have taken notice. This is good, but not great."

Gez stepped forward, "Rest assured. We are ready to do greater things."

Barabbas said, "I want to have no more part of this."

"And there is no need," Caiaphas responded, looking at him. "I have something else in mind for Dismas and Gestas. Barabbas, you are to remain at home and ensure your wife's safety."

"But what about these two attacking the Romans?"

"Ah, yes, this is what we will be discussing. I want them to attack *more* Romans."

"More?" Barabbas blared in shock. "That is absurd! This will bring more soldiers. We don't have an army to defend ourselves!"

Caiaphas was relaxed. He gently smiled, "Yes, it will bring more soldiers, but what I want is for them to attack someone specific, someone of significance."

"We are ready," I said with excitement.

I looked at Gez and saw the spark of hope inside of him. I had believed we would be arguing for our plan to happen, and here it was falling into our lap. Joseph Caiaphas understood the need to bring Rome under our rule.

Caiaphas said, "The information I give you tonight is not to be shared with anyone, including your men. The Passover week is of the highest importance, for many Jews will come to Jerusalem. I know of a dignitary coming from Rome itself who will be paying homage to Herod Antipas and his brother, Philip, the Tetrarch. They are good friends. I am acquiring his route as we speak, and will divulge this information to you once it is obtained. His arrival will happen before the Holy Week. You will attack this dignitary with all of your bandits. And I do mean *all* of them."

"We can do this," Gez spouted enthusiastically.

"All of them, except Barabbas of course. He will remain back at his homestead. Is this understood?"

Barabbas walked out of the room without a word. It was clear how he felt.

I said, "Caiaphas, we are in your debt for allowing us this great honor. We will make you proud and leave no Roman alive that day. The dignitary will be crucified and displayed for everyone to see, this I promise you."

The High Priest smirked and placed his hand upon my shoulder, "I know you will do well. I bless your plan to make this happen. This strike will take Rome's eyes off of the Jews, and hopefully bring order back once again. God is making a way for what is to come."

"I will tell you what is to come," Gez said, "more Roman heads. This will be only the beginning."

"Yes, yes, of course," he placated. "Now, if you wouldn't mind, I have some business to attend to. You will receive word as to when and where to attack. Prepare your men. Continue your raids, but lessen them a bit while you coordinate. I do know that your attack will take place near Jericho." Caiaphas turned and walked away.

Just before he exited, I asked, "Do you believe a Messiah is coming?"

In my peripheral, I saw Gez staring at me. Bewildered at my question.

Caiaphas stopped and turned, "Indeed I do."

"How will you know he is here?"

"God will inform us of his arrival. I must inform you though, you are Greek and the Messiah is for the Jews."

"Does a king not need servants?" I asked.

Caiaphas chuckled and then gave a slight bow, "Indeed he does. I will make sure you have a place in his court."

He turned and left. We were alone. Our thoughts engulfed us.

Gez said, "What do you care about their king?"

"I'm not sure, but it's nice to know that we won't be out of a job when this is all over."

We both laughed and exited the same way Barabbas had. The plan was in motion. We would finally get justice for all the years of pain and suffering. Rome would pay for all they had done, and the only form of payment we would accept would be their blood.

CHAPTER 41
SCYTHOPOLIS

TWO MONTHS FROM THE CROSS
-NESTOR-

SCYTHOPOLIS BUSTLED WITH people from all over the region. Nestled between the Jezreel and the Jordan Valleys, with green landscapes all around, it felt secluded from the rest of the world. Scythopolis was its own. Those who resided here remained in its womb, with no care for the outside dealings of Greek travelers, like ourselves, and our plights that took place somewhere far away. The city was part of the Decapolis, but somehow it was different. Perhaps it was because of its location and distance from the other nine prominent towns.

Looking around, I saw trees and plants that I had never seen before. It was so green compared to the minimal amount of foliage around our hometown of Hippus. Neither Philos nor I had ever seen or been to such a place.

People of all cultures sold and bought goods. Kids played openly in the streets, as mothers looked on from their various vantage points. Others washed clothes or prepared meals. Groups of men laughed. Roman soldiers marched to or from their posts. The hammering and stone-chiseling work echoed in the distance, as more buildings were in various stages of construction.

Loud cheers caught our attention. They came from deeper inside the city. It sounded like a great multitude of people yelling in unison.

We followed the sound and discovered an outdoor auditorium. A play was happening, causing raucous laughter and energetic boos. We entered to see hundreds sitting on stone steps in a vast semi-circle surrounding a lower platform. Actors dramatized a story that I couldn't understand. All I could do was look upon the hundreds of enthralled faces.

A tall gentleman in Greek robes startled me when he tugged on my sleeve, "You need to pay to watch. Are you going to stay?"

I didn't respond. The voices around me began to muffle. I saw Philos approach the man as I backed away. His lips were moving but there was no sound. I suddenly felt overwhelmed by the vast number of people. *"How were we going to find my son among such crowds as this? This is just a glimpse of what is before us in this city. How would we find what Max, the professional tracker, could not?"*

Sound began to return to me.

I'm not sure if I spoke the question out loud, but Philos answered, "God will help us find him." Philos ushered me out of the stadium.

"Are you okay?" he asked.

I half-smiled and continued to look at all the people. "I'm fine."

"Come, let us find Baruch's friend and get ourselves situated. All of this is quite overwhelming," Philos said.

"Indeed it is," I thought.

We found ourselves in the marketplace after a brief walk.

"Baruch said it would be the merchant selling rare oils," Philos said over his shoulder as we pushed and weaved through the patrons crammed in the streets.

We came across camels baring their teeth as they chewed cud and caged animals from near and far. Various fruits and nuts, tapestries and linens, cooked foods and breads, and anything else one could think of were displayed on carts and under tent awnings for buyers to see. This was the marketplace. Some people entertained the crowds with juggling or fire eating. Some merchants had dancers to woo patrons to further pleasures in back rooms. It was as if light and dark collided in this place. I looked into the eyes of several people and I wondered, *"What is their story? How did they get to where they are now?"* I surmised they were looking for life's answers just like the rest of us. *"Why are we here? What is the purpose of life? Better yet, what is my own purpose?"*

"Maybe they are simply living life, buying and selling, seeking wealth. But to what end? Are we not all in search of meaning deep inside, beyond the superficial worldly circumstances that govern our decisions?"

My memory took me back to when we encountered Jesus. When the darkness fell away, the first thing I saw was Jesus. He smiled at me. It was like being born all over again. *Life* had entered into me. Colors were so bright, so beautiful that my soul was filled with joy and peace as I took them in. Even the mundane rocks shone brilliantly. One second I was forever damned to darkness. The next I saw the world again after Jesus cast the demon, Legion, back to the pit of hell where it came from.

I don't know what came over me. My inner thought suddenly verbalized, "Do you know who you are?" I said out loud.

Philos turned to me and said, "What was that, Nestor?"

I didn't look at him but instead increased the volume of my voice, "Do you know who you are?"

Some people close by turned to look at me as I continued, "Do you know who you are? Do you know why you are here? Can you answer what is the meaning of your life?"

More people stopped talking and circled around me. Even vendors gazed our way.

"The Kingdom of God is at hand!" I yelled.

Philos gave me room, circling around me to create space. I knew he was supporting me.

"Where is this kingdom you speak of?" one shouted.

"A great light has come into the darkness of our lives. The Kingdom is the light and the one who preaches the Kingdom is named Jesus."

"Someone call the guards! We have another one!" a vendor called out.

"I'll take care of this one," a younger lad stepped up in front of me.

I looked into his eyes; the anger showed clearly on his face. "Do you know who you are?" I asked just before the younger man swung his fist. All I remember was falling backward to the ground.

I came to with Philos hovering over me, along with another man I had not seen before. He had a pudgy face and a short beard with russet-colored eyes.

"Nestor? It's okay. We are at Tuvia's home. Tuvia is Baruch's friend," Philos said.

"What happened?" I asked groggily.

"Just rest, my friend."

I passed out, unable to keep my eyes open. I could hear Philos' voice in the distance. Images flashed inside my mind. Max laughed, his voice garbled like he was under water, his maniacal face coming closer to me with his prominent white teeth showing. Then it switched to Vena holding Dismas in her arms when he was a baby. She looked up at me. I could see her saying something to me, but I couldn't hear her. *"What are you saying? I can't hear you. Vena, tell me."* Her face turned distraught as she tried to speak even louder. *"I can't hear you!"* I yelled back. *"Why can't I hear you?"* I suddenly felt like I was being pulled away from her. *"Vena!"* Darkness consumed me.

My eyes flared open. Sound came back to me as did the pain. I flinched, feeling a searing heat on the left side of my stomach. With great discomfort, gritting my teeth and growling, I sat at the edge of the bed. Dried blood was on my clothing. My face and ribs were sore. I lifted my shirt to see the bruising and winced in pain when I touched the gouge along my left eyebrow.

Philos slid from an adjacent room into view and quickly came to my side, "He is awake!"

"Yes, I'm awake. What happened?"

"You don't remember anything?"

"I remember entering the city, the play, the marketplace and then nothing."

"Yes, the marketplace. We were looking for Baruch's friend, but…"

"But what? What happened?"

"You began to tell people about Jesus, and they attacked you."

"They attacked me? But why?"

A new voice came into the conversation. His voice was light and jovial, "I will tell you what happened. Thugs who don't like this Jesus is what happened. Hello, my name is Tuvia and this is my wife Devorah. Welcome back."

"How long has it been?"

"Two days, Nestor," Philos said.

In shock, while trying to stand, I said, "Two days?" I fell back, grabbing my ribs.

Devorah came by my side, "You need to be careful. The bones are not broken but very badly bruised. You are welcome to stay. Your body needs to heal before your search continues." Her face was pleasant with a noticeable mole on the far side of her left cheek.

"Yes, thank you. Um, we are looking for—"

"Your son," she quickly replied. She continued, "Philos has shared a great deal with us and we are honored to host you in our home."

Tuvia added, "Baruch is our friend. Any friend of his is like family to us, so please rest. We will bring you food to eat and we will talk later. First, eat and get yourself cleaned up."

"Thank you for your hospitality."

The husband and wife left, leaving Philos and me alone.

Philos said, "Thank God you are okay. I had to fight them away to get to you. I had never seen such hostility."

"Nor I. This is a strange place we have come to."

"What provoked you to speak out like that?"

I looked at Philos, "I don't know. I was overwhelmed by so many people. Something inside of me wanted to or perhaps needed to get the message out. I am unable to describe it."

"I think I understand. I have felt something similar when I ministered to the people coming for a blessing at Baruch's. When the feeling comes over me, I am compelled to profess the love of God."

"Yes, that is it!" I jolted back in pain, grabbing my ribs once again.

"Careful, my friend."

The pain settled.

There was a long pause of silence before Philos said, "Nestor, I have been talking with Tuvia. He said there is a man we should speak to. Said the man knows a lot about the comings and goings of people in this area. He's a local who lives near a town called Aenon, not more than ten miles away."

"Who is it?"

"His name is Barabbas."

CHAPTER 42
THE OLD MAN

SIX WEEKS FROM THE CROSS
-NESTOR-

TWO WEEKS PASSED as I healed from my injuries. We kept a low profile while in Scythopolis, and found the city to be a melting pot of Jews, Greeks, and Samaritans. It was quite volatile at times. The Jews and Samaritans were not fond of one another, while the Greeks wanted to get along with everyone. Being full Greek myself, I understood my fellow men in their inclusion of both Jews and Samaritans.

The slow healing process had caused much anger to build inside of me. Most of the time I kept to myself in our borrowed room. However, my anger turned to an anxious excitement when it finally came time for us to venture to the town of Aenon to search out the man by the name of Barabbas. We left early morning and had to pass the Roman crucifixion site just outside of town. A group of bandits was recently apprehended by the Romans. All of them were killed.

"Try not to look," Philos reasoned.

"I have to. One of them could be Dismas."

The birds ruffled their feathers as they repositioned themselves on the shoulders of the dead men and continued to peck and dig into the rotting flesh. These bodies had been out here for weeks. The Romans would keep them there until the white-washed bones were all that was left. I couldn't be certain if Dismas was one of them as their faces were eaten and skin was falling off.

Philos consoled me, "Dismas is not here."

"I pray that God will end this barbaric way of the Romans," I said.

We hurried through the rows of crosses on either side of the road, not looking back. Our road ran along the contour of the Jordan River. It twisted and turned, hugging the ridgeline, sometimes dipping down closer to the river, which flowed swiftly from the rainy season.

Philos said, "This is the river that Tuvia and Devorah spoke of, where the one called John washed people. Rabbi Shem called it baptizing."

"I wish we could have seen this man, Philos, and all the great crowds he drew."

"Yes, it would have been quite a sight."

We continued to walk until I suddenly stopped and said, "Philos?"

He turned to face me. "Yes, what is it?"

"Let *us* be baptized."

"Are you serious?"

"Yes, we are here and this John was led by God to do it, so why not?"

Philos smiled, "Okay, yes. Let's be baptized."

We walked down to the river, with a bit of excitement, maneuvering the slope to a slow-moving section of water so as not to be swept away.

"Nestor, how does one be baptized?" Philos said as we stared at the river side-by-side.

"I don't know. Maybe we just bless each other while in the water. I will bless you first."

We dropped our belongings and disrobed down to our loincloths. I stepped into the water and quickly retreated, "That is cold!"

"Come on," Philos urged, smiling, "this was your idea."

I stepped in, determined, and then turned, "Hurry up."

Philos stepped in, fighting the intense cold also. He faced me. His jaw muscles were tight. We looked at each other, freezing, not knowing what to do, and began to laugh hysterically. I hadn't laughed that hard in a long time.

I splashed Philos and said, "I bless you!"

Philos retaliated with splashes, "And I bless you!"

We exited quickly, shivering. We put our robes back on as fast as we could. I rubbed my shoulders and legs briskly to bring warmth back into my body. Within a few minutes, we picked up our belongings and headed back to the road. As we approached, we noticed several people watching us.

I hailed them, "Well met."

An older man greeted us, "What brought you into the cold river?"

I looked at Philos, not knowing how to answer. We didn't know what we were doing.

Philos said gleefully with a tinge of nervousness, "We baptized each other."

The old man's face scrunched as his eyes narrowed. Younger boys in their teens who were with him looked at each other.

"Baptized? Are you a rabbi?"

"No, we are not," I said, "but we heard the man named John had conducted baptisms in this river. Had you seen him by chance?"

"Yes, yes, we have," the older man slowly said.

"What was he like?" Philos asked.

"Like? He wasn't *like* anything."

"What do you mean?"

"He was no *man*. He was a prophet sent by God and the Romans killed him."

"We were just saying how we had wished to have met him."

The old man scoffed, "And now you mock him with your antics."

Philos and I exchanged a glance before I said, "We meant no disrespect and to be honest—"

"Honest?" he interrupted. "You think what John the Baptist was doing was splashing people in the water? The Prophet was preparing the way for the Lord! Those who came to him were baptized with water! But someone more powerful than him is coming to baptize people with the Holy Spirit and fire!"

"Fire?" Philos said, surprised. "I don't understand."

"I believe the Christ has come."

I stepped forward, "Yes, Jesus of Nazareth. He is the Christ. We have seen him."

"Recently?" the old man asked.

"No, it has been quite some time now, but we hope to see him again soon."

"I am taking these boys on a pilgrimage to the Holy City. Passover festival is weeks away, but we are in hope of Jesus being there."

"Where do you travel from?" I asked.

"A small town called Cana. And you?"

"We are from the town of Hippus."

"Ah, I have heard of such a place. It is in the Decapolis region is it not?"

"Yes, I am sorry, but we have not heard of your town."

"No one has. Not even the ones who live there," he chuckled. "Tell me, there was talk of demons in that area cast out by Jesus. Is this true?"

Again, Philos and I looked at one another. I turned to face the man, "Yes, it is true."

He nodded his approval, "That is good. Very good. It confirms to us the authority that Jesus carries. Who other than the Messiah can command such forces? This information warms my aged heart."

I said, "We are heading to Aenon. Can we walk together?"

"Yes, yes. Let us walk and exchange stories."

Philos said, "We have quite a story to tell, my friend."

CHAPTER 43
AENON

SIX WEEKS FROM THE CROSS
-NESTOR-

I T TOOK US longer to reach the town of Aenon than expected. Our pace was slowed by the old man, named Arlan, but the travel was pleasurable as we shared stories of Jesus with him and the boys. He also told us an incredible tale. His son was married two years ago. On their wedding day, the very same Jesus we know had miraculously changed vats of water into wine. Arlan had not known about it, nor had his son, until the next day when he was told by his servants. He did not officially meet Jesus, but the bride knew Jesus' mother, Mary, and had invited her to the celebration. Apparently, in Jewish homes everyone was welcome, especially to weddings, so Mary's son, Jesus, came as well. It was an incredible story and showed Philos and me that God could even change the very nature of water into the sweet, bitey nectar of the grape.

We said our farewells as they continued on toward Jerusalem, and we veered to the town of Aenon. It was set against a beautiful backdrop with the flowing Jordan River snaking behind it. Dots of green bushes laced the sandy shores and clusters of trees draped over it in various sections, dipping green tentacles into the cool water. The dark, muddy look of Aenon stood out amongst the lighter sand color surrounding it as people and livestock moved in and out of its confines.

Roman soldiers were stationed at the entry, and tax collectors waited for patrons to pay the entrance tax even in this remote location. After paying our duty we entered.

Philos stopped someone passing by and asked, "Do you know of a man called Barabbas?"

"Yes, he frequents Aenon, but I haven't seen him of late. You could always ask Mendel."

"Mendel?" I said.

"He conducts Barabbas' business."

"Do you know where he is?"

"Yes, he is usually in the marketplace or at the synagogue."

"What does he look like?" Philos asked.

"Oh, he is the small one with a short groomed beard, dark hair and well-fed."

"Thank you for your time."

"Welcome to Aenon," he said as he moved away, "We don't get many visitors now that the Baptizer is gone."

There were only a handful of buildings, so we easily spotted the synagogue and marketplace. We decided to start where there were fewer people and ventured to the Jewish gathering place. It was a large complex in comparison to the other buildings. Pillars adorned the outside with stone steps ushering us a few feet higher than the street level. We entered the candlelit room.

My voice echoed, "Empty, Philos."

Before we could exit, someone called. He was in the back of the room in an alcove we had not seen, "Looking for someone?" An older gentlemen with a gaunt figure shuffled into view. His frail body moved only inches at a time. He was so ancient, I wasn't sure he could see us. His right hand slid along the back rail of a bench, feeling his way as he walked.

"We are looking for a man named Mendel?"

"Ah," he said, "Yes, good Mendel is in the back unloading supplies for the Cause. Come, come, follow me."

We did as instructed, albeit very slowly. We saw sunlight filtering through an open door up ahead. We were now behind the temple and noticed two men loading supplies from a cart into a cellar room. They slowed, then stopped upon seeing us.

Mendel was clear as day as his figure perfectly matched the description we received earlier.

The old man said, "These men are looking for you."

"I'm Mendel," the shorter one said, turning to face us. "What can I do to help you?"

The old man turned and shuffled slowly back inside. The younger teenage boy continued to take crated boxes off the cart while Mendel approached us.

"My name is Nestor and this is Philos. We have come a long way and were told you know someone by the name of Barabbas."

"Yes, he is a dear friend of mine. What is your business with him? I only ask because I handle all of his business in Aenon."

"We apologize. We are in search of someone and were told that he might know the person we seek."

"And who told you all of this?"

Philos said, "Tuvia of Scythopolis."

"Ah, yes, we have done business together. He is a good man. How is his wife?"

"Devorah is well. She is in fine spirits."

Mendel smiled, "So, who are you looking for, might I ask?"

I glanced at Philos as we had been down this road so many times, I blurted, "My son."

"Your son?" Mendel asked with concern. "How old is he?"

"He is around twenty years of age now."

"I'm confused. So he ran away?"

"In a manner of speaking. More like I ran from him. He never knew me because we were separated."

"Separated?"

Philos said quickly, "Perhaps we can tell this tale with you and Barabbas at the same time."

"I'm sorry, but Barabbas is away. I do not know when he will return."

He was responding to Philos, but staring at me. *"Why was he looking at me that way?"*

"Yes," Mendel said, "Barabbas would kindly receive you. He is a good man, as you can see. He donates greatly to the Cause."

"The Cause?" Philos asked.

He continued to stare at me and then broke away to focus on Philos. "Yes, the God of Abraham, Isaac, and Jacob. Barabbas and others have coined it 'the Cause'."

"Well, that is an interesting way of saying it," Philos responded.

"Yes," I said, "and we look forward to discussing it with Barabbas when we see him. You don't know when he's back in town?"

"Typically, he is here at least twice a week, but he is a busy man of late."

"So he travels quite a bit from his home to Aenon?"

"You can say that, but he also likes to spend time praying and seeking after God out in the wilderness." He pointed out toward the country. We followed his line of sight to the beauty of the rugged terrain beyond. "I wish I could have been more help."

Philos said, "You have been a great help. We shall try again, perhaps next week."

"Ah, very good. Well, back to work. Well met."

"And well met to you also."

We walked down the small street to the main road and before we turned out of sight we heard Mendel call out, "Oh, what is your son's name?"

I yelled back, "Dismas!"

There was a pause before he said, "I will keep my eyes open for your son."

CHAPTER 44
HE KNOWS SOMETHING

FIVE WEEKS FROM THE CROSS
-NESTOR-

A FULL WEEK HAD passed since our trip to Aenon. On the inside, I couldn't wait to leave Scythopolis, although Tuvia and Devorah were the loveliest of people. On the outside, however, I showed everyone, including Philos, my pleasantries, so as not to upset anyone with the turmoil I was feeling. I know Philos saw through to my heart. He would gently place a hand on my shoulder and squeeze just enough to let me know that he understood and was still with me.

We were preparing to head back to Aenon, but I couldn't shake the thoughts and images of this man called Mendel. There was something strange about him that I couldn't quite figure out.

I wasn't feeling at peace. I retreated from the household often to contemplate the anxious thoughts overtaking my mind.

Philos noticed and asked, "Are you all right, my friend? You seem distant of late."

I nodded, "I'm sorry."

"Nothing to be sorry about. I just want to make sure you're okay."

"Did you find Mendel to be strange when we left?"

"Strange? How so? He seemed to be a good man."

"Yes, *seemed*. I don't know. It's just…"

"Just what? Do you not want to go back?"

"No, that's not it. I just feel like he was hiding something."

"I didn't get that feeling at all. Let's find this Barabbas and see where it leads us next."

"Yes, you're right."

"I'm always right," Philos smiled.

We left the next day after saying our goodbyes to Tuvia and Devorah. Baruch truly had good friends around him, and we were thankful that he shared them with us.

Half the day passed uneventfully. Philos and I spoke little during our walk to Aenon. Many people, mainly Jews, were heading towards Jerusalem for the Passover celebration in four weeks. It would be nice to visit Jerusalem, not more than a few days to the south, but finding my son took precedence over everything. I dreamt, as I walked, of finding Dismas, traveling to the Holy City, and worshiping God together as father and son.

Philos disrupted my thoughts, "Aenon, straight ahead."

There it was. The small town with its few buildings and rooftops now visible as we came around the last bend.

"This could be the day," Philos mused.

I nodded and half-smiled, "Yes, this could be the day."

Aenon had little to offer except as a resting place to those traveling through the area. There was a small marketplace, a single synagogue, and few homes which undoubtedly belonged to the small number of merchants. I estimated there were more Roman guards than patrons in the marketplace, but it was hard to tell with the increased crowds stopping on their way to Jerusalem.

Philos and I made our way to the small alley behind the synagogue where we had first encountered Mendel. To our surprise, he was leaning against the wall as if waiting for someone. He perked up with a large grin once he spotted us.

"Good news," he said.

We hurried down to meet him, "What news do you have?"

"Your son. We know of his location."

I almost felt the wind knocked out of me, so incredulous was I at this news. This was the first time anyone had *known* where he was. Philos grabbed hold of me as my knees buckled.

I stumbled with my words, "You, you know where he is?"

Mendel continued to smile, "Yes, that's what I said."

Philos asked, "Well, where?"

"Tiberias, along the Sea of Galilee."

I breathed deeply and composed myself, "How did you come by this information?"

"Barabbas came into town a few days after you left and I discussed it with him. He knew of Dismas from parleying with a caravan leader coming from Tiberias. As I said, Barabbas knows a lot of people. Anyway, the caravan leader said a group of bandits waylaid a friend of his just outside of Tiberias and he overheard one of the names—Dismas."

"Is Barabbas here? Can we speak with him?" I asked.

"I'm afraid not. He had some business to attend to further south and I didn't ask when he would return."

Philos said, "Don't you handle his business?"

"Well, yes, but not all of it. Barabbas handles certain parts, while I handle the parts he doesn't like to deal with. I wish I could tell you more. Are you not pleased?"

I looked at Mendel and with all sincerity said, "Yes, of course. We are indebted to you and Barabbas. I hope to repay you both someday."

"Ah, no need for repayment. We are happy to help, especially a father in search of his son. It is a touching story. Maybe one day you can come back to visit, together of course."

"Yes, that is something I very much hope will come to pass. Well, we won't take any more of your time. We need to head back to Scythopolis with this new information and make way to Tiberias by morning." I confirmed my statement with Philos as we made eye contact.

"Very good, then," Mendel said. "Well met."

"And well met to you as well. May the favor of God rest upon you, Mendel."

With that, we began our trek back to Tuvia's home. This time our steps were hastened with hope. I caught myself smiling as we walked, letting my imagination take me to places I rarely ventured. I pictured the reunion with my son and the restoration of our hearts.

CHAPTER 45
LIES

FOUR WEEKS FROM THE CROSS
-DISMAS-

I COULDN'T BELIEVE WHAT I was hearing. Mendel just informed Barabbas that two Roman spies came to Aenon in search of me. "Spies?" I inquired.

"Yes, that's what I said. They came looking for you. They knew your name," Mendel replied.

Barabbas said, "And these two men were looking for me as well, you say?"

"Yes, they wanted to speak with you because you know a lot of people in this region. I believed it was a way for them to get more information."

"But this doesn't make sense. How would anyone know to look for Barabbas in order to find Dismas?" Gestas interjected.

"I know not, but I felt it my duty to give them false information and have them look elsewhere. They were very convincing individuals. I can't even speak of the lies they tried to employ for information."

"What lies?" I asked.

"Ah, it's nothing. They are gone now. We need to find—"

"What lies?" I insisted.

Mendel looked at Barabbas and then back to us. "They…"

"What lies, Mendel? This could have bearings on our plans."

"One said he was looking for his son. It's deplorable what these Romans will do these days."

"Son?" Barabbas said. "What do you mean?"

"I know not. The tall one said they were looking for his son, and his name was Dismas. That's what they said."

I was so confused. Roman spies trying to find me by saying they are looking for their son? It didn't make sense. I looked at Gestas, who shrugged. He was just as baffled as I was.

"Where did you send them?" Barabbas asked.

"I thought about sending them far to the north, but thought that might be suspicious, so I sent them to Tiberias."

"Tiberias?" Gestas scoffed. "It's only a few days away at most."

"I know, but if I sent them any farther, they might have been suspicious. I calculate they will be looking for you, us, whomever, but we will have concluded our mission by the time they find that you are not there."

There was a long pause, then Barabbas said, "He's right. You did good, Mendel. The Roman dignitary is coming in two weeks. These spies will be tied up scouring Tiberias while we will be lying in wait outside Jericho."

"Not you," Gestas reminded. "Dismas and I will be there, along with the rest of our men. You are to stay back at home and not be party to this. Your face is too recognizable."

"Yes, that is what I meant." I noticed he slightly stumbled over his words. I squinted at him, but his eyes locked onto mine, giving me a sense of certainty. Barabbas finally stated, "I know what I'm supposed to do."

"Then it's settled," I said. "We will gather the men and start out for Jericho tomorrow morning. Mendel, alert the cell groups to move in small squads. Have them make their way to the meetup location."

Mendel nodded and looked over at Barabbas for his blessing, which he received. Mendel headed out of the goatskin tent.

Barabbas stepped forward, "I don't like this."

My brother responded, "We've gone over this, Barabbas. We will do as Caiaphas planned. There is nothing you can do to stop it. If you do, you jeopardize Gaddi. Do you want her hurt, or worse, by the Romans? You know what they will do to her."

Barabbas nodded, took a deep breath, and left.

I looked intently at Gestas.

"What do you think?" he asked.

"I don't know. Spies looking for me and Barabbas just weeks away from our attack. It's…"

"It's nothing, Diz."

"Nothing? I hope you're right."

"I'm always right. Come on, we have firsthand knowledge of a major Roman dignitary coming to Jericho. This is everything we had hoped for and more. For the first time, we will be showing these dogs who the real master is. And this is just the beginning. Our mother's sacrifice will not go unpunished. This foreign disease will be eradicated once the people of this land take ownership and fight back."

"Do you think this Jesus of Nazareth will—"

"I don't care about Jesus. He talks and talks and talks but there is no action. He is not training warriors."

"You can't deny the miracles he has done, Gez."

"Miracles don't win wars, brother. Don't be deceived by this so-called Jewish Messiah." Gez stepped closer to me and placed his hands upon my shoulders. "Diz, we are so close. Let us focus on what is to come and not the "what if's." The Jews will show up, this I know. They are a stubborn people and they need someone to lead them."

"Are you saying we will lead them?"

"Perhaps." Gez took a step back. "I do know that we will uphold our part and show the world that Romans bleed just like the rest of us. Come, let us prepare our men and shift our thoughts to the task before us."

We exited the tent. Gez gathered our ragtag warriors. I watched him rally their wayward souls. Several cheers broke out as he inspired them with his speech. My mind sobered quickly. In two weeks, some of these good men would fall to the sword. It was at these times that I couldn't help but wonder what it was like to finally embrace death. What was on the other side? Where does one's soul find rest? Perhaps there was another war to fight, perhaps we were destined for all eternity to live the same life we left behind. If that was so, then I will be a fighter; a warrior always in pursuit of what I perceive to be the truth. I had proposed my thoughts about this to Gestas one night. *"Perhaps each Roman we have killed will be waiting for us on the other side to continue to fight until we find peace."*

I chuckled to myself and remembered the sting of his punch across my jaw and his words echoing in my mind, *"There is no peace to be found, brother."* He leaned in as I tasted the blood on my lip, *"Remember that."*

He was right. He was *always* right.

CHAPTER 46
JESUS IS NOT HERE

THREE WEEKS FROM THE CROSS
-NESTOR-

"My God, Philos, where do we start?"

There in front of us was the bustling city of Tiberias, positioned on the opposite side of the Sea of Galilee from our home in Hippus. People came and went in droves. Camels and donkeys passed, led by their owners. Carts rolled in, filled with produce and product from the region. I turned to and fro to try to get my bearings. Roman soldiers marched in unison while others guarded the tax collectors who lined their pockets with portions of the citizen's contributions. Dust billowed up around us from all of the movement. Though there were clouds in the sky, the air was dry and the smell of fish and citrus permeated the atmosphere.

There was an incessant pounding as blacksmiths hammered metal and laborers chiseled stone, fabricating statues for the posh palaces of the elite. This city was in constant flux as it grew with people and infrastructure.

"Let us pray then," Philos said as he put his hand on my shoulder.

I looked at him surprised, "Now?"

"Yes, why not?"

I thought, *"This is strange. Praying right now, in the middle of the road with everyone walking here and there. His impromptu suggestion startled me, but I suppose if God has brought us this far, perhaps he would give us a sign."* We bowed our heads.

Philos started, "God, we ask for your guidance. Help us navigate this city to find Dismas. Without your help it will be impossible, but we know that all things are possible with you. Help us. Guide us."

He paused and I knew that he had finished so I began to pray, "Thank you, God, for all your provision. Thank you for bringing us this far. Thank you for saving us from the clutches of darkness and we thank you now in advance for what is to come."

I wasn't finished with my prayer, but someone came up to us and tugged on my robe, "Do you follow Jesus of Nazareth?"

Both of us looked up from our bowed position to find a beggar standing before us. He smelled of rancid meat. His soiled clothes, torn and stained, draped loosely on his frail body. His face had deep lines embedded from his forehead and cheeks down into his neckline.

"Yes," I replied. "We do."

"He is not here."

"Oh, thank you, but we are not looking for him."

"Jesus is not here," he repeated.

I looked at Philos and he shrugged. "Thank you," I said again.

"Jesus is not here."

"You said that already." I was trying to be polite.

"Yes," the beggar said, "But did you hear me?"

Philos said, a tad irritated, "We heard you. Jesus is not here."

"He said that you would give me money."

I was shocked, "Who said?"

"Jesus."

Again I looked at Philos. I was perplexed. "Are you saying that Jesus of Nazareth told you to say this?"

"Yes. He said you would give me money."

I suddenly thought, *"This beggar is tricking us."* Sternly, I said, "Don't lie to us, stranger. You say this to others coming and going into town so you can get money from them. Isn't that right?"

"I said what He told me to say. You give me money now."

"No. We are leaving. Come on, Philos."

We walked away, periodically looking over our shoulders. The man stood there watching us. People crossed between our line of vision. The further we went, the less we could see of him but the man remained steadfast, staring in our direction, not moving. *"What a strange man,"* I thought. *"Does that tactic actually work?"* I pushed him from my mind and tread deeper into Tiberias. Philos and I found an inn and secured a room, informing the keeper that we would be there on a day-to-day basis, not knowing for sure when we would depart.

I sat on the straw mat bed and looked up at Philos, questioning him with my eyes as to what to do next.

"I know not, my friend, but I trust God will lead us. Be patient," he said.

"That is not something I am good at, Philos. Patience is your gift, not mine.

"The innkeeper told us to see a man by the docks in the early morning. A Jewish man named Zebedee. All we can do now is wait. Why don't you get some rest."

"I will rest if you decrease the sound of the city."

After we chuckled, I looked at Philos seriously, "Philos, I sense we are close to finding him. He's here. He has to be."

"I pray so, Nestor. I pray so."

I lay down, staring up at the ceiling, contemplating, calculating, and wondering. Philos rummaged through his pack and ate some of the figs we purchased from a local vendor just outside the inn.

"Ah, these are good," he mumbled. "Nestor, you need to try these."

I peered over at him, "Maybe later."

"Ah, your loss then." Philos continued to murmur enjoyment as he consumed one after another.

Morning came early for me. I was up before the sun. I couldn't wait any longer and nudged Philos awake.

"Philos? It's time."

He groggily opened his eyes and squinted at me, "It's still dark."

"I know. We need to get to the docks early. I do not want to miss this Jewish man."

"They said he arrives after morning meal time, which is still far off."

I didn't respond, as I knew he was right, like always. But Philos sat up nonetheless and said, "This could be the day."

I smiled broadly and helped him to his feet. Within minutes we were outside in the cool air whipping off the sea.

"Dock four is the one he said to go to. It's located at the far end," Philos pointed out the direction.

Most of the boats were now on the open water as the fishermen started early. The sun was just dawning, casting beautiful pink and orange clouds on the horizon. The wood planks we walked on were thick, but well-worn. Fish guts and scales were embedded into the fibers of the wood. Dents and scratches along railings showed proof of the many boats that had slid along the skeletal framework of the docks. Some boats were still tied and bobbed back and forth in the water, sloshing about. Seabirds waited patiently for the fishermen to return to port and offload their breakfast.

We came to the end of dock number four to an empty slip. I sat on the edge to wait. Philos joined me.

"Do you remember us wanting to become fishermen?" I asked.

"Yes, and accountants, farmers, innkeepers, and...what was the other one? Oh, yes, Roman soldiers."

I laughed, "Yes, I did have some grand plans, didn't I?"

"*We* had some grand plans, not just you."

"I'm sorry."

"For what now?" Philos questioned.

"I'm sorry for not fulfilling any of those plans."

"What are you talking about? We lost nineteen years if you've forgotten."

"No, I haven't forgotten. If only God could reverse time." I looked off into the Sea of Galilee.

"He has given us the most important plan of all; finding Dismas."

I gently grabbed his shoulder, "Thank you."

"Question is, what will we do after we find him? Maybe this Zebedee will give us jobs." Philos laughed.

More time passed and we began to see fishing boats approaching. "It looks like they will be coming in soon," I said.

"Yes, I think you are right."

"The keeper said that this man knew a lot of people in the area, but doesn't live here. Is that right?"

"That is what he said," Philos responded.

"Well, all we need is a little direction. I pray he can give us some names to follow up on."

"God will show us."

There was nothing to say after that. We waited and eventually one of the many boats approached our area. We weren't certain if it was our contact, so we hailed him.

"Well met!" I yelled.

The twenty-foot long hull speared through the small swells. The morning sun blared overhead, lighting up the faces of the many fishermen on board. We could see one of them squinting at us in the sunlight.

"I already paid my taxes," an old sea-faring voice bellowed.

"We are not collectors."

"Is that so? Who are you then?"

The boat was still thirty feet away and we saw two other men helping to slow it down to slide into the dock. Other boats were now pulling into port and some had already begun offloading the fish into baskets for the market.

"We were told to speak to Zebedee about finding someone."

"I'm Zebedee. Just hold there a minute."

We waited as they came alongside. One man, leaner than the others, jumped out and secured the line by tying it down to a wooden piling. A second man with bulging muscles joined in at the other end, fastening a second line around another piling.

"How did you fare today?" I asked.

Zebedee jumped onto the dock and looked us over, not responding to my question.

"Who told you about me?"

"The innkeeper named John."

"I named one of my sons after him. He is a good man and lifelong friend. You help me offload these fish and then we will talk."

I tried to interject, but he cut me off, "You can learn a lot from someone's work ethic. No talking, just offloading, then we talk. Understand?"

Suddenly, a dripping basket loaded with fish was pressed into my chest and I reactively grabbed it. The smell almost knocked me over into the water. Philos and I both helped, and about an hour later we had finally finished. Judging by his graying hair and sun-leathered skin, Zebedee was maybe fifty, but his strength was like that of someone thirty years of age.

"Come, let us walk. I have business in the market, and you will tell me the reason you have sought me out as we go along." Zebedee didn't wait so Philos and I hurried to his side while dodging other fishermen and their catch of the day along the dock.

"My name is Nestor and this is Philos. We come from Hippus."

"Hippus you say? What brings you here?"

"My son."

"Explain."

"I was separated from him when he was born and now I search for him."

"How long have you been searching? Better yet, what does this have to do with me?"

Philos said, "It is quite a tale and we don't have time to tell you before reaching the market."

"So why me, then?"

I said, dodging another worker, "John the Innkeeper said you know people in this area. We are hoping you might be able to direct us to someone who would know of bandit activity in the area."

He stopped, "Bandits? You think I deal with scum like that? I'm a businessman who has built my business by the strength of God and hard, honest work. I don't deal with bandits."

"Zebedee," I pleaded, "Forgive us and please don't take this the wrong way."

"Too late," he said as he continued to walk away.

"No, please," I grabbed him to stop. "We are also followers of the God of Abraham, Isaac, and Jacob."

He looked sternly at us and said, "You have been with Jesus of Nazareth, am I right?"

"Yes."

"He has brought nothing but trouble upon my family."

"What do you mean?"

"My two sons follow him now. They are his disciples and I fear for them. I wanted my sons to have a rabbi to teach them the ways of God. This Jesus, however, brings difficult teachings that challenge the way we have always been taught."

"Do you not believe he is the Messiah?"

"Messiah?" he paused. "I had thought, perhaps, at one point, but now, I don't know."

"What about the miracles and signs?" Philos said. "Do they not prove that he was sent by God?"

"It is not just a simple matter to believe. The rabbis have always taught us that a Messiah will bring freedom, like when Moses brought us out of Egypt. I only see Roman oppression increasing. Look, I don't have all the answers. All I want to do is put food on my family's table and leave behind something for my sons."

I looked at him and said, "As do I. I need your help finding *my* son."

He paused as he stared at me, "Your eyes. They remind me of a boy I met a long time ago."

I looked over at Philos and then back to Zebedee, "What was this boy's name?"

Puzzled, he responded, "Dismas."

I fell to my knees, shocked at hearing someone say my son's name. Zebedee said, "You know this boy?"

Philos answered as I began to cry, "Dismas is his son. When was the last time you saw him and where?"

"He was just a boy that I rescued out of the sea. He stayed with us for some time in Capernaum. Dismas and his brother, Gestas. Are both of the boys yours then?"

"No," Philos responded, "Dismas was placed into another family. He and Gestas grew up together never knowing the truth."

Zebedee let out a heavy breath, "Come, let us talk more privately."

He helped me to my feet, and I embraced him. This Jewish man had rescued Dismas, had seen him with his eyes, had intimate knowledge of him. He had stories to tell me. He had touched him with the hands that held me now.

We found ourselves in a back room away from patrons at the innkeeper's place. We spoke for quite awhile, first listening to his story. Dismas was in Capernaum for four years. Four years!

"Then he vanished," Zebedee concluded. "I never saw him again."

"Thank you," I said. "Thank you for taking care of my Dismas. I now feel a little closer to my son through your stories."

Zebedee said, "So why bandits? You said you wanted to know who to talk to about that. What do these people have to do with your son?"

I answered, "I fear that Dismas has gone the way of banditry. We were told that he has been seen in this area. We don't know anyone here, but were led to speak with you."

"Well, I don't have direct contacts with this underground group but I can put out some inquiries."

Philos said, "That would be most helpful. Any information would be good. We don't want to get you involved with these people, though. We don't know what will happen with us, but we trust in God."

"As do I," Zebedee said. "So, you met my sons then on the beach that day when Jesus came to you?"

"That day was quite a blur, to be honest, but I do remember John's face. It was soft and caring."

"Mmm, yes, that is John. He has always been close to his mother, while James leaned more in my direction. You put those two boys together though, and they are quite a team. I'm blessed they travel with Rabbi Jesus, even though I contradict myself for saying so. I don't understand Jesus' ways, but I trust in God. I long, as a father, to one day see my boys teaching in the temple."

I touched his shoulder and said, "I also pray for this to happen."

"Well, I must get going. Stay here at the inn. I will send word once I find something. Don't worry about paying. I will arrange everything with John."

"We are very thankful. May the peace of God be with you."

"And with you also."

Zebedee left. Philos and I sat in the quietness, reliving what had just happened. I stood and said, "I'm going for a walk."

Philos understood, giving me a nod. It was late afternoon. Not knowing where to go, I found myself walking through crowds of people, criss-crossing here and there. A singular man came into view. It was the beggar. He stood in the same spot we had left him the day before. He was looking right at me as I approached.

"Jesus is not here."

CHAPTER 47
IT IS TIME

ELEVEN DAYS FROM THE CROSS
-DISMAS-

I HEARD THE WAGON wheels churning over the rock and sand. The horses breathed heavily. The odor of warrior's sweat permeated my sense of smell. The time had arrived. This was our moment to strike at the monster known as the Roman Empire. Their brutal tactics for world domination were ingrained into everything and everyone. Our destiny was clear, to thwart this enemy, to bring justice to the people, and to satisfy our thirst for their blood to be spilled.

Eighty-two of our men lay in wait as the brigade rolled closer and closer to our trap. The story of these Romans wouldn't end here. This day would be recorded in history as the day that launched the defeat of the great Roman military. The entire region would see that they do bleed and they can be beaten. The people would then rise up and join us to slay this Roman dragon once and for all.

These thoughts brought a smile to my face; not of joy, but of satisfaction for the forthcoming revenge.

I watched the dawn approach as I lay beside my brother, who twirled his dagger in the palm of his hand, flipping it over and under; a move he had practiced for years. Looking back up to the heavens, I watched the fading stars twinkle. Suddenly, I saw a shooting streak of light soar across the sky, leaving a blazing spectacle in its wake.

"Did you see that?" I whispered.

Out of the corner of my eye I saw Gez nod.

"It's a sign," I said.

Gez punched my shoulder, "No it's not. What's going to happen is the sign. A sign for everyone."

I nodded. He was right. He was *always* right. Signs are what we believed in when we believed in the gods. It was our destiny to create a true sign that others would talk about for generations. After today, we would execute what the supposed gods should have done. After today, we would be immortalized, too. In my mind, I could smell the ink penned on the parchment by the historians. I watched as they rolled up the scrolls to pass on to the generations to come.

I could hear them saying, *"Dismas and Gestas, heroes who rose up and birthed the revolution that would catapult the expulsion of evil from the land; the ones who brought healing to all those traumatized by slavery."*

It was our time to show everyone that the true miracle comes from fighting against tyranny, not healing a leper. Let the eyes of all the common people see the miracle of today and grab hold of it like a sword to wield wildly against our enemy.

Gez tapped me and I abruptly came out of my daydream. Leaning out to take a peek, I saw Roman soldiers in two lines leading the parade. Two wagons, heavily adorned with gold and silver were pulled along by four horses. Banners waved in the wind. Silk drapes covered the windows, hiding the dignitary we sought. There were roughly thirty warriors, but with the element of surprise and our eighty men, we would easily take them. Victory was heartbeats away. A little closer, just a little closer. The anticipation was thick.

There it was—the flaming arrow soared into the sky above us. My heart skipped a beat. Adrenaline coursed through my body as I rolled to my feet and slunk in next to a Roman soldier. Five steps in, I plunged my dagger into his side. I felt the familiar warmth of his blood cascade over my hand and then the chill of the early morning air forced the heat away as I pulled the blade out, threw him to the ground, and then swiveled to the next. Groups of our men poured in from their various hiding places. A dagger whisked by me and slammed into a soldier nearby. I followed the trajectory backward to find my brother's hand extended. He pulled forth another and flicked his wrist to let the knife loose, striking with deadly accuracy. The Roman sentries were frozen in surprise.

Within two minutes, thirty Roman dogs bled on the ground.

Our strike was quick and efficient. Our victory was at hand. I looked around and didn't spot one of our own to have fallen. All that remained were the wagons and the dignitary inside. Our men grabbed the horse reigns and settled them. Gez and I approached the second wagon. Before I pulled the door open, one of our men yelled, "These aren't warriors!"

I froze in place and slowly turned. As I looked, more and more helmets were pulled away from the dead to reveal that these were not Romans, but gagged commoners. The blade of recognition slammed into my soul. These were the very same people who had helped us inside the towns. We had done business with them. These were merchants who smuggled weapons for us. These were servants who loaded and offloaded contraband alongside us, and now they were all dead by our hands. Our frenzied state caused us not to notice the painted gags that blended in with the skin of their face. Why hadn't we seen this? We were blinded by our revenge.

In a panic, I turned to the door and yanked it open. Inside was Mendel. He was gagged and bound, beseeching us with his eyes. I removed his gag.

He coughed and said, "I'm sorry."

In that moment, I knew we had come to our end. My heart sank.

"It's a trap!" someone yelled behind us.

Roman soldiers stormed in around us. Our men tried to fight off the initial onslaught, but were overtaken by the sheer number and skill of these particular warriors. These were no ordinary fighters; no, these were the elite forces.

Gez grabbed me, "You need to escape, brother!"

I locked eyes with him. On the outside, yes, I wanted to run, but deep down I knew it was too late. Our fate was sealed. It had always been sealed. It was only now that we succumbed to the truth of it. "No, my brother, we go to the afterlife together."

He knew it to be true as well. Relinquishing his grip, he nodded.

"Come, let us take as many of these dogs with us as we can."

My vengeful smile returned. We entered the battle with no fear.

Dodging, sliding, twisting, maneuvering between bodies, we danced the dance of warriors. One fell, two, then three, until finally, a sword slashed across my arm. I backhanded the offending soldier. Gez plunged his dagger into the fighter's neck, releasing a geyser of blood.

A second wave of Romans came forth. Unlike the first wave, these wielded not swords but man-catchers and nets. We would not be captured and be enslaved to them. We could not.

Our men, our loyal men, fathers and sons, died at our side by the dozens. The remaining survivors were now being apprehended.

There were just too many of them. A hundred Romans surrounded the ten of us who were corralled together into a small group, back to back, circling to try and find space to escape, but the grip of this beast tightened.

"Lower your weapons!" a commander on horseback yelled.

The red plume on his gold helmet stood out amongst the rest. Bronze reflected in the light from his armor banding laced within the leather. Silver bracers with gemstones adorned his forearms. There was no doubt that this was the leader of the brigade.

"We will not!" Gez yelled in defiance and then spat in his direction.

One of the soldiers lunged in hard with a pole to strike Gez in the stomach, but Gez stepped aside, pulled the fighter in and ran his blade deep into his gut. Gestas continued to stare intently at the commander while his soldier bled to death at his feet.

"Who is next?" Gez yelled.

The commander looked over at a group of his fighters and nodded. Weighted nets came flying in and covered several of the men. These nets had hooks woven into them, so the more you fought or struggled, the more the metal hooks would gouge into your flesh and tighten their grip into you.

"I say again, lower your weapons!"

I was about to take a step forward, to take them all on alongside my brother, when an infuriated roar echoed from behind. The Romans turned heads in unison. Emerging from the bend was Barabbas, the mighty Barabbas. In his hand was a long spear stretching out eight feet in length. I had never seen Barabbas with a weapon. He had never shown any inclination towards wielding such a thing. From my vantage point, he appeared to be a giant as he puffed his bare chest out and bared his teeth in a bear-like growl.

"Enough!" he bellowed.

At the very least, Barabbas had caused a hundred Roman warriors to freeze in fear, which was no small task.

The commander swiveled his horse to look directly at the beast of a man.

"Barabbas, you have no play here. Go home."

"What?" I thought. Gez looked at me. Barabbas knew this man or the man knew of him. *"What was going on?"*

"Let them go! Take me instead!" Barabbas blared.

The commander responded, "You know as well as I do that battle never goes according to plan. No need for further bloodshed. I will, however, give one back to you. You might want to talk things over with him, however." The commander nodded to a nearby soldier, who reached inside the wagon and yanked Mendel out the door and onto the ground. He cut his ropes, setting him free, and then kicked him toward Barabbas.

Our friend froze in place. Barabbas looked to be on the verge of crying. "Why, Mendel? You…"

"I had no choice, my friend."

"Friend?" Barabbas barely croaked as the word caught in his throat. "Mendel, why?"

"You were not supposed to be here, Barabbas."

"And where was I supposed to be? Look at what you have done. All of these people are dead."

"Barabbas, they told me that they wouldn't hurt anyone. They said they would capture them with nets. They lied to me."

"No!" Barabbas roared. "No, Mendel! You lied to *us*!"

Mendel cowered, recoiling as he came face to face with what he had done. Shame blanketed his heart as the tears fell to the ground at his feet.

The commander said, "Barabbas, I'm giving you a chance to turn and go back. Pontius Pilate only wants these ruffians and no more. Their time of banditry has ended."

Barabbas' eyes fell to the ground, "What will happen to them?"

"Don't ask things you don't wish to hear. Just go home."

"What will happen to them?" he said more forcefully.

The commander looked around and then back at Barabbas, "They will be crucified. Some here at the gates of Jericho and some in Jerusalem, to send a message."

"I ask that you take me instead."

"That is not part of my orders, Barabbas, nor would I submit to a commoner such as yourself."

It was the way the Roman stated the word 'commoner'. He knew Barabbas somehow. They had a history.

"Take me instead. I beg of you."

"Begging is what your kind does best. Rome, however, does not beg. We take. I give you one last chance to turn back the way you came. What say you, Barabbas? Choose wisely or you force my hand."

Barabbas met the commander's eyes. "I have a message for you to give Pontius Pilate."

"And what is that?"

Barabbas pulled back his arm and released his spear. It whistled through the air and slammed into the Roman leader knocking him off of his horse. Nets flew at Barabbas; he stood still and let them come. I could see his face. Something had changed. He became like a statue without feeling or remorse. Soldiers went to their leader's aid, but I knew he was dead before he hit the ground. Then nets covered us, as well. All we could do was stand still. My eyes never left Barabbas. *Why had he come? What compelled this good-hearted man to leave his wife and aid us? Why had Mendel betrayed us?"* The question why became the noose around my neck. Then my thoughts shifted to despair.

Fate, destiny, future, what did it matter? Every man will come face to face with the finality of his life. No one knows the number of days as he travels his own road. I certainly did not. But at that moment, I no longer cared.

We were hit in the back of our legs, causing us to fall to our knees. A hook caught my left cheek and yanked at my flesh like a fish on a line. I didn't cry out. I wouldn't cry out. Yes, we were like fish to the gods and someone had a fine catch this day. My goal now was to hope the gods choked on my bones when they dined on us this night.

Gestas started laughing like a crazy man. His high pitched squeals caused the soldiers to beat him more severely. There was no getting out of this with the demon-crazed ploy again. Finally, they knocked him unconscious. The hooks embedded deeper.

"Curse the gods," I whispered. "Curse them all."

It turned out that the shooting star we saw earlier was a sign after all. It represented my life, with one exception; my life had no sparkle. It had nothing. It meant nothing. I had no family; well, no true family. I had nothing. Now the monsters I grew up with had returned. The shadows had come for me and all I could do was close my eyes and let them. *"Come quickly, I beg. Come quickly."*

CHAPTER 48
RACE AGAINST TIME

THIRTEEN DAYS FROM THE CROSS
-NESTOR-

"HE JUST STOOD there, Philos. In the exact same spot we left him the day earlier. It was as if he was waiting for me to return."

"And he said that same thing again?"

"Yes, he said that Jesus is not here. What do you think? Do you think he knows something?"

"Nestor, what could he possibly know?" Philos said as he turned to look out our room window onto the street below.

Zebedee had spoken to the owner of the inn and we found ourselves upgraded to a nicer room with actual beds, food, and a wash basin.

He turned back to me and said, "Let's wait on Zebedee and see what comes from his contacts."

All I could do was nod. What choice did we have? We would either wait for the Jewish businessman who knows the area or go to a beggar on the streets who was asking for money. It wasn't a hard choice, but I couldn't get him out of my mind.

Two days passed. We settled into our room, afraid to leave and miss any possible news. The knock on the door startled us. Philos answered. It was John the Innkeeper, a heavy-set man with a long beard that he parted and twisted together at the ends in several dangling tendrils. Much like his belly, his curly hair bounced as he spoke.

"I have news."

We did not respond, but ushered him inside and closed the door.

John leaned in and said quietly, "Zebedee received word that a group, calling themselves Tzedakah, is willing to meet with you. This is not a safe group to be talking to. Their name might mean "justice", but their rules are not civilized."

"It's possible they know something. We have to try," I said.

"Where are they located, John?"

"Kafr Manda, about twenty miles west of here."

"Twenty miles?" Philos questioned.

John added, "These are Samaritans," and then he spat on the ground, "Not only that, they are thugs who steal, kill, and destroy all those who contest them. All, except the Romans, of course. They stay clear of Rome and Rome stays clear of them. They are not to be trusted."

I looked at Philos and then back to John, "We understand. God will protect us." Even after I said that, I didn't truly believe it. I remembered being beaten nearly to death back in Scythopolis.

"You are to go to the Rayiys Shaytan hill near the town of Kafr Manda."

Philos asked, "What does Rayiys Shaytan mean?"

"It is Arabic for Demon's Head." Then John left.

"That sounds fun," Philos said sarcastically.

"We have to try, my friend."

"I know. Come, let us gather our things and get supplies. We will leave at first light."

It was late afternoon when we walked out of the inn. More people were now traveling toward Jerusalem as the Jews prepared for Passover, their Holy Week. We walked in silence, watching the camels and carts being loaded with items as people packed up for their journey. Suddenly, Philos stopped and grabbed my robe. I looked over at him. He was staring at something. I followed his gaze. There in the distance was the beggar.

I squinted and said, "He is in the same place, Philos. He hasn't moved."

"I know," Philos whispered, not diverting his eyes from the stranger.

We approached the filthy man who stood in the exact same spot we encountered him three days before. He watched us and then repeated, "Jesus is not here."

"Why do you say this to us?" I asked.

"You give me money now."

Without a word, Philos pulled forth a shekel and placed it in his hand.

"Jericho," was the beggar's response.

"What about it?" I asked.

"Jericho."

"You said that already, but what *about* Jericho? What are you talking about?"

"He will be in Jericho."

"Who will be there?"

The beggar didn't answer.

Philos questioned, "Jesus? Is that who will be in Jericho?"

"Jesus is not here."

"Yes, and you're saying that he will be in Jericho, but why?"

The beggar ignored Philos and stared into my eyes. I locked into his gaze and felt a strange kind of connection. I felt compelled to repeat his words, "He will be in Jericho." My words were barely audible, but upon speaking them, I knew their meaning. I turned to Philos.

"Philos, Dismas is in Jericho, not Jesus."

"What are you talking about? How do you know this?"

"I don't know how, but I do."

"This is crazy, Nestor. How can you be certain?"

"Philos, we have to go to Jericho," I said, frantic.

"But what about Kafr Manda and the information we just received?"

Suddenly, a donkey brayed directly behind us. We both jumped and turned simultaneously. The donkey, wandering the streets of its own accord, snipped at me as if I were concealing an apple in my robes. We stepped away. It meandered off, looking for food elsewhere. I looked at Philos. Without words, we communicated much. Where was the animal's master? We turned to face the beggar, but he was gone. I looked around in all directions. He was nowhere to be seen.

"Where did he go?" I asked.

"I know not." Philos' head whipped about, looking as well.

"We are going to Jericho and we are leaving now," I said firmly.

"Now? As in, right now?"

I took off at a fast-paced walk toward the city gate.

I heard Philos a few paces behind, "Yes, I see you meant right now."

I didn't say anything and kept walking.

Philos caught up with me, grabbing my shoulder to show his support. "This could be the day," he said.

I smiled at him as we left Tiberias behind.

We made it a mile before Philos asked, "I know that you believe Dismas is in Jericho, but can we reason together about this? To be honest, I don't share your confidence and I'm concerned."

As he spoke, I felt anger building. *Why couldn't he see it? That beggar was a messenger and Philos couldn't or wouldn't see it.* We walked a few strides while I settled myself to respond.

I said, "If Dismas is not in Jericho, all the blame will fall on me."

Philos stopped me.

"I'm not looking to protect my feelings, Nestor. I want us to find Dismas. But I want us to look at the facts."

In frustration I said, "Then go to Kafr Manda! I'm going to Jericho!"

"Why are you so angry?"

"And why don't you trust me?" I quickly retorted.

"Nestor, after everything we have been through, you don't think I trust you? This isn't about trust."

"Then what is it? Why don't you believe?"

"Believe what? Believe that a beggar was sent to deliver us a message from...from—"

"From who, Philos? Say it."

"From God."

There it was. I didn't respond right away. I let the words hang in the air.

Philos took a deep breath and exhaled. "Nestor, I want to believe, but we need to review what we know to be true."

"And what is that?"

"Mendel told us that Barabbas was recently in Tiberias, not Jericho, where this reputable man, well-known in the region, stated he heard the name of Dismas. Jericho is in the opposite direction." Philos pointed. "Why would Barabbas say otherwise?"

"I don't know!" I said frustrated.

Philos continued, "We have good information that Dismas is in this area, not Jericho. A beggar, that can barely speak a full sentence, saying strange things like, "Jesus is not here" and "Jericho", doesn't persuade me."

"But, Philos," I pleaded. "That beggar disappeared before our eyes. You can't deny this."

Philos sighed and said confidently, "I can, Nestor. There were a lot of people. He could have easily blended in."

"Come on! You were there!"

Philos raised his hands saying, "I do find it strange, but—"

I turned away in frustration, "I'm going to Jericho!"

Philos gently grabbed me, "Nestor, please." But I pushed him away, a little more roughly than I had intended. I heard Philos fall and grunt in pain, causing me to turn to see what had happened. He was on the ground holding his foot, grimacing.

I rushed to his side, "What happened?"

"My ankle," he managed to say through gritted teeth.

A passing wagon saw our misfortune and assisted me in helping Philos.

"Where are you headed?" I asked the Jewish man, knowing already he was bound for Jerusalem.

"Jerusalem, for the Passover. I'm taking my three sons." His boys stood just behind him. They ranged in age from ten to late teens.

"Might we get passage with you? Our destination is Jericho, which is on your way to Jerusalem. We can pay."

The man, in his forties, looked at his sons, then back to us. "There is no need to pay. We are going that way, but all I can offer is a ride in the hay cart."

"That is kind enough. Thank you."

They helped me with Philos, carrying him to the back of the cart. He groaned in pain from the movement. We positioned him to be as comfortable as possible. I climbed in next to him and then we were moving. Several minutes passed in silence between Philos and me. The sound of the cart rolling over the uneven dirt road and the clop of the two donkeys faded. My mind was elsewhere. *Could I be wrong? Was I foolish to be chasing words spoken by a simple beggar or was that truly a message from God?* My heart burned that I was right. I had no choice. If I went to Kafr Manda now, I would not be able to think about anything but Jericho.

"I'm sorry," Philos said after a while, snapping me out of my thoughts.

"Nonsense, my friend. It was my fault."

"Nestor, you realize that I will go wherever you go? This isn't about me. It never was. I'm with you, whatever the cost."

I looked at Philos, "I know you are. I'm sorry for not stopping to listen. It wasn't fair of me to do that to you. And it is my fault your ankle is sprained." I paused while I looked out the back of the wagon. "I can't logically explain my decision to go to Jericho, and perhaps nothing is there, but I have to find out."

"Then I am with you, my friend. And it wasn't your fault, it was the rock I stepped on."

There was a long pause as we listened to the wagon wheels turning over the uneven road. I finally asked, "How bad is it? Will you be able to walk?"

"It will be fine," he said, clearly still in pain, as every jostle of the cart told me.

I knew then it was going to be a tough journey for both of us, and I needed to be patient with Philos in his condition. Inside, I fought a deep-rooted frustration. *"Why now to sprain his ankle? We need to get to Jericho fast."* I felt to be in a race against time and my patience was being tested.

"Yes," I said. "Yes, you will be fine."

We stopped to rest for the evening. The father and sons helped build a fire and shared some of their food with us. We took our residence in a soft patch of sand, lying on straw mats with a single blanket to share. Philos fell asleep, and I was thankful. He needed his rest. I, however, could not find sleep that night.

I lay back, looking up into the night sky. Gazing upon the sparkling shimmer of the numerous stars, I wondered how God had created them. What seemed like only minutes turned into hours. I watched the fading stars twinkle and then suddenly saw a shooting streak of light soar across the sky, leaving a blazing spectacle in its wake. I looked over at Philos, but he was still asleep. The father and his sons slept soundly as well. I stared at his boys, nestled closely together, next to their father. My heart stirred. I wanted to be with Dismas. I needed to be with him.

Settling back, I wondered about my son. I wondered if he had seen this same blazing streak of light. I wondered what he was doing at this very moment. I took out the lion figurine and ran my fingers gently over the blemished object.

I whispered, "Dismas, your father is coming for you."

CHAPTER 49
DARKNESS

SEVEN DAYS FROM THE CROSS
-DISMAS-

"PERHAPS THE JEWS *like being slaves,*" I thought to myself. *"Perhaps the multitudes that celebrate this Holy Week, this Passover, lean too much on an invisible god to do their bidding. A god that will never come."* All I could do was ponder these thoughts. To confess any of them to my atheos brother would only bring ridicule and a flood of opinions.

We were both chained in a dungeon cell somewhere within the walls of Jerusalem. It took days of travel locked inside a cage for us to arrive here. Gestas hadn't said much during that time. Something in his eyes told me he had given up. We both had. But I couldn't turn off my thoughts. Why couldn't I stop thinking about things that didn't matter?

Again, what was the purpose of our lives, only to end this way? How did the gods decide which family or which culture we would be born into? What was the meaning of any of it? My mind would not, could not, stop thinking of the endless possibilities of one's fate in life.

I had thought that hate would win. I hated the Romans. They hated us. There could only be one winner; clearly, we had lost. I wondered if love could win, but I recalled that love was murdered before my eyes. The image of the lifeless body of my mother being dragged away played over and over in my mind. I loved her, but now my love had faded into this numb state of confusion. I had loved many people, at different levels, a father and mother, a brother, a friend, an acquaintance, a woman I slept with, a warrior standing by my side in battle, a vendor selling me my favorite food. But none of these expressions of love had won anything. Here I was, chained to a wall, waiting for the eternal darkness.

They fed us once a day, and not more than a rat could survive on. We were startled at the jingling of the jailer's keys, fearing the inevitable beatings that would follow. I curled into a ball in one corner. My brother took the opposite corner. Hay, encrusted with fecal matter, lay beneath us. It was dank and moldy and the air was cold. I could feel the sharp, frigid air penetrate my lungs like a knife into my chest. Repeated bouts of coughing told me that a fever was quickly approaching. What would it matter? Death by fever would be no more painful than death by the Romans. These dogs had mastered the art of brutality and slow deaths were their trademark.

"Dismas," my brother whispered, then coughed loudly. "Dismas," he said again.

"I'm here."

"Good, I don't want you to die before me." His voice was raspy.

"Is this now a race, too?" I asked.

"No, we shall die together. Remember?"

"I remember, but our fate lies…" *"Where?"* I thought. *"Where does our fate lie?"*

Gestas began to laugh. A high-pitched cackle that turned my face sour at hearing it echo. Then he began to cough.

Gez said, as he tried to gain control, "Fate is a myth. Fate is the discovery that life is a myth, my brother."

I finally contested him, "There must be something after this life. But what?"

"You know what it is."

"I don't."

"Yes, you do. Every man does."

"What are you talking about?"

"Darkness."

"Darkness?" I repeated.

Gez said sharply, "It is darkness that awaits everyone. Every star will fade to darkness. Every day will turn to night. Every man will sleep. Every memory will be lost. Every emotion will fall away. It's the darkness, brother, yes, the darkness. It comes for us all; don't you see it?"

I curled up tighter as I listened to his barrage, trying to push it away. In the end, he was always right, and my mind received his words into my soul. His words, like a battering ram to the wall of my mind, broke down my defenses and the walls exploded open. Hopelessness flooded in like a horde of monstrous demons screaming, *"We are Darkness!"*

CHAPTER 50
SENTENCED

ONE DAY FROM THE CROSS
-DISMAS-

THE ROMAN GUARDS shoved me back against the wall and beat my ribcage repeatedly. I clutched at my side, groaning, but soon began to giggle, which unleashed more brutality from our captors. My hate was stronger than the pain.

"That's it, my brother!" Gez said. "Laugh in their faces!"

Eventually, they ushered me back into my cell, slamming the cage door shut, and locking it.

"Keep it up," the guard said. "You will break. Everyone does." Then they left.

Enduring our Roman hospitality for days, our spirit of defiance swelled. We were held in the same room, dangling in individual cages, like caught birds, next to each other. Our cells were in the center of a large underground chamber with cut stone block walls and a single iron door leading out. It had been that way for the last couple of days. They placed an extra portion of food into only one of our bowls, which happened to be mine. I refused to eat more than my brother, throwing the remainder at the guards in protest. The Romans would torture us, not only physically, but emotionally as well, though, at this point, we were far beyond any emotional games that could pit us against one another. They did, however, give us extra water than we expected, but we knew it was for some reason we had not yet seen.

Periodically, we saw other prisoners brought in, but all of them were taken away, and we never saw them again. We heard the guards talk openly about their wagers on how long a prisoner would last, and then the cheers or moans, depending on the outcome.

It was the Jewish prisoners that fared the worst at the hands of the Romans. If only the Jews would rise up together and fight! But why even entertain the thought? What did it matter?

The iron door opened, and someone we had not expected to see ever again was pushed through; Barabbas. His face was battered severely. His beige robe was riddled with blood; torn and frayed from obvious beatings. Two guards, hulking men, man-handled a withdrawn Barabbas with ease, slamming him against the wall and chaining his wrists.

"See you later, darling. Look forward to our next moment together," the guard said as he puckered his lips in a pretend kiss. His cohort slapped him on the back and both laughed heartily on their way out. The door slammed, echoing loudly.

Barabbas looked up and saw me, "Dismas? Is that you?"

I didn't respond but just looked at him.

"You are still alive. Thank God."

That single word set my brother ablaze.

Gez shouted and lunged between the bars, clawing to reach him, causing his cage to swing, "God? There is no god, you pathetic fool of a man!" He retracted his arm and stared at Barabbas.

"I'm sorry, Gestas. This was not how it was supposed to end."

"And how was it supposed to end?" Gez questioned.

"It doesn't matter," Barabbas leaned against the wall.

It was quiet for a few minutes as both of them settled back into the numbness of the situation we all faced.

I finally broke the silence, "What happened, Barabbas? Why did Mendel betray us?"

He looked up at me, his left eye nearly swollen shut, "They crucified him before I could find out. They crucified all of them and made me watch, over and over and over."

"They are the lucky ones," Gez whispered.

"Why did you come when you knew to stay behind? You must have known something," I said.

He sighed heavily, "It was Mendel. He was acting differently than before. I thought someone was watching him. He gave me the plans and was adamant about me not being there, much more than was necessary. I knew then that he was hiding something. I went only to watch from a distance, but then I saw the treachery unfold. The caravan, the Roman soldiers massing, our people dying..." His words faded.

"Why are you still alive?" Gez asked.

I said brazenly, "It is Caiaphas who keeps him alive, brother."

Gez spat in Barabbas' direction. "Caiaphas betrayed us. Mendel was his puppet. Tell me, Barabbas, how does it make you feel that your brother-in-law betrayed you *and* your wife?" Gez' voice was full of contempt.

Barabbas said nothing.

"Oh, *now* the big man remains quiet," Gez taunted. "I will tell you how you feel. It is how we all feel. Empty."

Barabbas looked at Gez, "Empty? No, it is great sorrow. I can only ask for forgiveness and pray that God will find mercy upon us."

"I will never forgive you!" Gez stated, placing his face up against the bars. "You can pray and seek mercy all you want, but the darkness comes for us all." Gestas pulled back, launching into his hideous cackle, which turned to coughing before silence apprehended us once again.

"Your hate of the Romans brought this upon us," Barabbas said.

"Our hate?" Gez questioned.

"I was too blind to see. Or perhaps I saw, but did not do enough to stop it."

I said, "Our hate came to us when we were but children, and it grew stronger with every second that passed. Watching our father die, then our mother, then our friends. All that remained was our hate. Vengeance drove us."

"Vengeance is not for us. It belongs to the Lord," Barabbas said.

Gez spat out, "Your god is pitiful if he allows men to sin and does nothing."

"I had thought God led me to you both out in the wilderness. Perhaps I did not hear him correctly."

"You are laughable to say you hear god," Gez retaliated.

"His ways are not our ways," Barabbas countered. "Do you remember me telling you that God is revealing your story and we are to find out what it is?"

We didn't respond, but I remembered that morning at the table when Mendel spoke of John the Baptist and the possible Messiah.

Barabbas continued, "You wanted to hear this man crying out in the wilderness. He was preparing the way for something greater than him. John's story was being told to the world."

"What are you talking about, Barabbas?" I asked.

"Your story. What will it say when you end this life? This world contends to be the writer of our stories. But it is in the heart of men to *re-write* them. It is in your heart to write your own story. Don't you understand? You decide how it ends, not the Romans, not me, not anyone."

"You are pathetic like the rest of the Jews," Gez said. "Our stories end with crucifixion. Our blood spilling down that wooden pole for all to see. Our shame is the end of our story."

"You have resigned in your heart then as to how your story will end."

"We can't wish ourselves a different story, Barabbas. What you speak of makes no sense," I responded.

"Perhaps not, but none of us have gone this path before. I look to the one who created all things and not to the minds of those who only see themselves the victim."

Just then the door opened and the guards stepped inside.

"It looks like you have a visitor, darling," the guard said as they unshackled Barabbas and led him out of the room.

The silence was like a large stone being rolled over our tomb, cutting us off from the outside world. My thoughts were despairing, but my heart battled with hope that the words of Barabbas could be true. *"What is my story?"*

I was an orphan living in a make-believe family who found out his father was possessed by a demon. I lived my life in search of vengeance, for I believed that was the only way to fill the hole in my heart. Revenge made me feel a part of something. I just wanted to belong, to be known, and my wrath was my way to channel that longing.

I never wanted my story to be like this, but what choices did I have? And what choice do I have to make my story any different, considering where I am now? For surely I will die an agonizing death, nailed to a cross and ridiculed by onlookers; those who saw me only as a criminal.

My sentence was before me and Death was its name.

CHAPTER 51
UNLIKELY WARRIORS

THE DAY OF THE CROSS
-NESTOR-

THE FEELING CAME again, stronger than before. Urgency versus peace created in me a divine tension I had never experienced. Philos told me earlier he sensed it, also. He now stood in prayer by the open window. There was a strange light shining upon him. At first, I thought it to be a heavenly aura, but quickly realized that was not the case as I stepped outside the front doorway to the home where we were staying. I looked up at the partly cloudy sky to see colors ranging from magenta-orange to a bruised blue-green. The air was heavy and still. It was like the calm I had felt at the Sea of Galilee just before breaking winds would rush down the hillside to create monstrous waves.

I whispered to the heavens, "What waves come our way, Lord?"

I couldn't shake the need to hurry to Jerusalem, but Philos had sprained his ankle and pressuring him to walk faster wouldn't help either of us. Nonetheless, we needed to get to Jerusalem. My son was close. The Roman dignitary we met in Jericho had indicated so.

The strange weather still had me perplexed as I slowly made my way to the road just outside the home. The clouds, changing colors before my eyes, some dark gray, others red and purple, swirled together and then split apart. The winds high above appeared to be uncertain as to their own direction. Yet, I felt no breeze at all. It was still; unearthly still.

I looked through the open window and my dear, loyal friend continued his prayers to the God of all gods. Our hearts were filled with hope and it was the only thing that carried us through each day. Our hope was in Jesus. Only he could bring my son back to me. I believed that Dismas, upon seeing me, would know the truth of who Jesus is.

A slight vibration under my feet caused me to look down at the ground. At least I thought it was a vibration. I looked at Philos again but it had not stirred his determined prayer. Peering around, none of the others in this small village of Bethany seemed to take notice.

"Ah, you're up and about," a female voice said behind me.

I turned to see Martha with the entry rug in her grasp, preparing to beat dust from the weave as part of her daily chores.

"Yes," I responded. "Strange weather, don't you think?"

"Oh, I hadn't noticed." She stopped to look, squinting. "Strange, indeed." She looked at me without a second thought of the sky's bizarre nature, "Breakfast will be ready shortly." Then she continued on with her tasks. Martha was not one to be distracted from her chores; that was for certain. *What a blessing she and her sister Mary had been to Philos and me,* I thought.

"Will you be staying another night?" she called while placing the mat back in front of the doorway.

"Unfortunately, no. I feel the pull of Jerusalem."

She turned toward me from the door of the house. I could see the concern on her face as she thoughtfully approached me.

"It was but six nights ago that our Lord Jesus blessed us with his presence. I had prepared the meal."

She paused and gently placed her hand upon her chest. Her voice softened as emotions filled her, "I won't ever forget that night. He told us *not* to go to Jerusalem. I feel it in my bones, a stirring inside of me. It is the same stirring that Mary and Lazarus feel, as well. Even now they are in prayer and have been so for days."

She stopped and lowered her eyes to the ground to hide her tears.

I said, "What about you, Martha? What is it that you feel?"

She looked up, "Me? I don't know how to describe it, but I feel…" I saw her struggling with her emotions before she said, "I apologize, the words escape me. I beg you and Philos to stay another night."

"I feel so close to finding him, Martha."

"Jesus isn't hard to find, my dear. Just follow the crowds."

"No, finding my son. I mean yes, I do want to see Jesus again, but thoughts of finding Dismas consume me. After our encounter in Jericho, I know we are close. *This* is the stirring that pulls me toward Jerusalem."

She paused briefly, "Then go, my dear. Find him. But first, I will pack you some food." Martha turned and headed inside.

"Jerusalem is not far," I called after her.

Her head popped back out the front door, "You must eat no matter the distance."

"Thank you, Martha."

Just as we finished, Philos took a hobbled step outside and exhaled a deep breath while grinning blissfully.

Martha said, "Ah, I have seen that face before. The Lord has blessed this one."

Philos nodded, "The Lord has blessed us all." He noticed the odd weather and looked up at it, whispering. "Strange."

"My friend," I responded, "It is time for us to depart to Jerusalem. Are you ready?"

He walked over to me, placed both his hands on my shoulders, looked intently into my mismatched eyes, and said, "Yes, it is time. Your son is there. He has to be."

"Not before I pack you some food!" Martha called from inside.

Philos said, "She is a good soul."

We headed back to gather our meager belongings. Martha gave us bread, dried fruit, and some type of cake tucked in a thin piece of cloth.

She smiled, "If you see Jesus, tell him, if you can, that we love him."

I nodded, "Of course. Please give our kindest regards to Mary and Lazarus."

"You are always welcome here, Philos and Nestor of Decapolis."

With that, we were off. My heart soared at the thought of being united with my son, who had been lost to me for so long. Countless times I have relived the idea of seeing him face-to-face and sharing my heart with him. Would he accept me? Could the love of God reach even that far? These questions haunted me, but my reminder was always my encounter with the one named Jesus. A name to be above every name. He had come to find me across the sea. A bright light had shown in the darkness. The clutches of evil relinquished their grasp and I was set free. *"Yes, he is the Messiah."* He came to save us. My son's darkness could be no darker than where I was. The draw that I felt was not toward the city of Jerusalem, but toward destiny. Fate drove me forward much like the relentless winds above.

The future is always in front of us, never seen. My thoughts were consumed by that which was unseen. At any given moment, my son could appear before my eyes, and the mere thought pushed me forward even faster.

"Hey, do you mind?" Philos yelled.

Jarred from my thoughts, I stopped and turned to see my friend many paces behind me, nursing his left ankle.

"I realize you have some urgency," he continued with labored breath.

I attempted to apologize for my quickened strides, but Philos would not have any of it.

"But perhaps you could indulge me and find it in your heart to stay in step with your dear friend?" he asked sarcastically.

"Yes, of course," I said as I quickly walked back to his side.

"Good, I have certainly enjoyed our adventure of late. I'd find it meaningless if we were to part now."

"I have no intention of parting from you, Philos." I pulled his arm over my shoulder and let him lean into me as we walked together.

As we continued, Philos said, "Jerusalem, the Holy City. I have imagined its greatness. I feel something strange, however."

I stopped and looked hard at Philos. "What is it?" I pressed him.

His gaze never wavered. He simply said, "Be ready to fight, my friend."

"We are not warriors, Philos."

"Are we not? Do we not contend against principalities beyond our mortal eyes? We lived in that realm for a great many years, don't ever forget that." Philos' grip tightened as he clasped my shoulders.

I stared at him as his words reminded me once again of what we were truly up against. This world we breathe in, walk in, live in, is not all there is. There is another realm that exists far beyond what we see in the natural and even imagine in our thoughts. Demons abound in that realm. So do the angel armies of God, in even greater numbers. Indeed, there is a war at hand. Somehow, God had strategically placed us at the center of it. I would fight and fight even harder for my son, Dismas.

Philos saw my eyes, understanding, and nodded his approval. He relinquished his grasp. "Come, Jerusalem calls for us."

CHAPTER 52
THE CITY OF PEACE

THE DAY OF THE CROSS
-NESTOR-

I FELT THE HARD, flaky, limestone surface under my feet as we climbed higher and higher, skirting the Mount of Olives. This long and arduous road started in Jericho, passed by Bethany, and concluded in Jerusalem. I focused on my labored breathing, caused by the steep climb. With each step, my staff bit into the hardened ground. Philos was just ahead of me. There were many travelers along with us on this day. A day with no wind, yet the strange clouds swirled above with more of the strange colors I had never seen the sky produce before. Deep greenish-gray to indigo, washed on the edges with purple.

Bandit raids were almost non-existent between Bethany and Jerusalem because of the strong Roman military presence, so I had no thought of anyone attacking us. My thoughts were consumed with finding my son. The Roman dignitary of Jericho had captured a large band of rogues who had assaulted a political caravan. Many were crucified outside the walls of Jericho, but a few were brought to Jerusalem to be sentenced. I know nothing of Roman politics or law but I do know that they march to their own beat, marked with brutality.

"Jesus, help me," I whispered.

Philos stopped and looked back, "What was that?"

"Nothing, my friend. You seem to be walking a little better."

"Ah, it's just an ankle. The Lord blessed me with another."

Philos turned and continued on. After Jericho, finding out that Dismas was one of the captured, Philos changed a bit. He was more... open. Open to the leading of God, that is. He apologized profusely for not trusting me that Dismas was in Jericho. My friend had stood by my side since we were children. He had lost so much, just as I had, and through it all, he still remained. Could this be the completion of our journey together? Where would we go after finding my son? Would Dismas come with us? My hope and prayer was that he would. But would it be even possible? Dismas was now in the hands of the Romans. I'm hopeful that I will be able to plead my case to the magistrate for his release. I submitted my thoughts to God, placing them in his gracious hands. These were hard times. But the Messiah had come, and hope loomed brighter than ever before. Indeed, a great light had shone.

"Nestor."

I looked up from my walk and saw Philos leaning against a rock, staring off into the distance. We had been hugging the side of the mountain in a steep ascent for quite some time. Philos looked back at me and smiled.

"Come," he said.

I took the few remaining steps and what I saw took my breath away. My eyes feasted on the vista before me. There, across the valley, stood the majestic Holy City. My eyes digested the huge limestone brick walls surrounding the homes of the lower city quadrant. My gaze shifted immediately to the gold temple that towered a hundred feet or more above everything else.

Philos too, was awestruck, "It is the perfection of beauty. A joy for me to see with my own eyes."

I didn't respond. I don't think I could have. The limestone colors ranged from white to pink and from yellow to orange-brown. Immense bricks, honed to stand the test of time, were resurrected in the most majestic piece of human art that mankind had ever known. Were there no limits to what man could do?

Thousands of hearty souls resided inside this compact city and it was then that I suddenly felt the pangs of anxiety. Impossibilities flooded my heart and mind. The gravity of not only finding my son, but actually being able to speak to him, or save him, overwhelmed me with doubts. The dark clouds swirling above became ominous.

Philos clutched my shoulder and said, "We will find him, Nestor."

He knew me. His words comforted me like a cool drink of water in the desert. I acknowledged him with a slight smile and a nod.

"Come, let us go find him."

We were not but ten minutes into our walk down the mountain when Philos said, "I realize now, I actually prefer going uphill rather than down."

He had slowed considerably. His ankle was clearly troubling him as he fought against the momentum.

"Sit, my friend. Let us rest a bit." I pulled him to the side, joining him on a flat-topped boulder. A group of twelve or more people was heading our way from the city. They wore an assortment of colored robes and shawls. With them were two donkeys loaded down with numerous rolls of fabric, filled sacks, and cooking equipment, which clanged and rattled at each clop of their hooves.

"Strange weather," I said to them.

One stopped and looked up. He nodded and kept going without a word. The others never slowed.

"Do any of you know if a group of bandits were brought in recently?"

A younger man wearing an off-white robe and worn sandals stopped and said, "Bandits? Have you not heard?"

The entire group of men stopped now.

"Heard what?" I asked.

"You wouldn't understand, being Greek."

Philos said, "We follow Jesus of Nazareth as well."

"It is over. The Romans have won."

"Won what?" I asked.

"They have captured the Messiah, Jesus, and even now they march him to his death."

I immediately stood, "How is this possible? The Romans have Jesus?"

"Yes, our land is doomed. Not even the Messiah could defeat them. We are heading north. Perhaps beyond Capernaum. We suggest you go back. This is not a safe place for anyone who follows Jesus."

I gently grabbed hold of his arm, "What about any bandits? Did they bring any in?"

"Bandits are brought in daily, my friend."

Another of the men in the group said, "He speaks of Barabbas."

My eyes jolted toward the older man. The wrinkles on his face were like wind blown dune ripples. "Yes," I said, "this man you say, Barabbas. I have heard his name spoken before. Do the Romans have him?"

"The Romans let him go."

"Why would they let him go? I was told he was the bandit leader."

"We don't have time for this," the younger one said and pulled away from me. "Let's go." They began to walk up the hill.

The old man delayed and took a step toward me. His eyes, a former blue, but covered with the milk of time, looked deep into mine. "I still believe in Jesus. I have seen too much not to believe. He must be the Messiah. I know not the ways of God, but why send the Messiah only to be killed? Jesus has awakened us. My heart leaps at the thought of all he has done. My sons leave out of fear, but I leave to be with my sons." He paused and looked a long second at me and then continued, "Barabbas, even now, rallies people in the courtyard of the Gentiles, if he is who you seek."

"No, I am in search of my son, who traveled with him."

The old man sighed, "If he was taken with Barabbas, then I fear the worst. His gang will be executed. Even now two of his men lead the way to Golgotha with Jesus."

"What is Golgotha?"

"It is a hill on the far side of the city outside the walls. It is the place the Romans crucify criminals, to send their message of fear."

"Crucify," I whispered and looked away at the city below.

Philos said urgently, "Go, my friend! Do not delay on my behalf! I will find you!"

I couldn't speak as I stumbled down the hill. My speed increased until I was in a full sprint. I had no time to take in any of the beautiful surroundings and architecture of the city. Nothing mattered, except the thought of losing what I sought and have chased for months. I prayed that my son was not one of the two that would be nailed to the wood beams and hung for all to see. This was no longer Jerusalem, the beautiful City of Peace, but a prison that contained my son somewhere within its walls.

CHAPTER 53
BARABBAS

THE DAY OF THE CROSS
-NESTOR-

I RAN ACROSS THE bridge to a large, wide-open gatehouse. There was no time to take in the view of the Kidron Valley. People were coming and going. Roman guards were stationed all around. I took three or four stone steps at a time, bypassing a line of patrons on the left, while dodging citizens leaving on the right. The smell changed from the natural odors of the land to something I had only experienced in the marketplace throughout my travels. This time it was amplified a hundredfold. Not just a musty mixture of dung, old men, and food. It was so much more—pungent perfumes, incense, burnt offerings, and the distinct smell of blood.

"Halt!" a Roman stepped out in front of me with a long spear to block my entrance. "Where do you think you're going, Greek?"

Startled, I held up my hands in surrender and backed up a step. "I need to find my son," was all I could say through labored breathing, sweat dripping down my face.

"Yes, well, everyone is looking for someone, now, aren't they? Get in line and pay your taxes!" He gestured back to the line of people, forty deep, waiting to gain entrance. I saw two men sitting behind a desk collecting money and other items from the people.

"But I don't have anything to be taxed."

"Where did you come from? Why are you running?"

"Jericho. I'm looking for my son."

Another guard with a black emblem of an eagle on his shoulder stepped over and said, "Problem?"

The subordinate guard responded quickly, snapping to attention, "No, sir! This Greek, I mean, man, is looking for his son and appears to not have any taxable items with him."

"Then perhaps you should just collect the entry fee and let him enter."

"Yes, sir!" He refocused on me.

I pulled forth a denarius and handed it to him.

"Welcome to Jerusalem. Move along."

I started to go, but stopped. I looked around at the hundreds of people who were milling about in the courtyard of the temple. I truly had no idea in which direction to go or to whom I should inquire. I clutched the lion figurine in my robe pocket and whispered, "Lord, help me. Guide me."

I turned back and said to the captain, "Excuse me, sir."

He turned and gave a slight smirk, "What is it now, patron?"

"Uh, this is my first time here."

"I'm not a tour guide. Get lost."

"No, that is not what I meant. My apologies."

"Then I suggest you get to what you do mean."

"I'm trying to find my son and I know that he is here."

The guard sighed heavily and said, "What is his name and how old is he?"

"His name is Dismas."

"Age?"

I knew this soldier wouldn't understand once I relinquished this information. I hoped he was a family man himself so that he would take pity on me because of my situation. The only problem was my child was fully grown. All I could do was trust God.

"He is," I paused, "he is twenty years of age."

"Twenty? I'm not in the mood for such a game as this, Greek. These are troubling days and I don't have time to be dealing with your *grown* son."

I pleaded with him, "Do you have a family, sir? I only ask because I lost my son at birth and have not seen him since."

He looked at me hard, "Pray, tell. What do you mean lost him?"

I didn't have time to go into the entire story, grand and epic though it was, so I blurted out, "I was oppressed with demons and walking in darkness for many years until Jesus came."

That single word; not demons, but Jesus, caused him to shift uncomfortably. I pressed on, "Jesus saved me and for months I have searched tirelessly for my son, whom I lost at birth. He is everything to me, so I beg of you, please help me."

"Do you not know what happened this very morning? Jesus was sentenced to death, and even now carries the cross he will be executed upon."

"Men outside the city informed me. I am deeply troubled by this news. My Dismas traveled with another called Barabbas."

"Barabbas?"

"Yes, my son has made some poor decisions in life. I blame myself because I was not there for him."

The guard looked intently at me, took off his helmet, clutching it at his side. I saw compassion in his eyes. He leaned in and said, "I am a father, myself. Know this, we do the best we can, but our children will make their own decisions at no fault of ours. No different than our own fathers. Don't take guilt upon yourself or it will become your gravestone."

I nodded in agreement and asked him once again, "Do you know where he is?"

"Barabbas and his gang of bandits were brought in for sentencing. All were supposed to be put to death by crucifixion, but..."

"But what?"

"All were sentenced except for one. Barabbas was set free by the Jews and in his place they sentenced Jesus of Nazareth. The Jews are a baffling people." He placed his helmet back on his head, positioning it appropriately. "Barabbas is in the Court of the Gentiles." He pointed in the direction.

"Thank you," I said, quickly heading that way. As I walked, I called behind me, "I have a friend who will be coming through this gate! His name is Philos and he has a sprained ankle! I hope—"

He cut me off, "He will get in with no trouble, and I will point him in the right direction. May the goddess of luck give you favor this day."

I entered the temple district. Swallowed by the sea of people, I dodged bodies crossing my path from all directions. Finally, I came into a vast open area where people were selling animals to be offered as sacrifice. People were everywhere, from what seemed like every nation. Cripples, beggars, the blind, and zealot temple guard patrols, clearly not a part of the Roman elite, also milled about.

A larger gathering of people attracted my attention on the far side of the courtyard. Thirty-foot pillars, set every ten feet, held up the red-tiled roof area that surrounded the temple district. Steps led up to an elevated platform where a man stood, looking extremely distraught. He was a bear of a man dressed in tattered loose clothing with an open robe too small for his large frame. His hands gestured in grand fashion as he appeared to be telling a story to the crowd. More people gathered closer to hear him.

His baritone voice projected. So did his contempt for Rome, "You see I stand for righteous justice! Those we lost along this path will not die in vain! They will be remembered for all time, when the mighty fall."

This was Barabbas. There was no doubt in my mind. He was clearly speaking against the Romans without saying it openly.

Barabbas continued, "Today, we will lose brave men, brave sons, but God is with us. God was able to rescue me, and he will surely rescue more."

The mention of God caused the people to cheer in acceptance. These were Jews looking for hope and inspiration to brighten their darkened world.

I had no time to waste, so I challenged Barabbas, "Where is my son?"

The crowd slowly quieted.

I said more forcefully, my eyes locked onto Barabbas, "Where is my son?"

The crowd turned in my direction. People parted as I stepped closer to the front. Barabbas licked his chapped lips, squinting to get a better view of me, the intruder. A noticeable scar over his left swollen eye and across his cheek brought attention to his mud-brown-colored eyes.

Again I asked, "Where is he?"

"Who are you?"

"My name is Nestor and my son is Dismas."

There was a pause. Then Barabbas let out a roar of laughter. Others in the crowd chuckled.

"Dismas, you say? His father is dead."

I put another bold foot forward and began to walk up the five steps. Again, the crowd hushed. I am tall for a Greek but this rogue warrior towered over me. I swallowed hard and declared, "Let there be no doubt, I am his father!"

Barabbas looked into my eyes for a long moment. His demeanor changed as he leaned in and whispered, "What are you all about? Diz never spoke of you."

"My son never knew me. We were separated at birth."

"Twenty years? Where were you? Imprisoned? Slave labor?"

"I was once dead. Now I am alive, because of Jesus of Nazareth."

Barabbas turned back to the crowd who waited to find out what this confrontation was all about. "This man is a Jesus follower! We have seen what Jesus has done across this land. But when the time came to fight, he rolled over and gave himself up. The so-called Messiah will be buried alongside the others who called themselves Messiah, but Barabbas remains. We remain! I have favor with God, let there be no doubt! The High Priest has blessed me. God answered my prayer and bestowed mercy upon me."

The crowd cheered and yelled his name repeatedly. I leaned into him, "Please tell me where he is and I will be gone."

"Diz was more than a good soldier to me. Whoever you are."

"Please," I begged.

Barabbas looked back at the crowd who continued to cheer. This caused the Roman guards to send in a patrol, which began to disband the people.

"Dismas, if I could speak to him but once. Grant me this."

"I had many sons until these Roman pigs killed them."

"And so you understand, every beat of my heart belongs to my son."

The guards were now at the steps, heading toward us.

"Where is he?" I pleaded in urgency.

"You are a Jesus follower," he smirked. "Then follow Jesus."

I was shoved aside and ordered to leave the area, as was Barabbas. Four guards ushered Barabbas down the steps and led him to the nearest gate out of the temple district. Many followed him, but I stayed in place, unable to move. Barabbas' voice echoed in my mind, *"Then follow Jesus."*

I understood his meaning—my son was one of the two that would be crucified with the man who saved and healed so many in these last few years. The reality of this truth took my breath away.

Jesus of Nazareth had authority over demons and over death. This had to be a showdown between God and Rome. The sky above swirled in anticipation. What others had said about Jesus going to his death was not the truth. Jesus was going to show his true power. Hope bubbled up inside of me.

I said under my breath, "My son will be there to see this firsthand, and so will I."

CHAPTER 54
FOLLOW THE BLOOD

THE DAY OF THE CROSS
-NESTOR-

Jesus had to save my son. The Messiah, the Christ, the Son of God, was about to display his might over the Romans, and anyone else who came against him. My time of searching for Dismas had come to an end. I would finally be reunited with my son! I would be able to share the rest of my life with him telling him all about Jesus of Nazareth.

"Where is Golgotha?" I asked several people as I made my way out of the temple district. Some ignored me while others pointed the way.

I traveled the winding corridor of limestone-paved streets, continuing to ask directions along the way. This place was a labyrinth. I estimated many people had lost their way within its confines; physically and spiritually. Hostility was in the air. It could be seen on all the faces that I passed. Some small groups argued vehemently, ready to come to blows, while Roman guards stood watch close by.

There was a large contingent of soldiers about. I reasoned they were there because of Jesus and his followers. I heard the Messiah's name whispered as citizens walked by me, but none openly declared it.

Two older men wearing priestly garb stood off to the side of the street, conversing with one another. I approached them in hopes they could inform me of the direction.

"Golgotha?" I asked.

They stopped talking and looked at me quizzically.

The purple-robed man said, "Are you one of his followers?"

His question was one I had heard before, but there was a distinct hint of venom in his voice.

I responded with a bit of hesitation, "I am."

His bushy eyebrows raised as they looked at each other with sinister smirks.

He turned back to me, "You are a Greek, no?"

"Yes."

"I'm curious, why do you follow this Jewish man?"

I had seen these types before. They grappled the people with their words and held them hostage. I had no time for this.

"Where is Golgotha?"

He was clearly not amused with my deflection of his question. He said disdainfully, "Follow the blood." He turned and walked away with the other following close behind.

At first, I had no idea what he meant, but then I looked at the ground and noticed the large red droplets, some smeared. Larger crowds were heading toward me from the opposite direction. I realized then that these people must have been part of the crowds sending Jesus to the site of his crucifixion.

I stooped down and poked at a large droplet of blood. Suddenly, my mind was hit with grotesque images of Jesus being brutalized by Roman guards. The flashes subsided and the site and smells of the streets of Jerusalem returned.

I heard my name being called, "Nestor!" It came from the crowd behind me, but I didn't see anything.

Again, my name was called, "Nestor!"

Emerging from a large group of people was my longtime friend Philos. I embraced him and said, "Thank the Lord you found me."

"Did you find him?" Philos asked.

All I could say was, "Come. This way. We must hurry."

"Just remember my ankle, my friend."

Philos and I took off down the narrow crowded street going against the tide of people. Pushing and dodging, we made it to another inter-section. I moved in the direction the people were returning from.

It was uphill most of the time. The streets snaked back and forth, weaving an intricate web.

"Did you find him?" Philos shouted from behind me.

"I did. He is with Jesus."

"With Jesus?"

"Come. No time to explain. We must hurry."

The crowds began to dwindle the further up we went. There were women weeping along steps. A group of men laughed heartily, slapping backs as if in triumph. The patrols of guards decreased as we got closer to our destination.

Philos passed me as I tried to navigate through a group of people on the left. He chose to pass on the right and made it through easily. I then realized he was walking normally.

"Your ankle?" I called to him.

Philos stopped and turned toward me, then shock registered upon his face. He lifted his foot and rolled it back and forth and up and down.

"It is healed!" he gasped.

As I looked at the miracle before me, I spotted a smear of blood on the outside of his foot just above the ridge of the sandal. He also spotted it.

"Am I bleeding?"

"No, it is his blood."

"Who's?"

I looked with wonder at my friend, "*His* blood."

Philos nodded, "Come. It is time."

The crowds of mourners grew, their cries resounding along the path. It was as if they had experienced a death in their own family. Did they not know that Jesus, the Messiah, was about to conquer this city and this land? They should be rejoicing, for soon their tears would turn to joy. They were blinded by only what they could see.

There ahead of us was a city gate leading outside the wall. The ominous clouds continued to brew above us and became darker. I could now feel the wind whirling and rushing through the area. Something was amiss. Guards shielded their faces from the fierce wind funneling through the gate entrance. Philos and I clutched one another and fought through to the other side. Once there, I spotted a hillside to our right. I tried to look in that direction but the pelting sand, kicked up from the wind, caused me to flinch and cover my eyes.

It was at the top of this hill that I would find my son. I began to run. No wind, sand, or storm would stop me. Nothing in all the world could prevent me from setting my eyes upon him. I didn't know if Philos was behind me but my legs would not stop pumping. My muscles strained under the pressure, but I would not be stopped. All these years had boiled down to this day, this place, this one moment.

The wind decreased the further I climbed. I looked up longing to see what everyone else stared at. A hundred people were down on their knees in clusters on the hill while hundreds of others stood by watching. It was the horror of what was before them that seized my heart. My run ended abruptly like a final breath of life. Philos plowed into me from behind but I took no notice.

"No," he said under his breath.

Jesus was nailed to a cross. There was nothing recognizable about his face, but we knew. Blood covered him from head to toe. His face was mangled, bruised, battered, and cut open. I knew who he was because of his sheer presence. He was our Messiah. He was our King.

I don't remember walking but found myself closer. I was captured in a dreamlike state of being; taken from the palace of hope to the depths of despair.

I was about to sink even lower.

My eyes focused on the cross to the left of Jesus. I had never seen the man before. I don't know how I knew, but just as I knew who Jesus was, I knew he was my son. It was my Dismas.

CHAPTER 55
IF YOU ARE THE CHRIST

THE CROSS
-NESTOR-

PHILOS AND I stood there in utter horror and shock. Not only was the Messiah brutally nailed to the wood beams that held him several feet in the air, but my son, my Dismas, also clung to life. How could this be happening? All this time in search of him, only to come to this ending. I was his father and yet there was nothing I could do. The helpless feeling balled up inside my stomach and nausea almost overwhelmed me. My mind dulled the noises around me and I struggled in disbelief as I tried to wish this event away. This was torture. These images would haunt me to my grave. *"What was the point of Jesus saving me? How could God possibly reconcile this?"* In mere seconds, I traveled from the road of hope to the road to hell. My heart and soul were pierced as the darkness began to swallow me.

Roman guards to the left of me caught my attention. Blood was splattered across their armor, legs, and arms. A purple robe lay on top of a cluster of boulders, displaying the prize as dice were tossed at the base of the rocks. They were throwing lots for Jesus' belongings. The clattering of the dice caused me to wince. It sounded like they were rolling them inside my head.

"Son of a whore!" one yelled as another laughed heartily in

triumph and scooped up the garment. He waved it around at the others to flaunt his winnings.

I turned my attention to the other sounds. Sobs emanated from the group of women closest to Jesus. There was a man standing behind them who seemed familiar to me, but I couldn't place him. They were his followers, no doubt. I could discern no other followers in the groups that gathered. It seemed most were hurling insults. People came and went, spitting in Jesus' direction or yelling obscenities, mocking his teachings. I prayed they would stop. I wished I could stop them, but I could not bring myself to move. At the same time, I wanted to yell at my Messiah and question him harshly, *"Why? Why!"* I wasn't sure I could speak even if I wanted to. My eyes moved from person to person as my mind tried to grasp the reality of what I was witnessing. I longed for someone to yell, "WAKE UP, NESTOR!" I needed someone to slap me in the face and snap me out of this nightmare, but the moans from the three people suspended above reminded me that this was not a dream but reality.

Romans had perfected the art of torture. Crucifixion stood at the pinnacle of the evil that could be perpetrated upon a person. I had seen the dead hanging from the wooden posts, but never went close enough to see the truth of what happened to a man before he died. Each one labored for breath and was forced to raise himself up by his impaled feet to catch but a gasp of air. Slowly he would sink back down. It was less than the length of a finger, but even the smallest of movements brought immense pain. I knew this would go on for hours. We were in the early stages of this brutal Roman ritual.

I heard chimes, and my eyes diverted to the sound. Walking up the small incline was a parade of Jerusalem's religious elite. I had no idea about rankings within Jewish hierarchy. But I understood enough that these men, dressed in expensive robes with golden sashes and expensive jewelry, carried authority.

One of the priests stepped forward. He had a disgusting smile on his face and said for all to hear, "He saved others and yet he cannot save himself!" He looked around at all the people as if preparing to speak a sermon to the flock. Many laughed at his statement. He turned toward Jesus and said mockingly, "Let the Christ, the King of Israel, come down now from the cross that we may see and believe!"

Another priest shouted right behind him, "You, who would destroy the temple and rebuild it in three days," he spat on the ground and continued, "save yourself, and come down from the cross!"

No one spoke or laughed as they awaited the response. We all held our breath, looking at Jesus in anticipation. The priest continued his haughty speech, "You see. He is just a man." He turned away from the scene and walked back the way he had come. The other priests followed behind.

I had not noticed it before, amongst all the carnage, but nailed above Jesus' head was a wooden sign, written in Hebrew, Latin, and Greek. It read, 'Jesus of Nazareth, The King of the Jews'. Just then, a soldier dipped a sponge-tipped spear into a jar, filled with some kind of liquid. *"Perhaps water,"* I thought.

The soldier barked, "Here, you pathetic fool! You can't save yourself so let me help you out a little!" His cohorts chuckled and mumbled comments to one another that I couldn't hear. The dripping sponge touched his lips but he turned away. "Come on, then. If you are the King of the Jews, then save yourself." He walked back to his comrades and chided further, "The sign says 'King of the Jews,' does it not?" More laughter ensued.

I was mesmerized by all the happenings. It was as if I had left my body, taking account of each person's words and actions, yet somehow oddly removed and unable to react. I avoided looking upon my son. What was left of my conscious mind pushed back, no, *buried*, all thoughts that this man was Dismas, my son. If I could separate myself and keep numb to what was happening, then the pain might subside. If I could just be an innocent bystander, then maybe it would stop searing my heart.

The criminal furthest from me cried out horrifically, jarring me back to reality. He slipped back down after gasping for air, helplessly trying to slow the suffocation he was experiencing. I forced my eyes to look away. I wanted to leave and never look back, but I knew I had no choice. There was no running from this. I was but a mere mortal and no amount of running or prayers would change what was happening before me.

I glanced back at Philos, who was dumbfoundedly transfixed. I followed his gaze and noticed that the less swollen eye of Jesus was focused upon him. Wait, not him. He was looking at me. His look pierced me. It took my breath away. *"What was he looking at? He was disgusted with me, he had to be. He was...no, those eyes spoke a different story about me than I had ever thought about myself."*

I had seen that look before. It was a look that brought you to your knees. No man could withstand that look. They would fall, no doubt, to their knees, physical or spiritual, but the wiser would fall to both. I crumbled to the ground and sobbed. In an instant, Philos was at my side, holding me. Through my guttural sounds as my insides turned inside me, I heard Jesus piercing through my sobs. It was so clear, just like on the beach of Galilee when he saved me from the clutches of evil all those months ago.

"Nestor, this burden is not yours to carry."

Through tears, I choked out, "Lord, why?"

His voice, so powerful and soothing, like honey, *"Nestor, give me the why."*

"I can't!"

I could hear Philos trying to comfort me. He was unaware of my exchange with Jesus. No one could know that the Jesus they saw before them was speaking to me through my spirit just as clearly as if he were standing right next to me.

I could relinquish neither my pain, nor my questions. *"Lord, why? Why did you bring me all the way here to witness this horror? My son. He is my son. Why? Just answer me, I beg of you. I don't understand."*

"Fool!" A loud voice far away jarred me out of my conversation. It wasn't the voice of Jesus, but the other thief. *"What was his story?"* I wondered. *"How had these two boys ended up here?"*

The thief coughed and sputtered again loudly, "Fool! What are you? Are you not the Christ? Save yourself and us!" He began to cry. No, that was not crying. He was laughing a horrible cackle.

Dismas joined him in laughter.

My son echoed his words, "Yes, what a fool. You announced 'round the land that you're a king." He coughed and then continued, "No king now, just a common criminal." They both laughed again. High-pitched cackles laced with pain. It was evil to the core.

I sighed heavily. I had no strength in my body to stand. Philos continued to hold me. I thought while looking at him, *"Oh, friend of mine, why do you stay?"*

Suddenly, Dismas stopped laughing as if someone had slapped him in the face. I looked quickly and saw that he was entranced by Jesus. Jesus had looked toward Dismas from his perch. It was the same look Jesus had given me. There was power in his gaze. I wrestled again with this reality. Jesus was no mere man. And yet, I could see plainly that it was a man nailed on the cross, bleeding like all others. What king would allow such an atrocity to happen except for one who had been conquered? If Jesus was not a man and was not a king, then what was he?

My attention was drawn back to my son. *"What was happening inside Dismas?"* I wondered. *"What could Jesus be imparting to him through his eyes, through his thoughts?"* It was apparent that not even Jesus' look of love was going to change this course of events. It was hopeless. Hours seemed like days upon this hill of Golgotha.

My heart sank even lower. I had stood at the top of a glorious mountain waterfall, after being freed from my demoniac prison; hope for a new life filled me, hope for the triumph of Jesus reigning as Messiah and king inspired me, hope of being reunited with my precious son consumed me. Standing now at the foot of the crosses that were perpetrating the agonizing, torturous death of my Savior and my beloved son caused me to plunge over the falls, crashing so hard upon the rocks below that it felt as if my very soul had shattered into a thousand pieces. The crashing water churning over me, pulverizing me. I disappeared into myself, into a dark abyss lined with the shadows of nothingness. Darkness swallowed me.

A breeze, no, a whisper, brushed by me in my darkened state. I tried to ignore it, but the words echoed inside of me. They were words of life and power. The voice of Jesus. He simply said, *"Be ready."*

CHAPTER 56
THE PAIN

THE CROSS
-DISMAS-

M Y NAME IS Dismas, feared by no one, known by no one. It is strange that, at the twilight of your death, you recall your life and all you have done. I find it all to have been meaningless. What does anything matter when you are facing a dark journey of passage into an unknown realm? From the lowliest of lepers to the highest of kings, all will ultimately face the same darkness.

"What is beyond this veil? Nothing, perhaps. Or do we start over?" My mind wanders in this labyrinth of thought. But what do my thoughts even matter, considering how I hang upon this cross? No amount of torture from these Roman dogs will break my spirit. I will not gratify them by crying out in pain. It will not happen.

It is hard to breathe. I chuckle and cough at the thought, as I come back around to the question; has anything about my life mattered? I'm hours away from whatever is next. Good riddance to this world and this life. Good riddance to these people crying at the foot of this so-called Messiah, and good riddance to the ones who ridicule him. I heard about this man called Jesus. Who hasn't? I heard the testimonies from the people who said they were blind and now they see or were once lepers but were now healed. There was even talk of a man being raised from the dead.

I try to gather saliva in my mouth to spit toward this man who hangs in the center of Gestas and me, but my mouth is too dry. I need to breathe and have to push against the nail embedded in my feet. The pain! I bite my lip and push. The taste of my blood fills my mouth. I'm not going to cry out. I'm not going to cry out. Breathe, Diz, breathe. Oh, the glorious intake of air in my lungs. I tell myself, *"It was worth the pain."*

I go back to wondering who this man was, this Jesus. Beaten and broken beyond recognition. I have not seen anything like it in my lifetime. This man, who claimed to be the Messiah to the Jews, now fights to take his last breaths just like I do. I don't like looking at the people who came to gawk, so I stare at Jesus. His entire body is covered in criss-crossing slashes; gaping wounds exposing muscle and sinew. Blood, so much blood, trickles down his body, down the post, and to the ground. He shouldn't be alive, but he is. He even refused the wine concoction that was offered to reduce the pain, not once, but twice.

I looked to my far left and there was my brother, Gestas, my dear Gestas. How did we get here? I know the answer. But, oh, how I wish that he had escaped. He would never have abandoned me, though. We have lived together always. Now we shall die together, side-by-side.

I remember Aziz, from years ago, when he had picked both Gestas and me to be part of his elite group. Aziz had shocked the Servant community when he was only to pick one, but instead picked us both. Aziz had said, *"I have seen in a vision that when one dies the other will as well."* It sounded so poetic then, but how do I truly feel about it now? Gestas was my brother and my best friend. He taught me that a brother is not always blood, but one that stands by you no matter what. The latter bond is the strongest.

"Oh no, Gestas, don't cry out, no, don't let these Roman pigs hear your scream! Fight, damn it!"

Yelling at him to stop would be meaningless. Let him scream. The pain. So relentless is this pain. It doesn't subside. Over time, it elevates to a new level. Those Roman dogs know this and have exploited it. How many have I watched suffer in this same position over the years? Dozens, perhaps. Even then I wondered what it was like. I even had dreams of it happening to me.

I wanted to cry out to all the gods, *"I am here! Finish me!"* No words came out but I used this buried anger to stay resolute in hiding my pain.

Suddenly, I heard my brother, "Fool! What are you? Are you not the Christ? Save yourself and us!" Then he began to laugh. Oh, that cackle, so hideous it makes me cringe, and yet absurdly infectious at this point. I couldn't help but laugh with him.

I echoed his sentiments through my laughter, "Yes, what a fool. You announced around the land that you're a king. No king now, just a common criminal." Our laughter increased and I remembered how Barabbas said we laughed like hyenas in heat. It made me laugh even more.

My head swiveled with an unexplainable draw to look toward the man we laughed at. Our eyes locked. I instantly stopped laughing. There was something different about this man, something deep in his stare that I could not understand. It was not condemnation. Was it pity? No, not pity. Perhaps it was compassion. No, that was not quite right either. I had seen this look before. My mother came to mind. She looked at me this way. This was the look of love. Yes, this man was looking at me with love. But, why? Suddenly, I was more consumed by what this man thought of me than I was with the pain. It made no sense, but this love was almost as uncomfortable as the pain. Yet, I could not look away.

"I'm here for you," a voice said in my mind. It was gentle, but powerful.

I tried to look away but couldn't. What was this voice? It was at once foreign and familiar. It was a person that I had always known, always wanted to know, yet didn't know, all wrapped up in one. It was someone I had looked for, but never found. It was someone who knew me and loved me, utterly and completely. *"Wait, what did he say?"*

"I'm here for you, Dismas," the voice came again.

He knew my name. *"How? I never met him before."* I asked in my thoughts. *"What are you talking about? Why are you here for me?"*

"The pearl," he responded.

Suddenly, the story about Jesus that old man on the road to Jericho told me came to my mind. I had mocked that man. Days later we were caught and arrested. How did this Jesus know? Who was he? No, this voice couldn't be him. It was obvious that my mind was failing, and I could no longer discern reality. *"The pearl? What did the old man say about that story again? Something about a merchant who found one and sold all that he had to get it? Why would my mind bring me that story as we hang here? What does it even matter? I am not a merchant and I have no need for a pearl."*

The pain flooded back. Oh, the pain! I needed another breath, but this man called Jesus would not stop looking at me. He was staring into my soul. I still couldn't look away.

"I will give you a sign," Jesus said to me with no words coming from his mouth.

"What sign? What are you talking about? Our death is imminent and you talk of signs."

Suddenly, a calm came over me like gentle waves on the Sea of Galilee. This peace brought me back to my childhood, before the dark times. It was a time when I was free to be me, explore my thoughts, and pursue adventure alongside my brother. Throwing rocks down The Well or sloshing through the mud in the fields to rescue pigs for Father. These memories came to the forefront of my mind. I liked these thoughts. They made life matter to me. These memories, not of pain, suffering, and separation of family, but of joy, freedom, security, and belonging in a loving family, *these* memories brought hope.

His voice returned inside my mind. He simply said, *"Be ready."*

CHAPTER 57
I'm Ready

The Cross
-Nestor-

I DON'T KNOW HOW much time had passed. It could have been a couple of hours, but it might as well have been days. I just wanted it to be over. I felt that when it did end, when my son dies, I would end along with it. I imagined that my body would just fall lifeless, as if I were somehow connected to the men on the crosses before me.

"Be ready for what?" I asked myself. What could Jesus do now? Shouldn't he have already done it?

The women to my right continuously wept; loud bursts of emotion with unintelligible words erupting periodically through their wails. These followers had been with Jesus for quite some time. But where were his disciples? Perhaps the lone man standing behind the women could be one. He had a soft face, young in appearance, but at the same time, I could tell there was something Jesus-like about him. I don't know how I sensed this, but it was as if I knew that he had been with Jesus. The man never openly cried out but I could see the tracks of tears trailing down his face into his brown beard. Wait, I do recognize him. His name was John. Yes, that was what Jesus called him. John, Zebedee's son, had helped us, and had spoken kindly to us on the beach that day we were set free.

Right now, watching these people distracted me from my son.

And so I watched them. Periodically, John would stoop down and console one particular woman who was in the center of the small group. She seemed to be of importance to him. It was hard to discern faces from behind the coverings, especially from where I was standing. They rocked back and forth in their grief, every now and then reaching their hands out toward Jesus, longing to touch him, to help him.

At one point, John leaned down toward the woman and the timbre of his voice carried just far enough for me to discern, "Mary, mother of Jesus," he said.

My face contorted at the thought. *"Mary, mother of Jesus."* This woman was Jesus' mother? Why was she here? A mother should not have to endure such a horrific tragedy. Instantly, I realized that I was in the same situation. We were both trapped and couldn't escape that our children were slowly dying a torturous death before our very eyes. I was sure she, like me, desperately wished she could take his place. A mother and her child. A father and his.

This woman birthed Jesus. She raised him. She must have known that he was special. What had she seen that others had not? Her tears were more like prayers, each drop a call to God to bring her son down off the cross and back into her waiting arms.

The memory of my wife, my sweet Vena, suddenly flashed through my mind. Tears welled up and began to run down my cheeks. My Vena could have been here by my side watching our son go through this. Oh, thank you, God, for sparing her this brutal cruelty, this overwhelming grief.

Philos whispered to me from behind, "The crowds. They have lessened."

I wiped away the tears and scanned the area. Yes, hundreds had come to gawk but now only a dozen or so remained. Those who had come to witness the spectacle had no relationship with the accused. It was easy for them to turn their backs and walk away. I had earlier wished to leave, too. But now, after all that had happened and with more yet to come, I knew I was where I needed to be.

Suddenly, a surge of conviction came upon me and I stood. Philos helped me to my feet and I locked eyes with his. Shame was what I confronted. My shame was what prevented me from looking upon my own son and...fear. Fear of Dismas rejecting me.

I said firmly, "A son needs his father."

I felt some strength enter me as Philos' hands grasped my shoulders tighter.

"I'm ready," I told him, not really understanding myself what I meant. It came out again, "I'm ready."

Philos had no words, but nodded. I could tell he was uncertain as to what I meant. I could see the worry in his eyes. Perhaps he questioned whether I was going to do something rash. Or maybe he thought I was ready to accept the hopeless situation that was before us and finally say goodbye to my son.

I repeated those words in my mind, *"I'm ready."* I turned towards Jesus and saw that he was already looking at me.

Our connection went beyond words. In that brief moment, we exchanged so much, yet to anyone looking at us, nothing at all. I looked at my son.

Something had happened to me in the momentary connection with Jesus. I emerged from that moment no longer afraid that Dismas would reject me. I was no longer afraid that he would be angry with me. I was no longer afraid that he would hate me.

I approached my long lost son.

"Dismas," I croaked. He couldn't hear me. I could hardly believe that I was finally here, mere feet away, looking up at my son who had lived twenty years of life without me.

"Dismas!" I said louder.

He grimaced in pain as he peered down at me. Squinting, he knew neither who I was, nor why I approached him. I longed to know what he was thinking. He would not speak as he had to take shallow breaths in order to keep alive. Why would he waste any breath on a stranger?

I could feel the tears welling up and all I could say was my son's name, "Dismas."

Why couldn't I say it? Why couldn't I say, *"It is me. Your father."* He was my son, after all. Shouldn't he know the truth?

I could tell he was confused that I knew his name and through his pain he was searching for a memory of me.

Dismas had seen me when he was ten, but it was not the real me. He had seen the demon who resided inside of me. My flashes of memory over these months revealed to me it was Dismas on that shore. Though only a brief memory, it was enough to sustain me for the next several months leading to this point in time.

Jesus came to the shore of Galilee and banished Legion. His mission was never Legion. Jesus was there for me and Legion was in his way.

I'm here for my Dismas and these nails, this pain, and this

circumstance are in *my* way. I pulled out the lion figurine and raised it high for him to see. Oh, the glory of seeing his face recognize what I held before him! This simple wooden sculpture captured my son's attention. God only knows who carved it. I don't know why it meant so much to him, but it was all I had to make a connection. It was what he left behind ten years earlier and it was my lifeline to him.

His eyes were fixed upon the object. My tears flowed freely now. *"Look at me, son. Recognize who I am."* This was my silent plea from the depths of my heart. Slowly, ever so slowly, his gaze lifted to me and I nodded, letting myself grasp this glimmer of hope.

I yelled, "Dismas! I'm your father! Truly, it is I! I found you and I'm sorry I am too late! You deserved better!" I could tell my words were getting through to him. "Don't speak, son. Just listen. Your mother and I loved you. We never chose to give you away. Jesus saved us and I know that he can save you as well. Believe in him, son!"

I watched as Dismas looked toward the lion figure and then back to me. Our surroundings faded around us as my son and I exchanged this precious moment.

There were no more words. There didn't have to be. I moved the lion toward Jesus. Dismas followed with his eyes. Would he recognize that I was the demon-possessed man who now held the figurine he lost on the shores of Galilee all those years ago? Would he understand that Jesus saved me? My Savior stared intently at Dismas.

"Jesus," I said in my mind, *"you saved me all those years ago. My deepest prayer, the only prayer that matters, is before you now. I beg of you, Jesus, save my son."*

CHAPTER 58
REMEMBER ME

THE CROSS
-DISMAS-

I HEARD MY NAME and it jarred me from delirium.

"Dismas!"

There was a man I had never seen before looking at me strangely. If my feet were not nailed to this cross I might have kicked him in the face just for the fun of it. I had no tolerance for others outside of my people. What did he want? It's not like I had any money. This thought almost caused me to burst out laughing. I always thought I was funny. But Gestas never thought so.

"Wait, how does this stranger know my name? He was no Roman magistrate. How did he know me? Was this someone I had stolen from? Did he seek retribution? Too late, the Roman dogs got to me first. Why is he crying? This was no man seeking revenge. He knows me. He really knows me, yet I had no recollection of him."

The more I stared at him though, the more I felt something. It was something slightly familiar.

The drifter slowly pulled forth what no man could have ever resurrected from my past. It was my father's gift to me; the lion. How was this possible? It was lost ten years ago to the Demon of Ghasa on the shore of Galilee. Yet, here it was in this stranger's hand.

The man yelled, "Dismas! I'm your father! Truly, it is I! I found you and I'm sorry I was too late! You deserved better!"

"My father?" I thought. *"What is happening? How is this possible?"* I did not understand.

The stranger continued, "Don't speak, son. Just listen. Your mother and I loved you. We never chose to give you away. Jesus saved us and I know that he can save you as well. Believe in him, son!"

Slowly, he moved the figure toward Jesus and my gaze locked into those powerful eyes once again.

"The pearl of great price," Jesus spoke inside my mind or my own mind brought the words, I knew not. It wasn't the normal voice of my thoughts, the one I hear when I talk to myself. It was a voice of extreme authority, wrapped in indescribable peace.

"The pearl?" I repeated in my mind.

"A merchant found this pearl and sold everything," Jesus communicated.

What did it mean? What was this Jesus about? I'm a Greek. He's a Jew. Why did he look at me? Why did he care?

"I am here for you, Dismas."

"Why?" I asked.

"You are the pearl."

"I'm the pearl?" I couldn't fully grasp this simple, yet profound thought. With a single word, Jesus of Nazareth had healed people from all over the region in the past three years. There were rumors of his power over demons, as well.

I looked back to the stranger who held this prized possession of mine. If this Greek man came from my home, could it be possible that he wrestled it from the demon? It was not possible. No man had ever subdued them, and no man could, not even the mighty Romans. Who was this before me with my figurine in his hands?

Wait, was this...no it couldn't be. My heart stopped for a second as I looked at his eyes. Was I hallucinating, or were his eyes different colors, like my own? Was this the demon coming back to finish what he started ten years ago? But this was no demon. This man before me was crying. I could see his tears streaming down his face.

My mind replayed that encounter from so long ago. Two demon-men, naked, scarred, dirty, bleeding wounds, torn patches of beard, gnarled hair sticking out in all directions. This man was bigger, well-fed, but still his face, yes, his face was similar. There was another man standing close behind him looking at me, as well. He also looked familiar. These *are* them. They must be. These are the Demons of Ghasa. How could this be possible?

If that was the truth, then this man, this stranger, was...my father. He was my blood-related father. I did not want to believe this. My eyes deceived me. But my heart burned to believe it was true.

I looked at Jesus. This Jewish Messiah had stepped into Gergesa and done what? He commanded the demons to leave? It seemed impossible, yet here was the man standing before me, gazing at me with such emotion. I had seen this look before. It was the same look my father, the one who raised me, had. He believed in me and loved me, no matter what. This man was looking at me in the same way.

Gestas had revealed the truth to me of who I was and where I had come from years ago. That moment we became closer than blood brothers. We became inseparable.

I shifted my gaze toward my brother, Gestas. He was watching this transaction. I could see the rage in his eyes. His eyes jarred away from me and looked at Jesus.

Gestas yelled, "Hey, you! Are you not the Christ? Save yourself and us from death!"

My brother looked back at me with a bloody smile. I could tell he wanted me to join him once again in the mockery of Jesus. He wanted me to be on his side. Over the years we had argued our points. We didn't always agree, but we always came together no matter the outcome. Gestas was *always* right. But this time it was different. I was drawn by the power of Jesus. Jesus' eyes bored into my soul. I felt he longed to hold me in his arms and I, from the depth of my soul, longed for the same. What I wouldn't give to be held, to be loved, truly loved.

In my final moments in this world, my heart stirred awake, a feeling that I had buried long ago at the Great Loss, the murder of my mother. I fell into darkness. Darkness had consumed me. I cared for nothing but revenge. I took control of my own destiny and now here I was. Jesus' destiny led him here, also.

Jesus told me that he was here for me. Was this true? Could it be possible that this man who healed the sick, raised the dead, and who banished demons with a word, could be here for me? My heart burned to believe in Jesus, more intensely than the pain I currently felt. What was happening to me? In my mind, I wanted to curse everyone and everything, but in my heart, I wanted to go where Jesus was going. I could see in his eyes, he was going *somewhere* and I longed to be with him. Was it possible?

My resolve strengthened as hope rose inside me. Gestas *had* always been right, but now I knew he was wrong. There was more to life than what we believed to be true, what we've seen with our eyes. I couldn't go to the darkness with Gestas. I wanted to go where Jesus was going. Surely darkness was not his destiny.

I yelled what could've been my final words. Losing strength, I called out, "Gestas, have you no fear of God? We are under the same sentence of judgment. We are suffering justly. We are getting what we deserve for what we have done, but this man has done nothing wrong."

I had no more words for him. I could only attempt to send him a message through my mind, *"Oh, my Gestas, my brother. Please follow me. Let us not be broken apart on this final day. This Jesus was beyond our understanding. We always dreamed of what it would be like beyond the veil of life. The mystery of death and that final voyage of discovery was now before us. Follow me, Gestas. I beg of you, follow me."*

I pleaded with my eyes for him to follow me. He stared hard at me for a long moment. His gaze burning into me and mine into him. It was our way of battling and this was a battle of life and death.

I turned toward Jesus of Nazareth, the Messiah to the Jews, and blared, "Jesus, remember me when you come into your kingdom!"

Jesus spoke clearly and without labor. His words were not inside my mind but spoken for all to hear. His words were so powerful, "Truly, I say to you, today you will be with me in paradise."

It was like refreshing water flowing over me. I knew at that moment that he spoke truth. I would be in paradise with him. Darkness was not my destiny. Had Jesus always known this would happen? Had he always known that he was destined for the cross to rescue me?

In this world, that now fades before me, there are many kingdoms; Romans, Greek, Jew. Why couldn't there be another kingdom? The kingdom called Paradise.

In my final breaths, my thoughts went to Barabbas. He spoke often of everyone having a story. He spoke of how the world around us contends to write our story, but it was in the hearts of men to re-write them. My heart chose to follow Jesus.

I always thought a story must be written onto parchment, but it was instead to be written on the heart. My mind drifted off as if I was dreaming. The pain subsided. All the cares of the former world disappeared. A bright light burst forth in my inner darkness. I ran to the light and on the other side of it, as it enveloped me, was Jesus. His face ignited in pure joy upon seeing me. I ran into his arms.

"Welcome home, Dismas. Welcome home."

CHAPTER 59
THE ROMAN ROAD

THIRD DAY AFTER THE CROSS
-NESTOR-

WHAT SHALL I say to you? Should I tell you of the earthquake that shook the region at his death? Or, perhaps, the confirmed dead people who were suddenly brought back to life from their many graves speaking the name of Jesus, whom they had never met? Not one of those stories compares to my story. A father in search of his son; a father doing everything in his power to find him and save him. This was my story, but was my son saved? I know not. Even now, with the overwhelming grief that I feel, I wrestle with the fact that he is gone. He died on that cross alongside Jesus of Nazareth, the Messiah, the one that brought signs and wonders. That man now lies within a tomb. And my son, buried by my hands, in a grave. These were the things that I pondered, walking almost aimlessly down this Roman road back to Hippus.

"What happened, Philos?" I whispered. "Tell me this was but a dream."

"I'm afraid not, my friend."

"I heard him, Philos. In his own voice, I heard Jesus say today Dismas would be in paradise with him. Then we watched their horrific deaths. I don't understand."

"Nor do I."

At this point, a man came alongside us. Though my head turned to acknowledge him, my heart did not care. I expected the stranger to pass, but instead, he walked beside us.

The stranger suddenly asked, "What are you discussing as you walk along together?"

I looked at him as we continued to walk. He was a young Jewish man, healthy beard, standard clothing, with a face that was soft and welcoming. He seemed almost familiar to me.

"Have we met before?" I asked.

"It's possible. Perhaps through our exchange of stories we will uncover the answer to that question. You both seem troubled by something, deep in thought and conversation. I would like to hear what has happened to cause you to be so disheartened."

"Were you not in Jerusalem?" I asked.

He responded jovially, "Yes, I was just there."

Philos said, "You must be the only one in the entire region who has not heard then."

"Heard what?"

I exchanged a subtle glance with Philos before he responded, "Jesus of Nazareth was what happened. He was a great prophet who with but a word commanded demons to leave. He loved and helped many people, and yet the priests and rulers arrested him. They crucified him three days ago. We were discussing how we thought he was the Messiah, the Christ of the Jews. We don't understand, with all that we have seen and experienced, why he died, if he was truly the Messiah."

There was silence for a few moments, and I noticed that the man maintained a jovial spirit despite the news.

"Do you know something that we do not?" I asked. "You seem in high spirits even after what Philos has explained to you."

He looked at us and smiled, "Yes, I do know something."

"Then please tell."

"What if I told you that Jesus is alive?"

"Then I would say that you did not see what we have seen," I said.

"Did not Abraham receive instruction from God to sacrifice his only son, Isaac?"

"You are a rabbi?" Philos asked quickly.

Without hesitating the stranger continued, "And did Abraham follow God's instruction, even though he did not know what would happen? Could it be that you followed the instructions of God, not knowing the full intent of the Father?

I said, "I suppose. But you speak as if you know with certainty. I lost my son. He died with Jesus."

"Can I impart a grand story to you both as we walk? I have much to tell you."

I indicated that I wanted to hear more. This man spoke with an authority unlike anything I had ever heard except from Jesus himself on that fateful day he came upon the Gerasene shore. Perhaps this Jewish man had walked with the disciples.

He began his story and spoke with clarity and emphasis. His words washed over my grieving soul. The more he talked, the more my spirit became aligned with hope, faith, and love.

Hours went by, yet I experienced no fatigue walking the road. He introduced revelation after revelation about Jesus of Nazareth. Many things we had never heard, other things confirmed what we had seen. This man was very knowledgeable and did not relent in telling us all he knew. His words were like water to my parched heart and honey to my bitter soul.

"Therefore," the man continued, "he saw the joy ahead of him, so he endured death on the cross and ignored the disgrace it brought him. Then he received the highest position in heaven, the one next to the throne of God."

I watched him look up into heaven with exuberance upon his face and say, "Did not Jesus of Nazareth say that on the third day he would rise?"

There was silence. We could not answer such a question. We had not heard Jesus speak this in our limited time with him.

Philos whispered, "Today is the third day."

The Jewish man smiled brightly, as if Philos had answered the question correctly. I stared blankly, waiting for him to say more.

"Tell me, Nestor, what was your son like?"

"Had I told him my name? I must have."

"My son?" I asked.

"Yes, tell me about him."

"Well, I don't know where to start. Let me see. He was...taken and raised with a family right after his birth and—"

"No, tell me about *him*." He emphasized the last word.

"I don't know what you mean."

"You know your son. You have seen him in your mind and heart. A father always knows his son. Speak of what you know."

I looked at him, puzzled, and searched inside myself to come up with the correct answer.

"He was hurt and misguided, and a thief."

"No, those are things of the world. Now speak of the son the world did not see. Speak the way a father sees what no one else does."

At this point, I stopped walking. The sun was setting. Philos placed his hand upon my shoulder. The Jewish man stepped in front of me, lifted my head to look into his eyes and said simply, "Speak truth."

"My son was named Dismas."

He smiled at me and said, "Yes, tell me more."

"He was full of hope and wonder."

"Yes," he nodded at each of my words as they continued to come freely.

"He was in search of truth and was a great warrior of that truth. He found good in all those he encountered and helped them understand who they were destined to be."

I couldn't understand all the words flowing out of me but each word came from my heart and I let them come, without restraint.

"My son did great things, and was called to greatness by his father."

"Yes, Nestor, keep going. Don't stop."

"He received love and never knew a day without it. He was destined to slay giants and conquer every enemy set before him. I tell you that Dismas, my son, reigned mightily as a king of righteousness. He did not fail."

"Where is your son, Nestor?"

Without hesitation, I yelled, "He is in paradise! He is with God!"

The stranger, yet not a stranger, set his hands on each of my shoulders and nodded. Tears welled in his eyes. I heard Philos sniffling beside me, but my eyes would not leave this man.

He said, "I'm proud of you."

"Who are you?" I asked as tears began to well up in my eyes.

He smiled and held my gaze, then gently pulled away and said, "It is time for me to leave. But don't worry, I have gone and prepared a place for you."

"Prepared a place for us?" Philos asked.

"Show me the lion figure you hold in your possession."

"How do you know this?" I asked.

"Show me."

I slowly pulled it out and presented the scarred, scratched, and broken figure. "It was my son's."

He took it, looked it over as he twirled it around in his hands. "It has seen better days."

"I think my son made it."

"No, your son did not make this, but I know who did."

"You do?"

He handed it back to me and said, "Yes, a carpenter from the small town of Nazareth."

"Nazareth?" Suddenly, upon saying this word my eyes opened, and I saw this man for who he truly was; the very one who had turned my life around. It was Jesus! He stepped back and held out his hands. I saw the holes as the setting sun behind him illuminated them. His eyes sparkled without any light reflecting upon them. A glorious glow brightened from within him as brilliant rays spiked out in all directions.

"I must depart."

"Don't leave us!" I pleaded.

"John the Baptist called out in the wilderness 'prepare the way'." The light became brighter around Jesus. "I will return when our Father deems. He is the only one who knows the time. In all you do, and with every breath you take, prepare the way for my return."

"What are we to do, Lord?"

"I have told you these things, so that in me you may have peace. In this world you will have trouble. But take heart! I have overcome the world." With that, he faded away before our eyes and the light diminished.

We both fell to our knees on this Roman road, lifting our hands to the heavens.

Philos and I embraced and cried, not bitter tears, but tears of joy. We had seen with our own eyes, had touched with our own hands, had heard with our own ears, the wonder, and majesty of the Christ.

"Was not your heart burning when he spoke before we knew who it was?" Philos asked excitedly upon wiping the tears from his eyes.

"Oh indeed, my friend. My heart burns still. We have much to do. The work of the Lord is upon us!"

"Where do we go now? I fear that I will not sleep for days."

"Let us return to Baruch and bring the good news of the risen Lord."

CHAPTER 60
AND IT WAS SO

-NESTOR-

AND IT WAS SO. Philos and I returned and proclaimed all that we had seen. Roman guards, tax collectors, prostitutes, commoners, and everyone in between opened their hearts to the truth. Churches were built and more Kingdom disciples of the Truth, the Way, and the Life spread throughout the region and beyond. Some of the disciples came through Decapolis and strengthened what was already upon us. Signs and wonders followed those who believed. The sick were healed, the lepers restored, the lame walked, and the captives of this world were set free through the love and sacrifice of Jesus Christ.

I lived many years with Philos by my side until we were each called home. Some glorious days. Some not so glorious. But our love and faith in Christ remained all the way to the end, or should I say, to our new beginning.

You might be asking, *"Were you able to see your son when you passed away and entered Paradise?"*

Indeed I did.

But that is another grand story for another time...

THE END

FINAL THOUGHTS

"SOME SAY THAT we can decide our own destiny, others say destiny is already decided for us, while still others say destiny is to be discovered. I believe it is a culmination of all three.

There's also a sense that destiny can be missed, which says to me that there are multiple possibilities for a person to uncover in life based upon their decisions. No matter the outcome, one shouldn't dwell on the past, for what is present and ahead is more important than the former.

I should know, for my life was not something I would want to live over again. But in the end I am where I am based upon a single decision in my heart to choose life instead of death. It's unfathomable to calculate every choice set before us and the ramifications they produce, good or bad, in one's life. There is only one in all creation that can understand the depth of destiny and he remained by my side all the way to the cross and his name is Jesus."

-Dismas the Redeemed

"I hate you! It's all your fault! Go to Hades!"

-Gestas

Acknowledgements

First and foremost, thank you to my wonderful and brilliant wife. With you in my life, everything makes sense. Your encouragement and insight into the making of this book has brought me to a whole new level in writing.

Huge shout out to all my beta-readers! You guys rock! Tiffany, Rikah, Suzanne, Sharon, Claudene, Manna, Karlet, Jill, Michelle, Sabrina, and Jan. Your valued insight helped to shape the final product. Blessings upon you all.

Thank you to the entire KWA family. All of your prayers and all of your encouragement have brought me great joy over these last two years bringing D&T to life. You are all world-changers.

Thank you to my daughter, Michelle, for developing the beautiful map. May your future books be highly favored with God and man.

Much appreciation, to my friend, Craig, for speaking life over this project and pushing me toward a title that grips you. 'Remember Me' wasn't it and you were right.

To Suzanne Carlson, my amazing editor, and friend, thank you! Your knowledge and skill brought strength to the book. Very thankful that God brought us together.

My devotion and affection is fully for God. Thank you, Papa, for bringing me this story from the vault of heaven and breathing life into it. You are the ultimate storyteller and I aspire to be more like you. May this story wreck people in a good way and may it propel them to search their heart for the answers they seek. I pray this book, this story, is a healing salve to those in need.

Brae Wyckoff is an award-winning and internationally acclaimed author, born and raised in San Diego, CA. He married his beautiful wife, Jill, in 1993, and they have three children and six wonderful grandchildren.

Brae's passion for mysterious realms and the supernatural inspired him to write The Orb of Truth, the first in a series of fantasy action adventures. His first book, The Orb of Truth, won Best Christian Fantasy Award and has been voted #1 in several categories, including Best Indie Fantasy Book, Epic Fantasy Worth Your Time, and Fantasy Book That Should Be Required Reading. Other award-winning books are, The Dragon God and The Vampire King.

In 2015, Brae released his first children's book, called The Unfriendly Dragon, after he teamed up with Disney Artist, Seth Weinberg.

Brae is currently the Director of Kingdom Writers Association (KWA) based in San Diego where he is working with writers of all levels to encourage and empower them to pursue their calling as authors. KWA is part of Awakening International Training & Reformation Center.

Brae has shared the stage with notable authors and public figures such as Paul Young, author of the Shack, Darren Wilson, author and film director, Dr. Mark Stibbe, author and speaker, Manna Ko, author and speaker, and many more.

You can contact Brae Wyckoff to schedule a speaking engagement at www.braewyckoff.com